THE CASKET OPENED EAS[...]

Ash Shandy lay inside. Death had mottled his skin with furry brown spots, like patches of fungus feeding on their host. Orient made a hurried check for signs of life using the standard techniques. They all came up negative.

Suddenly a violent fluttering burst through the quiet. Orient swatted blindly at a trio of frightened ravens swirling around his head. As the birds flew up to the ceiling, he noticed a subtle movement inside the coffin. He pointed the dim light toward the corpse . . . and froze.

Shandy's eyes were now wide open. Orient stood paralyzed as he and the dead man stared at each other in the dank stillness of the tomb.

Abruptly the flashlight went out.

"Hypnotically readable . . .
Frank Lauria has written the most
believable vampire and werewolf stories
I have ever read"
William S. Burroughs

D0840300

BLUE LIMBO

FRANK LAURIA

AVON BOOKS NEW YORK

BLUE LIMBO is an original publication of Avon Books. This work has never before appeared in book form. This work is a novel. Any similarity to actual persons or events is purely coincidental.

AVON BOOKS
A division of
The Hearst Corporation
105 Madison Avenue
New York, New York 10016

First Avon Books Printing: May 1991

AVON TRADEMARK REG. U.S. PAT. OFF. AND IN OTHER COUNTRIES, MARCA REGISTRADA, HECHO EN U.S.A.

Printed in the U.S.A.

RA 10 9 8 7 6 5 4 3 2 1

For Ellen Smith—with love and squalor . . .

In memory of Wang Weilin, unsung hero of the massacre at Tiananmen Square.

Chapter 1

LUCIEN ST. GEORGE WAS A BORN COOK.

In his hands the most ordinary provisions were transmuted into rare delicacies. Eggs blossomed into fluffy omelets, meats luxuriated in aromatic sauces, salads bloomed plump and fresh—even chipped beef on toast exuded the scent of exotic spices. Each dawn, the rich fragrance of his coffee wafted like musky perfume through the stale confines of the submarine.

That was what he'd miss most, Captain McGinn reflected wistfully. St. George brewed the finest coffee on the seven seas. But St. George's tour of duty was nearly over, and McGinn hadn't been able to convince his chief cook to re-up. To make his day complete, two new seamen were reporting for duty.

Sam McGinn hated changes in personnel. It disrupted routine and shifted the fragile balance of personalities that fused his crew into a battle-ready unit. His fondness for order was probably why he enjoyed being a sub commander, McGinn speculated. Cruising beneath the ocean surface for months at a stretch imposed a discipline that remained undisturbed by the passage of sunrise and sunset. Beneath the sea a submarine carried its own time.

A familiar tap at the door interrupted McGinn's thoughts. St. George entered, a wide smile breaking across his usually solemn expression as he set the tray on McGinn's desk.

"Here it be, Cap'n."

McGinn made a show of slowly lifting the white napkin covering the tray, but the succulent odor told him what was underneath.

"Your favorite, Cap'n," St. George said proudly. "Honey-fried chicken, Cajun cole slaw, black peas, corn buns, and strawberry shortcake." He leaned closer and lowered his voice conspiratorially. "I fried up three extra birds and stuck 'em in the freeze box—so you got somethin' to remember me by."

"Oh, I'll remember you all right, St. George. Who could forget the best damned cook in the Navy?"

"That's real nice of you to say, sir."

"I also said it in a letter of commendation that's now in your permanent file."

St. George beamed. "Might come in real handy when I'm lookin' for a situation."

"Well, if you ever decide to reenlist, make sure you contact me before you sign anything," McGinn said gruffly. "I don't want to lose you to some chickenshit admiral."

"Don't you worry, Cap'n," St. George assured. "I been teachin' my cousin Harold everythin' he should know. Come a week or so, you won't know I'm gone."

But as McGinn savored a moist slice of chicken, he was far from convinced. From what he'd observed, cousin Harold was a bit of a dolt. Still, if his new Chief Cook Harold Patterson proved to be half as good as St. George, he'd be grateful. Right now he was forced to hurry an excellent lunch because of two blasted seamen who'd been assigned to his command. Some whiz brain in Washington had the brilliant idea of sending two lubbers with no undersea experience to serve on the Navy's most sophisticated, and expensive, submarine.

The U.S.S. *Blowgun* was a Sea Wolf class attack sub, slightly larger, faster—and much quieter—than the older Los Angeles 688 class submarines. McGinn had commanded the vessel since its shakedown cruise and had grown to love it. In his opinion it was the most dangerous weapon in the armed forces. But for some inane reason the boys in the Pentagon insisted on using it for absurd experiments. Such as the one they were about to undertake within the next forty-eight hours.

McGinn poured himself a fresh coffee and reluctantly called Lieutenant (jg) Craig Early.

"Okay, Early, send up the new guests."

"Not to worry, Commander, they look shipshape."

"I'll be the judge of that, Lieutenant."

"Aye, sir."

Cursing his foolishness, Lieutenant Early replaced the phone and hurried off in search of the new crewmen. He should have known better than to try to buddy up the old man. Commander McGinn hadn't been exactly pleased with him since he learned the news about the damned experiment. At the moment, Early wished he'd never gotten involved.

Too late now, turkey, he fumed. Just stay cool and make the best of it. The old man could change his mind yet. And maybe this sub would learn how to fly.

As St. George eased his lanky frame along the cramped corridor, he had no regrets. He had accomplished everything he'd set out to do. The Navy had expanded his horizon and now he intended to explore it fully. He had almost finished packing when Harold dropped by to say his farewells. As usual, his cousin had been nipping at the rum bottle. And as usual, he was complaining.

"I still don't feel so good. Maybe I need some more of that soursap," he added hopefully.

"You'd do better for yourself if you laid off that overproof. The cap'n'll have you in the brig if he finds out."

"Shee, Lucien, I know what to do. Ain't I always done right by you?"

Normally the whining insinuation in his voice never failed to grate on St. George's nerves. But today he could afford to let it pass. He was about to kiss the Navy—and cousin Harold—good-bye. So he smiled and jerked his thumb toward the nose of the sub. "Look in the back of the freezer. I left a quart of soursap there for you."

Harold beamed appreciatively. Back in Jamaica, where both of them had been born, soursap juice was held in high esteem as an all-purpose tonic. Especially to counteract the wicked hangovers incurred by drinking overproof rum.

"I thank you kindly, Lucien."

"You damned well should. You got yourself the coolest berth in this man's Navy. So don't blow it."

Harold ignored the advice and leaned closer. "Say, cuz, could you let me hold a hundred or so? Just until payday."

"What the hell you need money for underneath the water, like you gonna be the whole next ten days?"

"Oh, you know, Luce, boys and me like to roll them dice just to pass the time. I swear I'll send you the bread first thing I get it."

St. George reached into his shirt pocket and extracted a tight wad of bills. He carefully peeled off two fifties and held them just out of Harold's reach. "Now you best remember one thing," he said quietly. "I don't like people that call me Luce."

"Sure, Lucien, sure," Harold said uneasily. He gingerly snatched the bills from St. George's hand and began backing out of the small compartment. "You have a nice trip home, now. And don't you worry. The money be in the mail next week."

St. George wasn't at all worried. He was certain he'd never see that hundred again.

He finished packing and headed topside, pausing frequently to shake hands with his shipmates, who seemed genuinely sorry to see him go. During his two-year stint aboard the *Blowgun* the tall, gaunt-featured cook had gained a modest reputation as a healer. He used native Jamaican herbal remedies to treat minor ailments, and his notable success with the more common social infections had earned him the admiration of half the crew.

St. George was approaching the control room when he spotted Lieutenant Early escorting two strange seamen to the captain's quarters. He'd already heard the scuttlebutt about two men coming aboard for some top-secret experiment, but he didn't believe the rumors. It didn't make sense to assign a pair of lab sailors to a high-megaton piece of hardware like the *Blowgun*.

Either the Navy Department was crazy or these men were aboard for another reason, St. George speculated, stepping into an alcove to let the trio go by. He studied the new crewmen as they passed, and decided his doubts were justified. They looked more like SEALS than lab rats. One was a blond surfer type with a goofy smile that didn't fool St. George. There was little goofy about the man's alert blue eyes, or the karate calluses decorating his knuckles like tiny leather patches. The other one was shorter and thick around the chest, like a wrestler. But there was an air of intelligence about his glum, vaguely pugnacious expression.

Whatever they were, it didn't matter anymore, St. George reflected as he ambled toward a narrow shaft of sunlight spearing through an open hatch. By the time the

Blowgun pulled out of King's Island, Georgia, he'd be long gone.

Actually, when Commander McGinn finally met his new crewmen, he was forced to agree with Early's brash appraisal. Both Kent and Garin seemed seaworthy enough in their crisp white uniforms. They carried themselves with an air of confidence befitting submarine men. And he was pleasantly surprised to learn they'd qualified in the upper percentiles at computer school. He always needed hands who knew the right buttons to push. However, as far as he was concerned, they had yet to prove themselves where it counted. Under the sea.

"Welcome aboard, men," he said brusquely. "As you'll come to learn, this submarine is a highly sensitive vessel. So until you get used to her, keep your hands in your jeans or you may live to regret it. Am I clear? Good," he added without waiting for an answer. "Now, then. You'll find I'm hard but fair. How hard, how fair, is up to you. Understand? Now, until further notice you're both assigned to the torpedo room." He nodded to a short, amiable figure standing in the doorway. "First Mate Blum will show you the ropes. Any questions?"

Lieutenant Early knew there wouldn't be, but he held his breath until they were outside. Apparently the old man had approved. Otherwise he would have given them his Woe Unto Those Who Screw Up routine. Suddenly feeling much better, he delivered his charges to First Mate Blum and went off in search of a cold beer. In his haste he failed to note the look of smug amusement that passed between Kent and Garin.

"Candyass," Garin muttered, watching him depart.

"Stow it," Blum cut in. "The lieutenant's good people."

Garin tilted his head and scowled. "I'll let you know."

Blum scowled back. "You'll soon know who's who on this ship, mister."

"Don't pay no mind to my bonehead buddy here," Kent said affably. "He's got an attitude about officers."

Blum relaxed a bit and nodded. "Yeah, most of 'em's chickenshit for sure. But McGinn is fair enough. And Early's better than most. In fact, he's got a kind of secret weapon."

"Yeah, that kid?" Garin said, glancing at Kent. "What the hell's he got?"

But Blum caught the look, and since he was still put off by Garin's arrogance, he decided to go by the book.

"I said too much already. Anyway, you'll know all about it by the time this cruise is half over. C'mon with me. I'll show you your berths and get you squared away."

"Uh, any chance we can get some chow?" Kent ventured. "We didn't get but a snack on the damned plane."

Blum's natural dislike for airplanes softened his disposition. "Sure, the crew's mess is open. At worst they'll rustle up some leftovers."

"Good cook?" Garin inquired, hoisting his sea bag.

"Dunno yet. Matter of fact, he just took over today."

"No shit. What's his name?" Kent said. "In case we have to butter him up. It's a joke, get it? Butter up the cook."

"I got it." Blum sighed, moving toward the corridor. He couldn't decide which annoyed him most, Garin's arrogance or Kent's phony good humor.

As it happened, the chief cook wasn't in the best of humor himself that afternoon. Patterson's eyes were red-rimmed and his voice was hoarse. "Goddamn dinner bell ain't for two hours yet," he replied gruffly when Blum requested chow for the new arrivals.

"Hey, look, anything will do," Kent persisted. "Sandwich, leftovers, anything. We're starvin', man. We'll be glad to cover you for the inconvenience,'' he added, lifting a folded bill into view.

Patterson squinted at the bill, then at Kent. "Keep your damn money, boy. I'll rustle up somethin'. But don't acquire no habit. I run a tight burner."

He turned toward the galley, then stopped. "Where you think you're goin'?" he snapped at Kent, who had started to follow.

"Well, uh, I thought you said . . ."

"I said I'd rustle somethin' up. I didn't invite you inside. 'Less you want KP, my galley is permanently off limits. That clear?"

"Hey, sure. No problem." Kent's boyish grin was wasted on Patterson's departing back.

Blum didn't say a word, but he had a feeling he was going to get along with Patterson just fine.

Later, while unpacking his gear, Kent was still fuming.

"If you hadn't been so fucking pushy with Blum, he might have told us what's up with Early."

"Who cares?" Garin retorted. "What could he tell us that we don't already know?"

"Now we'll never know, will we?"

"Anyway, we got to meet Patterson."

"Hey, easy," Kent hissed. He looked around at the deserted bunks. "No need for names. Not for what I got for him."

"He really pissed you off back there, didn't he?"

"So what if he did?"

"So remember. We wait until we're at sea. We want a captive audience."

Kent sat on his bunk and studied his nails.

"Don't worry. I plan on taking my time on this one. He'll be beggin' to tell me long before I'm finished."

"Outstanding," Garin grunted.

"What about . . ." Kent lowered his voice, ". . . the skip?"

"What about him?"

"Well, we do have to tell him his shit-heeled cook is busted, don't we?"

Garin leaned closer. "We're not here to bust him, homeboy. Once we get a full confession, orders are to terminate. Any problem with that?"

Kent eased back in his bunk and cradled his head in his hands. "You know the thing I like best about submarines? The weather's always good."

Harold Patterson hadn't taken a drink for forty-eight hours, but sobriety seemed to disagree with him. Ever since the *Blowgun* had pulled out of King's Island, he'd been as sick as a swamp hog. He'd guzzled the entire bottle of St. George's soursap juice to no avail. After serving breakfast he'd been forced to check himself into sick bay, well away from his rum supply.

Since then he had dozed fitfully, feverish dreams galloping across his brain and pain twisting his belly. Albano, the pharmacist's mate, had diagnosed the ailment as intestinal flu and administered a combination of antibiotics and mild sedatives. But when he checked later that evening, Patterson's condition had worsened. A pasty gray pallor dulled his dark, sweat-glistened face, making his yellowed pupils seem like distant beacons in a fog. And although he was still conscious, his hoarse responses to Albano's questions were barely audible.

"Where does it hurt?" Albano droned.

Patterson passed his hand from his chest to his groin. "All down here . . . pain keeps movin'."

Albano cursed his Sicilian luck. He didn't relish having to tell Commander McGinn they'd have to scuttle the cruise because he couldn't make a proper diagnosis. Especially if Patterson's complaint proved to be minor. The old man would bust him down to deckhand and send his ass to the Gobi Desert.

"Listen, Harold, there's a couple of buddies waitin' to see you," Albano said hopefully. Perhaps a friendly visit would aid his recovery.

Patterson squinted as if hearing news from another planet.

"You know, the new dude Kent and his pal," Albano prompted. "Kent says he knows you from the Blue Parrot bar."

Patterson's eyes suddenly went wide. "Water, man . . . get me water."

After he drank he seemed calmer, and more alert.

"Tell that boy I'll see him in a few minutes, okay?" the cook whispered, settling back on his pillow.

"Is he feeling better?" Kent asked when Albano came out of sick bay.

"He said he'll see you. But he's real weak. Don't excite him. Maybe only one of you guys should go in."

"Anything you say," Kent assured him. "We're here to cheer up the poor bastard."

Garin put his arm around Albano's shoulder. "You like good scotch, old buddy?"

Albano perked up. "Do boats float?"

"So happens there's a thirty-year-old jug of Ballantine standing at attention in my locker, which happens to be unlocked. So why don't you just help yourself to a snort or three while we bullshit with ol' Harold."

"Well, okay, but don't overdo it. I'll be right back."

"Think the scotch will hold him long enough?" Kent asked when Albano was out of earshot.

"Don't worry, it's jacked up. One drink and he'll still be smiling when we get back. Now let's squeeze this scumbag for some names and numbers."

Patterson stared in wide-eyed fascination as they entered sick bay and approached his bunk.

Kent gave him a mischievous wink. "Hello, Harold. We're here to talk about Blue Parrots. We can do it the fun way"—he lifted his hand to show him the hypodermic—"or the hard way." He smiled and produced a serrated combat knife. "It's up to you."

Patterson continued to stare at him blankly.

Kent stopped smiling and moved closer. "Think fast, Harold. You're looking at permanent damage plus life at hard labor—if you're lucky enough to get past me. And I hate traitors."

"Hold it a second," Garin muttered.

Kent shot him an annoyed glance. "What the fuck for?"

"Look for yourself, homeboy. You are talking to a dead man."

Kent studied the unblinking figure for a long moment. "Dammit. Now what?"

"First we lose the needle and the blade," Garin said coolly. "Then we join Albano for a drink, and tell him Harold seemed very depressed."

In a way, Patterson's sudden demise solved Albano's dilemma. Even though he had erred in his diagnosis, at least he hadn't been forced to abort the cruise. Procedure was quite specific in these cases.

In the event of death at sea, subject is zippered into a body bag and kept on ice until the submarine returns to port. Since McGinn's orders were to maintain absolute radio silence for seventy-two hours, he ordered Patterson's body to be stored in the large freezer on the lower missile deck. And since Albano mentioned that Kent and Garin were friends of the deceased, McGinn assigned them to look after the remains.

"He must weigh three hundred pounds," Kent groaned as they heaved the body bag onto a shelf in the food freezer.

"It does give us an excuse to shake down his personal effects," Garin reminded him.

"Horsecock. Now we're stuck with this stiff during the whole experiment."

"So what? It's no damned secret. Our friend in Washington approved it to begin with."

"Yeah, well, suppose this Lieutenant Early is some kind of scam artist," Kent persisted. He nodded at the body bag. "You know it'll look bad if we come back empty-handed."

Garin sighed and slammed the freezer door shut. He knew there was a certain logic to what Kent said. "All right, I'll stay and cover you while you nose around. But be extremely careful, homeboy. Empty-handed is bad. Fucking up is terminal."

Both Garin and Kent had been briefed on the *Blowgun*'s experiment before they left Langley. Code-named Earlybird, it was a low-priority project initiated by Dr. Shandy's department, which was well known for its brainstorms. Such as training dolphins to plant magnetic tracking devices on enemy submarines.

But Earlybird was the dippiest yet, Kent reflected as he made his way to the upper deck. The way he'd heard it, Shandy met Lieutenant Early at some embassy cocktail party. Early told Shandy he had experienced telepathic contact and Shandy bought the package. Somehow Shandy managed to sell the Pentagon on giving it an expensive test. Still, Kent had to admit the project idea touched one of the Navy's most sensitive nerves—the crucial problem of maintaining total silence on a nuclear sub to avoid detection. So if Early actually did succeed in making telepathic contact with someone on shore, the Navy would have an ace up its sleeve.

Ass is more like it, Kent gloated. It shouldn't be difficult to hang Dr. Shandy, and maybe even Early, for misuse of official funds on this harebrained ESP scheme. He'd raise enough of a smoke screen to obscure their bad timing with Patterson.

The project was simple enough. The *Blowgun* would set a completely random course in the Caribbean. In fact, every move the ship made would be recorded on tape, called the "white rat" by the crew. After each patrol the tapes would be sent to civilian specialists for study to see if the ship had fallen into detectable patterns.

At the same time, Lieutenant Early had a navigational chart of the local waters in front of him. His contact in New York had the same chart. At thirty-minute intervals Early was to transmit the *Blowgun*'s position telepathically. At the end of a three-day period, the results would be checked against the sub's actual course.

The odds were against him, Kent calculated. And when Early blew it, they'd have Shandy by the balls. The first thing they'd do would be to leak the details to the press.

While the ship was in its ultra-quiet mode, all nonessential machinery, including the ice-cream dispenser, would be shut down. And all crew members not on watch were to be confined to their bunks. However, because of the special nature of their duties, Kent and Garin were always on watch. With the exception of the radioman, the crew manned their normal stations during the experiment.

For this reason Kent was alerted when he saw Blum hovering near the captain's quarters, a long distance from the torpedo room.

"Sorry to hear about your buddy," Blum said, emphasizing the last word.

"Yeah, well, he wasn't exactly . . . uh, have you seen Albano?"

"If he ain't in sickbay, try the head."

Kent ignored his abrasive tone. "Say, what about this ESP stuff? Is that the secret weapon you meant?"

Blum suddenly looked worried. "I never said nothin' about ESP."

"Of course you didn't. But scuttlebutt is that there's some kind of mental telepathy stuff going on. So after what you said, or never said, about Early . . ."

Blum put a finger to his lips and pulled Kent into an alcove.

"Nothin's ever secret on a sub," he muttered. "Okay, c'mon back to my quarters before you get us both in trouble. You tell me what you heard and I'll tell you what I know. Maybe between the two of us we can figure out what the hell we're really doin' on this patrol."

Garin was having second thoughts about letting Kent walk around unattended. His partner had a tendency to be impulsive. Better to wait until things settled down. After all, the experiment would last seventy-two hours. If Kent made a rash move, the Patterson thing could blow up in their faces.

He flipped through an old *Penthouse,* but his mind kept going back to the corpse in the freezer. The bastard was lucky, Garin thought ruefully. At least he croaked at the right time. For him. If only he'd lived another thirty minutes . . . Garin's dour speculations were interrupted by a scraping sound behind him. Knowing the area was off limits to most crewmen, since it housed both provisions and half of the sub's twenty-four nuclear missiles, he assumed it was his partner.

"Kent? So what's the scoop?"

But when he turned, there was nobody there. He put the magazine aside and checked the corridor. It was deserted. As he returned to his chair, he noticed the freezer door was slightly ajar. Thinking it might have popped loose when he slammed it, Garin tried to push it shut.

The door didn't budge. Apparently something had lodged in the jamb. He slid the door open and checked, but the runner seemed clear. As he stepped inside, Garin caught a shadowy movement in the corner of his vision. Then something cold gripped his throat.

The hands were terribly strong. And icy. Like frozen metal cables choking off his breath. Reflexively he lashed back with an elbow and connected with solid flesh, but the hands crushing his windpipe did not relent.

With desperate quickness he dug his thumbs underneath the fingers clamped around his neck, grabbed one—and yanked down hard.

Just as he'd been taught, he felt the sharp snap of broken bone. But when he tried to twist free, the pressure on his neck increased. Panic swam through his brain and he kicked back wildly as waves of agony pounded at his lungs.

The realization that he was about to die swelled inside his belly and he thrashed from side to side, mouth gaping in a soundless scream for air. Suddenly he felt his bladder void and his awareness collapsed, sucking him into the black, bottomless silence.

The first thing Kent noticed when he returned to the storage area was that the air purification system wasn't functioning properly. Then he saw the black shoe protruding form the half-open freezer.

"Not funny, Garin," he muttered, moving closer. "C'mon, I got something to tell you."

As he neared, recognition jolted his instincts and he reached for the knife holstered at his ankle. Garin was sprawled on the floor, eyes bulging in sightless surprise and tongue stuffed through rigid blue lips.

A faint shuffling sound jerked Kent's head back. There was someone in the missile room. Crouching slightly, he moved to the open door. He saw a tall, naked figure bent over a missile tube. He wasn't ready for what he saw next.

The man who turned toward him was Harold Patterson.

Kent's thoughts ricocheted crazily from Garin to Patterson. This isn't real, I've been drugged, he told himself, watching Patterson lurch closer. As the dark shape loomed in front of him, Kent jabbed blindly with his knife. He felt the blade punch flesh but the figure pressed forward. Patterson swatted the knife out of Kent's hand and grabbed him by the hair. Clamping a huge hand over Kent's mouth, he smashed his skull against a steel beam.

He let Kent's inert weight slip from his fingers and pushed the outer door shut. He moved directly to the missile tube and slid open the metal housing to reveal the solid-fuel base of a nuclear rocket cradled in its electronic nest.

After a momentary pause he located a panel marked "Caution/Range Safety." There were three buttons on the panel. He pushed the two outer buttons, then the center and right buttons in sequence, activating a tiny, flashing red light.

Then he closed the housing and shuffled back to the freezer compartment.

The first to notice that a small Sea Hornet missile had been primed was Computer Technician Kislak.

"Jesus, Commander," he blurted, staring at the screen. "We got a problem in lower missile."

"Deactivate the entire section," McGinn barked when he saw the blinking light on the graphic. "Disarm all warheads."

"All systems disarmed," Kislak droned, rapidly punching the keyboard. "Still getting an alarm signal, sir."

"Probably a computer glitch," McGinn decided. After all, it took four keys to launch a nuclear missile. And three of the keys were in a safe to which not even he had the combination.

He was only half right. The commander had forgotten about the Range Safety Package on the Sea Hornet. This was the control mechanism used to destroy the missile in the event it went off course. There was very little he could have done, in any case. The device detonated the rocket within ninety seconds. As it was, McGinn's order to disarm all warheads prevented the sub from being dissolved into radioactive soup.

The explosion ignited the rocket stage, blasting the missile through the tube. Both the lower and upper compartments were immediately vented to the sea, and the main electrical system failed a few moments later. The *Blowgun* listed to one side as a huge fist of water rammed through the gutted hull, and the half-darkened submarine began tilting slowly toward the ocean floor.

Chapter 2

". . . AND WHEN HE GOT UP TO GO INTO THE street, he found the world had changed."

The line had stuck in Orient's mind ever since he ran across it in a story by Paul Bowles. Over the years it had returned to him often, in many tones of meaning. But never with such cold clarity.

The city had changed in ten years.

In better times it had always managed to retain a certain wit, which endowed the massive skyline with a shade of dignity as it passed through its countless incarnations. Today, however, the glass towers seemed barren and dull, as if New York's legendary spark had been snuffed under its own weight. The city's style had been corrupted by pomposity, its curiosity consumed by excess, its rare intelligence reduced to base cunning.

Most likely it was simple attrition, Orient speculated unhappily. In a thousand years the city would be a field of ruins like Pompeii. An odd side trip for tourists on their way to Disneyworld.

Orient stared out the window as the cab threaded through the evening traffic on Park Avenue. Even the deep sunset light cascading down the cross streets like liquid gold failed to rouse his usual admiration for New York's natural wonders. He had barely been in the city two weeks and he was nearly broke. At the moment, he had enough money for a ticket back to Rome and three months of frugal glory.

Of course, he could always resume practicing medicine at some understaffed hospital willing to overlook his erratic professional history. But he wasn't sure his long-dormant skills could rise to a life-and-death test. And anyway, he felt too burned out to deal with the paperwork.

With all his misgivings, Orient was looking forward to seeing Sybelle again. Uppermost among the things he had missed during his self-imposed exile were close friends. And while he often disagreed with his flamboyant colleague, Orient considered Sybelle Lean to be one of his most cherished allies. On numerous occasions she had pulled him out of a tight spot with the timely delivery of a scented envelope stuffed with cash to some remote corner of the world. She had a knack of reaching out when he most needed it. Like tonight, for instance.

Orient wasn't really clear about how Sybelle knew he was staying at the Chelsea Hotel. But he expected she'd explain over drinks and one of her sumptuous dinners.

When the cab stopped for its second red light in two blocks, Orient paid the driver and strolled leisurely to Madison Avenue. He browsed the sleek shop windows as he walked uptown, marveling at the sheer bulk of riches warehoused on the stretch of concrete between Sixty-first Street and the Whitney Museum. The men and women promenading on the avenue were also sleek and richly attired, making him aware of his own well-worn black jeans and scuffed leather jacket.

He didn't mind the contrast, but a few of the opulent matrons seemed pained when they glanced at him in passing. Then again, Orient mused, it was quite possible their pained expressions were a permanent fixture, like bobbed noses and tummy tucks.

Orient was comforted by the knowledge that some things hadn't changed in his absence. Sybelle still resided in an immodestly elegant town house off Seventy-fourth Street. The squat, red brick structure had been converted from a defunct fire station, allowing plenty of space for Sybelle's esoteric lifestyle. The pale blue card above the brass bell read:

SYBELLE LEAN
Psychic Consultant
BY APPOINTMENT ONLY

He pressed the button and heard what sounded like wind chimes somewhere inside. Moments later the door swung open, and Orient saw the familiar mass of frizzy red hair framing Sybelle's cherubic features. But their reunion fell far short of his expectations. Sybelle's face was sickly white, and the dark circles around her green eyes overshadowed her wan attempt at a smile.

"Owen, darling, at last." She gave him a hurried kiss. "I'm so happy you're finally here. Come in, everyone is waiting."

"Everyone?" Orient echoed as he followed her down the hall. "Is something wrong? You seem out of sorts."

Sybelle paused. "Right on both counts. There is something wrong—and I feel like hell. Now come along, darling. Time is of the essence."

"Who's waiting for us?" Orient persisted, but she had already opened the door and was ushering him into the library.

As soon as he entered, a large, white-maned gentleman with a dour, bulldog expression lurched to his feet and extended his arms.

"Let's get goin', Owen," he blared. "We missed you."

Orient would have recognized the foghorn voice and shopworn greeting in the midst of a typhoon. Former U.S. Senator Andy Jacobs had been a family friend since childhood.

"Good to see you, Senator," he said as they embraced. "It's been too long."

"Damned right. You've been out of circulation for a dog's age, boy. You planning to stay?"

Orient was about to answer, then noticed the two men sitting quietly on the couch. Both were strangers, but he knew who they were instinctively.

Sybelle cleared her throat. "I, er, don't believe you've met Mr. Westlake and Dr. Shandy."

Both men stood at the same time. The older of the two, a barrel-chested man with a receding hairline and piercing gray eyes, extended his hand. "An honor to meet you at last, Doctor. Sybelle has been telling us some fascinating things about you."

"No doubt she has," Orient said, giving Sybelle a tight smile. "Now perhaps someone will explain why we're all here."

"Of course, Owen. Of course," Andy Jacobs said gravely. "You see, Mr. Westlake and Dr. Shandy are with the Navy Department. Naval Intelligence, to be precise."

Orient's expression didn't change, but he felt a perceptible rise in his pulse rate. He continued to stare at Sybelle, who wavered for a moment, then met his gaze squarely.

"They're here at my invitation, Owen. And so is Andy. I thought the senator could serve as a sort of counsel, or mediator . . ."

"Counsel? Am I on trial here?"

"No, dear. I am," she said wearily.

Something in her voice penetrated his confusion. For the first time he realized Sybelle desperately needed his help.

"Perhaps I can explain . . ."

Orient turned in time to catch Westlake scowling threateningly at his associate. The younger man ignored him and resolutely went on. He had a tendency to squint, which, along with his Vandyke beard, gave him the air of an enthused diamond cutter examining a prize gem.

"I'm Dr. Ashton Shandy, scientific liaison for Project Earlybird, which Commander Westlake heads up. I'm also a great admirer of your research work."

"Well, that explains everything," Orient said curtly. He moved closer to Sybelle and took her hand. "What's all this have to do with you?"

"It so happens Project Earlybird has to do with telepathy."

Orient let her hand drop. "And you're advising them."

"Not her, Doctor," Shandy interjected. "The subject in question was Lieutenant Craig Early. Ah . . . *is* Lieutenant Early," he amended hastily, noting Sybelle's stricken look.

"I taught Craig your technique," she blurted out. She watched Orient's face for a reaction. There was none.

But all of Orient's senses were suddenly aware of the silent undercurrents circling the room. The tensions between Westlake and Shandy. Sybelle's desperate fear. Shandy's smug certainty. Westlake's hostility. Only Andy Jacobs stood apart, like some gnarled oak tree at the edge of a whirlpool.

The senator regarded Orient glumly. "Give her a break, Owen. It's not entirely her fault."

"I'm afraid it is," she murmured.

"Give *me* a break," Westlake cut in. "We're getting way off base. Human lives are at stake here." He jabbed a finger at Orient. "Listen up, Doctor. We've got a crippled submarine with one hundred and forty-three men aboard, stranded somewhere between Florida and Cuba.

And we need you to help locate it. In fact—ridiculous as
it may sound—you're the only chance those men have."

Shandy's back stiffened. "An accuracy rate of seventy-
seven percent is hardly ridiculous."

"Shove your percentages. All right, Dr. Orient, those
are the facts. Right now the men on that sub have a forty-
hour air supply. So whatever your decision, please make
it fast. The Navy has better things to do than wet-nurse a
goddamn seance."

Orient studied him for a moment, weighing the possibilities. Some deep instinct harbored an intense distrust of
the commander. He glanced at Andy, who shrugged
mournfully.

"How can I refuse such a heartfelt appeal?" Orient said
finally. "Of course I'll do anything I can. For the men
down there—not the almighty Navy. So, Commander,
since time is our common enemy, I suggest we get to it.
First I'll need to have a brief conference with my col-
leagues. In private."

Westlake seemed disappointed. "Please make sure it's
brief."

"You and Dr. Shandy must be famished," Sybelle fluttered, herding the two men toward the door. "Let me fix
you a marvelous snack. Everything's all prepared." She
glanced at Orient uncertainly. "I'll be right back, darling."

"Now, exactly what the hell is going on here, Andy?"
Orient demanded as soon as they were alone.

The ex-senator jerked his head toward the door and put
a finger to his lips. "Place may be bugged."

"I've got nothing to hide. How about you?"

Andy Jacobs shook his head. "I cut a deal on your
behalf, Owen. In return for your help in this matter, the
Pentagon is willing to drop any outstanding criminal
charges and curtail all surveillance at once. And oh, yes,

I've also put paperwork through on the release of your complete file under the Freedom of Information—''

''Does the fact that I've committed no crime have any bearing on this marvelous deal?''

Andy managed a bleary-eyed smile. ''None whatsoever, my boy. I know what you've been through and I'm proud of you. But it's time to come home now. Time to forget and go on with your life . . . your work.''

Orient looked away. ''Perhaps you're right, Senator. Anyway, there's no time to argue the point, is there? But I still don't understand how you and Sybelle got involved with Naval Intelligence.''

''Well, you might say I got into this through the transom.''

''The fact is I called him,'' Sybelle declared, striding into the room. ''I was the one who got mixed up with Project Earlybird. And I was the one who betrayed your trust.''

''Listen, Owen, she's—''

''Please, Andy, I have something very personal to discuss with Owen.''

His jowls bulged with indignation. ''Great,'' he muttered, stalking to the door. ''I get to eat with the sharks while you two kiss and make up.''

Sybelle took a glass from the shelf above the bar. ''When the intelligence people told me you were . . . available, I asked Andy to represent your legal interests. I hope I wasn't too presumptuous.''

''Presumptuous,'' Orient repeated. ''You watch me burn my bridges and go underground for ten years to protect my work from the CIA. Then you turn around, break your vow of secrecy and deliver me to the very people who have been trying to destroy me. And you write it off as presumption.''

''More like abject despair. You see, my partner in Project Earlybird—Lieutenant Craig Early—is my son.''

She tried to pour herself a brandy, but the glass slipped from her trembling fingers. "I know it was terribly wrong, Owen . . . but he's down there . . ."

Orient slowly reached out and took the decanter from her hand. "I'll do everything in my power to find him," he said softly. "We can sort the rest out later. Right now we'll need some place more secluded where we can get to work."

Relief flooded her pale features. "Yes, of course. My studio. It's already set up. I've been trying to . . . reach Craig on my own."

Orient managed a tight smile. "Good. I can use your experience. I'm a bit rusty these days."

The studio proved to be ideal for their purposes. Since Sybelle used the room to conduct her psychic readings, it was both comfortable and well-equipped. Among the amenities were various charts of the area where the *Blowgun* had been cruising.

"Actually, the first stage of our little experiment went quite well," Sybelle explained, settling down in a black leather chair.

Orient gestured at the nautical charts littering the table in front of her. "Are these part of the project?"

"Yes." She pointed to a chart marked with a red fluorescent pen. "We were using this one when they told me about the accident."

"Are they certain there was an accident? Sometimes subs lose contact . . ."

"I know. When they dive too deep underwater. That was exactly the reason for Project Earlybird. To find alternate means to communicate . . ."

Sybelle took a deep breath and shook her head. "Anyway, the whole thing was simple, really. Like a little game."

Orient fished a silver cigarette case from his pocket and extracted a hand-wrapped cigarette. "Tell me about it."

"The *Blowgun* set a totally random course, complete radio silence. Every fifteen minutes for a six-hour period, Craig would transmit his position to me telepathically. They have some sort of tape device aboard that registers their position. Craig and I have the same charts. When I received his message I marked the position on my chart." She slid an ashtray across the table. "Anyway, they said we did quite well the first day. Over seventy percent accuracy. I should have known something terrible was going to happen when they told me one of the crewmen had died."

"Why didn't the sub turn back to port?"

"They said the deceased was being shipped back home. Somewhere in the Caribbean, I think."

Orient studied the burning tip of his cigarette. "Who's 'they'?"

"Ash Shandy. He was the original head of the project. Westlake stepped in after the accident."

"There's one thing I don't understand. If the submarine was maintaining total silence, how do they know there was an accident?"

"Apparently the *Blowgun* managed to radio for help for almost three minutes before it . . . went dead. Oh God, Owen, I could feel it when it happened. My blood went cold."

"Exactly where was the sub before they lost contact?"

She leaned across the table and pointed to a large red X marking the black swirls of a nautical chart. "Their last tape reading was eighteen hours before the accident. It put them right here—between Florida and Cuba." She indicated another X, a short distance away. "This was my last telepathic reading, but it can't be verified. Westlake has planes searching the area now."

Orient stubbed out the cigarette and studied the chart.

Its intricate lines were difficult for a layman to decipher. To complicate matters, they also had to consider charts of the surrounding waters. The *Blowgun* could be anywhere within a radius of one hundred miles. He looked at Sybelle. "Any luck with your recent efforts to contact Craig?"

"I don't know. Since this happened. . . . I can't be sure."

"What about the seventy percent?"

"I don't follow."

"You had a seventy percent accuracy rate, correct?"

"What about it?"

"Then you should know if you contacted your son or not. Relax and think back. It's important."

Sybelle made a visible effort to compose herself. After a few minutes she shook her head. "I thought I did once. But maybe I just wanted it very badly. At any rate, whatever I sensed was awfully faint."

"Do you have something in the house that belonged to Craig? An article of clothing, a toothbrush, anything he might have used?"

"Why, yes. He left some T-shirts in the guest room."

"Please fetch one. The most worn."

"Oh, Lord. That means running the gauntlet past Westlake and Shandy all over again. Westlake keeps insisting you allow them to observe."

"Just as well," Orient said, unbuttoning his shirt. "While you're busy keeping them at bay, I'll have time to warm up."

When Sybelle left the room, Orient removed his shirt, shoes, and trousers, then knelt on the thick blue carpet. Limited by time, he focused totally on his spine as he went through an abbreviated set of stretching exercises designed to tune body and mind. As his concentration deepened, he began a four-count breathing pattern that pumped oxygen into the brain and sent pulses of electricity through his bloodstream.

Slowly, as if carefully banking a glider, he swung his concentration to the base of his skull and felt the brain cells light up like runway flares. He took the silver case from his shirt pocket and placed it beside him on the floor. The case had been given to him by the master Ku when he had completed his studies in the Tibetan mountain retreat and was ready to resume his place in society. The curious mandala design etched on its face was the symbol of his destiny as a monk of the cities. It was his function to seed the telepathic technique among those few who qualified. It was also his duty to preserve its integrity at all costs, Orient reflected. He could only pray he wasn't being duped into betraying that sacred trust.

He picked up the nautical chart and spread it out on the floor. He had just lit a pair of candles when Sybelle returned with a stained, gray athletic shirt.

"I should have thought of this myself," she said, easing down onto the rug. "Of course it will be easier to contact Craig by using something personal of his as a *point d'appui*. Thank God you came."

She pulled her dark red smock over her head and tossed it aside. The black leotards she wore underneath attested to the Yoga regimen that kept her plump curves firmly toned. Without any preamble, she took a few moments to stretch out her limbs, then deftly slipped into a lotus position.

"Owen, I'm still worried about something," she confided. "Even if we do manage to reach Craig—how will we pinpoint his location? I don't really understand these charts, and there's a distinct chance I may misinterpret any numbers or coordinates he sends."

Orient fingered the pendant hanging from a thin gold chain around his neck. It was a shard of ice-blue crystal set in a black metal collar. "We can solve that problem

by using the dowsing method. First stage, we contact
Craig. Then we let him guide us directly to his position
on the chart.''

Sybelle clutched Craig's old shirt against her chest. "I
pray to God you're right.''

Orient took her hand. "We'll give it our best, and
more.''

He continued to hold her hand as they began the primary breathing pattern, focusing on the faint throb of her
pulse. He cleared his mind of everything else, letting their
pulsebeats merge into a single rhythm.

His senses embraced Sybelle's aura, fusing with her
tentative orbit. He mentally probed the vibration emanating from Craig's shirt and felt a surge of momentum
as Sybelle locked on her son's energy. Their momentum
gathered intensity as she swung out in search of the energy source. For a sickening instant they dropped through
the void. And suddenly it was there.

A faint, oddly familiar vibration tugged at their orbit.
Sybelle's quick surge of emotion tilted their balance, but
Orient managed to steady their teetering link with Craig.

Without waiting to test their fragile connection, he immediately projected an image of the nautical chart Sybelle
had marked. At the same time, he removed the gold chain
and held it in his outstretched hand, letting the pendant
dangle over the chart.

The crystal shard hung motionless as they remained
fixed on the tenuous thread of energy binding them in
time. Then, very carefully, Orient shifted poles from ac-
tive to passive.

As he tuned his senses back on himself, a flicker of
tension leaped across the momentary vacuum, and the
crystal pendant began to sway back and forth.

Chapter 3

LIEUTENANT CRAIG EARLY WAS HAVING TROUBLE keeping his nerves from coming unwrapped. The emergency generators were maintaining their life-support systems, but the radio was still malfunctioning. Although he knew the accident hadn't been his fault, he couldn't overlook the fact that the rescue team would have their accurate position if not for his damned telepathy experiment. What started as a game had become the *Blowgun*'s albatross.

A stillness had settled over the crippled submarine, and Early had the impression the crew was waiting for him to perform some sort of miracle. Having no other option but to keep trying, he stayed with the pre-agreed schedule. Every fifteen minutes he transmitted their position telepathically to his mother. Even before the accident blew out the missile room, Early found that the effort required to focus his concentration left him drained. But now, as he faced sure death, it took all his strength just to stay in the cramped compartment and stare at the chart.

So he felt a deep sense of relief when the timer signaled his shift had ended. Unfortunately, as soon as he stepped into the corridor he ran into Commander McGinn.

"Any progress?" McGinn growled.

"It's hard to know, sir."

"Well, keep trying." McGinn started to move past, then paused. "You feeling well, Lieutenant?"

"Yes, sir. Why do you ask?"

"Because unless we've sprung another leak, you seem to be sweating bullets."

Early looked down and saw that his shirt was drenched to the skin. "Guess it's a little stuffy in there, sir."

"I can imagine. Carry on."

"Uh . . . sir?"

McGinn eyed him impatiently. "What is it, Early?"

"Sorry about the radio."

"How do you mean?"

"If it hadn't been silent so long, because of my experiment . . ." He let the sentence dangle, waiting for McGinn to come down on him.

Instead the commander shook his head and chuckled. "You know, Early, about a year before you came aboard, the Navy Department had us under radio silence for forty-three days to test a new air conditioner. Anyway, Sparks managed to send out a Mayday for almost three minutes before the radio went dead. The accident wasn't your fault. And you can do more for us than air-conditioning. Right now you're our lifeline. Luckily we also managed to send up a disaster beacon. All you have to do is lead them to it."

The exchange left Early feeling encouraged. McGinn's little pep talk made a strange kind of sense. For the first time he actually believed his experiment had value. He thought about what McGinn had said while he toweled dry and changed his shirt.

As it happened, a large part of his problem was the air-conditioning. Or lack of it. There simply wasn't enough oxygen in his cramped work space.

It occurred to him that he might be better off starting

his basic breathing pattern before he entered the small compartment. To test his theory he casually took a few long breaths and found it fairly easy to work into a deep, deliberate cycle. The Yoga breathing dusted off his weary brain, so he continued the pattern as he went off in search of some fruit juice.

By the end of his thirty-minute break, Craig felt primed and anxious to get back to work. As soon as he entered the small room he sat on the floor, facing the nautical chart taped to the wall. He was already relaxed, so he took his time, going through each step the way he'd been taught. He became totally passive as he stared at the chart, trying to absorb it into his consciousness. A phrase rippled across his mind—what McGinn had told him about the disaster beacon.

He visualized an orange neon beacon bobbing on the clear blue water. The mental image trailed along as he shifted his concentration and focused all his senses on the precise spot on the chart where the sub had gone down. He projected the image of a bright orange beacon onto the chart and instantly felt a snap of recognition.

At the same time, his concentration was battered by a sudden rush of fear. He fought back the raw panic clawing at his belly and continued to press the image of an orange beacon onto the exact longitude and latitude of their grave, until his will collapsed from exhaustion.

When Early left the tiny compartment his uniform was again drenched with sweat, and his senses were numbed by deep depression. He couldn't be certain what had happened in there. But he knew it would be a long time before he gathered the courage to try it again.

As he made his way back to his quarters, the faces of the crew seemed starkly pale in the dim light. As if they were already dead.

Chapter 4

ORIENT COULD FEEL COLD SWEAT OOZING FROM Sybelle's palms as the crystal pendant swung in small arcs above the chart. He detected a slight muscle tremor, but she gripped his hand firmly and held her inner balance.

He intensified his concentration, carefully beveling into Sybelle's orbit until he felt the weight of their combined energy. Then, using Sybelle as a direction finder, he cast across the void for Craig.

Her pure link to her son gave them an instant connection.

Almost simultaneously, a noxious sense of evil pervaded his awareness. It spread rapidly, clogging his belly and lungs with venomous panic. The foul presence wound around his concentration, threatening to topple their orbit.

Fighting a reflex to bolt, Orient focused on the pendant dangling from his fingers, and rotated abruptly to a totally receptive state.

The shift wheeled their orbit inward, generating a sudden flux of gravity that pulled the pendant taut on its chain. The crystal shard quivered, then dipped toward the chart like a magnet to iron.

The fine hairs on the back of his wrist lifted as a wave of static electricity swept from fingertips to shoulder. And vanished.

Orient pulled away from Sybelle and pressed the crystal into the chart, marking the exact spot.

Sybelle opened her eyes. "Why did we break contact?"

He pointed to the deep indentation on the chart before circling it with a red marker. "Mission accomplished—I think."

"Owen, are you sure? It all seemed to happen so fast."

"The sooner we check, the sooner we can try again."

She looked away. "I felt something in there. Something cold . . ." She forced a smile. "I pray we won't need a return engagement."

He gave her a reassuring hug. "Come on. Let's put the Navy to work."

As expected, Shandy was eager to contact the rescue patrols, but Commander Westlake still harbored doubts.

"This position you marked puts the *Blowgun* about forty miles east of Cuba. The waters in that particular area run between fifty and a hundred fathoms at most."

Orient shrugged. "So what's your point?"

"Their radio would function at that depth. That's my damned point."

"Look, Commander," Orient said patiently. "I was told the radio signaled a Mayday for three minutes. Which seems to indicate that whatever caused the *Blowgun* to malfunction caused the radio to malfunction. So let's not drag our feet. As you informed me, human lives are at stake. If I prove wrong, you can fire me."

Westlake smiled. "You damned well better hope you're right. Or you can forget that little amnesty deal."

Orient returned the smile. "So much for honor among thieves."

As Westlake stalked off in search of his special telephone, Dr. Shandy approached Orient and Sybelle, rubbing his hands excitedly.

"God, if you guys are on target, this will be an absolutely huge breakthrough."

Still smoldering from the exchange with Westlake, Orient glared at him.

Sybelle stepped between them. "Tell me, Dr. Shandy, how long will it take the rescue team to reach the *Blowgun*?"

He seemed upset by the question. "Well, perhaps nine, er, twelve hours at most. For the rescue ships, that is. Be assured our search planes will be there much sooner."

Her brows shot up in surprise. "Why so long? As I recall, the very last position I charted with Craig was in the same general area. The rescue ships should certainly be there by now."

"Yes. Of course." He peered at her solemnly. "But, er, the fact is Commander Westlake chose to deploy all search teams over a probable route computed by headquarters."

"A computer?" Sybelle exploded. "You've been wasting all this time on a fucking printout?"

His face reddened. "Westlake's orders. He's always been extremely hostile to this project. He thinks—"

"To hell with what he thinks. Is Senator Jacobs still here?"

"Why, yes. I'll get him," Shandy offered, grateful for an excuse to escape Sybelle's wrath.

As he left, Sybelle turned to Orient and grasped his hand. "Thank you, darling."

"For what?"

"When you stood up to Westlake, it made me realize what sort of pompous bastards we're dealing with. All this time I've been so afraid for Craig I . . ."

"Not your fault. It's the way of the world."

Sybelle paused and looked up and down. "You know, you have changed a bit, Owen."

"Let's hope for the better."

Before she could reply, Andy Jacobs came storming into the room. "Sybelle? Owen? What the hell's going on?"

"Nothing at all, Senator. Except our Commander Westlake has been lying through his teeth. Not only has he reneged on his deal with Owen, but he's got our rescue ships out of position. Instead of my reading, he's been using some damned computer."

"Somebody talking about me?"

Sybelle turned to glare at Westlake, who was standing in the doorway. "Yes, as a matter of fact . . ."

"Excuse me," Andy said calmly. "May I have the floor?"

The edge in his voice drew Sybelle's attention. "Well, of course. I yield to the senator."

"Ex-senator," Westlake reminded her.

"Now that's true," Jacobs said, removing his glasses. "But I can promise you one thing. If you are responsible for any obstruction whatsoever to Craig's rescue, I will devote the remnants of my humble career to nailing your hide to the tallest flagpole on Capitol Hill."

"I have ordered all search teams to the area indicated by your Dr. Orient," Westlake said flatly. "It all depends on his accuracy."

But for the first time since the crisis erupted, he appeared worried.

It was getting extremely warm inside the *Blowgun*.

The cooling and circulation systems were running on low power to conserve energy, and the body heat generated by one hundred and forty frightened men was becoming a factor.

The first thing McGinn had done after the accident was to take a head count. To his relief only seven men were missing. However, the remaining crew was confined to a space roughly two-thirds the size it normally occupied.

Food presented no problem, nor did air, although one of the main oxygen tanks had ruptured, limiting them to a week's supply.

By that time some of the men would begin to crack under the intense pressure, McGinn thought glumly. In fact, he wasn't sure he'd last the course himself. He hoped he wouldn't have to use the .45 he now wore holstered at his waist.

Oddly enough, their most crucial concern was having sufficient water. Most of their potable reserves had been lost, forcing McGinn to impose severe rationing.

The commander worked hard at keeping the crew's morale high by inventing projects to keep them busy. He also called meetings every six hours to update the situation.

In truth, their situation hadn't changed since they hit bottom, McGinn reflected. Sparks still hadn't managed to fix the radio. The watertight compartments had maintained full integrity after the missile and torpedo rooms flooded, but at best they provided a brief standoff against the waiting sea.

"With rationing we should have enough air and water for at least a week," McGinn told his assembled officers. "Our main priority is establishing radio contact—our highest priority is getting out of here. So if any of you gentlemen has an idea, even a bad one, speak up. No matter when the notion strikes. One more item. From now on, all officers will be required to wear side arms."

To Lieutenant Early, the directive was the most ominous thing McGinn had said. It conjured images of madness, mutiny, suicide, and murder.

"Any special reason everybody's packing a pistol, sir?" Blum asked the moment Early appeared in the computer section.

Early hesitated, knowing the other crewmen were listening.

"Keep this under your hat," he told Blum. "The old man gave orders to shoot any prowling fish on sight."

The general laughter wafted like a cool breeze through the stuffy compartment.

Just before Early took his shift in the chart room, Commander McGinn called him aside. "If we get out of this I'm writing you up for a commendation."

"Well, ah, thank you, sir. But why?"

"Any man who can joke under fire is my kind of officer."

The compliment didn't make Early feel any less scared as he prepared to continue his experiment. It all seemed so absurd. So hopeless. The stifling heat inside the chart room closed around him like a shroud. And as Early went into his breathing pattern, he began to pray.

A metallic clang roused him from his meditation.

The compartment wall quivered as something struck the hull. Fearing the wall was about to give way, Craig left the tiny compartment and went to inform the commander.

McGinn took the news calmly enough, but he hurried back to the chart room immediately. As they approached the compartment, another clang resounded through the corridor, and McGinn drew his .45.

Craig froze when he saw the commander heft his weapon and step inside the tiny room. A moment later he heard the loud bang of metal striking metal. He peeked inside and saw McGinn swatting the hull with the butt of his pistol.

"They found us," McGinn said hoarsely as he batted the wall again. "Thank God. I lied about the water. We would have run out in forty-eight hours."

Chapter 5

ORIENT FIRST HEARD ABOUT THE *BLOWGUN*'S
rescue on television. The news flash interrupted a late-
night screening of *The Treasure of the Sierra Madre*. He
left the guest room and hurried to wake Sybelle. But when
he reached her bedroom he found the door open, and Sybelle on the phone.

"It's Dr. Shandy," she announced excitedly. "He says
Craig is safe."

Orient lingered in the doorway until she hung up.

"When do you get to see Craig?"

"Dr. Shandy said it might be a few days."

"Why so long?"

"I'm sure I don't know, darling. But I must say you
don't seem very excited about Craig's rescue."

Orient gave her a hug. "Of course I am. I just heard it
on the tube. Why do you think I rushed in here?"

"My devastating charm."

"That too. Perhaps you should phone the senator and
give him the good news."

"You give him the good news, darling. I'm going to
pop a bottle of champagne for the occasion."

"That's great. Really wonderful," Andy Jacobs bellowed when Orient phoned. "But why in hell didn't the Navy boys contact Sybelle before they informed the damned media?"

"It does seem a bit funny."

"Funny as a four-card flush. Look, I'll drop by for breakfast. You make sure Sybelle doesn't drink all the champagne before I get there."

The senator arrived promptly at seven a.m., and for the next few hours he sifted through his little black book and placed phone calls to various cronies on Capitol Hill and at CIA headquarters in Langley, Virginia. Long before noon, however, he decided it was time for a celebratory drink. Sybelle whipped up an impromptu brunch of toasted bagels, cream cheese, and smoked salmon, along with a large pitcher of champagne and orange juice.

"It's the damnedest thing," Andy told them morosely. "They're all clamming up on the *Blowgun* incident. Apparently most of the crew got out and are on their way to some unknown port in the Caribbean. There's a rumor that the Navy is attempting to raise the sub."

By two that afternoon, the news coverage on the Navy's dramatic rescue of one hundred and forty men trapped aboard the crippled submarine had reached saturation. Every channel showed the official stock footage of the special bathysphere that attached to the *Blowgun*'s escape hatch and shuttled the crew to the surface over an eleven-hour period. Despite Sybelle's fears, the rescue ships had arrived three hours after the *Blowgun*'s disaster beacon was sighted by a search plane.

It was widely noted that the *Blowgun* had sunk off the Cuban coast. And a few TV newscasters mentioned that the submarine was fortunate to have gone down in relatively shallow waters. But for the most part the medium confined itself to rerunning the same footage of the same smiling crewmen emerging from the bathysphere and boarding the rescue ship. There was no mention of Project Earlybird.

"Television has managed to erode the freedom of the press more effectively than any dictator," Andy Jacobs grumbled, relighting his cigar.

Sybelle sat up and reached for the phone. "Now that's a good idea," she said, rapidly punching a number.

"Who are you calling?"

She ignored Andy's question. "It's Sybelle Lean for Dr. Shandy. Tell him it's urgent."

"Shandy?" The senator shook his head. "You've already called him three times since this morning."

Sybelle covered the mouthpiece and smiled. "This time I have something to say."

"Oh, he's not? Will you please give him a message?" she asked sweetly when she was finally taken off hold. "Just inform Dr. Shandy that if I don't speak to him by three-thirty"—she paused to check her watch—"then I will be speaking to the press.

"Please don't worry, Owen, darling," she assured him after hanging up. "If Shandy doesn't call back—and we all know he will—I swear I'll keep you out of it."

At that very moment Orient was seriously wondering whether it wasn't time to move on. He had accomplished what Sybelle had asked. Her son was safe. All the rest meant nothing to him.

It wasn't quite true, Orient admitted ruefully. One small debt remained outstanding. Westlake had made a deal. And he intended to collect his winnings.

He decided to wait for Shandy's reaction before making any decision. He didn't have to wait long.

Dr. Shandy returned Sybelle's call within twenty minutes. Two hours later he jetted in from Washington for a private conference.

"One should never underestimate the power of the

press," Sybelle crowed as they waited for Shandy to arrive.

"Just remember, dahling," Andy muttered, "the sun don't shine on the same dog's ass every day."

"You're just jealous," she sniffed. But when Shandy arrived she sat back demurely and let the senator handle the meeting.

"First off, why all the secrecy surrounding this affair?" Jacobs demanded when they were all seated.

Shandy shrugged. "Quite simply, we wish to avert a radiation panic in the area. Which is precisely the reason we need to raise the sub—so we can prove the *Blowgun* suffered a non-nuclear accident."

"Makes sense, I suppose," Andy conceded reluctantly.

"What about Craig?" Sybelle prodded.

Andy Jacobs blinked at her unhappily. "Yes. Exactly to the point. Radiation panic doesn't explain why Ms. Lean has not been allowed to communicate with her son."

Shandy pulled at his beard. "Lieutenant Early, as well as the other crewmen, is being debriefed. Which is SOP in these cases. Standard, ah, operating . . ." His voice withered under Sybelle's fiery glare.

"I demand to know where he is. After all, we did locate the submarine for you."

Orient winced at the word "we," sensing he was about to be drawn into the conversation.

"Rest assured we are extremely grateful for the invaluable services performed by you and Dr. Orient."

"In that case," Andy Jacobs growled, "perhaps you'd be so kind as to demonstrate that gratitude. All she wants to do is speak to her son."

Shandy stroked his beard. "I can't tell you where he is unless . . . uh, may I use your phone in private?"

When he returned he was grinning proudly, revealing small white teeth. "I still can't tell you where your son is. But I am authorized to take you there."

Sybelle stared at him. "I don't get it."

"If you agree, we can fly both you and Dr. Orient to see him. However, I cannot reveal our destination until after takeoff."

"How do I fit into this?" Orient inquired.

"Oh, please, darling. I need you. And I do so want you to meet my son."

"Besides which, I believe you have unfinished business with your friend Commander Westlake," Shandy added with a smug smile.

Orient was tempted to wipe it off by declining the invitation. But that would only disappoint Sybelle.

"Fine." He sighed. "When do we leave?"

"As soon as you're ready. My car's outside to take us to the airport. I have a jet all warmed up."

"You seem pretty sure we'd come."

"Please don't misunderstand, Dr. Orient. I stopped off here on my way to . . ." He glanced at Andy Jacobs. "To visit Commander Westlake at the debriefing center."

"While you boys thrash out the details, I'll go pack," Sybelle announced, heading for the door.

"I'll give you a hint," Shandy offered. "Pack for tropical weather."

Orient looked at Andy and shrugged helplessly. They both knew it made little difference who arranged the trip, or why. Someone had to tag along and look after Sybelle.

Chapter 6

IT DIDN'T TAKE ORIENT LONG TO PACK.

He had moved his things from the Chelsea to Sybelle's guest room the day before. But as the Gulfstream IV corporate jet taxied toward the runway, Orient couldn't rid himself of the nagging feeling that he was being manipulated.

Oblivious to his brooding, Sybelle chattered excitedly as the jet rolled onto the tarmac, but Orient remained wrapped in his thoughts.

As promised, Dr. Shandy revealed their destination soon after takeoff. Unsnapping his seat belt, he strolled down the aisle of the spacious executive jet and leaned up against Orient's chair.

"In less than four hours we'll be landing in Montego Bay," he said with a flourish. "This little Gulfstream does better than five hundred knots. Same model actually broke the around-the-world speed record. Almost seven hundred knots."

Orient studied him carefully. "How long before we can actually see Craig?"

The question seemed to puncture Shandy's convivial air.

He squinted at Orient disapprovingly. "I'm afraid that's up to Commander Westlake."

Sybelle's mood also changed abruptly. "Isn't that why we're on this damned plane—to see my son?"

"Of course. Of course," Shandy assured her hastily. "No doubt you'll see Lieutenant Early as soon as we land. I was merely pointing out that from here on, this matter is completely under the jurisdiction of the commander. Project Earlybird is technically finished."

Orient looked at Sybelle. "Perhaps you'd better inform Dr. Shandy of our arrangement."

"Arrangement?" Shandy echoed warily.

Sybelle gave him a dazzling smile. "Owen had an idea something like this might happen, so we arranged to contact Senator Jacobs by phone at a certain time. If he doesn't hear from us by then, he is instructed to contact the media and give them the details of Project Earlybird."

"Well, uh, what time would that be?" Shandy asked in a shocked tone.

Orient shrugged. "We'll let you know."

The stewardess entered with a drinks wagon. Shandy waved her over and ordered a double vodka without waiting for his guests.

"You must understand that Westlake has always been hostile to the project."

"Oh, we're quite aware of that," Sybelle said sweetly. "I'll have a scotch, thank you."

Shandy mellowed a bit after his first drink. He ordered a second and loosened his tie. "Westlake isn't going to like this," he confided after the stewardess left. "But I'm sure you won't have any trouble. The one thing he doesn't want is publicity."

Orient sipped his wine. "Any particular reason? One would think you'd be up for a citation."

The casual probe struck a nerve. "Yes, one would think so," Shandy said vehemently. "However, since Westlake didn't believe Earlybird would work, my, uh, our success with this project will be accorded minimum priority.''

Although Orient felt extremely relieved that Westlake wasn't anxious to publicize the incident, he sensed Shandy was holding something back.

The jet began its descent shortly after midnight.

As the plane banked in a steep circle, Orient could see a necklace of landing lights in a valley between two large mountains. "Are you sure this is Montego Bay?" he asked acidly. "There used to be a harbor."

Shandy managed a weak smile. "Quite right, Doctor. Montego is a few miles south. The commander thought it best we use a private landing facility. It's all right. Trust me."

"Trust you?" Sybelle exploded. "Everything you've told us is somewhere south of the truth. What the hell is going on?"

Shandy heaved a sigh and stared down at the blinking lights. "A salvage team has raised the *Blowgun* and is towing it here to Jamaica. Westlake has quarantined the crew until the sub arrives. That's all I know."

"What about us?" Sybelle persisted.

He peered at her sadly. "Uh, I believe you'll both be quarantined as well."

As expected, when Shandy explained the details of Sybelle's "arrangement" with Senator Jacobs, the commander blew his stack.

Westlake stormed into the small office where Sybelle and Orient were waiting. "If you people think I'll submit to blackmail, you are sadly mistaken," he announced.

"We've been sadly mistaken ever since we agreed to take this trip," Sybelle said calmly. "You used my son as a ploy to lure us into what your cohort so tactfully refers to as 'quarantine.' ''

"As I recall, you were the one who insisted on seeing Craig immediately. Again, under threat of exposure."

"Naturally. So you decided to cut us off from the press with this little scheme. Fortunately, Owen had the foresight to suggest an escape clause."

Westlake leveled his finger at Orient. "What do you want here anyway?"

Orient shrugged. "We have a deal, remember?"

"I remember. And I intend to honor my word to you and Mrs. Lean—"

"Ms. Lean," Sybelle purred.

"Yes, of course. Rest assured that you will be reunited with your son—if you play by the rules."

"They seem to have changed," Orient said quietly.

"All we ask is that you sign an agreement to refrain from revealing any details of Project Earlybird for at least eighteen months."

"And if we don't sign?"

"Why, then Ms. Lean will be allowed thirty minutes with her son—as promised—and you'll both be flown back to New York."

"Thirty minutes?" Sybelle said indignantly. "That's hardly enough time to say good-bye."

Westlake smiled. "The reunion can be stretched to forty-eight hours, should you decide to sign."

Sybelle bit her lip and looked questioningly at Orient.

He drummed his long fingers on the desktop. "Why this vital need for secrecy? If you've raised the sub, you can certainly prove the accident was non-nuclear."

Westlake scowled. "First of all, no one else knows we've raised the sub. Second, nobody knows it's being towed here. Which is precisely why we quarantined the survivors."

He folded his arms. "Now that is all I can tell you. Unless, of course, you sign . . ."

"Oh, give me your damned agreement," Sybelle said in exasperation. "Then take me to my Craig."

Having sworn himself to secrecy years before, Orient had no compunction about signing, only curiosity.

He knew Westlake would never disclose the full truth unless it served some devious self-interest. Orient detected little trace of integrity beneath his flinty, tight-lipped expression. "I don't suppose you actually brought my file with you?" he inquired.

"And here I thought you were a mind reader," Westlake said, looking over at Shandy. "Where did you stash it?"

The bearded researcher gave Orient a smug smile. "In your safe."

"Very cute," Orient congratulated. "You carried my file from Washington, and me along with it. All right, where do I sign? And how soon do I take possession?"

"Right now, of course. My office is right down the hall. Dr. Shandy, please give him the agreement."

Pleasantly surprised, but wary, Orient followed them to a larger, more comfortably furnished office and watched as Westlake pushed aside a wall painting and began to spin a combination lock concealed behind it.

It occurred to Orient that his life was about to turn with it.

Moments later, he stared at the two thick manila envelopes stacked on the desk; they seemed a meager harvest for a decade spent as a fugitive.

"As you know, Dr. Orient, I was skeptical of this experiment. However, on behalf of the men you saved, please accept my personal commendation."

"Accepted, Commander. Now when can I return to New York?"

Westlake checked his watch. "Thing is, the courier plane won't be back until tomorrow night. Anyway, I thought you agreed to stay on with your friend. You'll be our guest, of course.''

Orient realized he was in no position to object, even if Westlake's offer masked a subtle form of kidnapping. Still wary of the sudden rush of hospitality, he decided to probe a bit deeper. ''You're very kind. But now that I've signed your secrecy pact, you might tell me what it is I can't talk about.''

Westlake lit a cigarette. ''Our primary investigation of the wreckage indicates sabotage. As does the testimony of the crew. Someone deliberately tried to destroy the *Blowgun*. Someone aboard that sub.''

Orient was suddenly sorry he had asked. He recalled the shock of revulsion when he encountered the ravening evil that hovered over Craig's telepathic aura. It was a presence that could only be termed supernatural. And a memory he intended to forget.

''Well, if you're correct, whoever did it was obviously quite willing to die for his cause. A fanatic like that shouldn't be difficult to weed out,'' Orient added hopefully.

Westlake smiled. ''Problem is, Doctor, there were only three men who actually had access to the detonation area when it blew. Two were my own men. And the other one was already dead.''

Chapter 7

Sybelle was working on an industrial-strength headache.

It was all her fault, she brooded. She had agreed to participate in Project Earlybird in a vain attempt to assuage her maternal guilt. Unfortunately, the price had been excessive. And now Owen had to pay.

Even worse, she had allowed herself to be manipulated. That's what really made her angry, Sybelle fumed, rummaging through her handbag for an aspirin. She felt shamefully used by Shandy, Westlake—and her own unruly emotions.

It had started out innocently enough. Craig had always shown a marked psychic talent, even as a child. After the divorce Craig went to live with his father in Alaska, which naturally caused Sybelle considerable pain. So when the opportunity to work with her son on Project Earlybird came along, she jumped on it. The whole thing hadn't seemed so complicated at the time.

Dr. Shandy had invited her down to the naval base at King's Island, Georgia, for some simple experiments. Craig had decided to use his telepathic skill to wrangle a new assignment. To be sure, teaching him the technique had been her own stupid decision, Sybelle conceded ruefully.

She herself had to take a vow of strict secrecy before Owen finally consented to teach her the technique of telepathic communication. But during a rare summer vacation with Craig, she realized her son had inherited some of her psychic abilities, and in a burst of motherly enthusiasm she undertook to teach him the basic principles of telepathy. Craig learned quickly, and by the time their visit ended he had become reasonably adept at sending mental images. His receptive senses needed more work. Still, over the years he managed to retain his facility, despite the fact that he was surrounded by insensitive louts—from his Alaskan fishing buddies to his father.

If one looked up the expression "macho pig" in the dictionary, he would find her ex-husband's picture, Sybelle thought glumly. It was his fault Craig had entered the Navy instead of continuing his musical studies.

But she was the one who had broken her vow, she reminded herself, washing down the aspirin with a glass of white wine. And as such, she was totally at fault for whatever problems Owen was now having with Westlake. The antagonism between the two men was painfully evident. Owen had suffered mightily at the hands of the CIA in the past, and now she had managed to betray him as well.

Fortunately, Owen had a forgiving nature—as well as a healthy instinct for survival. His insistence on protecting them against Westlake's devious tactics had served them well, Sybelle reflected. After all these years, Owen Orient was still the most uniquely fascinating man she had ever encountered.

Not to mention handsome, she mused, moving back to the bar to refresh her wine. Time had only served to accentuate his penetrating green eyes and sharp, sculpted features. He still exuded the slightly dangerous aura of an exiled aristocrat living by his wits.

Sybelle strolled over to the glass terrace door and stared out at the flowering plants. She had been quite surprised when they'd ushered her to her suite. The place seemed more like an old colonial hotel than a military station. But she couldn't really appreciate Westlake's hospitality until she was allowed to see Craig.

"Mrs. Lean?"

Sybelle looked up and saw a stolid young man in a tan safari jacket standing at the door.

"Ms. Lean," she corrected.

The reply seemed to confuse him. He glanced around the room as if expecting to see someone else. "Uh, yes. Your son is here. Please come with me."

"Why all the fuss?" Sybelle asked as she followed him down the carpeted stairway. "Couldn't my son simply come up to my suite?"

"Orders, ma'am."

Even her annoyance at his curt tone failed to deflate her mounting anticipation as he stopped at a room almost directly below her suite.

The moment her escort opened the door she saw Craig standing at a far window. Then she saw the other two men. Ignoring them, she rushed inside and threw her arms around her son. "Oh, Craig, thank God. Thank God it's all over."

"It's okay, Mom," Craig whispered, holding her tight.

"I'm afraid it's not quite 'all over,' Ms. Lean."

The reedy voice grated at Sybelle's comprehension like nails on a blackboard. She jerked her head up and glared at the man who had spoken. He was wearing a white linen suit and sported a thick Hitleresque mustache. His watery eyes squinted disapprovingly through designer sunglasses. "This happens to be a serious case of sabotage and your son is involved."

"Oh? It's my understanding that my son helped save your damned submarine—not sink it."

The other man in the room came closer. "Indeed he did, ma'am. I can attest that young Craig is a four-star hero. You should be very proud."

"Well, thank you, Mr.—"

"Mom, this is Commander McGinn. He's the skipper aboard our boomer—er, our submarine."

McGinn bowed. "My pleasure, ma'am."

"If you people are finished congratulating yourselves, we have work to do," the other man snapped.

Sybelle smiled. "And exactly who the hell are you?"

"Beston Holstein, Naval Intelligence. I'm in charge of debriefing all personnel on Project Earlybird."

"Well, that's very nice, Mr. Holstein, but I'm afraid I've already been debriefed by your Commander West-lake."

"Hey, now, Beston," McGinn put in amiably. "Ms. Lean hasn't seen her son since the rescue. Let's give them a chance to catch up."

Holstein wearily removed his glasses. "Please, Commander. You're treading on my deck here."

McGinn's jaw clamped shut. At that moment he resembled a red-faced lion. But while he seemed to back off, Sybelle could tell he was seething.

"Now, then," Holstein went on, "suppose you give me the details of your little experiment."

"You forget I'm not under naval authority."

Holstein gave her a nasty smile. "True, you're not. But your son still is."

Sybelle glanced at McGinn, who seemed to be having trouble containing his anger, then at Craig, who stood with his arms folded, staring at Holstein. Suddenly she remembered something and became fearful. Craig's expression had been remarkably similar the day he decided to punch his baby-sitter. "Don't worry, Mother," he said quietly. "I can handle it."

Sybelle glanced around the suite. "Do you mind terribly if we sit down?" Without waiting for an answer, she headed for a large white couch.

"How exactly did you pinpoint the *Blowgun*'s location?" Holstein demanded, following her.

Sybelle made herself comfortable and motioned for Craig to join her. "I'm sure you've been told the details by my son."

"We've been briefed as to the nature of the experiment. What we need to know is what happened at your end. In New York."

"Why not ask Commander Westlake or Dr. Shandy?" she suggested sweetly. "They were right there."

"Not quite. You and your friend Orient were secluded."

Sybelle pounced, eyes flashing. "Oh? Then you have spoken to Commander Westlake. Divide and conquer, is that the game? Owen was right. He said you people would try to renege on our agreement."

"We agreed to reunite you with your son, and here you are," Holstein said impatiently. "Now tell me about this Dr. Orient."

"Dr. Orient is here on the premises, darling. Better ask him yourself."

"I warn you, Ms. Lean, this could be a short reunion. And your son's naval career could become quite unpleasant."

Sybelle put a restraining hand on Craig's arm and stood up.

"That is quite enough. Since I entered this suite you have done nothing but harass and threaten. As far as I'm concerned—this does not qualify as a reunion. Now I wouldn't want to tread on your deck, but I'm sure that, upon review, your conducting a debriefing in front of un-

authorized personnel will be judged to be extremely un-
professional. You may inform your Commander Westlake
our deal is off—terminated. I'll be in touch with Senator
Jacobs immediately.''

Holstein's expression went from disdain to dismay. he
paused to wipe his glasses, then attempted a smile. ''I'm
afraid you're overreacting, Ms. Lean. All we wanted to
do was clear up some, uh, outstanding details. Certainly
we can take this up at another time. I'll leave you two
alone for the evening and we can discuss it in the morning.
Over brunch, perhaps.'' He replaced the glasses and
started backing out of the suite.

He was nearly at the door when McGinn stepped in his
path.

''Before you go, Beston, I'd like to remind you of something.''

''Which is?''

''Lieutenant Early is a highly valued member of my
crew. He happens to be a brave and loyal officer. I fully
intend to put him in for a commendation.''

Holstein shrugged. ''Why tell me?''

McGinn leaned forward until his chin was only a few
inches from Holstein's tinted glasses. ''Because if I hear
that anyone has taken liberties with his future assign-
ments—or makes any attempt to embarrass him—I will put
my rank on the line. Am I being perfectly clear?''

Holstein managed to muster a sneer as he hastily slipped
out of the room. McGinn turned to Sybelle and gave her
a conspiratorial smile. ''Well, now I know where Craig
gets his nerve. You're quite a warrior under all that feminine charm. Remind me not to get you angry.''

She grandly waved the compliment aside. ''I abhor
bullies. The man has no sense of tact. Anyway, you're
certainly no slouch in the self-defense department.''

''Occupational reflex,'' McGinn confided. ''But rest

assured, Holstein won't bother Craig after I speak to a few people here.''

"Tell me, Commander, exactly what is this place—a Navy base?''

"Tell you the truth, Ms. Lean, I haven't a clue. Far as I can figure, the Olympia Club is some sort of spook farm.''

Sybelle looked at Craig. "Olympia Club . . . spook farm?''

"The Olympia Club is the name of this establishment,'' Craig explained, winking at McGinn. "And spook is navalese for intelligence agent.''

Macho mumbo jumbo, Sybelle fumed. Just like his father. But she felt too good to make an issue of it. In fact, she rather liked Commander McGinn with his flinty manner and faraway blue eyes. "I suppose this place is filled with your crew members,'' she ventured, hoping to draw him out.

McGinn seemed puzzled by the remark. "Oddly enough—no. The few that were shipped here are officers or tech specialists. From what I understand, some of my men were taken to our base in Cuba, and the rest were flown back to King's Island. You'd almost think they're trying to break up my crew before the smoke has a chance to clear.''

"Make sure you cover your rear,'' Sybelle said solemnly.

He grinned and took her arm. "That's how I got my command.''

"How long can you stay down here, Mom?'' Craig asked.

"I'm not quite sure, dear.'' She looked him over appraisingly. "I must say you look remarkably well considering your ordeal. You are far too handsome to stay a bachelor much longer.''

She was pleased to note that Craig blushed slightly. "Mom's always trying to marry me off," he murmured.

McGinn lifted his arms in mock surrender. "After the way she handled Holstein, she can do whatever she wants."

"Well, I'd love to go somewhere for dinner," she said hopefully.

McGinn's smile became apologetic. "I think Craig will have to enjoy that privilege alone. The only place you can go is the club's dining room, but it's excellent. I have to get myself ready. They're shipping me out of here in a couple of hours."

"So quickly?" she said, unable to suppress her disappointment. "I mean one would think they'd give you a holiday or something."

"One would think so," he growled. "But no. They want to fly me to Newport. Perhaps next time you'll allow me to take you to dinner."

"I'm looking forward to it, Commander."

"Good." He turned to Craig and clapped him on the shoulder. "Take very good care of her, Lieutenant. She's one special lady." Then his expression became solemn. "You're a damned good officer, Early. But, if you'll pardon my butting in, I think your future is elsewhere."

Craig beamed. "Coming from you, sir, I'll take that under serious consideration."

As she and Craig walked to the dining room, Sybelle felt both grateful and frustrated. It would have been nice to explore her new friendship with Commander McGinn a bit further. She wondered why the Navy was in such a rush to have him transferred. She'd never even found out if he was married.

Chapter 8

LATER, WHILE BEING DRIVEN TO HIS QUARTERS, Orient had time to reflect. Although he felt reasonably sure Westlake was telling the truth, he knew better than to ever trust him. At the moment, however, he was more concerned with his destination.

From what he could gather, they were careening along some sort of crude jungle road. Occasionally the car would emerge from the dense tunnel of vegetation and he'd catch a glimpse of the moonlit sea, far below.

"I'm in no hurry, friend," Orient said as the car slid around a gravel corner and descended into the shadowy forest.

The driver turned and gave him a gap-toothed grin. "That's all right, mon. We soon there."

Reassured by his confidence, Orient settled back and regarded the two manila envelopes on the seat beside him. He wasn't certain whether to destroy them or save them for evidence. He also wasn't certain they were the only copies. That would be too much to expect of Westlake.

As Orient watched the headlight beams bounce down the steep, rutted road, he pondered their situation. The one thing he could be sure of was that Westlake hadn't enticed them to Jamaica as a reward for their service. He wondered if Sybelle's son was considered a witness or a suspect.

To Orient's surprise, instead of taking him to a military compound, the driver delivered him to a stately tree-shrouded hotel called the Olympia. Not only had a suite been reserved in his name, but the desk clerk informed him the dining room was still open.

Famished after having avoided most of the synthetic food served on the plane, Orient left his suitcase with the clerk and headed directly inside.

Despite the late hour, the restaurant was full and the hostess told him it might be a long wait. Then he spotted Sybelle at a corner table, talking to a young man with a shock of red hair that could only belong to her son.

Hunger overcame his reticence, and he decided to barge in.

"Oh, there you are, darling," Sybelle called out as he approached. "Craig, this is the special friend I've been telling you about. Owen, what on earth do you have in those envelopes?"

"Postcards, pamphlets, suntan oil, the usual tourist amenities. Mind if I join you?"

Craig stood and extended his hand. "Mind? I'd be honored, sir. If it hadn't been for you and Mom . . ." He shrugged and looked around for his drink. "Please sit down."

"Have they got your entire crew quarantined at this place?" Orient inquired, looking for a waiter.

"Actually, only about twenty or so. Mostly officers. The rest are either in Cuba or Georgia."

It occurred to Orient how little he knew about Westlake's end of the operation. But since he'd retrieved his file, his curiosity had diminished considerably. He finally caught the waiters' attention and ordered grilled swordfish with peas and rice, and a Red Stripe beer.

"Craig is leaving for Japan in forty-eight hours," Sybelle said unhappily. "I do wish he'd reconsider."

"Rather a quick transfer," Orient observed.

"Actually, it's kind of a reward," Craig told him, wavering between pride and modesty. "Sub Commander McGinn put me up for commendation, so they offered me a choice of assignment."

"He was cited for bravery," Sybelle interjected, patting Craig's hand.

"As well he should. It took a cool head to keep sending after the accident." Orient waited for Craig to comment on the *Blowgun*'s sabotage, but the young officer ignored the hint.

Instead he returned to the subject of his new assignment. "When they made the offer, I knew exactly where I wanted to go," Craig confided. "It's been a dream of mine for years. And now I'll actually be playing piano with the Navy orchestra."

"Well, I certainly like it better than submarines," Sybelle sniffed. "Don't you agree, Owen?"

Orient's response was diverted by the arrival of his food. The swordfish was excellent, as was the company, but soon after dining he decided to call it a night.

Finally, alone in his room and unable to sleep, Orient opened the manila envelopes. Along with the copious paperwork, they had enclosed a single computer disk. Putting the disk aside, he began reading the tightly worded documents in his file.

They went back a long way, to the years just before the Vietnam War. Then he had been an unknown psychic researcher, tucked away in the Riverside Drive town house he'd inherited from his family. During the early seventies he broke one of his cardinal rules—that of never exposing his work to public scrutiny—when he cured the paralyzed daughter of the then Vice President of the United States. Although they managed to keep publicity at a minimum, the CIA became interested in his research. As the war escalated, they became increasingly aggressive. In an effort to obtain four videotapes that contained the core techniques of his telepathic research, various agents tried money, threats, treachery, and finally violence, resulting in the arson of his town house—and his going underground for the next decade.

Since then he'd been around the world twice, and all the low points in his journey were mapped out in his file. Friends who sold him out, women who betrayed him, others who died along the way. There was a brief gap of two years, when a female agent, sent to turn him, fell in love instead. But those years of constant running wore their tenuous bond dangerously thin, and they decided to part while there was still something left.

In a curious way, the file provided Orient with a real continuity to those otherwise lost, rootless years. Fascinated, he pored over the neatly typed documents for hours, tracing his strange past as if leafing through a family album.

The morning sun revealed his location with stunning clarity. From his bedroom terrace he could see a wide expanse of blue sky and sparkling green water, edged by a crescent of white sand. Looking down, he noticed a few brightly colored umbrellas dotting the beach at the base of a flower-strewn hill. The vivid scenery was underscored by the glorious chattering of birdlife nesting in the lush vegetation surrounding the hotel.

Every bit as cheering was the discovery that the shower worked perfectly. There was even a thick terry-cloth robe hanging behind the door. Added to that was the prompt response of room service to his breakfast order. By his

second cup of coffee, Orient was beginning to feel like
the winning contestant on a game show.

The phone interrupted his musings. It was Sybelle calling from the lobby. "Good morning, darling. Feel like a
nice swim? Craig had to go to some dreary meeting."

"Give me ten minutes."

"Fine. I'll meet you on the veranda."

Before leaving the room, Orient looked around for a
place to hide his file.

The computer disk was easy, fitting neatly in the pocket
of his robe, but the bulky manila envelopes posed a problem. Then he happened to glance out the living room window and found a solution.

He hurried down two flights to the lobby and walked
across a side patio to a group of palm trees where an
elderly gardener was burning dried leaves in a garbage
can. The man stopped and saluted as Orient approached.

"Nice mornin'," he said amiably.

"Yes, it is. Mind if I throw this stuff on your fire?"

"Housecleanin', eh? Go right ahead, then."

Orient took the documents out of their envelopes and
fed them slowly into the flames, making sure all of them
were totally consumed. When everything, including the
manila envelopes, had been reduced to ashes, he saluted
the gardener, tipped him five dollars, and strolled back to
find Sybelle.

She was conspicuously ensconced at a corner table on
the wide, roof-shaded veranda, dressed in a pink bathing
suit and matching turban, intently applying sun cream on
her milky white skin.

She looked up and gave him a surprised smile. "Well,
don't you look well rested and handsome. I believe this
little vacation is just what you needed."

"I already feel years younger," he said, giving her a
kiss. "Ready to hit the water?"

"Am I! It's been at least a year since my body touched the sea."

"Did you say Craig had a meeting?" Orient ventured as they walked to the beach.

"Yes. Something about cutting his orders. He leaves tomorrow evening."

"Seems abrupt."

"Well, he has to go somewhere. Jamaica isn't exactly hospitable to American military influence. That's why everyone here is required to wear civilian clothing."

"Just what sort of place is our little hotel?"

"From what I've gathered, the Olympia Club is some kind of private diplomatic reserve. I understand there's a fence and guards, but I didn't see anything or anybody coming in last night. Did you?"

"It was too dark. And we were going too fast."

"No matter. We won't be here long enough to explore." She tossed her turban and robe on a nearby deck chair and started running toward the shimmering blue water. "Last one in is an albatross!"

After a brief swim Sybelle was forced by the intense sun to seek relief under a beach umbrella. Orient lingered in the calm, crystal water, taking the opportunity to carefully study his surroundings. Certainly nature had made sure the Olympia Club would remain a private enclave, he noted. Wedged between two steep cliffs, overlooking a tree-curtained bay shaped like a hairpin, the hotel was an ideal fortress.

It also provided the usual amenities expected of a vacation resort, such as a palm-shaded bar and smiling beachboys. The guests seemed like ordinary tourists, except for the fact that most of them were single males. Orient counted fifteen men and three women, Sybelle excluded. Of the three women, one was a windsail instructor. The other two were bikini-clad blondes, as slim as matching greyhounds, accompanied by a trio of portly males in flowered shirts.

For the next hour he and Sybelle lazed beneath their umbrella watching people swim, windsail, parasail, and drink. But while more male guests appeared, the number of women decreased significantly when the blondes departed with their escorts.

"The men around here seem to run to type," Sybelle mused, sipping a rum punch.

Her perception was quite accurate. The males roaming the beach were between twenty and forty years old, most slightly balding, with sun-reddened skin and thick rolls around their waists—a consequence of the many beers they consumed during the morning. Their spirited language made it clear that they were members of either a football team or a military unit. They avoided any contact with Sybelle and Orient, almost as if embarrassed by their presence.

While Orient enjoyed the silky water and the exotic tropical setting, he did miss his privacy. He decided to swim out past the narrow neck of the bay in hopes of finding a secluded beach where he could stretch out and meditate.

It didn't take him long to reach the edge of the tree line, and as he swam into view of open sea, he saw two things.

The first was a long barge, carrying what looked to be an enormous crate, being towed by a gray freighter. The second was a small black powerboat bearing down on him.

The Jamaican behind the wheel cut the engine and drifted closer to Orient. "Sorry, sir. No guests allowed past this point. Bad fish around here. Sharks and the like," he said cheerfully.

Orient waved and began swimming back to the beach. The boat followed for a few yards, then veered out to sea.

"Security here is tight," he told Sybelle when he returned to the umbrella.

"I saw the boat chase you. Don't worry, darling, we'll be leaving this charming isolation booth tomorrow."

Orient put on his robe. "I'm ready for an early lunch."

"I'm staying a bit longer," Sybelle said wistfully. "It's not fair. Two minutes in the sunshine and you've got a gorgeous tan. I have to baste all day for just a hint of pink."

"Try coming out from your umbrella."

"Don't be silly. I'd burn like a red flare. Besides, I'm having lunch with Craig. He's taking me for a drive."

In a way, Orient was grateful for the time alone. As he strolled back to his room, he decided to do some stretching exercises before lunch.

When he opened the door to his room he felt something. The vague sense that someone might be inside.

He stood in the doorway and scanned the empty room.

Someone had made the bed and removed the breakfast tray, but everything else seemed to be there, including the watch, wallet, and passport he'd carelessly left on the bureau. Dismissing his intuition, he took a rolled-up cotton exercise mat from his suitcase and went out to the bedroom terrace. As he unfolded the mat, white padding spilled out through a long tear in the cover.

Somewhat confused, he went to the closet and took his silver cigarette case from the inside pocket of his leather jacket. It was then he discovered the jacket lining had been neatly cut along the seams. Orient studied the jacket for a moment, then checked the sports coat hanging beside it. The coat lining was slit at the seams.

Orient extracted a hand-wrapped cigarette from the silver case and looked for a light. As he smoked he wandered slowly around the sunny room searching for more evidence that someone had been there. Since all Orient had with him was a change of clothes and a bathing suit, and since the intruder had ignored the few valuables he possessed—he could only conclude that his mystery guest had been looking for something one could slip inside a coat lining. A list that included cash, jewelry, even drugs. He put his hand in the pocket of his robe and found the answer.

The computer disk Westlake had given him, along with his files. Satisfied he knew what the intruder had been seeking, Orient snuffed out his cigarette.

A warning tremor resonated inside his probing awareness like distant thunder. The next twenty-four hours prior to their departure were to be taken slowly, and very cautiously. By burning his file he had reduced his problems to a minimum. Now his only concern was where to hide the disk.

By the time he came downstairs for lunch, he had solved the dilemma.

There were only a few people seated in the large dining room when he entered. But one of them was Commander Westlake. Orient went directly to his table and sat down.

"Tell me, Commander, just what do you expect to find that you don't already know?"

"Beg pardon, Doctor?"

"My room was searched. Why?"

Westlake drummed his fingers on the table. "What did they get?"

"Nothing. But that's not the issue."

"The issue is, Doctor, I did not order your room searched."

"I was under the impression the Olympia boasts bullet-proof security."

"So was I," Westlake said grimly. "You just can't get good help these days."

"Inside job?"

"Dammit, what else?"

Orient studied him. Westlake's gray eyes were glazed with fury, and his thick fingers were crushing his napkin into a tight ball. His reaction seemed way out of proportion for a simple burglary.

"Is there something going on we should know about?" Orient asked quietly.

Westlake tossed the napkin on the table and sat back.

"If you care to take a ride with me after lunch, maybe I can color in a few squares."

Having lunch with Westlake was like dining with the Washington Monument. What small talk he generated was all pointed in the same direction.

"You know, of course, the agreement you signed also prevents you from talking about this private hotel of ours."

"I'd hardly make a credible informer. I'm not even sure of our exact location."

"Credible enough to force the Olympia Club to shut down."

Orient smiled. "You have a way of making everything sound vaguely like a threat."

Westlake smiled back. "Occupational hazard. I recommend the jerk chicken," he added as the waiter appeared.

"Too heavy in this heat. Fresh fish is more like it. With cole slaw."

"Might be good," Westlake conceded. "White wine?"

"Red Stripe for me."

"Fine." Westlake turned to the waiter. "Make it two of everything. Beer, fish, cole slaw. Now then, Doctor . . ."

Orient didn't hear the rest. His attention was abruptly diverted by the entrance of the two lithe blondes he had seen on the beach. Both women were beautiful, but one of them stilled his breath.

She moved with the indifferent elegance of a snow leopard. Although it was high noon, the glow of her long silvery hair made it seem as if she was walking in moonlight. She suddenly paused and turned toward him, as if sensing his presence. Her canted gray eyes scanned the room; then she turned back to her companions.

"Are you feel well, Doctor?"

Orient exhaled slowly and met Westlake's concerned scowl with as much detachment as he could muster.

"Just thinking about the burglary," he lied. "We were on the beach when it happened."

Westlake's concern faded to boredom. "I thought we agreed to discuss it after lunch."

"So we did," Orient said, trying not to look at the blond woman.

The struggle continued, but he was saved by the excellent food, which tilted his attention to the business at hand. Still, he lingered over coffee, hoping for an opportunity to study her. Westlake glanced at his watch and signaled the waiter, who immediately hurried over with the check.

This should have impressed Orient; instead all he felt was frustration at his inability to regain his composure. Her image gusted through his mind like an ocean wind, scattering his thoughts.

"Ready?" Westlake barked, dropping some Jamaican dollars on the table.

"That reminds me," Orient said, relieved to find something to focus on. "Where can I get some money changed? The desk clerk doesn't seem to know."

"Your money's no good at the Olympia. Just sign for what you want. Tips are included." Westlake turned and headed for the lobby.

"What if I go sightseeing?"

Westlake kept on walking. "You can't leave the grounds. You entered Jamaica illegally. If they check you, they'll arrest you, amigo."

Orient slowed his pace. He stared at Westlake's departing back as the words gradually penetrated. Some minutes later, while following Westlake down a steep hillside trail, he realized that was merely the bad news. The good news was that he had managed to exit the dining room without stumbling over the lady with the moonlit hair.

Chapter 9

WESTLAKE LED ORIENT AWAY FROM THE BEACH, taking him along a crude path that cut across the gardens, then curved steeply down through an uncultivated patch of jungle. In a short time they reached a clearing that overlooked a small cove concealed by dense vegetation.

There were steps cut into the stone cliff leading down to the water. Waiting at the base of the steps was a black powerboat.

Orient hesitated. He'd been under the impression they were going by car.

"Perfect day for a little ride out to sea," Westlake said, ushering Orient to the stairway.

"Good afternoon, suh. Nice to see you again," the boatman said in greeting. He was the same man who had warned Orient back to shore earlier.

As Westlake stepped into the boat, Orient settled into a rear seat from which he could watch both of them. The boatman put the engine on low throttle and eased the vessel past the curtain of overhanging vines.

Emerging into open sea, Orient spotted the barge and freighter he'd seen earlier. Apparently they were anchored a few hundred yards offshore. The powerboat began to buck as it picked up speed, heading directly for the tethered vessels. When it reached the freighter, the boatman swung around the prow and cruised alongside, to the barge.

Up close, its cargo appeared even more massive: a crate the length of a seven-story building buttressed by steel planks. As they approached, a door opened at the rear of the crate, and two men in denims hurried to lower a rope over the barge's stern.

Westlake preceded Orient onto the barge and went right through the door without waiting. The two men pulled Orient aboard and escorted him inside.

Eyes adjusting to the sudden gloom, Orient squinted through the dim light for Westlake. Then he made out a sinister black shape looming in front of him. Its sleek outline resembled that of a giant shark, but a million times more lethal. Slowly, it dawned on him that the crate housed a nuclear submarine.

"This is the *Blowgun*," Westlake said proudly, stepping out of the shadows. "We didn't want to leave her in Cuba. Whole fucking island is wired. So we rigged up a floating hangar and towed her here. Our boys are going over her piece by piece. Care to take a tour? After all, you did help save her."

Orient didn't have any choice, but he had learned to be wary of Westlake's invitations.

As he followed the intelligence officer over a short connecting bridge, Orient saw that the sub was actually floating. He could also see the huge, jagged hole near its prow.

The interior of the sub was somewhat larger and more comfortable than he had imagined.

"Dr. Shandy is waiting in the control room," Westlake said, leading the way.

As far as Orient could tell, there was no one else on board. Their footsteps echoed in the long passageway.

Shandy was seated at a computer console, squinting intently at the luminous screen when they entered the compartment. He smiled and waved them over.

"I've punched up a diagram of the sub so you can see what happened, Doctor. We had to plug up the missile room with plastic foam. That's where it blew."

"Back up a bit, Ash," Westlake said curtly. "Let's give him the full picture. As you know, the *Blowgun* was cruising in total radio silence, in a random pattern, while Lieutenant Early attempted to transmit the submarine's position through, er, psychic means."

Shandy started to say something but Westlake ignored him. "What you don't know, Dr. Orient, is that during the experiment a crew member expired in the infirmary. Being under strict orders to maintain radio silence, Commander McGinn opted to preserve the body in the commissary freezer pending completion of their mission." He peered at Orient to make sure he understood.

"I'm with you so far," Orient told him.

"Good. Then let's gather round the computer and see what Dr. Shandy can tell us."

The screen showed a detailed diagram of the forward section of the submarine. As Orient looked on, Shandy located the freezer area with a white arrow.

"This is where the body was, uh, stored. As you can see, it's adjacent to the lower missile room." He moved the arrow. "This is where the missile exploded. As I said, we pumped foam in there to keep the sub buoyant. But we combed the room thoroughly before doing so," he added, glancing at Westlake. "At the time of the explosion there were only three men in the freezer area, the two seamen assigned to stand watch over the remains—and the corpse itself."

Orient looked at Westlake thoughtfully. "You mentioned the two guards were your men."

"Correct, Doctor." He leaned closer. "I assigned them to keep tabs on Patterson. That's the dead man's name."

"Why?"

Westlake weighed the answer. "We have reason to believe he sold information to foreign agents."

"Is that why he died?"

"Believe me, we wanted him alive. Patterson died of natural causes. But I can't say the same for my men."

"How so?"

"One of them, Garin, had bad bruises on his throat. He'd been strangled. The other one, Kent, died of massive head injuries. We ran an autopsy. No water was found in their lungs, or in Patterson's either. All three men were dead *before* the blast."

"Perhaps they were killed *by* the blast," Orient suggested.

Westlake shook his head. "Not Garin. Kent maybe. But definitely not Garin. I saw the body. He'd been strangled, all right."

"Oh, I almost forgot this," Shandy said. "It was found near Patterson's body."

Orient looked down at something in Shandy's outstretched hand. It was a small black cross adorned with a red ribbon.

"What do you think it is, Doctor?" Shandy asked, fingering his beard.

"I'd like to go back ashore, if you don't object," Orient said evenly.

Westlake shrugged. "Sure. I'll call for our boat."

"Dr. Orient, is something wrong?" Shandy asked.

"You're damned right there is."

Westlake snatched up his portable phone. "Bring it around. Now," he barked. Then he turned to Orient. "Now, then, exactly what is your damn problem?"

"I don't like being double-teamed, Commander. That's my damn problem. You set me up for this little debriefing.

No doubt you suggested that Craig take Sybelle elsewhere to make sure I'd end up with you as a lunch date."

"Very perceptive, Doctor. But the point is I did not have your room searched. Which is why I'm worried. The same people who sabotaged this sub probably broke into your room. Which means it's one of our own."

"With all due respect, Commander, that's your problem."

"I suppose it is too much to expect that a man helps out his nation."

Orient looked at him in disbelief. "You expect me to find your traitor?"

"Not at all. I was merely hoping for some professional advice. Not much to ask from an American. But then, you have a history of running away from confrontation."

Although Orient knew Westlake was deliberately baiting him, he felt cornered. And very angry.

"What do you expect, Commander, 'The Star-Spangled Banner'?"

"As I said, Doctor. Just some professional advice."

Orient took a deep breath. "All right, then. From what you've told me, and from what I've observed . . ." He paused to consider the ominous black cross Shandy had shown him. "My best advice would be to reexamine Patterson's body."

"Be sure I'm going to take it," Westlake said flatly. "Got that, Shandy? Reopen Patterson's file."

"Actually, there is a rational scenario."

Westlake scowled. "Talk to me, Doctor."

"Kent strangled Garin, then was killed in the blast."

"We've considered that. But the position of the body, and the fact that Kent had unsheathed his weapon—a knife—indicate otherwise. We found no knife wounds on Garin's body."

"What about Patterson?"

Westlake nodded at Shandy. "Check it out."

"Now, Commander, have I earned the right to go back to shore?"

Westlake gave him a tight smile. "Certainly, Doctor. Right this way."

On the return boat trip Shandy carried a clipboard, occasionally jotting notes although very little was said. Finally, while climbing the steep trail leading to the Olympia Club's spacious gardens, Orient decided to ask.

"What time do we fly home tomorrow?"

"You're on the red-eye. About twenty hundred hours."

"That late?"

"Don't worry, Doctor, our business here is finished. By tonight the *Blowgun* will be on her way to King's Island, Georgia. So relax and enjoy yourself."

But as Orient walked back to his hotel room and cautiously opened the door, he wished he could leave with the *Blowgun.*

He found the computer disk safe in its hiding place as a coaster for an ashtray, but a vague apprehension buzzed around his instincts like a mosquito. Most disturbing of all was the tiny black cross Shandy had found near Patterson's body. Of course, he had recognized it immediately as a voodoo hex. But he refused to identify it for Shandy. Let them punch it up on their computer, Orient brooded, stretching out on the couch. He intended to forget he'd ever seen the damned thing.

After a short nap and a long shower, Orient felt hungry. He planned on room service, but the phone rang before he could order. "There you are, darling," Sybelle trilled. "We missed you this afternoon. Let's have dinner."

"Why not?" Orient said casually, but his blood began pumping at the possibility of another encounter with his moonlit lady.

He dressed carefully, cursing the thief who had slit the

lining of his dark blue blazer, and the damage time had inflicted on his social image.

Certainly dining with Sybelle amplified his modest style. Her red hair was swathed by a black band and she wore a loose-fitting black dress tied with a blazing red sash.

"Craig will be delayed," she announced, scanning the room before she sat down. "What have you been doing all afternoon?"

"I did a little sailing. Where did Craig take you?"

"We went to Port Antonio for lunch, which was marvelous. It's a long drive, though."

"Has Craig discussed what happened aboard the sub?"

"Not really. He seems rather reticent on the subject. It must have been very traumatic for the poor darling. My, my, who is that stunning woman with Dr. Shandy?"

Orient knew who it was before looking up. She was dressed in blue silk and wore her white-blond hair pulled back, accentuating the smooth line of her neck.

A familiar bearded face loomed up in his line of vision. Orient impatiently leaned aside to follow the lady's progress, until he realized the beard belonged to Dr. Shandy and that the lady was approaching their table.

"Good evening, Sybelle. You, too, Dr. Orient," Shandy said expansively. "Allow me to introduce my wife, Tristan."

He stood awkwardly and extended his hand. "Owen Orient."

Her cool touch sent a tingle from palm to spine. Their eyes met for an instant and he tumbled into a crystal sea flecked with lightning. He felt relieved when Sybelle drew her attention. He really hadn't been prepared for Tristan.

"Do join us," Sybelle cooed. "I need a little girl talk."

Tristan's pale smile illuminated her face like candlelight. "I'd be delighted, thank you," she said, her voice a husky wisp of southern smoke. "It's been so long since I've discussed something that isn't classified."

Shandy grinned and held a chair for her. "Well, then, shall we order cocktails?"

Orient usually avoided hard liquor, but when Tristan asked for an overproof and cola, he couldn't resist having the same. Aware that he was too smitten to attempt rational conversation, Orient listened to Shandy recount the unsung exploits of his intelligence unit. Shandy occasionally pumped him for information about his psychic research, but Orient politely dodged all queries.

"Know anything about the occult?" Shandy inquired.

"Some. But I'm more interested in practical applications. Medical, not military."

"Anyone for another round?" Tristan asked.

Orient looked at his glass. It was half full. On impulse he gulped it down and ordered another. It seemed like a good idea considering his unsettled emotional state. He could feel the rum burn away the tension as it spread.

Shandy, like Sybelle, was drinking rum punch, which seemed to melt his professional restraint.

"Remember that little object we found near Patterson?" He glanced at Sybelle and Tristan chatting together, then lowered his voice. "The black cross."

"Yes, I remember. Why?"

"I have reason to believe it's an occult cross. Voodoo, to be exact."

"Really? What makes you think so?"

"There's a Jamaican technician here at the club who knows about these matters. He saw it and made the ID. Gave me some background. Fascinating stuff, voodoo."

"Yes," Orient said. "Fascinating."

"They call it Obeah here in Jamaica," Shandy confided. "Many of them still practice it."

Tristan leaned over his shoulder. "Are you boring Dr. Orient with technical jargon, dear?"

"Not at all, Mrs. Shandy. Your husband was just telling me some fascinating aspects of his work."

"Please call me Tristan."

He felt as if he had been nominated for high office.

"Yes. Please call me Owen," he said lamely. He looked to Sybelle for help and found her grinning at him mischievously.

"Owen has been a bachelor too long," she teased. "He's uncomfortable around lovely women."

It was either her remark or the overproof rum, but for some reason Orient felt his shyness fade.

"I am out of practice. But I'll try to catch up."

"You should visit us in Virginia," Tristan suggested, looking into his eyes. "The ladies there will be only too happy to further your progress."

"Think about it seriously," Shandy chortled. "Tristan has a flock of single girlfriends."

Orient kept his eyes on Tristan. "I'm considering it quite strongly."

"Ash told me you're one of the heroes of Project Earlybird." She turned to Sybelle. "And you're the heroine."

"Classified, pet," Shandy reminded her. "Better change the subject."

Tristan pursed her pale lips into a mock pout. "But you've already told me. Unless you lied."

Her expression suddenly clouded. Orient turned to see what had disturbed her, and saw Westlake advancing toward them.

Shandy jumped to his feet. "Why, Commander . . ."

"Sorry, ladies," Westlake said briskly. "I'm afraid we need Dr. Shandy. You're invited too, Orient, if you care to join us."

Orient really didn't, but Westlake's urgent tone made it difficult for him to refuse. And the alternative made him too uncomfortable.

After offering his apologies, he followed Westlake and Shandy outside.

He climbed into the backseat of a black Mercedes SEL waiting at the entrance.

"What's the problem?" Orient asked as Westlake slipped behind the wheel.

Westlake snapped on his safety belt. "On *your* best advice we ordered medical to reexamine Patterson's body."

"So?"

"So we've just been informed that Patterson's body is missing."

Chapter 10

THEY DROVE IN RELATIVE SILENCE. DARKNESS was settling and Orient could see the lights of a departing ship far across the lead-gray sea. Somewhere along the way Westlake turned on the radio and they listened to the tinny rhythms of reggae music as a purple curtain lowered over the red-streaked sky.

A short time later Westlake coasted to a stop in front of a square, low-roofed building about two miles from the Olympia.

"Infirmary," he announced. "Your ball, Shandy."

Orient trailed behind them as they entered a spacious lobby with a white linoleum floor that reflected the fluorescent light. There was a large white desk in the center of the room. Behind it was a young Jamaican nurse. An American security guard stood behind her. The guard snapped to attention when Shandy and Westlake approached the desk.

"Who is in charge here?" Shandy demanded.

"Dr. Chin is head of staff," the nurse responded, picking up the phone.

Dr. Chin appeared within minutes of her call. "I was informed you were coming," he said gravely.

Shandy pointed at the security guard. "Is someone always on duty?"

Dr. Chin removed his glasses and smiled. "No, security wasn't authorized until after the . . . incident."

"Show us where it happened."

The doctor led them along a white linoleum corridor to a room labeled "Storage." The temperature inside was below freezing. When the door closed behind them, Dr. Chin began to speak, his breath coming in ragged clouds. His monotone suggested he had conducted the tour many times before. "On this side we store our plasma, certain medicines, perishable items. Over there"—he pointed to a row of metal drawers built into the far wall—"is where we store patients who are deceased." He walked over to the wall and began pulling out drawers. "Two days ago your people consigned three bodies to us. Today we have two."

He regarded the men accusingly. "You should have provided security earlier. However, my staff is available for questioning."

"In due time." Shandy peered at the corpses in the first two bins. "Care to have a look, Dr. Orient?"

At that moment Orient was wondering why he had agreed to come along. "No, I wouldn't care to have a look," he said curtly. He turned to Westlake. "If you don't mind, I'll wait in the car. It's getting chilly in here."

He stood outside, breathing deeply, grateful to be free of the sterile confines of the infirmary. Actually, he knew only too well why he'd left the club to tag along with Westlake. The prospect of being alone with Tristan made him nervous. He felt like a schoolboy on his first date. Except Tristan was already married. To an agent of Naval Intelligence.

But why he'd accepted Westlake's invitation wasn't really important, Orient brooded, looking up at the full moon. The real question was why Westlake had invited him at all.

Westlake strode out of the infirmary, closely followed by Shandy. "There, now, gentlemen," he said, unlocking the car door, "that didn't take long. I'll have you both back in time to finish dinner."

"Why exactly did you ask me on this joyride?" Orient asked bluntly as they drove to the hotel.

"You suggested we check Patterson," Westlake reminded him. "We check and Patterson's gone."

"Which means?"

"Means you're thinking in the right channel. We might not have found out for days that his body was taken. Any ideas on the matter?"

"In my considered opinion, it's totally insane. That's my best reading, Commander."

"Shandy here thinks it's connected to voodoo."

Orient sat back and folded his arms. "Naval Intelligence is seriously considering voodoo?"

"Do you know much about it?"

"Not really," Orient lied, relieved to see the hotel up ahead.

"You'd better rejoin the ladies," Westlake suggested when they pulled up to the entrance. "I need to work out a few details with Dr. Shandy."

When Orient entered the dining room, he found Sybelle and Tristan chatting over coffee and cognac.

"How nice, you're back," Sybelle said as he sat down beside her. "Why all the excitement?"

Orient signaled the waiter. "There's been another robbery."

"Another? When was the first?"

"I didn't have a chance to tell you. My room was burglarized this morning."

"That's impossible," Tristan said in a hushed voice.

"Everyone here has been screened." She glanced at Orient. "The staff, I mean."

Their eyes met briefly, clashing like flint and steel.

"Did you lose any valuables?" Sybelle asked.

"I'm, afraid this thief picked the wrong pocket."

The waiter arrived and Orient ordered a cognac.

"Luckily I didn't bring much jewelry," Sybelle confided. "But it's still very unsettling."

"Of course it is. If you're not safe here . . ." Tristan let the question hang.

Orient shrugged. "I'm sure Commander Westlake will handle it."

"Are you a friend of Glen's?"

"Glen?"

"Westlake. I guess you're not."

"Actually, Owen became involved in your husband's project because of me," Sybelle explained. "We're old, dear friends. My son was aboard the *Blowgun,* you see."

Tristan gave her a sympathetic smile. "Ash is positively ecstatic at how well everything turned out." She turned to Orient. "And so am I."

Orient took a long swallow of cognac. When he set the snifter down, Tristan was still looking at him.

"It will all be over tomorrow," he said quietly.

Before she could answer, Dr. Shandy appeared at the entrance to the dining room and waved to her.

Tristan eased out of her chair. "Excuse me, I think my master beckons."

"Isn't she breathtaking?" Sybelle murmured as they watched her glide across the floor to Shandy.

"Very pretty," he said casually.

"Owen Orient, don't you try to be coy with me. You're bedazzled. It's all over your face. And you know what else?"

"There's more?"

"Tristan likes you too."

Orient turned aside, unable to mask his elation.

"Seriously, though, Owen, I want you to be prudent. After all, she is a married woman." Sybelle leaned closer. "And we don't know her very well."

Something in her tone attracted his attention.

"Do you know something I don't?"

"Just a feeling. Call it female intuition."

Orient had learned to heed Sybelle's intuition. Normally she preferred to promote the cause of romance.

A sudden wave of nausea reminded him that he had been drinking on an empty stomach.

"You don't look well, darling," Sybelle said anxiously.

"I forgot to eat. I'll be all right."

"Why don't I have them send a nice club sandwich up to your room?" she suggested. "With some ginger ale. Best thing for an upset stomach."

While Sybelle instructed the waiter, Orient sat grimly, trying to suppress the churning in his belly. He felt a slight vertigo as they left the dining room, but his whirling senses slammed to a halt when he spotted Tristan and her husband in the lobby. Unwilling to have her see him in his shaky condition, he made a concerted effort to focus beyond the sickness.

He felt his head clear, and walked toward the stairs, hoping the couple would be too engrossed in their conversation to notice. It was too much to hope for.

Tristan cocked her head as he and Sybelle approached. "Giving up so early? Ash is working overtime and I have nobody to talk to."

"Actually, I'm the one who's giving up," Orient said.

"Wish I could turn in," Shandy said ruefully. "I've got a stack of calls. And making phone calls on this island can get real ugly."

"Oh, yes, Owen told us about the robbery," Sybelle confided. "Simply dreadful."

Shandy squinted at Orient.

"The burglary in my room," Orient prompted.

"Oh, yes, of course. It's a major problem."

Sybelle looked unconvinced but the desk clerk saved him. "Telephone for Miss Lean."

"Excuse me a moment."

"Apparently Sybelle is having no trouble with the local phone service," Orient said, watching her depart.

"Sooner or later she will," Shandy grumbled. "You'll have to excuse me, Doctor. As you can well understand, Commander Westlake is out for blood."

Tristan stroked his cheek. "Poor dear. I thought things were going so well."

"They were until the, uh, robbery. Well, I'm off. Are you coming, dear?"

"In a little while. I want to look at the moon." She glanced at Orient, crystal eyes flashing with curiosity. "Are you interested in astronomy, Doctor?"

Orient cursed his bad timing. For the past few minutes he had managed to stave off the nausea, but now he felt it burning through his concentration. "I'm afraid I'm coming down with the local flu."

"It's going around," Shandy told him. "I feel a bit queasy myself."

Tristan's smile was like a veil. "Pity. It's such a clear night. See you later, Ash."

She moved to the side doors and Shandy tilted his head closer to Orient. "We've got to talk," he whispered. "Better come upstairs with me."

It was the last thing Orient wanted to do at the moment, but it couldn't be avoided. As they walked to the stairway he saw Sybelle hang up the desk phone.

"That was Craig," she announced. "He's sending a car for me. Will you be all right?"

"I'll be fine. Have a good time."

Sybelle pressed an ivory pillbox into his hand. "Here, take some aspirin. And don't forget the ginger ale."

Shandy began talking as soon as they reached the stairway. "Take your time. This is the only place that's not bugged around here. Bottom line is you need my help and I need yours."

Orient felt too groggy to argue the point. "What for?" he managed to say.

"You can't trust Westlake. He's out to damage this project. He's using you people."

"Why should I trust you?" Orient asked flatly.

"Because I've already done you a great favor."

Orient paused. "I don't get it."

"You will when you check out the computer disk." Shandy took Orient's arm and gently nudged him along. "I'm the one who slipped it into your envelope."

"Thanks. But why should I help you?"

"For one thing, I hold the access codes to that disk. Without them you can't open your file."

Orient wanted to tell him that he didn't really give a damn about his file, but a fresh ripple of nausea swallowed his anger. All he wanted to do was get back to the blessed isolation of his room and sleep.

"Let me think about it."

"Of course. We can discuss it on the beach tomorrow. Uh, come alone. Until then, Doctor." He bowed slightly, then strolled down the hall.

Orient continued up the stairs and had barely entered his room when a waiter arrived with the food Sybelle had ordered. When he was finally alone, Orient locked the door and poured himself a Jamaican ginger ale. The spicy, natural root tonic was quite different from the American version. And as Sybelle had promised, it effected a noticeable improvement in his condition.

Trying to absorb the overproof rum and cognac he had foolishly imbibed, Orient forced himself to eat half his sandwich. Feeling better, he prepared for bed.

But while he was brushing his teeth the vertigo washed over him. Dropping the toothbrush, he grabbed the basin with both hands. Weaving slightly, he staggered out to the bed and flopped down on his back. He breathed deeply as the room began to spin.

Then he realized that leaving the bathroom was a mistake.

He rolled off the bed and half crawled to the toilet, fighting back increasing waves of nausea. He thought he had made it, but just as he entered, a thick jet of vomit spewed from his mouth like water from a hose, spattering everything from walls to mirror.

The acid bile seared his throat and he turned on the tap full blast, as if the rushing water could flush his sickness. Putting his head under the faucet, he washed out his mouth. The cool liquid diluted the acids in his throat. He took a few deep breaths and felt his head begin to clear. Whatever his system had rejected would not be missed.

He found a glass and gulped down some more water. Then he picked up the phone and asked the desk to send up some cleaning utensils. A maid arrived promptly with the utensils but Orient declined her services, preferring to clean up his own mess. That was another mistake.

Before he reached the bathroom with the mop and bucket, a dull pain hit the base of his brain like a mallet. He sank to the floor as the pain began to pound his skull with escalating intensity. At the same time his heartbeat accelerated wildly.

His chest felt ready to burst under the pressure. His belly convulsed and a stream of water shot through his lips. As he crawled to the phone, it dimly occurred to him that he had been poisoned.

Gasping for air, Orient stretched out his hand, but the phone was too far away. He sprawled headlong, his mind swelling with the babble of a hundred chanting voices. Agony boomed from belly to skull as the darkness closed in. Nailing home the message that he was about to die.

Chapter 11

THE DRIVER CRAIG SENT WAS RATHER HAND-
some, Sybelle decided. But she didn't like the way he
handled a car.

It all came down to style. He was too fast and not quite
smooth enough to cut it. The car kept jerking from side
to side to every turn. Finally she leaned closer to the driver.

"Sir. Could you please slow down?"

He paid no attention.

She glanced through the windshield and saw the main
gate far ahead. From previous experience she knew the
car would be stopped for routine inspection.

The driver slowed down and switched off the lights.
Sybelle sat back, annoyed that Craig hadn't come for her
himself. As the car approached the gate, the driver shifted
gears and suddenly accelerated, hurtling through the
checkpoint with tires screaming. Frozen in the back seat,
Sybelle clung to the door handle as the car careened around
a curve, skidded, then shot forward. She looked back and
saw two Jamaican security men running after them, waving their rifles.

"Stop!" she yelled, but the driver went faster. The car

screeched around another curve and to her horror, Sybelle
realized they were roaring along a narrow cliffside road,
high above the sea.

She looked back, hoping they were being followed, but
there was nothing behind them.

"Where are we going?" she demanded.

The driver didn't answer, intent on the moonlit ribbon
of road ahead.

"Where are we going?" she repeated, a bit louder.

Without turning, the driver lifted his left hand. It was
holding a gun.

"Please shut up miss," he said curtly.

Considering his excessive speed, the crude road, and
the fact that he was driving without headlights, Sybelle
decided not to argue the point. But her mind cast about
frantically for some way out of the car.

Fortunately, the window on the driver's side was
open. Sybelle slowly unwound the red sash binding her
dress. The long strip of silk had two metal cinches on
one end. Carefully, she tied the other end of the sash to
the door handle, then tossed the metal cinches out the
window, like anchors.

They immediately set up a great clatter, bouncing up under the chassis and against the tire. The driver automatically
slowed down and looked out the window. At the same time,
Sybelle reached over and unlocked the door on the other
side, hoping the metallic din would cover the click.

It did. The driver slowed to a crawl and opened his door
to check the source of the noise.

Sybelle didn't hesitate. As he leaned out to inspect the
right side, she deftly rolled out the left door, hit the ground
wobbling on her high heels, and ran into the dense foliage
lining the deserted road.

The moment she found cover she began moving swiftly
through the shadowy underbrush, trying to be as silent as

possible. She changed direction, went on a bit farther, then paused behind a tree and listened.

All she heard was her own booming heartbeat. She struggled to take a deep breath and think calmly. On instinct she decided to forge deeper into the forest, away from the car. In the darkness, on foot, she had an even chance. Despite her damned heels.

Then she heard him thrashing through the bushes. The driver didn't have to be quiet. He had the gun.

Afraid her white skin would be easily spotted in the moonlight, Sybelle crept inside a thick cluster of vegetation and crouched low. She heard the thrashing sounds coming closer and tried to control her ragged breathing.

Moments later the sounds started moving away from her hiding place. Fearful they would return, she remained still. After long minutes she eased out of the protective vegetation and edged further into the forest. She heard someone behind her mutter a curse and took shelter in another clump of foliage. Basically she was employing a rodent technique—darting out and scurrying to the next hiding place. Yet it seemed to be working.

The forays out of her nests became more extended as she plunged deeper into the tangled forest. Luckily the terrain tilted downhill, which suited Sybelle's flagging endurance. She also discovered a narrow trail cutting through the dense undergrowth. The trail made it possible to put some distance between her and the driver. Moving easily, she hurried through the darkness, pausing every few minutes to listen.

About five minutes later she stopped cold.

At first all she heard was the muffled thump of a single drum, beating a slow, deliberate cadence. As it drew close, it sounded something like a funeral march.

Sybelle searched anxiously for a hiding place when the sound became more distinct. Then she saw the lights.

A long file of flickering torches threaded slowly through the forest like a glowing serpent.

Her damp skin felt chilled as she watched the bobbing line of torches, snaking toward her. She stepped off the trail and started to circle back when she heard a rustling noise behind her. She glanced around wildly and spotted a thick knot of bushes nearby. Stumbling, she ran to the bushes and crawled inside the fragile sanctuary. From her hiding place she could see the eerie procession wending its way closer.

The marchers were all dressed in white ceremonial robes, the men hatless and the women in white head cloths. When they reached the base of the hill, they stopped.

The men with the torches spread out in a semicircle, illuminating a wide clearing. They thrust the burning brands into the earth, then joined the other men.

The women stood in a group a short distance away. One of them carried a large black cross with a pointed metal top that gleamed in the torchlight. She brought the cross forward to a tall, gaunt man with dreadlocks standing alone between the two groups. The man took the cross, lifted it high above his head for all to see, then suddenly drove the pointed metal top into the ground. As Sybelle gaped at the inverted cross, she realized she had stumbled onto some sort of satanic cult.

Through the dancing light she saw two men approach, carrying a litter. At the same time the drum began its slow, funereal cadence, while the women filed one by one past the cross to genuflect and deposit a branch of dried leaves on the ground. When they were done, there was a bed of leaves at the base of the cross.

Watching the two men approach, Sybelle could make out something or someone on the litter, covered with a sheet. As the two men carefully placed the litter on the leafy bed, a second drum quickened the pace, softly at first, then more insistently, until the beat settled into a low, loping rhythm.

The women began a singsong chant led by the gaunt, white-robed figure. The men joined in, chanting in hushed voices as a third drum eased behind them. The women swayed from side to side while the gaunt man lifted his arms to the moon-flooded sky.

Cramped and frightened inside her flimsy shelter, Sybelle didn't dare try to move, fearing the driver was still out there stalking her.

Her eyes had adjusted to the gloom and, aided by the torches and a full moon, she was able to scan the area for her pursuer. She also feared being discovered by the worshippers, who seemed to be working themselves into a frenzy.

The gaunt man with snakelike dreadlocks stalked about the clearing, extolling his flock in a strange, chanting tongue while the drums intensified their muffled rhythms. Some of the women cast off their robes and were dancing around the litter, their bare breasts glistening in the torchlight.

Many of the men now removed their robes and danced half naked around the cross. The gaunt man strode off into the shadows, and when he returned he was holding a black rooster by its feet.

Sybelle suddenly began sweating profusely as she watched the gaunt man swing the rooster back and forth over the litter while his congregation chanted counterpoint to the galloping drums. Then he reached into his robe and pulled out a knife.

In one swift motion he slit the bird's throat and lifted it high above his head so that the blood spurted in a great shining arc, spattering the white sheet on the litter as it flowed into his open mouth. More of the women had removed their robes and were dancing with wild abandon around their gaunt priest, who flung the rooster's twitching carcass aside and lifted the blood-soaked sheet from the litter.

Underneath lay a naked corpse.

Sybelle could clearly see bright designs painted on the body. And when the gaunt priest removed his robe, she saw that his skin was also adorned with similar designs.

Suddenly a black-robed female appeared from out of the shadows, bearing a torch in each hand. Framed in the blazing light, she was extraordinarily beautiful. Even at a distance her high cheekbones, fire-streaked hair, and sea-blue eyes underscored her grace as she floated to the priest's side like a dark swan.

The woman gave him a torch, then moved behind the cross as he began to brandish the flame over the garishly painted corpse.

The drums fused into a single, charging force that incited the dancers to surreal extremes. The circle had extended, and some of the worshippers were whirling wildly only ten or twenty yards from Sybelle's hiding place.

Limbs aching, she watched the gaunt priest pass the torch back and forth, his braided muscles rippling in the light. Bending low over the body, he made a sign with his right hand. To Sybelle's horror, the corpse unclasped its arms and slowly lifted them to the sky.

A woman wailed in ecstatic awe.

The priest stood and triumphantly regarded his followers before lowering his arm and touching the torch to the litter's leafy bed. A tall yellow flame shot up like a flower and began to spread. His female acolyte ignited the other side of the now brightly burning bed and moved back.

As the flames mounted higher, the corpse's smoldering limbs began to bend and twist in a grotesque parody of dance. Gripped by terror, Sybelle saw the priest's hollow, hawklike features contort with raw power, his eyes wide and glassy.

Suddenly, someone nearby screamed.

Instinctively Sybelle turned and glimpsed the driver, edging through the underbrush, gun pointing directly at her. Prepared to die, she watched him come closer.

She saw them before the driver did. Sybelle shrank back as a blurred figure ran up behind him. Before the driver could get a clear shot, something struck him and he spun around. Then something else hit him hard. Sybelle held her breath as a quartet of sweating, wild-eyed worshippers advanced on him with stones and clubs.

The driver fired, hitting one of the attackers, but the others rushed him. One struck him on the side of the head with a well-aimed rock and the others pounced as he staggered back. Sybelle saw a club rise and fall, and she heard the driver groan. Then all four, including the wounded man, dragged the driver down to the clearing and cast him at the priest's feet.

With everyone's attention focused on the interloper, Sybelle took the opportunity to leave her hiding place and creep away, her cramped legs moving awkwardly. After a few yards her pain-stiffened muscles began to yield, and she got to her feet and began to run. She heard a high-pitched shriek somewhere behind her but kept stumbling blindly through the menacing shadows.

Another scream pierced the darkness, then a strange silence descended on the forest. The sound of her labored breathing and shuffling footsteps boomed in the dense quiet.

She ran for as long as she could before she stopped and listened. Somewhere through the wheeze of her own breath she could hear voices chanting.

Driven by stark panic, Sybelle bolted, her exhausted lungs heaving as she hurled herself headlong into the shadows. An intense pain seared her ankle and she fell heavily, her skull glancing against a tree trunk. As the darkness flooded her senses, she heard the chanting voices calling her name. . . .

* * *

Orient lay on the floor of his hotel room, flopping like a landed fish. His breath came in ragged gasps and his heart pounded wildly as he tried to crawl to the phone. Unable to make it, he grabbed a table leg and pulled himself to his knees. Sweat streamed down his face as sharp pains lanced his belly. In a desperate attempt to expel the poison from his body, Orient reached for a water glass. It was almost full. A few inches beyond stood the salt shaker that had come with his meal.

Fingers trembling, he unscrewed the cap and poured salt into the water glass, intending to gulp it down to induce vomiting. But as he carefully lifted the glass, an odd thing happened. The symptoms abated before he could drink the cloudy liquid. He felt better almost immediately.

A slow moment later it clicked. He hadn't been poisoned.

Salt water happened to be a basic defense against occult attack.

He set the glass down and poured some salt into his right hand. "I exorcise thee, creature of earth, by the Living God, by the Holy God, by the Omnipotent God, that thou be purified of evil in the name of Adonai," he muttered, letting salt trickle from his hand to the water.

"I exorcise thee, creature of water," he went on, sprinkling some of the water on his chest. "By the one God, that thou may be purified of evil in the name of Elohim Sabaoth . . . In the name which is above every other name, I exorcise all seeds of evil."

Instantly the intense pressure on his heart and lungs dissolved. He was able to breathe normally. The pain also evaporated, leaving him curiously light-headed. Orient tried to gather his thoughts, fearful of a lingering dread at the edge of his awareness. There was still something yet undone.

He had to find the magnetic link. Inhaling deeply, he

went into a slow, deliberate breathing pattern designed to focus his senses. He carefully began to dowse for an alien presence in the room, alert for any sign of attack. Then he felt it, an electric bristle crawling over the base of his brain like an insect.

Slowly, he got to his feet and let the energy guide him.

His senses drew him to a jacket hanging in the bedroom closet. Tucked inside the torn lining was a tiny black cross tied with a red ribbon.

A thin nail impaled a swatch of cotton on the cross. Looking closely, Orient could see strands of black hair on the cotton. Without a doubt they were his.

Orient knew exactly what had to be done. He took the cross inside and set it down next to the water glass. He sprinkled the purified water over the cross and repeated the words of exorcism. Then he crumpled a piece of paper, put it in the ashtray, and placed the cross on top. Finally he struck a match and ignited the paper. After making sure the flames consumed the cross entirely, Orient flushed the ashes.

When he had finished he surveyed the room. The damage was light, but ugly. A stench was rapidly developing from the still unmopped residue of the struggle. He couldn't sleep in it like that, and yet he knew he wasn't up to cleaning it, with all his good intentions. The only solution was to switch rooms for the night. After washing his face and brushing his teeth thoroughly, he decided to discuss the matter with the desk clerk.

As he left his room, Orient recognized a familiar voice drifting up the stairs. The words were garbled but he clearly understood their anguish. Tristan was near hysteria.

He hurried down the stairway and found Westlake holding a weeping Tristan with one hand while trying to dial the house phone with the other. As Orient approached,

Tristan left Westlake and fell into his arms, sobbing desperately.

"What happened?" Orient rasped, intoxicated by her scent.

Westlake stared at him thoughtfully. "Shandy just suffered a heart attack. I'm afraid it was fatal."

Chapter 12

SHOCKED AND SUDDENLY EMBARRASSED, ORIENT gingerly passed Tristan back to Westlake.

"I'd better take a look. Anyone try CPR?"

"Too late. I tried," Westlake assured him, dialing a number. "Hello, Bevo? Mayday. Get emergency over to the Olympia."

Orient moved reluctantly through the half-open door, steeling himself against what he'd find inside.

Shandy's body lay doubled up on the carpet in a fetal position. The stench was overpowering. Cupping a hand over his nose and mouth, Orient knelt to examine the inert figure.

Shandy's bearded face wore a fixed grimace of wide-eyed terror. It was far too late for CPR.

Suddenly Orient became aware of an alien vibration. He moved to an open window and inhaled deeply, repeating the slow, intense breathing pattern that helped fine-tune his senses. It was there, a hostile presence similar to the one in his room. It didn't take him long to locate it. Following his instincts, he homed in on Shandy's dresser drawer. There, concealed in the folds of a shirt, was an occult cross.

It was identical to the one he'd just burned.

"Come up with a diagnosis?"

Orient turned and saw Westlake standing in the doorway. "Where's Tristan?"

Westlake gave him a bored scowl. "Outside with Lieutenant Early. What about Shandy?"

"Looks like a heart attack, but it's too soon to know."

"How about poison?"

"Anything's possible. I also found this among his effects."

"Looks like one of those damned voodoo charms we found on the *Blowgun*," Westlake muttered. He gave Orient a long look. "And just what were you doing in Shandy's effects?"

"Checking for evidence of drugs. Or poison," Orient said, a bit too hastily.

Westlake caught it but let it pass. "Could this cross be related to Shandy's death?"

It became Orient's turn to stare. "Do you believe that?"

"I don't mean he died of the evil eye," Westlake growled. "Maybe it's some kind of calling card."

Orient shrugged. "Perhaps Tristan knows something about it."

Westlake didn't seem optimistic. "It all fits somehow. But only God knows how."

Orient didn't say anything. He knew, of course, that the voodoo cross had indeed caused Shandy's death, but he couldn't tell Westlake. At the moment, all he really wanted was to leave the Olympia Club, and Commander Westlake, far behind.

He thought about Tristan. Certainly he wouldn't forget her. Perhaps they'd meet somewhere else, at some better time.

Two men in medical whites entered the room. Both carried doctor's bags.

"Make sure you don't move anything," Westlake barked. "Where's the autopsy unit?"

The two medics looked at each other. "We weren't told we needed them," one of them said.

"Goddammit, mister, I don't want lame excuses. I want the autopsy unit. Now!"

The hapless medic hurried to the phone to comply.

"Touch that phone and I'll have you busted," Westlake roared. "Call outside. This is an investigation area. And you!" He jabbed his finger at the other medic. "Get in there and check the body. But if you destroy evidence, you're mine."

Orient followed the other medic out the door as Westlake continued his tirade. "I want this place dusted for prints, the body's clothing vacuumed, the works. Understand?"

When Orient left the room he saw Craig standing awkwardly beside Tristan, who was half reclined on a small couch in the corridor. Both men nodded. Tristan seemed to be in her own private reverie, so they spoke in hushed tones.

"She all right?"

"Well as can be expected, I guess," Craig ventured. "The desk clerk told me when I arrived."

"Does Sybelle know?"

"I'm not sure. I haven't seen her."

"Didn't she meet you after dinner?"

"Haven't seen her since lunch."

Orient's voice rose slightly. "Let me get this straight. You didn't phone earlier to tell Sybelle you were sending a car?"

"Not me, Doctor. I've been bogged down in paperwork since lunch. They still haven't cut my flight orders."

"Listen, Craig, do you have a car?"

"Is Mom in some kind of trouble?"

"I don't know, Craig. That's what I'd like to find out. What about the car?"

"No problem. Just let me check her room. Maybe she came back."

"Meet me in the lobby," Orient told him, certain Sybelle wasn't upstairs. He ducked inside Shandy's room and signaled Westlake. "You'd better get someone to stay with Tristan."

Westlake smirked. "I thought you'd volunteer for that."

"Her husband, your colleague, is dead, Commander," Orient said coldly. "So do your damn job."

Orient stalked to the staircase, his anger obscured by a flurry of thoughts. Shandy had succumbed to the same occult force that had attacked him earlier. As Shandy had speculated, the black cross was of voodoo origin. More properly, it was an Obeah hex. And now Sybelle had been kidnapped. Obviously whoever had launched this operation had decided to take full advantage of the lunar phase to generate an all-out assault. Orient didn't trust Westlake on this one. He had already booted too many chances.

He waited impatiently in the lobby until Craig hurried downstairs. "Mom's not there," he announced.

"Where's the car?"

"Out front. Where are we going?"

"Come on. I'll tell you on the way."

Craig drove a small BMW with a right-hand drive, which, as he explained to Orient, was standard issue at the Olympia Club. At the moment, however, Orient's thoughts revolved around finding Sybelle. "Do you need a pass or something to leave the grounds?" he asked Craig.

"I have one. But you still haven't told me where we're headed."

"Did Sybelle ever explain how we linked up to locate you?"

A slow smile spread across Craig's face. "Of course. Now I get it. You want us to hook up and find her."

"Can you drive and concentrate at the same time?"

The smile faded. "I'll give it a try."

"Fine. Then slow down and go into your breathing pattern."

For long minutes the only sound was the hum of the engine as they both focused on the calm center of being. Increasingly confident that they would locate Sybelle sooner or later, Orient tuned his awareness to Craig's dim, but steady, presence. In a short time he saw a closed gate with guards on either side, brandishing automatic rifles.

"Ask them if they noticed anything unusual tonight," he prompted.

"I'll handle it. Got some ID?"

As Orient dug into his pocket he felt something unfamiliar. He pulled out a small, oval object. Then he remembered. Sybelle had given him the ivory pillbox, full of aspirin, just before she left.

Craig leaned out the window and handed the guard his pass. "Did you men happen to notice a woman with red hair like mine come through here tonight?"

"No, sir," the man said, checking Craig's pass with a flashlight. The other guard stood a few yards away, his weapon poised.

"Security always this tight?" Orient asked, handing his wallet to Craig.

"Not that I know of." Craig turned to the guard. "Did anything unusual happen tonight?"

The guard shrugged and handed back their IDs. "Some jackass busted through here a couple hours ago. About ran us down." He waved to the other guard. "Yo, Harvey. Open up."

The other guard pushed a lever at the side of the stone wall and the gates slowly parted.

"Think Mom was in that car?" Craig asked softly as they rolled past.

Orient hefted the pillbox. "Wherever she is, we'll find her."

Orient had counted heavily on the psychic bond between mother and son to aid their search. But having an object she'd recently possessed, like the pillbox, provided a doubly strong link. He gripped the box tightly and expanded his senses.

Almost immediately he felt a frail, familiar vibration at the base of his brain and knew it was Sybelle.

Judging from Craig's surprised glance, he felt it too. The vibration seemed to get stronger when they reached the high cliff road. The full moon hung low in the clear sky, illuminating the wind-flecked sea. The road wound along the cliffs for a mile or so before reaching a fork. One way cut through the forest toward the city of Kingston. The other continued along the sea.

Orient pointed and Craig turned toward Kingston. But as they picked up speed, Orient felt his connection to Sybelle fade. "Hold it." He sighed. "Better try the other road."

Unable to turn on the narrow stretch of road, Craig backed up for almost a mile before reaching the fork. When they were finally moving forward along the cliffs, Orient sensed Sybelle's dim presence up ahead. A few miles later they saw the car parked at the side of the road.

Without speaking, Craig stopped behind it and they both got out to take a look. As they approached the car, Orient's instincts were seething. Every shadow, every sound, set off a dozen alarms inside his brain. Clutching the pillbox in his fist, he peered through the open window.

"Empty."

"She's around here somewhere," Craig muttered, almost to himself. "I can feel it."

Orient felt it as well. He circled the car like a dog picking up the scent. Then he saw the red sash hanging over the door and he was certain. Motioning Craig to follow, he moved toward the trees lining the road.

They picked their way slowly through the dense foliage, guided by the moonlight. Craig followed a few paces behind, his brow furrowed with concentration. Orient's senses continued to hum with conflicting signals.

They had covered about fifty yards when Orient felt a hand on his shoulder. He turned and saw Craig pointing somewhere off the trail. Without waiting he moved off. Orient followed reluctantly, uncertain of Craig's sense of direction.

It proved to be quite reliable. No more than ten yards away they found Sybelle huddled against the side of a tree, her chalk-white skin mottled with bruises and scratches. She was conscious, but barely coherent.

"Knew you were coming," she mumbled breathlessly. "Be careful . . . careful . . . they're back there . . ."

"Who's back there?" Orient whispered.

"Back there . . . down the trail . . ." She grabbed Craig's wrist. "We've got to leave here now . . ."

Orient helped him pull his mother to her feet. Although still wobbly, she was able to walk.

"You two start back," Orient said softly. "I'll take a look and join you at the car."

As soon as they parted company Orient regretted his rash decision. Alone, in the strange tropical forest, the shadows loomed larger and the smallest sound seemed menacing. He stayed on the trail, moving swiftly as his eyes adjusted to the gloom. He was also driven by fear. He felt it ripple the fine hairs along his neck as he moved down the hill, a nameless dread of the energy gathered somewhere in the darkness.

Suddenly he paused, aware of the dense stillness. He stepped behind a tree and listened for long moments before going on. His senses bristled as he edged down the trail. Although the area seemed completely deserted, evil hovered nearby like a swarm of bees.

Then he saw the clearing at the bottom of the hill.

It looked like a freshly pillaged farm. Smoke drifted up from a pile of ashes and there was charred wood and debris everywhere. Moving closer, he saw feathers, bits of white cloth, the headless carcass of a rooster, a burned cross, and the mutilated remains of a human being.

Orient could see that the victim was male, although his genitals had been cut off. However, judging from the lack of blood around the ragged wound, that hadn't been the cause of death.

What had probably killed him was the deep slashes in both his wrists. One hand was almost completely severed.

As a grisly encore, someone had inserted a plastic straw into the open artery.

Chapter 13

"ALMOST EVERY DROP OF BLOOD WAS DRAINED from the poor bastard's body." Westlake glared accusingly at Orient. "This was a ritual killing."

Orient shrugged. "You have Sybelle's statement. I believe she mentioned all that."

"But you haven't told me what *you* think, Doctor."

"I wasn't there."

"How did you know where to find her?"

"The same way we found the *Blowgun.*"

Westlake kept his eyes on Orient. "We need her over here to make a positive ID."

"Would it do any good to remind you that she's physically and emotionally exhausted?"

"It's vital we make sure the man you found is the same one who tried to kidnap her."

"She told you . . ."

"That she ran away when the voodoo cult captured the driver."

"You're sure it was a voodoo cult?"

"You're the expert, Doctor. You tell me."

"Telepathy," Orient said slowly, "is a science. You're talking occult, black magic."

Westlake smiled. It always worried Orient when he smiled. "And you don't believe in those things?"

"Let's say they don't interest me."

"We could use your help on this one. Pay you a handsome fee."

"Thanks, but no, thanks, Commander. All I want—"

"I know, I know." Westlake lifted his arms in mock surrender. "When does the shuttle take you back to New York?"

"You must be a telepath."

Westlake heaved a sigh and shook his head. "Just an overworked flatfoot up against a fucking crime wave. Sabotage, stolen bodies, kidnapping, two murders . . ."

"Then you do think Shandy was murdered?"

"I don't know what to think." The phone rang and he picked it up. "She's here? Okay, escort her back."

"Remember one thing, Commander."

Westlake shot him an annoyed glance. "Yeah?"

"When you show Sybelle the body, make sure his wounds are covered."

"Care to tag along?"

Orient didn't, but he knew Sybelle needed all the support she could get. "All right," he said wearily. "I'm game if she is."

The office Westlake had commandeered for the occasion was located in the infirmary and actually belonged to Dr. Chin. Like the rest of the building, it was cold and austere. Outside the infirmary it was cheerfully sunny; inside, it was always four in the morning.

"Good day, Ms. Lean," Westlake greeted her somberly when she entered.

"Owen! I was hoping you'd be here."

Orient went to her side. "Are you okay?"

"All things considered, I'm a wreck."

"They want you to identify the man I found down there."

"Yes, I know. I also heard about poor Dr. Shandy."

"Who told you?" Westlake snapped.

Sybelle whirled, green eyes blazing. "It's all over the hotel—or whatever it is you're running here. Exactly what have we gotten into, Commander?"

"Obviously the terrorists who sabotaged your son's submarine are behind all this. And your identification will be an invaluable help, Ms. Lean," Westlake added smoothly. "I do appreciate your coming down after your ordeal last night."

Sybelle beamed at Orient. "I was never so happy to see anyone as you two last night."

Westlake smiled. "Yes. Well, then, let's get this over with, shall we?"

It didn't take long. Dr. Chin opened the drawer; Sybelle glanced at the man's face, then nodded. "That's the man who tried to kidnap me," she said softly. "What did they do to him?"

"He died of a knife wound," Dr. Chin said, sliding the drawer shut.

Westlake took her arm. "I'll tell you about it on the way back."

"I'm not sure I really want to know."

To Orient's relief, Westlake refrained from going into details on the drive to the hotel. But to his surprise, the commander did reveal the dead man's identity.

"His name is Oswaldo Perez, a.k.a. Perro," Westlake told them. "We know him to be a Cuban agent."

Sybelle seemed stunned. "What on earth would a Cuban agent want with me?"

"The way I see it, the Cubans tried to sabotage the sub and, failing that, trailed the operation here." He looked at Orient. "Maybe Perro needed a hostage so he could deal."

"Deal for what?" Orient inquired.

Westlake peered through the windshield. "I guess we'll never know now, will we?"

"Whatever he wanted," Orient said carefully, "it's obvious these people think Sybelle and I are part of your operation."

"You're probably correct."

"Which leads me to this question, Commander. Why fly two unsuspecting civilians to a secret CIA compound in Jamaica when it would have been infinitely more secure to fly Craig to New York?"

"What's you theory, Doctor?"

"I think you seized the opportunity to use us as live bait. Which explains why you invited me to inspect the sub—and why you took me to see a corpse who wasn't there."

"Really, darling," Sybelle sniffed. "You didn't tell me any of this."

"There wasn't time between lunch and dinner."

"And yet," Westlake reminded him, "it was Ms. Lean—not you—these people chose to kidnap."

"She was vulnerable. Like you, Commander, they used her son as a lure." Orient didn't want to mention that he had also nearly succumbed to the Obeah hex that killed Shandy. He refused to serve as an advisor on psychic warfare.

"We've beefed up security," Westlake said.

"Please get me back in time to see Craig," Sybelle said impatiently. "He leaves for Japan this afternoon." She leaned forward and gave Westlake a cold stare. "I trust he'll be well out of the line of fire."

Westlake smiled. "Craig is a good officer."

Sybelle sat back and gazed unhappily out the window. "He'll make a much better piano player, believe me."

* * *

Craig was scheduled to fly via Miami to San Diego, where he could board a military connection to Japan. But he managed to squeeze in a late lunch with Sybelle and Orient after they returned from viewing the body.

Orient had grown to like and respect Craig during the brief time they had spent together. All through the search for Sybelle and the subsequent discovery of the murdered man, the young officer had shown uncommon sensitivity, courage, and self-control. Immediately after lunch Orient said his farewells, giving Sybelle time alone with her son.

"Nice knowing you, Doc," Craig said, slipping into a familiarity acquired sometime during the long night. "I'll write from Japan." He looked around to make sure no one was listening. "About the technique. Mom explained everything. I'll definitely honor her vow of secrecy. Depend on it."

Orient extended his hand. "Thanks, pilgrim. I will."

As he left the dining room and crossed the lobby, Orient noticed a Jamaican man, in a badly fitting suit, glumly surveying the guests while pretending to read a magazine. So much for Westlake's beefed-up security.

He continued to the staircase, slowly pushing his weary body toward his room and sleep. He was nearly there when he saw Tristan.

She stood in the doorway of her suite as if waiting for someone. Her black dress clung to the taut curves of her body, and her moonlit hair framed her pale, scrubbed features. Without makeup her face seemed startlingly young. And fragile.

Orient paused at the landing. "Are you all right?"

Tristan lifted her hand and he saw the cigarette tucked between her extended fingers. "Ash never liked me to smoke in the rooms," she said, almost to herself. "Anyway, I don't have a light."

"Did you think someone would eventually come along with a match?" Orient said gently as he lit her cigarette.

She stared at him intently. "I don't know what to think, do you?"

What could he tell her? That he knew her husband had been killed by an occult spell. That voodoo and espionage were somehow responsible for their meeting. That through his weariness and the long shadow of Shandy's death he could still feel the sensual tug between them.

"Actually, it doesn't make sense," she mused softly. "My coming out to smoke. Ash isn't here, is he?" She looked up at him. "Would you care for a drink?"

When he hesitated, her lips parted in a vaguely reproving smile. "Please, Owen. I need friendly conversation."

"I understand," he said quietly.

But as he followed her inside, Orient's thoughts were seething with doubts.

"Rum all right?"

"Lots of cola," he said, settling into an armchair.

He watched Tristan prepare drinks. The black silk dress enhanced her liquid grace as she turned from the sideboard carrying a tray and moved across the room. In one smooth motion she set the tray on the coffee table, eased down onto the couch, and touched the cushion beside her.

"Please don't be so distant, Owen."

Orient joined her on the couch and took the glass from her extended hand.

She lifted the other glass and looked at him. "To Ash," she offered. "He was a good spook. And he tried to be a good husband."

"To Ash," Orient said guardedly. "Please accept my condolences." He lifted his glass and drank.

The searing taste of overproof rum slashed through the cola. Orient wondered how much of the half-empty bottle Tristan had consumed that morning.

"I'm at least two drinks ahead of you," She said, as if

reading his mind. "I've been sitting here all day trying to . . . comprehend."

Orient nodded. "Yes, the shock . . ."

"Yes, the shock, the sudden emptiness, the arrangements . . ." She studied him for a second. "And the questions."

He met her gaze. "What sort of questions?"

"Owen, is it possible that my husband's death had something to do with this project you're working on?"

"Understand this, Tristan. I am not working on any project. I became involved in locating the *Blowgun* and that's it. As for Ash, has there been a doctor's report?"

"Cardiac arrest." Tristan snorted. "But the doctors will say anything Glen Westlake wants. Everybody knows it."

"Do you think it was something else?"

Tristan took a last drag on her cigarette.

"I don't suppose I'll ever find out." She tossed her head back, long silver hair catching the sunlight streaming behind her. The sudden illumination seemed to amplify the brilliance of her crystal eyes. A veil of smoke drifted between them, shading the chiseled contours of her face. She tamped out the cigarette and gave him a thoughtful smile.

"Will you be staying long?"

"We leave tonight."

Her smile faded. "Oh. I had hoped we could spend some time."

"Perhaps you'll come to New York." Orient extended the vague invitation, it occurred to him that he didn't know where he'd be in the next few weeks.

"I'd like that," Tristan said, her husky voice trailing off as she took his hand.

Her light touch sent a tremor through his senses. Orient took a deep breath and cleared his mind. But it was too late. They were already moving toward each other. Barely perceptible at first, their intense physical attraction slowly gained momentum.

Just before they kissed, their eyes collided, and Orient saw her violent need. Then her tongue darted inside his mouth, devouring his uncertainty. Her body arched against his and he eased her back onto the cushion. He inhaled her musky scent as the silk dress fell away from her smooth shoulders. As she drew him down to her pink-nippled breasts, the heat of her damp skin ignited a dormant pool of lust that incinerated his reason like a well fire. She tore open his shirt and he felt her lips moving across his chest. Senses steaming, he lifted her up and pulled her dress away. Her eyes burned into his as their bodies locked together with a convulsive shock that consumed their raging hunger.

Later, as Orient slowly climbed the stairs to his room, ashes of regret littered his thoughts and his skin felt oddly cold. Like that of someone who had just plundered a grave.

Chapter 14

The courier plane was late.

Orient and Sybelle were waiting impatiently on the side veranda when Westlake appeared with the bad news.

"Why can't we just go to the airport and wait there?" Sybelle demanded.

Westlake smiled. "Security reasons. Sorry." He turned to Orient and motioned him aside. "May I speak to you a moment, Doctor?"

Orient reluctantly followed him into the lobby.

"Right in here," Westlake said, walking briskly to a metal door located behind the hotel's front desk.

Orient was surprised to find a highly computerized office behind the Old World facade.

"Drink?" Westlake offered, moving over to a well-stocked sideboard.

"No, thanks. What's the problem with out flight?"

"No problem. It's just late, by about forty minutes. Anyway, it does give us time to talk."

"I'm afraid we have nothing—"

"Hear me out," Westlake interjected, filling his glass with ice and bourbon. He moved back to the desk and sat down heavily. "I had my men comb the area where they found the Cuban kidnapper's body. And where Ms. Lean claims to have witnessed a voodoo ritual."

"Are you saying you doubt her word?"

Westlake took a long swallow of bourbon. "Quite the opposite. A careful search of the area turned up charred human remains, which corroborates her story of seeing someone burned during the ceremony."

"A dead body," Orient amended.

"Not just any dead body. We checked out a set of bridgework and some charred teeth found at the scene, with our computer records. And we learned something quite startling. The body burned during this ritual was our missing Harold Patterson."

"*Your* missing Harold Patterson, not mine."

"So what's your opinion? About *my* present situation, I mean."

Orient shrugged. "Seems to me you've got more problems than you thought."

"Oh? How so?"

"If the driver who kidnapped Sybelle is a Cuban agent, then the voodoo people who killed him—and stole Patterson's body—are working with someone else. Which means there are *two* sets of players on the other side—the voodoo sect and the Cubans."

Westlake leaned back, smiling expansively. "Just exactly the reason I wanted to talk to you." He reached into his pocket and extracted a thick white envelope. "I'm prepared to pay ten thousand dollars in cash for any pertinent information you can dig up on this case."

"Why are you so intent on my input, Commander?" Orient asked curtly. "I believe I've made myself clear."

"Money talks, Doctor. And from what I've been able to see, you haven't much to say for yourself in that area."

"So you decided to become my benefactor."

"Not at all. Much as it hurts to admit it, I need a man with precisely your unique qualifications on this one."

"My research in telepathy hardly qualifies me to deal with voodoo."

"I know, I know. One is science, the other is occult. Shandy was always very careful to explain the difference."

Orient felt an angry edge slicing through his polite tone. "Well, thanks for your confidence. Now, if that's all, I'd better rejoin Sybelle. She must be getting anxious."

"Please consider my offer open, Doctor. I'll be in touch."

As Orient stalked back to the veranda, his sudden anger was tempered by decision. In the past he had always gone underground when confronted by men like Westlake. This time he was determined to stand and fight.

"What have you two been brewing up?" Sybelle demanded accusingly. "You've been keeping things from me, Owen."

Orient eased down beside her. "Yes, I have. But I promise to tell you everything when we're safely in New York."

"Oh, my God!"

"Well, I admit I wasn't—"

"Owen—over there!" Sybelle hissed. "It's him!"

Orient followed Sybelle's tightly jabbing finger and spotted a tall Jamaican man with dreadlocks leaning against a rear doorway. He was dressed in kitchen whites and smoking a narrow cigar.

"That's the man I saw perform that horrible ritual last night—the priest!"

Hawk-featured, with dark glasses perched on prominent cheekbones, and long limbs that seemed poised to strike even while at rest, the man in white exuded an air of controlled violence. He seemed to sense their interest, turning to meet Orient's stare before he flicked the ash off his cigar and strolled inside.

"I suppose we'd better inform Commander Westlake," Sybelle whispered.

Orient thoughtfully regarded the empty doorway. "Let me tell him. I'll explain later, okay?"

"Whatever you say, darling. I'll leave it entirely in your hands. Frankly, I'm tempted to fly off and forget the whole thing. But I suppose that's not very patriotic."

Westlake was at the bar, pouring another bourbon when Orient knocked.

"Oh, yes, Doctor. Still here, eh? Well, don't sweat it, the plane is on schedule."

"Actually, I came to see if your cash offer still stands."

"What do you have?"

"The identity of last night's voodoo priest."

Westlake smiled. "Seems to me that's something your friend Sybelle is more likely to know."

"But now I know too—and you don't. Do we have a deal, Commander?"

Westlake took the fat white envelope from a drawer and slid it halfway across the desk. "Now tell me," he said, keeping his hand on the envelope, "who is this priest? What's his name?"

"I don't know. But he works right here. In the kitchen."

"Describe him, please."

"I'll point him out, if you like."

"That won't be necessary," Westlake said sharply. Then, noting Orient's surprise, he softened his tone. He also lifted his hand from the envelope. "We don't want to alert him. The thing to do is follow him, until we get everyone connected with this. Please describe him to me."

"The man you want is tall, perhaps six-three, very slender, with a large head. He has prominent features, wears his hair in dreadlocks, and smokes cigars."

Westlake nodded. "That could only be one man. St. George, our chef."

The phone rang. Westlake took it. "You'll be pleased

to know your car is here, Doctor." He slid the envelope across the desk.

Orient picked it up and slipped it inside his jacket. "Sure you won't need more than my description?"

"As I said, there's only one man on our hotel staff who remotely fits that profile." He smiled and extended his hand. "Have a pleasant trip."

Plumes of deep red and purple fanned the evening sky as the car wound along the cliffs. Orient remained slouched in a corner, brooding over his final encounter with Westlake, while Sybelle stared out the window, adrift in a mild depression. She missed Craig terribly and felt vaguely betrayed by Owen's air of secrecy.

It was dark when they reached the airport where the Gulfstream jet waited. Five minutes after takeoff Orient fell asleep, leaving all of Sybelle's unspoken questions unanswered.

The next morning Orient treated Sybelle to an expensive breakfast at Sant Ambroseus, where he went over the relevant details of his experiences at the Olympia, omitting his interlude with Tristan. However, he did tell her that an Obeah hex was involved in Shandy's death. And that Westlake had attempted to recruit him. He also told her about the reward.

"And since you supplied the information for which the commander paid so handsomely, half the fee belongs to you," Orient said with a flourish.

Sybelle absently accepted the envelope, her mind still revolving around the events of the previous days. "Now let me get this right. You say a man died aboard the submarine, then his body was stolen—and he was the same man I saw being burned in that wretched voodoo ceremony?"

"So Westlake claims. Did Craig mention anything about the man's death aboard the sub?"

She sighed. "No, but you know how boys are. You have to drag everything out of them." She carefully spread some strawberry jam on a croissant. "And you're no exception, darling."

Orient looked surprised. "I've told you everything."

"Actually, I'm talking about something else now. Which is your annoying—and quite obstructive—compulsion about secrecy. Not once since you arrived have you mentioned anything about your plans. We're supposed to be friends. It's bad enough you disappear for years at a time without a word. Now that you've come back, you might share a little of yourself."

"Sorry. Guess I've been on the road too long. The truth is I have no plans."

"Then that settles it."

"Settles what?"

"I'm going to consider this five thousand dollars—that is what you gave me, isn't it? Anyway, let's consider it the first ten months' rent on your new apartment."

"Oh?"

"Yes. My place is too big for one, so I've decided to convert the guest room and the garage under it into a separate unit." She paused for a sip of cappuccino. "You might set up a new lab in the garage. What do you think?"

Orient took her hand. "I think I accept. And thank you."

"Thank me? You show up for dinner and I drag you into a raving madhouse of stolen bodies and God knows what all . . . not to mention the fact that you saved my son's life—and you want to thank me?"

He leaned closer and kissed her cheek. "Look at the up side. I'm no longer a fugitive. The CIA returned my file. I'm five thousand dollars richer. And I have a new apartment. Come to think of it, you keep a pretty mean secret yourself. In all the years we've been friends you never mentioned anything about having a son."

Sybelle's expression teetered between apology and defiance. "Let's just say I had my very good reasons."

He was immediately sorry he brought it up. "I'm sure you did," he said, signaling for the check.

"Anyway, Craig's on his way to Japan. And we're home safely. Let's hope we never see or hear from those people again."

Orient nodded, but as he watched the waiter approach, an image of Tristan flickered in his mind like candlelight.

Chapter 15

New York was enjoying an extended period of Indian summer. Inspired by the balmy weather, Orient took a few small steps toward rebuilding his life. He devoted the first week to converting Sybelle's garage into a laboratory, and began an extensive program of Yoga exercises to fine-tune his mind and body. He also made an appointment with Andy Jacobs to discuss some unfinished business.

"Let's get goin', Owen," the ex-senator blared, pumping Orient's hand. "Sorry to be short, but I'm due in D.C. tonight."

"Maybe I've caught you at the right time. I'm looking for some classified information. I need all you can dig up on a private CIA playground in Jamaica called the Olympia Club."

"Why is that?"

"It's a long story."

Andy sat behind the desk and opened his cigar humidor. "I've got fifteen, twenty minutes before the car arrives."

Again Orient omitted the details of his brief encounter with Tristan as he told Andy everything that had happened

121

to them in Jamaica. He also omitted any mention of the psychic attack that had nearly taken his life. There were certain things he couldn't confide to Andy.

"You must have been pretty damned busy," Andy rumbled, relighting his cigar. "You were hardly there a weekend. But what I don't understand is why you're still pursuing the problem."

Orient looked away. "Because the problem is bound to pursue me. Westlake wouldn't hand me ten thousand dollars out of sheer gratitude. And he didn't seem that surprised when I described the voodoo priest, who happens to be his chef, St. George—there's another name you may want to check."

Andy dutifully jotted the name in a small notebook.

"Anyway, sooner or later the other shoe will drop, and I need to be prepared."

"Damned right you do. Don't worry, Owen, I'll nose around while I'm up on the Hill, maybe call in a favor or two. We'll talk when I get back. I've got a little surprise for you."

Reassured, Orient escorted the ex-senator to his waiting car, then decided to walk across Central Park to the East Side. Recounting the nightmare events that occurred in Jamaica had stirred up noxious memories. He needed a stroll to clear his mind.

Encouraged by the refreshing autumn weather, a large segment of New York was jogging, cycling, rowing, horseback riding, skating, or just lying in the grass watching the world go by. The distant, tinny melodies of the Carousel mingled with the chirping of children at play and the occasional portable radio to weave a soothing tapestry of sound.

Orient veered off the curving lanes to an isolated rock partially obscured by an oak tree and sat down.

As he tried to absorb the beauty of the tranquil sanctuary in the midst of the looming city, his thoughts kept drifting back to Jamaica. In an effort to clear his mind he inhaled deeply and focused on the positive aspects of the present situation. He was grateful for the chance to resume his work, but he had to be vigilant.

As if in response to the thought, he noticed a wiry black man perched on a nearby bench, reading a paperback book. Oddly, the man was wearing dark glasses. Orient moved off the rock and wandered back to the path, following it past the Carousel. He saw an opening in the afternoon traffic and darted across the road to a stairway leading to the Chess Pagoda.

Orient liked to visit the secluded pagoda with its circle of stone chess tables. Its position, creating the hill, afforded a good view of the surrounding terrain. Sure enough, the man in the blue suit and dark glasses was just across the road, waiting for the light to change.

Orient hurried down the other stairway and kept going past the quaint Dairy, trying to maintain a safe distance from the man following him. To gain ground he risked ducking down a convenient but deserted stone stairway nestled behind some trees. From there he cut across to the Fifth Avenue exit and headed for Fifty-ninth Street.

He lost his man in Bloomingdale's, then went directly to the subway located below the department store and boarded an express to Eighty-sixth Street.

The sun had dropped below the skyline when he emerged and the air was chilled. Orient took a cab back to Sybelle's house, still brooding over what possible motive anyone would have to follow him.

Before the cab stopped, he had an answer.

Orient's room above the garage was quite spacious, with a private bath and a huge walk-in closet he'd converted to an office. Hidden behind a loose board that braced a tie rack was the computer disk Westlake had given him in Jamaica. Or had Shandy actually inserted it in his file? It didn't matter, Orient speculated. It was time to take a long, hard look at the dossier the CIA had compiled.

He found Sybelle in the large kitchen they now shared, blending tomato juice for her predinner Bloody Mary.

"Hello, dear. Care for a cocktail?"

"No, thanks, I'm on the wagon."

"Since when?"

"Since Jamaica. Actually, I need a favor. It's important I find an expert to decode the computer disk Westlake gave me."

"Why so important?"

"Because I caught someone following me today—and I have a feeling they're after the software. Anyway, it's high time I found out what they want so badly."

"Well, as it happens, I do have one client who is heavily into computers. But I'm afraid you two wouldn't hit it off. Duke has a hard time getting along with people."

"Duke?"

"Actually, his name is Bruno Berio. He's one of my more colorful clients."

"How so?"

Sybelle took an experimental sip of the blend and wrinkled her nose. "Needs a tad more horseradish."

"What about Bruno Berio?"

"Well, he needs a lot less horseradish—socially speaking, that is. The man is rude, abrasive, petty, vain, and totally outrageous. He's also a minor genius, and capable of great wisdom, insight, even tenderness . . . but very rarely."

"Sounds like my kind of man."

Sybelle pushed the idea aside with a wave of her lacquered nails. "You wouldn't like him, darling. Believe me."

"I'm not looking for a date here," Orient told her grimly. "Just somebody who can put the information on the screen."

"Oh dear." Sybelle sighed. "You're probably right. But remember, I'm doing this against my better judgment. I'll find his number after I have a proper drink. Come."

"What sort of consultation does Bruno Berio require?" Orient asked, following her to the small bar in the library.

Thoughtfully, Sybelle added Polish vodka to her mix. "Like everyone else, he has concerns about the future. I sometimes read the Tarot on his behalf."

From the set of her pudgy jaw, Orient could read that the subject was closed. Sybelle maintained a rule of strict discretion when it came to her clients.

She took a long swallow of her Bloody Mary and shut one eye. "A little less horseradish would have been perfect."

"Like Bruno Berio."

She shuddered and took another swallow. "Believe me, darling, Duke is far from perfect."

Right at the outset, Orient discovered what she'd meant.

The phone number Berio had left with her belonged to Nuclear Pizza in Greenwich Village. The gruff voice that answered the phone informed Orient that Mr. Berio would not be in until later that evening.

Orient took down the address, and after dining in an Indian restaurant on East Sixth Street, he strolled crosstown to Bleecker and MacDougal. When he found Duke's Nuclear Pizza, he understood.

A dazzling array of video games lined the red brick walls inside the pizzeria. Thankfully, the machines' sounds were turned way down, allowing the customers to enjoy the vintage jazz coming over the speaker system.

Orient seldom had occasion to play video games, but from the flashy graphics and artful hardware he could see they were quite sophisticated. And profitable, he speculated, judging from the knots of waiting players clustered around every machine. The players tended to be male, between fifteen and fifty, although there were a fair number of females in attendance. Male or female, most of them were eating pizza.

A bald, fierce-featured man stood behind the counter, expertly cutting fresh slices right out of the oven. Orient had to admit the aroma was exquisite.

He smiled. "Is Mr. Berio here?"

"Not yet," the man rumbled. "Wanna try a slice? It's dynamite."

"No, thanks. Do you serve coffee?"

"Is Amos famous? Best goddamn coffee in the Village."

The claim was no exaggeration. Not only was the brew excellent, it was served in a proper cup instead of a styrofoam container.

"Hey, Duke, you're up," someone called.

The bald man came out from behind the counter, wiping his hands on his apron. He hurried to one of the video games and pushed aside a young man at the controls. Immediately people from other machines began to drift over to watch him play. Orient finished his coffee and joined them.

The video game was called Gunga Din, and featured a turbaned figure trying to outrace, outclimb, and outwit his dogged pursuers through a series of mazes.

Each of the mazes opened onto a different graphic scene, such as the Temple of Kali or the Snake Pit, where the hero had to run a gauntlet of dangers. Duke smoothly went from level to level, cursing each fresh opponent and extracting cries of admiration from his circle of fans.

With consummate skill he completed the final maze and climbed the Golden Dome. As soon as the figure reached the top, fireworks erupted and electronic gongs began to sound. Suddenly an arrow pierced the figure and he fell. As the turbaned figure lay wounded, a quartet of angels floated down and carried him to heaven.

CONGRATULATIONS! YOU HAVE QUALIFIED FOR REINCAR-
NATION! read the message.

"Amazing," a girl whispered. "I've never seen anyone
get to this level."

Suddenly the scene changed. On the screen was an ap-
proaching galaxy and the announcement GET READY! YOU
HAVE BECOME STAR NINJA—THE ZEN SPACE EXPLORER
SEARCHING FOR SARTORI, PLANET OF WISDOM!

"Totally awe-inspiring," a young man said reverently.

Still cursing a blue streak, Duke tried to elude a horde
of alien enemies. But before he completed his run, the
Saturnian Spiders trapped him in a web of doom.

Duke stepped back and squinted at the screen. "Not
bad. New high score, even hundred and seventy-seven
thousand," he announced, savoring each digit. He glared
at a young man behind him and tossed a quarter on the
machine. "My hundred to your ten says you don't beat
it." Then he turned to Orient and shrugged. "Okay, now
I'm here. What is it you want?"

"You were recommended by Sybelle Lean, your consultant."

His piercing black eyes narrowed at the mention of her
name. "Over here," he growled, moving back behind the
counter. He leaned across and folded his large hands. "So
what's the angle?"

"No angle, Mr. Berio. I'm a friend of Sybelle Lean. I
need someone to open a computer disk and see what's
inside."

Duke eyed him suspiciously. "What are you, a fed?"

"I told you . . ."

"Yeah, yeah. How do I know you're not a bounty hunter
looking to shut down my operation?"

"I don't really understand. You can call Sybelle. She'll
vouch for me."

"And if she's wrong it's my ass. You don't understand,
right? Well, try this. There's a fifty-grand reward put out

on me by the corporate syndicate. That's how bad they want to bust my computer action. Capeesh?''

"Now I do. Look, you can take the disk with you. I'll wait here. Or anywhere, for that matter. Is that fair?''

"You ever hear of a virus program?''

Orient shook his head.

"That's a cute little bug that screws up your system—or maybe even gives out your location to another computer. Get it?''

"Cute,'' Orient agreed. "In that case, perhaps you can recommend somebody else who can help me.''

"There is nobody else. So what kind of material you got?''

"It's a government file on me, as a suspected subversive.''

Duke's dour expression lit up. "Yeah? Like what, CIA?''

"Something like that. I'm not really sure.''

"Lemme see the goddamned thing.''

Lips pressed in a scowl, Duke studied the computer disk.

"What you say your name was?''

"Owen Orient.''

"Wait here.''

Orient watched him move to a telephone on the wall and punch some numbers. After a few words he hung up and made a circle with his fingers. "Okay, Doc, she backed up your story,'' he muttered, removing his apron. He took the disk from Orient and headed for the door. "Hey, Artie, take over here. I'll be back in twenty minutes.''

After he left, Orient wandered about the room, watching the players at their various machines. Finally he broke down and tried one himself. As expected, it was far more difficult than it seemed. He took a flyer at the game Duke had played, Gunga Din, but couldn't get past the first maze. A few people drifted over to check him out, then drifted away.

He had invested at least ten quarters in a losing cause when he heard someone call his name.

"Orient here? Orient?"

He turned and saw the counterman waving the phone.

"It's me, Duke," the voice rasped when Orient took the receiver. "There's a phone booth on the corner of Seventh and Perry. Be there in five minutes."

"Can you tell me what this is about?"

"No."

He hung up, leaving Orient little choice.

Five minutes later he was standing at Seventh and Perry, waiting for the phone to ring. When it did, Duke directed him to the corner of Tenth Street and Fourth Street. Within minutes Duke appeared in person, to escort Orient into a basement apartment.

"Had you spotted all the way," he told Orient proudly. "Made sure you didn't have some fly on your ass. Like I said, the feds want to shut me down."

"How come?"

"They claim I'm operating an illegal transmitter—but the real beef is that I'm tapping their satellites." He unlocked the door and ushered Orient inside.

Except for a loft bed, the entire apartment was a mass of electronic equipment. All of it was in excellent working order, judging from the blinking lights, revolving patterns, and intermittent sounds emanating from the computer screens that decorated three of the brick walls.

"No wonder you're an expert at video games."

Duke snorted. "Video games—you mean Gunga Din? I should be an expert—I invented the goddamn program."

"What made you decide to invite me down?"

Duke shook his head sadly. "There's two problems. Whoever gave you this disk made damn sure you couldn't use it."

"How?"

"It's encrypted. I've already run through all the standard codes to access top-secret material, and none work."

"Which means?"

"Which means the motherfucker who programmed this plastic locked it up with some cute, personal-type code. And since those intelligence babies ain't that intelligent, it has to be something to do with your particular crime."

Before Orient could answer, he saw a dark shape at the far end of the basement room slowly rise. A large black Labrador wearing a studded leather collar padded warily toward him. It stopped about two feet from Orient and growled, lips curling back from sharp teeth.

"Don't mind him," Duke said, jabbing some buttons on his computer console. "He thinks he's a dog, but he's a pussycat."

Orient wasn't convinced until the dog lay down on the cement floor and rested its huge head on its paws, mournful eyes fixed on its master.

"Food's in the bowl," Duke muttered, squinting at the two screens in front of him.

The dog got up and trotted off to a far corner of the room that was obscured by a wall of electrical components. In a few moments Orient heard a noisy chewing sound.

"Now, then, Doc. The other problem is the matter of my fee. You might say it makes the first problem academic. Considering danger pay, I need a thousand now. Another thousand when I crack the program."

Orient counted out seven hundred-dollar bills. "Take this as a retainer."

"Deal." Duke dropped the bills on the desk. "So give. What kind of password could the bastards be using?"

Orient skimmed through a few possibilities. "Try Earlybird, Blowgun, double O . . ."

"I've already run down the permutations of your goddamn name, Dr. Orient,'' Duke snapped. ''Earlybird, and what was the other one, Blowpipe?''

''Blowgun.''

Duke punched in the code words, muttering to himself. Then he punched an order into a second console. ''This will spin out various combinations of the names you gave me and run them past your disk.''

After a few long minutes of staring at the screen and punching additional keys, he turned and glared at Orient.

''Braverman sent you, right? He's trying to show me up, isn't he?''

Orient lifted his hands in mock surrender. ''Look, I assure you—''

''All right, all right, forget it.'' Duke turned back to his console and furiously punched the keys. ''Shut up back there, you pig of a mutt,'' he ranted.

To Orient's astonishment, the chewing sounds ceased.

Duke glowered at the screen for a few more minutes, then abruptly shut it off. ''To hell with it. Come on, I'll buy you a good dinner.''

The chewing sounds resumed as Duke picked up his fee and walked to the door. He made sure all three locks were secure, than escorted Orient to an Italian restaurant on Bleecker, called Vanessa's. The place looked a bit upscale for Duke's casual attire, but he seemed to know his way around.

''The food here is spectacular,'' he confided as they were being seated. ''So what kind of doctor are you? GP, brain surgeon . . .''

''I used to practice. Now I'm in research.'' Orient picked up the menu.

''Oh, yeah? What kind of research?''

''Various things.'' Orient looked for the waiter. ''I think I'd like a drink. How about you?''

''White wine. So what kind of research?'' Duke repeated, his tone becoming truculent. ''Don't fuck with

me, Doc. This is your money and your ass. I figure whatever it is you do that makes the spooks so interested in
you is part of the access code. Get it?''

Orient weighed the possibilities. If Duke did succeed in
unlocking the disk, he would know anyway. And if he
didn't, a valuable opportunity would be wasted.

"Telepathy," he said finally. "My research centers on
telepathy and related sciences."

"That's really a wig, Doc. I've got an interest in that
stuff myself. I guess that's how you know Sybelle, right?''

Orient didn't answer. He stared past Duke in disbelief
as Tristan entered the restaurant, accompanied by another
woman.

Chapter 16

FOR A MOMENT IT WAS DÉJÀ VU, HIS MIND FLASH-
ing back to the first time he had seen her.

Now, as then, Tristan moved with feline grace, her silver hair starkly dramatic against her severely cut black
suit. The brunette woman with her wore a loosely cut linen
dress, also in black, liberally adorned with gold jewelry.
The two were deep in conversation as the host led them to
a table, so Tristan didn't notice Orient staring. But her
companion did, and registered her disapproval of his intense scrutiny by signaling the waiter. Suddenly all three—
Tristan, her companion, and the waiter—turned to look at
him.

"Excuse me a second," Duke muttered. "I'd better find
the men's room."

As he left the table Tristan stood and walked toward
Orient, her expression shifting from surprise to delight.
Orient met her halfway. He embraced her somewhat self-
consciously, then drew her to the relative anonymity of his
corner table.

"It's so wonderful to see you," she said breathlessly.
"What are you doing here?"

"Eating. What brings you to town?"

"I left a message on your phone machine that explains everything. I called as soon as I arrived."

His pleased grin betrayed his emotional involvement. He hadn't stopped thinking about Tristan since his return.

"Will you have time later tonight?"

"Why don't you and your friend join us now?"

"I don't suppose he'd mind," Orient said. But he wasn't really certain of Duke's reaction.

Orient escorted Tristan back to her table, where she introduced him to Adele Fletcher, a casting agent who was helping her develop a project. "I was stuck down in Virginia, settling Ash's estate and very depressed. So I decided to write a treatment based on some stories Ash had told me. You know, cloak-and-dagger stuff. Anyway, I sent it to Adele—we were college roomies—and she invited me to come up and discuss it."

"It's a strong property," Adele said knowingly. "I've already gotten a positive reaction from two majors."

"What happened to your friend?" Tristan inquired. "I hope he's not ill."

"Perhaps I'd better check. Excuse me."

Orient walked to the rear of the restaurant. But when he entered the men's room, it was empty. Neither the headwaiter nor the host could recall seeing Duke leave. Somewhat confused, Orient returned to Tristan's table. "My friend is very shy. He must have bolted."

"Is he afraid I'll bite?" Adele asked acidly. "Let's order. I'm starved."

Dinner proved to be a chore, forcing Orient to make polite conversation while burning to be alone with Tristan. Adele seemed to know every celebrity from Broadway to Malibu and spent the evening listing their names.

"So who's your favorite movie star, Owen?" Adele asked him over dessert. "I mean besides Cary Grant."

"I've always admired Colin Clive," Orient said solemnly.

Adele seemed flustered but managed a wan smile. From the corner of his eye Orient caught a glimpse of Tristan stifling her laughter.

Nothing deterred Adele, however, and she chatted on about the luminaries in her address book until the check appeared. "Listen, I've got some calls to make. West Coast time, you know," she said, reaching for her bag. "Let me leave you something for the bill."

"Please don't," Orient said, relieved she was leaving. "It's my pleasure."

"If you insist. Call me tomorrow, sweetheart."

After she left, both Orient and Tristan took a deep breath and stared at each other for a long moment. "I missed you," Tristan said softly. Abruptly she began to giggle. "Colin Clive indeed."

"I was sure she'd claim to be a close personal friend."

"Oh, Adele's always been star-struck. That' why she's so good at her job."

"I'm grateful she lured you to New York. Where are you staying?"

"The Gramercy Park. As long as we're here—how about taking me for a nice, long walk through romantic Greenwich Village?"

Orient took her hand. "What a good idea."

Although fighting to maintain its character, the Village had succumbed to change. Now Korean vegetable markets bloomed alongside the fragrant Italian salumnerias and pastry shops that dotted Bleecker Street.

They crossed Sixth Avenue and Orient led Tristan into a crooked little back street called Minetta Lane. They paused on the deserted street for a lingering kiss, then emerged from the quiet little mews into the tawdry bustle of MacDougal Street. Still holding hands, they strolled to Washington Square.

She pressed his hand and leaned against his shoulder. "Look, it's a blue moon," she whispered. "Second full moon of the month. We should celebrate."

"Okay with me. Any suggestions?"

"Your place will do fine. Or mine," she added, seeing his hesitation.

It occurred to Orient that Sybelle disapproved of his relationship with Tristan, and he still considered himself somewhat of a guest, despite the token rent she had accepted. That, and his natural bent for privacy, tilted his decision.

"Your place. It's less complicated."

They walked to Gramercy Park, moving leisurely past Astor Place and up Fourth Avenue. The balmy weather and full moon lured the usual share of eccentrics into the streets, but Orient and Tristan paid little notice, wrapped in their own silent conversation.

Later, alone in Tristan's suite, they danced to the music coming through the wall from the next room. Tristan's hair shimmered in the semidarkness and her eyes glinted like distant seas. As he bent close to kiss her, Orient inhaled her musky scent and his senses caught fire.

The touch of her smooth skin seared away his hesitation, fusing them together in a raging heat that lifted them both and left them glistening with sweat when their naked bodies finally fell back to earth.

It was a long time before either of them spoke.

Then Tristan found her cigarettes and struck a match. The flaring light shadowed the contours of her face, and when the flame died, her eyes were still gleaming.

"That was delicious, my love." She blew smoke at him. "Mind if I call you my love?"

"Only if you rub my back."

"I withdraw the offer."

"Perhaps I should withdraw from the room."

She put a hand on his arm. "Not yet. Please."

He pulled her close. "Hey, I'm just kidding."

"Maybe." She kissed him gently. "You're very sensitive, my love. Now turn over so I can rub your back."

"How long did you stay in Jamaica?"

"Just another day."

"Did Westlake go back with you?"

Her fingers dug deeper into his shoulders. "No. As a matter of fact, the son of a bitch let me take Ash's body back alone. I knew he hated Ash, but I didn't know how badly until then. He acted as if I didn't exist, beyond signing some paperwork."

"Then you haven't seen him since you got back."

"And I hope I never do. But if this treatment does what Adele claims it will, Commander Westlake should be very unhappy."

Orient rolled over and caught her in his arms. "Let's forget the shoptalk."

"You started it," she teased, slipping away.

As he pulled her close and kissed her, he felt the heat smoldering between them.

Much later, when it was clear he was staying the night, Orient decided to call Sybelle and cancel their usual breakfast meeting.

"Owen, where are you?" she demanded the moment she heard his voice. "Something terrible has happened."

"Are you all right?"

"Yes, yes, but burglars got into your laboratory and bedroom. Everything's a mess. Luckily I came back with a party of five. I think we scared them away."

Orient reached for his trousers. "I'll be right over."

"Something wrong?" Tristan asked, watching him dress.

"Nothing too serious," he said smoothly. "One of my lab animals seems to be ill."

"You mean you're leaving me for a guinea pig?"

"A hamster actually." He leaned over and kissed her. "I'll call you in the morning. First thing."

She drew him down for a more definitive kiss. "You'd better. Or you'll find me on your doorstep."

Sybelle's description of the situation proved to be slightly exaggerated. Orient hadn't really acquired much in the way of possessions since settling into his new quarters. So it took him less than an hour to sift through the litter and restore everything to its proper place. The burglars had missed, or ignored, the cash in his desk.

"Nothing seems to be missing," he told Sybelle, who hovered about anxiously. "And no major breakage. In a way, they did me a favor. The place is finally cleaned up."

"What do you suppose they wanted?"

"Only thing I can figure is the computer disk."

"You mean it's gone?"

"It's safely out of the way. Thanks to you."

The phone rang before she could reply. Uncertain, Orient checked his watch before picking up the receiver.

"Hello, this is Duke."

"What happened to you at the restaurant?"

"It got too crowded. Anyway, your job description worked. I accessed the information you wanted."

"When can I see you?"

"Now is best. My place. Ring once, then twice."

He hung up, leaving Orient balanced between elation and apprehension. Hopefully he would learn what his pursuers wanted. Perhaps he might even be able to do something about it.

All the way downtown Orient fought to dissolve the anger clogging his thoughts. Over the years he had become hardened to being followed, threatened, vandalized, burglarized . . . but the carefully constructed armor had begun to crack. And spilling out was a decade of bad blood.

To make certain he wasn't followed, Orient left the cab

on Sixth Avenue, then darted across Greenwich Avenue and headed toward Sheridan Square. He took the long way around the maze of side streets in that section of the West Village before doubling back to that odd corner where Fourth Street intersected Tenth Street.

He rang as instructed, and was surprised to see Duke's large, unfriendly dog standing there when the metal door swung open.

It occurred to Orient he didn't know the dog's name.

"Come here, stupid," Duke called. The dog backed away from the door, allowing Orient to enter.

As the door closed behind him, the dog trotted to his master's side.

Duke was seated on a padded chair in front of the computer console.

"How does the door work?" Orient asked.

"Buzzer code activates the TV monitor. If I like what I see, I spring the lock. Sit over here, Doc. You thirsty? There's a beer and a little cheese over here. I know you don't eat meat."

Orient eyed the neatly arranged repast spread out in front of the empty chair. "Why the royal treatment all of a sudden?"

Duke gave him a craggy grin. "I like your record, Doc."

He pointed at the dog, who was sniffing at the crackers. "Get away, moron, that's not your food."

The dog looked at him reproachfully, then padded off in search of his own bowl.

"Dumb-ass dog," Duke muttered.

"What's he called?"

"We're on a no-name basis. So like I said, I used the information you gave me to access the little fucker. The code name is Telepath."

Orient sat down and poured himself a beer. "Can I see what we've got?"

"What we've got is a real can of worms, Doc. The bastards really hounded you. You could sue the scum for the entire national debt."

He tapped the keys on his console and the file memos began coming up on the screen.

The information stored on the disk was more comprehensive and well ordered than the bulky file of papers Orient had destroyed. And as Duke had pointed out, the evidence was damning. It showed the systematic persecution of an American citizen who refused to sell his life's work to the intelligence arm of the military. But as the memos continued to roll across the screen, something caught Orient's attention.

One name kept appearing with regularity on the field reports and requisition forms. One name which over the years had graduated in rank from attaché to commander. Glen Westlake's.

Stunned by the revelation, Orient felt a hopeless rage steam through his thoughts. Then he noticed something else that made him pause.

"Can you run that back?"

Duke nodded and the document returned on the screen.

It was an expense memo, for an informant.

There was a photo of a man called Max Denton, who claimed to be a friend of Orient's during the years he lived in Rome. And while there was a significant number of expense vouchers totaling close to fifteen thousand dollars, Orient knew with cold certainty that he had never seen Max Denton in his life. The information supplied was totally bogus.

Which meant that someone had embezzled the money. And the authorization was signed by Section Chief Glen Westlake.

Suddenly it became crystal clear why Westlake wanted the disk. Andy why Shandy had given it to him. He'd wanted Orient to use it to destroy Westlake. Perhaps that was why Shandy had been killed.

"What another beer?" Duke asked.

Orient accepted, but strangely, instead of the exultation of victory, he felt a nagging sense of gathering evil. He shook it off and tried to think. No wonder Westlake had been so anxious to give him the ten thousand. He probably made a bundle on the deal. Then something else occurred to him.

"Didn't I mention you had most of the military access codes?"

"Yeah. It's like a game computer hacks like to play. Storming the castle, get it?"

"I'd consider it a great favor if you'd check out the name St. George for me. Try the Naval Intelligence roster."

With great fanfare, Duke began flicking switches and punching buttons. "This is where my operation taps into the satellites," he explained proudly. "I also got a computer hooked into a ham radio system that gives me a global network."

Unfortunately, after long minutes of searching the personnel lists of Naval Intelligence, he came up empty.

"No St. George here. Sure he's Naval Intelligence?"

"Not really. Just an educated guess. Forget it."

"Hang on, Doc. Maybe he's listed under regular Navy personnel. Let's check it out while we're here."

Sure enough, there were three men named St. George on the naval roster. And one of them, until recently, had been chief cook aboard the *Blowgun*. In fact, Lucien St. George's tour of duty had ended just before the submarine's ill-fated cruise.

"Bingo," Orient muttered. As it happened, Lucien St. George was born in Kingston, Jamaica.

"That the guy you want?"

"That's him." Orient took out a wad of cash and counted out fourteen hundred-dollar bills. At least Westlake's money was going to a good cause. "Thanks for the favor, Duke. I owe you one."

"I owe you one too. You gave me a hundred over."

"Give it to the dog."

Duke tossed a bill onto the console. "Forget it. I enjoy screwing the bastards. They're polluting my planet with their insane bullshit." He leaned back and took a long swig of beer. "Tell you what, Doc. I'm gonna fix this little disk so that nobody can use it to fuck you. Meet me back here in an hour or so. I've got to walk the mutt."

Orient was grateful for the opportunity to get some air. The gnawing anxiety he'd experienced earlier continued to nibble at his nerves. Unfortunately, the crisp night air failed to dispel his sense of foreboding. He walked west to the river, trying to assimilate the facts.

Since the beginning Glen Westlake had appointed himself his inquisitor, orchestrating his persecution by various agencies, including the FBI and the CIA. However, the one thing omitted from the disk was why Westlake had pursued him all these years. It seemed much more reasonable to simply assassinate him and be done with it.

But of course it wasn't that simple, Orient speculated, staring across the moon-flecked river.

There was the profit motive. And something else. If Westlake had him killed, he'd lose his chance at acquiring the telepathic technique. That was obviously what he'd been hunting so relentlessly. The one thing he couldn't buy.

As Orient turned and began walking east, he realized that the nagging anxiety haunting him all evening had escalated. Apprehension swept across his senses like a dusty wind.

Then he glimpsed the full moon, hanging low above the tenement rooftops, and he remembered. The last time he'd experienced this particular form of anxiety was in Jamaica. And it proved to be a dark premonition.

Abruptly, he began trotting back to Duke's studio, vainly looking around for a cab. He found one a few blocks east, but the maze of conflicting one-way streets made the going slow. He pushed some bills through the cash slot and headed for Tenth and Fourth at a dead run.

Breath heaving, he rounded the corner and sprinted to the basement apartment. Fear sliced his belly like a cold knife the moment he saw the open door.

He slid to a stop and moved carefully down the stairs. He heard a muffled growling and when he stepped inside he saw the Labrador pulling at a man's sleeve.

The man jerked back and grabbed a hammer from a nearby tool shelf. As the dog lunged, the man swung the hammer down on its skull with vicious force. The Labrador dropped like a sack of flour, blood running from its ears and the side of its jaws.

The man whirled and lurched toward Orient, hammer flailing wildly. Suddenly the weapon flew from his grasp.

Orient tried to dodge, but his feet were nailed to the floor. Limbs rigid with shock and belly churning, he gaped at the parched, death-mottled features of Ash Shandy looming closer—just before the pain smacked his awareness like a freight train.

Chapter 17

THE FLOOR FELT COOL.

Struggling against the leaden agony cleaving his brain, Orient lifted his head. He made out an inert form a few feet away. Long seconds later he recognized the dog. Then the memory came rolling in like a slow-motion tidal wave.

His mind reeling, he awkwardly pushed himself erect and checked the damage. A sticky wad of blood caked his temple, and his cheek felt quite swollen. He sat there trying to gather his tattered senses, but his thoughts remained at bay, drifting aimlessly between disbelief and depression.

But by painful bit, he reconstructed the events leading to his present condition. His mouth felt dry and he looked around for something to drink. He spotted the beer bottle he had left at the console and heaved himself to his feet. Still unsteady, he carefully made his way along the bank of electrical equipment. His arm jostled something and a sudden jolt of noise boomed through the basement room. Pumping dance music, loud and mocking, pounded his aching brain. With spastic urgency he clawed the buttons, jabbing them at random until the music stopped.

Grateful for the silence, he picked up the beer bottle. But before it reached his mouth he paused. Bottle suspended like a torch, Orient stared dumbly at the human hand protruding from a cabinet beneath the computer.

Very carefully, he set the bottle down and took a hesitant step backward. Moments passed before the realization penetrated his fogged awareness. *Duke.*

Not wanting to know, yet knowing, he steeled himself and bent to look beneath the cabinet.

He wasn't prepared for what he saw. Duke's body had been jammed into the small space, his limbs twisted grotesquely. His bloody face peered out from between his knees, one side of his bald dome crushed like an egg.

Orient fought back the nausea welling up in his throat and turned away. He was about to leave when he remembered. The computer disk.

After a brief but frantic search, Orient reluctantly conceded it had been stolen. He made one last pass, stopping short of examining Duke's corpse, then headed for the door, mind and body throbbing with abject defeat.

It took four stiff jolts of scotch to help him decompress his bruised brain and finally fall asleep. Even the clear light of morning failed to dispel the utter abomination he'd experienced. The horror putrefied in his memory like rotting meat. And his temple still ached from the blow he'd taken.

He found his silver case and extracted a hand-wrapped cigarette. As he smoked he tried to distance his mind from his emotions and extract only what he needed to function. All the rest was illusion, the shadows of his own fears. And he cast plenty, Orient conceded unhappily.

The reality of Westlake's rabid persecution frightened him almost as much as the confrontation with Shandy's walking corpse.

He put aside his cigarette and focused on the mandala

design etched on his silver case. His mind drifted back to the beginning, to the high mountain refuge in Tibet where he had been invested with the telepathic technique.

He settled back on the floor and began to slowly stretch his knotted body. At the same time he went into a deep breathing pattern that intensified his stretching and sent oxygen flowing through his blood. A thin film of sweat oiled his skin as he pushed his exertions past previous limits, tightening his focus on nothingness until it merged with being. For long minutes he relaxed on a sea of gravity, listening to the waves of time breaking at the edge of his mind. When he was finished he knew exactly what he must do.

Afterward he took a long, hot shower and dressed in fresh clothes. The old clothes he stuffed into a shopping bag. He intended to dispose of everything connected with the previous night. Feeling somewhat cleansed, he came down to the kitchen, where Sybelle was preparing breakfast.

"Oh, dear, what happened to you last night?"

"I was mugged—by Ash Shandy."

Her chubby features pursed with annoyance. "That's really not funny, darling, please . . ."

"I'm quite serious," he said with an apologetic smile. "Let's have some coffee and talk."

However, Sybelle left all food and drink untouched. She sat in openmouthed silence while Orient recounted the events leading to Duke's murder.

"Owen, it's incredible. If I hadn't seen that ritual . . ."

"It might be wise to visit a distant relative," Orient suggested.

Sybelle crossed her arms. "I refuse to let that slime Westlake run me out of my home."

"Well, perhaps it won't be necessary. After I see Andy Jacobs, I might be taking a short holiday."

"But why, darling?"

"For one thing, it will draw the heat away from here."

Sybelle leaned over and kissed him. "Please allow me to cook you a gorgeous breakfast," she said firmly. "Oh, and by the way, Andy called earlier. He's back in town."

Later that morning Orient sat in Andy's library and retold the story of Duke's murder. But this time he omitted the encounter with Shandy's corpse, and emphasized the information Duke had extracted from the computer disk.

"Glen Westlake has a lot of power on Capitol Hill," Andy said gravely. "I did some checking while I was there and the word is he's our next Secretary of the Navy."

Orient stared at him. "No wonder he wanted that disk so badly."

"Now that he has it, perhaps he'll drop you in favor of some loftier missions," Andy rumbled.

"Doubtful. Someone did try to terminate me in Jamaica. Maybe him."

Andy carefully lit a cigar. "Speaking of Jamaica, I also inquired about your Olympia Club."

"And?"

"Seems it's not a CIA enclave after all." He paused to examine the tip of his cigar. "It's actually the official Caribbean headquarters for the DEA."

Orient blinked. "The Drug Enforcement Agency?"

"That's what I said."

"But Westlake has a permanent office there. He's . . ."

"Easy, Owen," Andy growled. "It's not unusual for the Company boys to use the DEA for cover. Technically, the CIA can't operate in Jamaica. But the drug boys have the local government's full cooperation."

"Neat arrangement."

"Nothing neat about it." Andy exhaled a thick cloud of smoke. "Just old-fashioned corruption."

Orient shrugged. "It's a game Westlake plays extremely well."

"How so?"

"In that computer file were records of payments to informants that didn't exist. Either he was being conned, or he was padding his expense account."

"Wouldn't surprise me," Andy muttered. "Costs a lot to move in Washington's social circles."

"Funny, I never imagined Westlake as a socialite."

"Oh, he's quite well known on the party circuit," Andy assured him. "They say his charming wife has independent means."

"Apparently I've acquired an important enemy."

"Always said you can judge a man by his enemies. Anyway, now for the good news."

Orient seemed surprised. "Good news?"

"Remember I told you I had a little surprise? Well, here it is. That house of yours that they burned had a little insurance. And you still own the land it stood on. As you know, land on this island is at a premium. Conservatively, it's worth at least a half million. I've got your insurance money stashed in a CD account in your name. Cash value at the end of the month comes to seventy-seven thousand, nine hundred dollars." He took a long drag and blew a puff of smoke in Orient's direction. "Between one thing and another, you're a man of means yourself."

"I see," Orient said ruefully, looking away.

"You don't seem very happy, Owen."

"Actually, this comes at a bad time. Look, Senator, I'd like you to do me another favor. About an hour after I leave here, please give me a call at home—telling me I'm dead broke."

Andy glowered at him. "I don't get it."

"I'm counting on the fact that Westlake has my phone tapped. Part of a little plan I dreamed up this morning."

Andy mournfully regarded the ash at the end of his cigar. "You know I'll do anything I can to help, Owen. Just be damned careful. These bastards are killer sharks and it's their pool. They'll chew up any influence I might have. Understand?''

Orient understood he had no choice. Sooner or later Westlake would decide to eliminate any loose ends that might embarrass a high-level member of the Cabinet. And judging from the swiftness of Duke's assassination, it would most likely be sooner.

"Don't worry, Senator,'' he said lightly. ''I still have an ace in the hole.'' But as he walked back across the park, Orient wondered if he wasn't holding a joker.

A short time after Orient arrived home, Andy Jacobs called in as arranged.

"Hello, Owen,'' he rumbled amiably. ''I've got bad news. I've been going over your finances and I'm afraid you're flat broke.''

Orient tried to sound shocked. "Are you sure of that?''

"Quite sure. Sorry, but the estate is bankrupt.''

After he hung up Orient called Tristan. She wasn't in, so he left a message and went downstairs in search of Sybelle. He found her in the small drawing room where she received clients. The door was half open and she was seated alone at a lacquered Chinese table with carved dragons for legs, shuffling a Tarot deck.

Orient knocked lightly.

"Come in, darling. I've been waiting for you.''

"Did we have an appointment?''

"Not really. But I had a feeling you were coming—to tell me you're going away immediately.''

Orient's expression was part surprise, part admiration. "Been reading my mind, old dear?''

"No, the Tarot cards.'' Sybelle tossed the deck onto the table. "Here, shuffle them.''

Orient did as she asked, having learned over the years to respect her intuition. He also knew the Tarot cards served as a medium to channel Sybelle's strongest powers.

"Now deal out seven cards from left to right. Then pick two more cards and put them aside."

Again Orient did as she instructed.

Sybelle paused to center herself before reaching out to turn a card. The first card was the two of wands. The second was the two of swords; the third, the three of cups.

She looked up, her green eyes digging into is.

"I can't go on. There's something you're keeping from me." She reached out and flipped over one of the cards he had set aside. The Empress.

"It's something to do with a woman," Sybelle said quietly.

Orient shrugged. "I have been involved with Tristan. It started in Jamaica and I ran into her last night."

"Last night?"

"Yes, while I was having dinner . . . with Duke . . ." Orient's voice trailed off as the implication echoed through his brain.

"All right," Sybelle murmured, turning over the fifth card. The Magician. She put it beside The Empress and went on to the sixth card. The Moon.

The seventh card was The Wheel of Fortune. The eighth, The Ace of Pentacles.

Sybelle studied the cards for long moments. "You seek to confront a powerful enemy. But you have three enemies. Exposing them will be your first task. You will need to find a friend. Finding this friend will be your second task. But whether you fail or succeed, you will suffer beyond endurance. Accepting this is your third task."

She hesitated, her hand hovering above the final card. Then she turned it over.

A naked man and woman stood chained to a graven image of a horned beast with catlike features, crowned with a pentacle. It was the card called The Devil.

"Remember," Sybelle said, her voice low and hoarse, "more than your life is at stake."

As she sat back, eyes half closed, Orient realized his heart was pounding. He understood Sybelle had entered a mild trance during the Tarot reading, and he waited for her to ease out of it.

"Tristan, eh?" were her first words when she recovered. "I should have known from your hangdog expression. Are you in love with her?"

"I don't know. It doesn't really matter right now, does it?"

"I suppose not." She sighed. "I'm sorry, Owen. I just feel so damned helpless."

Orient took her hand. "You've helped me more than anyone else could. Forewarned is forearmed."

"I hope so, darling. If anything happened to you, I couldn't bear it. But . . ." Her voice faded and she looked away.

"But what?"

"But I'm afraid something will happen to you."

Orient slowly pulled his hand away from hers, uncomfortably aware that his skin felt ice-cold.

Chapter 18

TRISTAN WAS STILL OUT WHEN HE CALLED, SO Orient decided to take a walk to the East River. The sun had fallen and beads of light cascaded over the dusty purple skyline as he strolled along the wide promenade overlooking the river. Usually he enjoyed the view from the walkway curving around the mayor's mansion, but tonight it made him feel very small, and very vulnerable.

While watching a police boat cruise past the lighthouse, he wondered if anyone had found Duke's body. On his way back home he stopped at a corner phone and called the precinct house in Greenwich Village. He reported the murder of Bruno Berio in his basement studio, then hung up. But as he continued back to his own apartment, Orient couldn't help blaming himself for Duke's death.

The phone was ringing as he unlocked his door.

"You promised to call first thing in the morning," Tristan reminded him when he picked up.

"Where were you all day?" he countered.

"Oh, meetings with Adele, lunch, shopping, the usual. If you missed me so much you would have called earlier."

"Let's discuss it over dinner."

"Thought you'd never ask. Uptown or down?"

"We've got a very nice, very noisy restaurant up here called Mezzaluna. Italian okay?"

"I adore pasta. See you there at eight."

While showering, Orient became aware of a tingle of anticipation. Exactly the reason he'd asked her to come uptown, Orient brooded. It decreased the risk of his walking her back to her hotel.

He was a bit taken aback when Tristan announced over drinks that she was flying back to Virginia that night.

"Why so soon?" he asked, lifting his voice above the din created by frenzied Italian waiters serving trendy customers in a room the size of a hallway.

"I've got a rewrite. And some urgent business concerning the estate." She smiled and took his hand. "I'll be back as soon as I'm finished. Meanwhile there is the telephone."

"Was . . . is your husband buried on the estate?" Orient asked awkwardly.

Tristan cocked her head to one side and stared at him. At that moment she looked like a Victorian schoolgirl.

"What a curious question," she said, pursing her lips. "As a matter of fact, Ash's will specified that he be placed in his family mausoleum in Southampton. Why?"

Orient shrugged. "We . . . got together so soon after it happened. You've never told me how you feel about it. Never had the chance, really."

She squeezed his hand and leaned closer. "I know. It seems as if our relationship is a series of violent encounters. I'll admit I was, and still am, intensely attracted to you. My marriage to Ash had been over for years. We kept up the pretense for the sake of his career. Ash had been good to me, so I agreed. But even that didn't work. We decided to divorce a month before his death. The Jamaican trip was supposed to be a farewell holiday." She raised her glass. "Let's drink to fresh starts."

The penne proved to be exceptional, as was the wine. After indulging in a sinfully rich zabaglione for dessert, they left the noisy restaurant and walked hand in hand for a few blocks, enjoying the quiet.

"I should be back in two weeks," Tristan said softly. "Can you wait that long?"

Orient nodded and kissed her, knowing it might be the last time he saw her. "I'll miss you a lot," he murmured. "Take care of yourself, okay?"

Without waiting for an answer, he stepped into the street and hailed a cab. As the cab rolled to a stop, Tristan pulled him close and kissed him fiercely. "I'll miss you too, my darling. Call me."

Then she stepped inside and pulled the door shut. She looked back and waved as the cab sped away and faded from sight.

Orient had trouble sleeping that night, burdened with loose ends, dangling questions, and a precarious future. Still, at least one question had been resolved, he reflected. Shandy's burial place was less than two hours from the city. Which brought up other questions. He finally drifted off to sleep, possibilities bouncing through the endless corridors of his dreams.

He awoke early and went through his Yoga and meditation before breakfast. As usual, Sybelle was puttering around the kitchen, but she didn't smile when he entered.

"I suppose you saw Tristan last night," she greeted him.

"Yes, why?" he said evenly.

"Just fact-checking my cards."

"Look, I know you don't approve, but it's academic. We won't be seeing each other for a while."

Sybelle's head swiveled. "Oh, why not?"

"We both have business to attend to—which reminds me. When you got involved with Shandy and Westlake on

Project Earlybird, did they give you a number to contact them?''

"Why, yes, Westlake did, as I recall. Any special reason you want to speak to him?'' she asked apprehensively.

Orient smiled. "I've decided to take Commander Westlake's offer of gainful employment.''

"But, Owen, if you need money that badly, I can—''

"It's not really the money,'' Orient told her. "I've come to the conclusion that the only way to protect myself from Westlake is to join him.''

Sybelle started to protest, but Orient waved her off. "Sooner or later Westlake is going to terminate any potential threat to his political career. I'm certainly a threat, and possibly you are too.''

"Of course,'' She sighed. "But I'm still awfully worried about you, darling. My cards never lie, you know.''

Orient phoned Westlake right after breakfast. Knowing it might be at least a day before he received an answer, he went about his business.

With Sybelle's help he rented a car that afternoon and, after chauffeuring her to a series of gourmet food shops, deposited her at home and drove off alone to Southampton.

Somewhere in Long Island he stopped at a roadside hardware emporium for a few tools, then continued on to his destination. Although uncertain of Shandy's exact location, Orient knew Southampton was a small community. Somebody would remember where a local hero lay buried.

The task proved to be slightly more difficult than he'd thought. There were a number of cemeteries in the area, as well as churchyards and private burial plots. Finally, after making two house calls without success, Orient decided to look up a mortician.

He found an ad in the yellow pages for a funeral home established in 1923. Assuming the director would know the area, Orient paid a surprise visit to the Hampton Haven of Eternal Rest. There he was greeted by Mr. Milton Goode.

"Goode with an *e*," he confided, extending a damp hand. "Now, then, are you a relative of the deceased?"

"Actually, I'm here on behalf of a client who passed on two months ago."

A short, pudgy man with thick glasses that magnified his bleary stare, Goode hastily retracted his hand. "Oh? For what particular reason?"

"I'm an attorney," Orient told him. "I represent the estate which maintains the plot. I believe you handled the services. Dr. Ashton Shandy is the name."

Angry pink blotches suddenly colored Goode's pasty features. "I *should* have handled the services," he rasped. "We have provided discreet, dignified interment for the Shandy family for almost seventy years. However, someone saw fit . . ."

He peered accusingly at Orient. "Saw fit to entrust Dr. Shandy's remains to that Johnny-come-lately outfit in Bridgehampton."

"No wonder there's a foul-up." Orient said smoothly, blessing his luck. "What's the name over there?"

Goode wagged a triumphant finger. "Makes no difference. They went out of business three weeks ago. Shows you, doesn't it? Fly-by-nights."

"But we, uh, had a perpetual care plan for Dr. Shandy . . ."

"I'm afraid you got taken," Goode said smugly, ushering Orient to the door. "Everyone knows that the Shandy family already has perpetual care. Their plot is one of the showpieces of St. Jeremy's Cemetery."

The Shandy plot was actually an ornate mausoleum, whose facade resembled the Parthenon, adorned with sculpted angels on either side of the metal door. As Goode had promised, the tree-shaded landscape was perfectly maintained. A polished copper slab above the entrance attested to the Shandy family's honors and accomplishments in the political realm.

Orient, however, had a greater interest in the mausoleum's precise status in relation to the fence. Not wishing to attract attention, he scouted the area briefly, then drove off in search of a restaurant.

It was almost dark by the time he finished eating and came back to St. Jeremy's.

The cemetery crowned a wooded hill a short distance from town. A single road curved past the gates, around the cemetery, and back down to the highway leading to New York.

Orient cruised slowly past the gates to the far end of the grounds, where he parked in the shadows and waited.

He surveyed the area for some time, checking for signs of security guards and monitoring the passing traffic. As the sky darkened he left the car, toting an athletic bag filled with a doctor's kit and the tools he had purchased at the hardware store. The bag wouldn't fit through the wrought-iron bars, so he removed the kit and the tools—a crowbar, hammer, screwdriver, flashlight, and wrench—and tossed the bag over the fence. Then he grasped a low-hanging tree limb and swung himself over.

Once on the other side, he pulled the tools and the doctor's kit through the bars and put them back in the bag. Moving as quietly as possible, he picked his way through the shadowy tombstones, pausing every few minutes to check his bearings. During his earlier visit he'd fixed on a few prominent landmarks, but at night everything took on different proportions. Certain objects seemed larger, others disappeared completely. Orient was forced to move closer to the road which cut across the grounds, exposing him to possible detection by a security guard.

In a few minutes he reestablished his position and

ducked back under the trees. He scanned the area carefully, then headed directly for the Shandy mausoleum.

As soon as he reached the massive stone structure he opened the bag and went to work. First he used adhesive from his physician's kit to tape the glass panel above the door lock. Using the hammer, he cracked the glass, which broke with a minimum of sound. Then he peeled the tape away, taking the broken glass with it. He reached inside and felt around for an inside knob. When he turned it, the lock clicked open.

The metal door groaned in the stillness as he slipped inside. It was quite dark, the sole source of light being an open, circular window in the domed ceiling. Orient switched on his flashlight only to find it provided dim illumination. Apparently the hardware sales man had included used batteries. Concerned that the light would fail completely, he took a quick survey of the room.

The mausoleum housed nine granite crypts, two of which were empty. The contents of the other seven were identified by engraved marble plaques. One senior Shandy had served in Congress, another as mayor of Southampton. The plaque for Dr. Ashton Shandy III lauded him as a "Physician, Scientist, Warrior, and Pride of Yale."

Orient set the flashlight on top of the crypt and took the hammer and screwdriver from his bag. With the screwdriver he dug along the edge of the heavy stone cover until he found a space to insert the tip, then hammered the blade deeper underneath. He fished a can of machine oil from his jacket pocket and carefully squirted oil into the space on each side of the screwdriver.

He worked his way along the edge and, after lubricating all four sides of the crypt, he reached down for the crowbar. After wedging the tool beneath the stone cover, he slowly pushed down on the crowbar and turned. As the cover lifted it swiveled on the oiled sections. He repeated the process until the stone cover rested on an angle, its corners extending well past the edge of the crypt.

The exposed corners gave his hands enough purchase to push and slide the heavy cover to one end. The ragged sound of his labored breathing hung in the musty air. He had placed the flashlight on an adjoining crypt and its faint glow barely outlined Shandy's casket. He picked up the light and pointed it directly into the crypt. The casket inside was elevated, so that its top stood about waist-high to Orient.

A sudden flurry of movement overhead jostled his senses. He swung the light upward and saw the shadowed flapping of wings. He turned the light back on the casket and looked for the closing screw. There was none. When he tried the crowbar he found he didn't need it. The casket's hood opened easily.

Ash Shandy lay inside, looking exactly as he had the last time Orient had seen him. Death had mottled his skin with furry brown spots, like patches of fungus feeding on their host.

Orient made a hurried check for signs of life using an electrically amplified stethoscope, a portable blood pressure gauge, needles under the skin, the standard techniques. They all came up negative. But when he checked the mirror he'd placed over Shandy's lips, Orient noted a very faint cloud.

He also took note of Shandy's torn sleeve, and the jagged teeth marks in his wrist and hand, inflicted by Duke's dog.

Suddenly a violent fluttering burst through the quiet. Orient swatted blindly at a trio of frightened ravens swirling around his head. At the same time he caught a subtle movement inside the casket.

As the birds flew up to the ceiling, Orient pointed the dim light down, and froze. Shandy's eyes were wide open.

Orient stood paralyzed as he and Shandy stared at each other in the dank stillness of the tomb.

Abruptly the flashlight went out.

Fighting back raw panic, Orient fumbled for the butane lighter in his pocket. When he managed to ignite the flame, Shandy's eyes were still open. And he was rising from his casket.

Stifling a cry, Orient staggered back, tripping over his athletic bag as Shandy reached out for him. Holding the lighter aloft, Orient frantically tried to locate the door in the faint, flickering light. Shandy was almost out, but the crypt's granite cover blocked the hood of the inner casket. With an awkward shove Shandy sent the heavy stone cover crashing to the floor.

Screeching furiously, the ravens attacked Orient with renewed intensity. Unable to see in the choking dust, he lashed out at the birds with his free hand while he scrambled to the door, lighter held high. Shandy stumbled after him on stiff legs, arms extended. Somehow Orient found the door and pushed. It didn't open.

In his panic he'd pushed instead of pulled. As he jerked at the knob he realized it was too late. Shandy had reached the door and was clawing at him with dirt-caked fingers.

Reflexively Orient cocked his fist to strike. Then he stopped as Shandy did a curious thing. He stretched out his hand for the lighter. In that instant Orient knew.

Shandy was drawn by the light, like some shambling, decay-mottled crocodile.

Orient threw the lighter at him, then flung open the door and dove into the cool, fresh night air. A few quick steps away from the open door, he looked back, half expecting to see Shandy following him. Instead he stood motionless in the shadow of the entrance, just waiting.

Realizing Shandy was waiting for the light to guide him, Orient began moving toward the safety of the trees.

"Hold it right there!" a voice croaked.

Orient whirled and saw a uniformed guard bearing down on the mausoleum, the bright shaft of his flashlight cutting through the darkness. Almost immediately Shandy left the doorway and shuffled toward the light. Trapped between the approaching guard and the oncoming horror of Shandy's walking corpse, Orient pressed himself against a tree trunk, wildly looking around for a hiding place.

"Charlie! Charlie! Intruder section seven! Repeat, section seven, pronto!"

Orient peered past the light beam slashing the shadows and saw a walkie-talkie pressed to the guard's jaw. He turned in time to see Shandy's patched features looming closer.

In desperation he threw himself out of Shandy's path, crawling behind a nearby tombstone.

"All right, you! Stop right there!" the guard yelled.

Certain he had been spotted, Orient lifted his head above the tombstone and saw the guard backing away in panic as Shandy shuffled toward him, his hands reaching out for the flashlight.

"Mayday! Mayday!" the guard shouted. "Charlie, where are you?"

Suddenly a pair of headlights pierced the darkness as a van squealed around the bend, jumped the curb, and came barreling toward them, spraying dirt and pebbles everywhere.

The guard stumbled backward to avoid the van, but Orient saw Shandy veer directly into the oncoming beams, arms extended as if trying to embrace them. The van swerved, brakes screeching, but too late. The crunching impact sent Shandy's body cartwheeling high in the air. It came down heavily on the van's roof, caving in the metal shell and spraying thick streaks of blood across the shattered windshield.

For a long moment it was very still. Then the guard's tremulous voice cracked the silence.

"Charlie, you okay?" he called hoarsely, tugging at the door handle. The door opened and the driver half fell into his arms. As the guard helped the driver out of the van, Orient began moving swiftly toward the fence.

He edged along the trees until he found one with limbs low enough for a man in his exhausted state to climb.

When he dropped to the other side of the fence, he twisted his ankle. Hobbling slightly, he dragged himself to his car and crawled inside. Without turning on the lights, he started the engine and slowly pulled away.

He didn't stop until he reached the city.

While waiting for a light to change somewhere on Third Avenue, he realized his hands were trembling uncontrollably. He pulled over to the curb, left the car, and hailed a passing cab. Still shivering from some deep, unnameable sense of dread, he remained huddled in a corner all the way home.

Chapter 19

SUNLIGHT SLANTED THROUGH THE BLINDS AND birds were chirping in the tree outside his window as Orient glumly made his way to the shower. His sleep had been haunted by grisly dreams and his mind oozed morbid thoughts. A brisk shower banished the dreams, but the dark thoughts lingered like a summer flu.

His visit to St. Jeremy's had produced one vital link of evidence. Shandy hadn't really died until the moment he collided with the security van. An eight-week-old corpse wouldn't bleed all over a windshield. Unless it were alive.

Sybelle had gone out earlier, leaving him a note. As Orient read it, the last two words jumped through his brain: *Westlake called.*

He felt a momentary pang of frustration until he turned the note over and saw the number scrawled on the back. The area code was 804, which meant Langley, Virginia.

When he called the number, a female on the other end informed him that Commander Westlake would return his call at a prearranged time. She then gave Orient a choice of three convenient hours. He picked the earliest time available, then went down to his lab and spent the next couple of hours straightening out the disarray caused by the break-in. He was almost finished when Westlake called back.

"Is there some problem, Doctor?" he asked brusquely.

"No problem. I just wondered if you're still in the market for a consultant."

There was a noticeable pause at the other end.

"Well, I certainly would like to talk about it. I'll be in New York late tonight. Can you meet me at about twelve?"

"Depends where," Orient said evenly.

"I'll be at the Waldorf Towers. Penthouse suite. Make sure you bring ID."

He hung up before Orient could ask why.

He learned the reason that night after being stopped by two neatly dressed young men posted in the hallway leading to Westlake's suite. One of them frisked Orient and checked his credentials, while the other stood a few feet back, his hand gripping a pistol holstered inside his jacket.

"Sorry about the bodyguards," Westlake said affably when he ushered Orient inside. "Can't trust security here. Drink?"

"Soda water will do," Orient said, looking around. "Mind if I use the bathroom?"

Westlake pointed to the bedroom. "Suit yourself."

Orient checked to make sure both the bedroom and the bathroom were empty, but as he went back to the sitting room, he wondered about the closets.

Westlake smiled when Orient entered. "Don't worry, we're alone. Of course, there's always the possibility that we're being bugged."

More like a probability, Orient thought. But he said nothing. After all, he was counting on the probability that Westlake had tapped his phone.

Westlake came back from the bar with two glasses and handed one to Orient. "Sit down, Doctor. I must say I'm somewhat surprised by your change of heart."

"Nothing's really changed. You need a consultant and I need a job. It's that simple."

Westlake sipped his drink. He was wearing reading glasses, which gave him an owlish, almost harmless air as he stared at Orient. But there was a predatory glint in his steel-gray eyes, and his smile had a nasty twist. "Nothing's that simple, Doctor. You haven't explained how you intend to help me."

His smug tone made it clear to Orient that his ploy had worked. Westlake had indeed tapped his prearranged conversation with Andy Jacobs and believed him to be bankrupt. Now he was turning the screw.

"What about that matter in Jamaica?" Orient asked.

Westlake seemed disappointed. "Yesterday's news. What about your research on telepathy?"

Orient set down his glass and got to his feet. "Sorry for wasting you time, Commander. I thought your offer covered other areas of expertise."

"Don't be so impulsive, Doctor," Westlake advised. "I'm prepared to fund your research quite generously. Say two hundred thousand the first year."

"I thought we understood each other on that point," Orient said, moving to the door. "I also thought you needed my expertise, as you put it, on other matters."

"Please sit down," Westlake said resignedly. "I should have known you'd never bite the apple. Let's talk some business."

Orient paused. "What sort of business?"

"The problem we discussed in Jamaica."

"All right, what do you propose?" Orient said, sitting down.

"First, tell me how you view my situation in Jamaica."

"Well, as I mentioned before, you seem to have the voodoo faction on one side and the Cuban agent on the other. Since you weren't overly surprised when Sybelle

identified the cult priest as your very own chef, St. George,
I would venture that his activities are known to you."

Westlake lifted a cautioning hand. "I'll admit knowledge of St. George's influence as a religious cult leader.
But not murder—or human sacrifice." He took a large
swallow of whiskey. "That's something I cannot condone,
or even comprehend."

"Then why is St. George still in your employ?"

"How do you know that?" Westlake snapped, his af-
fable manner congealing to pure ice.

"Just an educated guess. As I said, you didn't seem in
any rush to apprehend him. So I assume he's a necessary
part of you operation."

Westlake smiled. "A necessary evil. You're quite as-
tute, Doctor. As it happens, St. George provides a crucial
function as a liaison to areas in Jamaica which are otherwise inaccessible. That, and the fact that there's no hard
evidence . . ." His voice trailed off as if the rest were
understood.

Orient didn't believe him. Westlake had conveniently
neglected to mention that St. George had served on the
Blowgun. However, he reserved his opinions. "Since you
obviously don't want this St. George apprehended, I don't
see how I can help you."

"Ah, but you can," Westlake said, lowering his voice.
"You see, Doctor, I'm in the business of manipulation, and
St. George is out of my control." He paused to sip his drink.
"St. George keeps his people in line through a combination
of fear and awe. But I don't comprehend his weapons. You
do. And that's what I need. Someone who can identify and
record the techniques this man is using. Naturally, because
of our association with St. George, it wouldn't be proper to
put one of our agents on it. Nor would it be effective. You,
however, could put those special talents of yours to work.
Sort of fighting fire with fire."

It was Orient's turn to lift a warning hand. "I'm not in

this as a warrior, Commander. My specialty is gathering intelligence. You'll have to fight the fire yourself."

"Agreed, Doctor. Does this mean you'll take on the project?"

"Provided we can agree on a fee."

Westlake gave him a sympathetic smile. "Let's say five thousand a month and expenses."

"Let's not," Orient said sharply. "As I recall, Sybelle was kidnapped right inside your protected compound. And you man left the Cuban badly in need of blood. The very same man you want me to investigate. Sorry, Commander. Danger pay on this project is worth double the amount you quoted. With a three-month guarantee. First month's fee in advance, plus five thousand for expense money."

"I should think your advance would be sufficient to carry you."

"Look, Commander, I intend to stay as far away from you, your agents, and your bankers as possible. No doubt the entire island knows who you are. I do this alone, in my own way, or not at all."

"All right," Westlake said wearily. "Fifteen thousand in advance. But until you come up with something tangible, the well stays dry."

"Agreed. I'll need a message drop in Jamaica for my reports. And the phone number of an emergency contact."

"You seem to know this business very well for an amateur. So hear this. I expect weekly memos, even if it's a weather report. What I especially want is hard information on any and all aspects of St. George's operation—especially of an esoteric nature. Failure to provide this information will result in termination of our agreement. Clear?"

"And loud," Orient said coolly. "But there's something I don't understand."

"Which is?"

"Why did you pay me ten thousand dollars for information you already had?"

Westlake smiled. "I wanted you to get used to easy money. Which reminds me. Your first payment."

He went into the bedroom for a few minutes and returned with a manila envelope containing fifteen thousand dollars and a blank petty-cash voucher. "I left the official vouchers at the office," Westlake explained. "Just sign this and my secretary will type in the amount."

Orient signed, without mentioning the phony expense vouchers in his file. So far Westlake didn't seem to know he'd accessed the information on his computer disk, and Orient intended to keep it that way. If and when he nailed Westlake, it would be for something more substantial than embezzlement.

"Now that we're on the same side, perhaps you'll call off your dogs," Orient said dryly.

Westlake looked surprised. "How do you mean?"

"I mean the people who broke into my apartment a couple of days ago."

"I assure you, Doctor, they weren't my people."

Orient watched closely for any sign that Westlake might be lying. But he seemed genuinely concerned.

"Obviously the other side knows your identity."

Orient shrugged. "A minute after reaching the Olympia Club we were spotted. All things considered, you people should hire private detectives."

"Very funny, Doctor. But since you're our man in the field, the joke's on you. I suggest you take this along on your holiday."

He opened a desk drawer and pulled out an automatic pistol. "This is quite efficient. It's made of special plastic to elude metal detectors at airports."

Orient tucked the manila envelope into his inside pocket and stood up. "No, thanks. Never use the stuff."

"You'll wish you did," Westlake said quietly.

Chapter 20

ALL THE WAY DOWN TO THE LOBBY ORIENT wondered if Westlake had really been taken in by his ploy. The whole matter seemed to have been handled too easily. Then again, Westlake had rabidly sought to secure his services for over ten years.

"Sought to control him" would be a more accurate description, Orient reminded himself grimly. Joining Westlake's team hadn't been the worst decision he'd ever made. At least he had the means to fight back.

He walked up Park Avenue for a while, trying to arrange his thoughts. He passed a jewelry shop that featured Tarot cards in its window display and recalled Sybelle's warning. Three enemies. The first was, of course, Westlake. Probably St. George figured in there as well, Orient speculated. One thing was certain. The third enemy would appear soon enough.

When he arrived at the apartment he found Sybelle waiting up for him. She didn't seem happy.

"Owen, I've been worried sick," she scolded.

His brows went up. "Did something happen?"

"No. Not in the way you mean."

"How, then?"

She clasped her hands nervously. "I've been having strong premonitions, darling. And last night I had a dream. About you."

Sybelle took a small wood box from the sideboard and held it out to Orient. "That's why I went out early this morning. To get this."

He took the box and opened it. Inside, nestled in a bed of black velvet, was a crude metal cross, held together with what seemed to be braided strands of black thread.

"It's made of silver coffin nails and human hair," Sybelle explained. "It's been blessed by a Catholic archbishop, a Celtic witch, and a Macumba priest. You wear it pinned inside your shirt, against your skin."

"Where did you find it?" Orient asked guardedly. He knew protective amulets could actually produce negative effects due to association with evil people or unholy rituals.

"Don't worry, dear," Sybelle assured him. "I got it from my own psychic tutor. She's an extremely dedicated, positive force."

Orient kissed her on the cheek. "You're an extremely positive force yourself. Thanks for the thought."

"Better put it on right away," she suggested. "There's a safety pin in the box. It's been blessed as well."

"Before I forget," Orient murmured as he attached the cross to the inside of his shirt, "I have something for you too." He reached into his jacket, extracted the manila envelope, and counted out fifty one-hundred-dollar bills.

"Five thousand," he said quietly, pushing the stack of bills across the table. "Advance rent."

Sybelle's heavily shadowed eyes went from the money to Orient's face. "Where on earth did you get it?"

"Westlake. I'm officially on his payroll. I'll be leaving sometime next week."

"Jamaica?"

He nodded.

"Promise me you'll be careful, darling," she said in a small voice. "I feel so desolate about getting you into this."

He shook his head and grinned. "Actually, Westlake got me into this. So it's only fair he get me out."

Orient spent the next seven days preparing himself.

Not only did he intensify his Yoga and meditation exercises, but he spent hours in the library and in occult bookstores like Samuel Weiser's, searching out certain tomes on the practice of Obeah, Lucumi, and Macumba. His main concern was Obeah, of course, as the form favored by Jamaicans. However, he knew that Cuban Lucumi and Brazilian Macumba were branches of the same voodoo ritual, their prime difference being that they were actually separate tribal languages. Their common source was the West African territory whence all voodoo sprang, like a poisoned river.

While at the library Orient also checked back issues of all the local newspapers for any mention of Duke's murder or the accident that had killed Shandy for the second time.

Finding none, he decided to ask Andy for another favor.

But first he had to explain the unexplainable.

"Now let me get this straight, Owen." The burly ex-senator gaped at Orient as if he had suddenly grown an extra nose. "You say Shandy got out of his coffin, chased you out of the mausoleum, and got run down by a security van?"

"Incredible but true," Orient said ruefully.

"But how, dammit, how?"

He shrugged. "As you might know, zombis, the living dead, are an integral part of the voodoo legend."

"Legend is one thing," Andy growled. "This is serious shit."

"So is Bruno Berio's murder."

"And you think Shandy killed him?"

Orient lifted his hands in surrender. "I know for certain Shandy killed the dog. Everything else is conjecture."

Andy went to the mahogany bar next to the ceiling-high bookcase and poured a healthy measure of cognac into a snifter.

"Sure you won't join me?"

"I'd better stay in training. Now that I'm working for Westlake, his enemies are my enemies. Which includes his colleague St. George, the Cubans, and most of the free world."

"Not a bad move, though," Andy speculated. "At least you have a lifeline."

"I have a feeling that when I reach out Westlake will cut all ties."

Andy's scowl deepened. "Wish I could exert some pressure on your behalf. But my leverage isn't what it used to be."

"There is something else you can do for me."

"Name it."

"Don't mention this thing about Shandy to Sybelle. She's frightened enough. Hopefully my departure will take the heat off the home front."

"I understand," Andy rumbled regretfully. "I'll keep close touch while you're gone to make sure she's all right."

"I appreciate it, Senator."

"Nonsense. You're the one who's going off to war, so to speak."

Later, as Orient's cab crossed Central Park and rolled past the Egyptian tomb encased behind the Metropolitan Museum, Andy's words drummed at his thoughts like rain.

The next day Orient met Andy for a late lunch at J.G. Melon's. The ex-senator wore a dour expression as he squinted through the sun-streaked windows. After the waitress took their order, he turned to Orient and shook his head.

"I'm afraid what I've got won't be of much help."

"You look worried."

"I am worried, Owen."

"That bad?"

"You tell me. I phoned the precinct captain downtown, who happens to be an old acquaintance. He swears they checked out your anonymous tip. And they found no body—no evidence of any crime at all—at your friend's apartment."

"Is he sure they got the right place?"

"Basement loft, filled with computer equipment? Tenant goes by the nickname of Duke?"

"That's the one," Orient admitted reluctantly.

"I also called an old school chum in Southampton. Happens to be the mayor there."

"I know," Orient said warily. "There was no accident reported at St. Jeremy's Cemetery."

"Oh, but there was."

"Finally we've got something. Did they identify the body?"

"Bodies, you mean." Andy paused as the waitress returned with their drinks, a scotch for him and a ginger ale for Orient.

"Bodies?" Orient repeated as she left.

Andy tossed down his drink in one swallow. "Yes. Two security guards at St. Jeremy's were killed when their van overturned and caught fire. Very little left to identify."

"But what about Shandy?" Orient blurted out.

Andy shrugged and signaled the waitress for a refill. "Either way, Shandy is dead. Odds are his body is back where you found it. Your friends seem to be quite thorough."

Disconcerted by the news, Orient stared across the dimly lit bar, trying to suppress the fear coiling inside his belly. The feeling that he had taken on much more than he could handle burrowed through his thoughts like a tapeworm, consuming what little remained of his courage. The waitress arrived with Andy's scotch and he had a sudden urge to order one for himself. Instead he sipped his ginger ale and waited for her to leave. Almost everyone lived in fear. The trick was to live with it.

He wondered if St. George feared the inhuman horrors unleashed by his rites. Perhaps he's afraid of himself, Orient thought ruefully.

"Seriously, Owen," Andy said firmly, "you might want to reconsider that trip to Jamaica."

Orient managed a small smile. "Actually, you caught me in the act."

"Then you will tell Westlake to stuff it?"

"I'll think it over," he promised.

But that night, as he watched the smoke from his hand-wrapped cigarette curl around the bedside lamp, Orient knew he had no choice.

Chapter 21

EZILI WAS ABOUT TO KILL HERSELF WHEN THE Loa came to her. The god touched her strongly and without warning while she was visiting the cove for the last time.

Ezili loved walking along the deserted cove. She used to come there with her mother when she was a little girl. The cove had been her private enchanted forest, populated by heroic knights and fire-breathing dragons. And she, of course, was the virginal princess pining for her true love.

Her earliest recollection was being there with her mother crooning a fairy tale that began, "Oh, my child, don't you know, before people learned to talk they used to sing . . ."

That was once upon a time, she thought sadly. Now she was all grown up and she knew the cove was nothing more than a secluded stretch of beach, tucked between a cricket green and a new restaurant. The restaurant was St. George's idea. Even in this small thing he had betrayed her.

She had shown him the cove a year or two earlier, while he was still in the Navy. And while he still maintained a semblance of humanity. At the time, he'd promised he

175

would keep her special place a secret. But a few months before he left the service, construction began on the restaurant.

Even then she hadn't any idea it belonged to St. George. She didn't find out until recently, along with more brutal evidence of his true nature.

Ezili didn't understand how a person could change so. When she first met Lucien St. George, he was a wild boy, but he had a deep tenderness. He also had great power. She had been attracted to his immense potential as an Obeah healer.

She herself had been born with the power. Like her mother, Ezili was a *Quatre Yeux*. A clairvoyant destined to be a master priestess.

Although she was sent to be educated in England, Ezili always knew that someday she would take her place beside her mother as a mambo healer.

Lucien St. George had changed all that, Ezili reflected, looking across the water to the darkening horizon. Just as he had perverted everything in her life since his return. When he first proposed the rite to Loa Baka, Ezili thought he was joking. Everyone knew that invoking Baka was to call down the most evil—and feared—god in the Obeah hierarchy.

But Lucian hadn't been joking. And to prove it he had taken her mother hostage to ensure Ezili's full compliance with the rite. And to make things worse, she'd just learned she was pregnant with St. George's baby.

She thought back to the beginning, when she'd first met Lucien St. George. It was during an Obeah ceremony to Legba. At the time, she had been mounted by Legba himself and was attempting to cure a little boy of malarial fever. However, she was having little success. In fact, it seemed the child was near death.

St. George had suddenly appeared at her side, his gaunt features glazed by ecstatic possession. From certain quirks in his behavior, Ezili could see he had been mounted by Papa Ogun, the warrior Loa. He put his hands on the child's belly and began a strange, guttural chant. In her ultrasensitive state Ezili could feel the immense power gathered in St. George's slender body. To her amazement, the child recovered almost immediately. The fever broke, and the boy's shivering chills gave way to peaceful slumber.

Later, after the ceremony, the gaunt healer seemed quite relaxed, as if what he had done was an everyday occurrence.

"The boy is going to be all right," Ezili told him shyly.

" 'Course he is. Had the best healer on the island, didn't he?"

"You're certainly not modest."

"Ain't rich either. But I have earned my braggin' rights on that boy's life. Unless you want a piece of the credit."

Ezili felt slightly embarrassed by his blunt retort. Especially since he was absolutely right. He had not asked for money. "I don't want a thing, thank you, Mr. . . ."

"St. George. Lucien St. George. And I don't want a thing either, miss. Except maybe to take you dancin' tomorrow night."

Telling herself she was more curious than attracted to the brash young man, Ezili accepted. According to local custom, St. George called at her home and paid his respects to her mother before escorting her to the dance. At that time he was still a gentleman, Ezili recalled. And quite charming, in a rude sort of way.

Having taken full advantage of her European education, Ezili was quite sophisticated for her years, but despite his lack of formal training, St. George seemed far wiser. This was due partially to Lucien's father, who was a *Bocor,* or medicine man, of high repute in the Blue Mountains. From him St. George had inherited three generations of esoteric knowledge, and little else.

"When my daddy died, everything he owned was in his *macoot*," St. George told her, referring to the shoulder bag filled with medicinal roots and herbs employed by the *Bocor*. Although he was smiling, Ezili detected a bitter edge to his tone.

However, in almost every other way she found Lucien the most fascinating man she had ever known. In a few weeks she was in love with him. Unrequited love, she noted now, watching the sun dip below the horizon.

"You're too young," he had told her. "Besides, I just joined the U.S. Navy."

"But how . . . why?"

"My mother was American, you know. I was born there myself. And I got a lot of catchin' up to do. If you're still waitin' when I get back, then we can have a talk."

Ezili had waited, and on his first leave he surprised her with an engagement ring, a turquoise stone from the Persian Gulf he claimed matched her eyes. Her mother objected to the match, but because St. George would be gone for at least a year, she relented, hoping Ezili would change her mind.

She wished to God she *had* changed her mind, Ezili thought, arms folded against the chill evening wind coming off the sea.

She was not unaware that men found her beautiful. Or of her nickname on the Jamaican streets. But she believed there were higher aspirations than mere physical beauty. And with St. George she thought she had found a partner in that quest.

Lucien had returned from that first cruise brimming with plans for a healing center and church in the mountains. But a short year later, his plans were slightly altered.

St. George came back from his second year a rich man by island standards. He told Ezili he'd won the money gambling. He took a forty-five-day leave before shipping out on submarine duty, and during that time he bought two pieces of property. One was a large parcel of land on Mount Diablo, above Ocho Rios, that included an abandoned church. The other was the cove.

When St. George told her he intended to restore the church and use it to house their healing center, Ezili objected. Everyone knew that abandoned churches, and their adjacent graveyards, carried a curse.

But Lucien had changed a great deal during that second tour. He had read widely while confined to his submarine, and had traveled to exotic ports. He returned a self-assured man of the world who knew exactly what he wanted. Certainly she didn't have the will, or the desire, to oppose him.

In fact, just before St. George shipped out on his next cruise, Ezili and her mother helped organize a special ceremony to purify Lucien's new church.

From that day, things started to deteriorate. Lucien came home twice after that. The first time he organized a large ceremony, promising that everyone who participated would have his wish granted. Both Ezili and her mother were shocked when St. George offered a blood sacrifice of two black roosters to the Loa Guede. Her mother left immediately, but Ezili foolishly stayed and found herself swept up in the sexual climax of the ceremony. The next day, ashamed of having betrayed her vows as a *Quatre Yeux*, she quarreled with St. George and begged him to stop.

"Stop?" He stared at her as if she had gone mad. "Ask the people who attended my service if they want me to stop. I've been trying to put this together most of my life. And nobody wants it to stop."

Unfortunately, he was correct. As promised, those who had participated in the blood rite had been granted their requests. And they were eager for more. Lucien held at least two other ceremonies at his newly acquired church, and while Ezili declined to attend, she knew he was attracting a huge congregation.

She also knew she couldn't continue their relationship. Before St. George returned to duty, Ezili gave back his ring.

"Think it over," he urged. "At least until I get back."

But Ezili had made up her mind. However, so had Lucien. He made a special trip home shortly before his discharge and told Ezili he needed her. It took a master priestess of her skill to balance—and control—the vile forces he intended to invoke. When Ezili refused, he and his hired thugs took her mother hostage.

In the end it was that simple, she observed bitterly, wading ankle-deep into the cold surf. One day three strange men broke into their house and took her mother away at gunpoint. From that moment on she had been St. George's slave.

No longer, Ezili vowed, wading farther into the water. Tonight she would be free. Because she intended to die.

She was preparing to plunge into the dark water when the Loa came to her. The god touched her suddenly, with only the dimly familiar buzzing inside her skull as warning.

Her brain throbbing with voices, Ezili fell to her knees in the shallow water as the presence filled her. Slowly a single voice emerged from the babble . . . a voice with a crystal tone.

"Help is on the way, child," the voice crooned. "Even now a stranger draws near. But you must kill the demon before it grows inside you. Use the birds . . . the birds . . ."

Then it was quiet except for the droning surf.

Although dazed by the visitation, she recognized the voice of her patron and protector, the Loa Ezili. And as she staggered back to the beach, she numbly understood what she had to do.

The next night Ezili stood inside St. George's church as he prepared for the *Mange Guinée*, a special ceremony in which caged birds were imbued with hexes. At the proper moment during the loathsome rite, they were set free to wing their curses to the intended victims. The rite was intended to rid St. George of his enemies and solidify his power in the county.

However, Ezili secretly but her own hex on one of the birds just before the ritual began. She cursed her unborn child, to induce a miscarriage.

Later, as she stood in the churchyard watching the newly released birds wheeling madly in the torchlight, frightened blind by the thundering drums, Ezili could hear her mother's childhood refrain circling in her memory: ". . . don't you know, girl, before people learned to talk they used to sing . . ."

Chapter 22

THE HOSTESSES ON AIR JAMAICA'S FLIGHT 250 were fickle. They dispensed their services with regal disregard for most passengers, concentrating on those few they favored. Their allegiances changed rapidly during the short flight, but Orient managed to hold the loyalty of a well-coiffed Eurasian lady named Kimberly until they landed at Montego Bay.

He tried to thank her as he left the plane, but she ignored him. Accepting her rejection as a minor portent, Orient resolved to take nothing for granted. After walking a gauntlet of young women singing the praises of Jamaican rum, he passed through customs and emerged into the heat and hustle of the sidewalk. He threw his bag into the backseat of the first available taxi and asked the driver to take him to Ocho Rios.

Typically, Westlake and Shandy had lied about the exact location of the Olympia Club. According to Andy Jacobs's information, the Drug Enforcement Agency stronghold was located somewhere between Goldenhead and Port Maria.

Goldenhead, or Orocabessa, was only a few miles from

Ocho Rios. As they drove along the scenic coastline, Orient wondered exactly how he would carry out his mission. As a last resort, he could always contact Westlake at the Olympia, but it would seriously jeopardize his cover. And being unarmed, unconnected, and completely unfamiliar with the terrain, he knew that anonymity was his sole advantage.

Orient sat back and tried to enjoy the glittering expanse of jade sea and turquoise sky floating past the car window. Near the end of the first hour he felt himself begin to decompress from the grueling pressures of the past few weeks.

Everything seemed scaled down to human size against the vibrant landscape—the roadside bars, the children swimming in tree-shaded coves, the exotic flowers clustered everywhere, the goats grazing peacefully in the lush green fields. Stripped of illusion, everything came down to human size, Orient observed. If he could somehow maneuver St. George into a one-on-one confrontation, he might have a chance of surviving.

Figuring it was easier to get lost in a crowd, Orient had chosen the Sunset Hotel for its central location. Perched at the end of a large parking lot, the hotel fronted a cramped shopping mall that had seen better days. However, as advertised, Orient's room overlooked a clean white beach shaded by palm trees, and the shower worked.

After changing into black nylon swim trunks and a black sweatshirt, Orient went downstairs to take a swim. The heavily saline water stung his eyes, but he felt the city grime peel off his skin as he floated under the cloudless sky.

The intense sun finally drove him back to his room, and after a long shower he went out in search of a cool drink. The hustle began in the parking lot and continued as he walked with a succession of street peddlers offering everything from souvenirs to vice.

Like Montego Bay, Ocho Rios existed solely for tourists and retired gentry. The white stucco storefronts and artificial marble plazas that lined the main drag had a tired, faded quality, like outgrown toys left behind by the smart money.

It seemed to be promenade hour, for a brightly dressed throng of Jamaicans crowded both sides of the street. Orient moved with the flow until he came to a wide alley called James Avenue that angled down toward the beach. From what he could see, it was almost exclusively a native thoroughfare. Moved more by boredom than curiosity, Orient turned down the alley.

He heard loud reggae music coming from a storefront up ahead. As he drew near he saw it was either a bar or a record shop. There was some confusion due to the faded condition of the sign outside. The name seemed to be Jack Ruby's, and peering inside, he saw a bar and tables. A brightly colored mural of Bob Marley, Jamaica's foremost reggae artist, decorated the entrance, and the bar itself was sparsely, if comfortably, furnished.

Orient strolled to the bar and took a stool. Feeling a bit jet-lagged, he ordered an overproof and cola from the burly, broad-shouldered barman. It being late afternoon, the place was empty except for a thin Jamaican girl studying her nails with a sullen expression. To be sure, the place appeared vaguely disreputable, but Orient felt comfortable. He sipped his drink and watched the parade of Jamaicans pass by the windows while he listened to sweet reggae music coming from a ghetto blaster behind the bar.

The rum spread warmly through his body, dissolving his tension. He didn't really need to confront St. George, Orient mused, but merely identify whatever occult techniques the priest employed. Actually, his first order of business should be to get himself a good guide. He recalled Sybelle's advice at the Tarot reading. He also needed to find a friend.

"Another drink?" the barman asked.

"This is fine."

The barman gave him a sly smile. "You got a good head, sir. This rum we serve is one hundred ninety proof."

More customers drifted in, all of them obviously at home in the restaurant. As Orient signaled for the check, a group of Jamaicans entered. There were two women and three men, all laughing at something one of the females was saying. When they saw Orient their laughter paused momentarily, then grew louder as they sat down.

Their brash, almost arrogant demeanor suggested they were tourist hustlers, with the exception of one of the females. She was young, perhaps twenty, with dusky gold skin and long, red-streaked hair that framed her exquisite features. Her grave azure eyes and pouting bee-stung lips shaded her expression with the brooding sensitivity of a Modigliani portrait. Something else nudged Orient's awareness. A tug of recognition, as if he had met her somewhere in his travels.

Orient paid his bill and prepared to leave, trying to ignore the nagging sense of familiarity aroused by the lovely Jamaican girl.

Once outside in the teeming mass of humanity that now crowded the cramped street, Orient found that the barman had been misinformed. He definitely did not have a good head for one-hundred-ninety-proof rum.

The flight, the swim, the strong sun, and the rum combined to make him suddenly very tired. Picking his way through the stream of tourists and Jamaicans competing for the narrow sidewalk, Orient managed to make it back to his hotel. By the time he got to his room, the fresh evening air had cleared his brain. Even so, the moment his head touched the pillow, he was asleep.

Orient woke up early the next morning. After performing a short series of Yoga exercises, he put on his bathing clothes and went downstairs in search of breakfast.

The hotel restaurant boasted strong coffee and weak service, but its oceanfront location made the wait bearable. When he finally finished breakfast, he wandered over to the small public beach and chose a picnic table in a remote corner. Despite the slow service at breakfast, it was still early and very few people were out. Orient took his silver case from the waterproof pouch belted around his waist and extracted a hand-wrapped cigarette. Along with the case, his newly acquired pouch contained his cash and passport, a Swiss army knife, a flashlight, a box of waterproof matches, and the cross Sybelle had given him.

As he smoked, Orient gazed across the sea and pondered his reaction to the beautiful Jamaican girl in Jack Ruby's cafe. When he finished the cigarette, he slipped off his running shoes and sweatshirt and walked into the sea. While floating in the clear green water, Orient tried to relax and focus on the task ahead. Then it dawned on him. The Olympia Club was on the water. He could easily recognize the place if he saw it from a passing boat.

As if in response to the insight, a voice hailed him.

"Hey, buddy. Beautiful day for scuba divin'."

Orient looked up and saw a tall, muscular Jamaican, wearing an old Brooklyn Dodgers baseball cap over sun-bleached dreadlocks, standing at the prow of a weathered blue boat. The vessel sported a patched, faded denim awning as well as a massive homemade engine that resembled an oversized vacuum cleaner.

"Lord Buckley at your service, sir. I got the sweetest boat in these parts. Come see for yourself."

Orient hesitated, then impulsively swam over to the boat and climbed aboard. The interior was upholstered in a variety of fabrics and patterns, but Orient noticed that a few of the bright swatches were actually voodoo flags. The designs on the flags were Obeah talismans.

"So you want to go scuba divin'? Or maybe do a bit of fishin'?"

"Depends. Think you can take me up the coast to Goldenhead?"

"You mean Orocabessa. Sure, mon. Take you all the way to Port Antonio if you want."

"How much for the day?"

Lord Buckley lifted his cap and scratched his head.

"Two hundred American, mon."

Orient was in no mood to bargain. He unzipped his pouch and peeled a hundred-dollar bill from the thick roll inside. "You'll get the second when we come back. Deal?"

Lord Buckley studied Orient with somber brown eyes. "You a smuggler?"

"Just out to see the coast past Orocabessa, maybe up to Port Maria."

The boatman shrugged and took the hundred. "Guess you can't be smugglin' much in that little pouch. But no pickups, agreed?"

"Agreed. But I need to pick up my shirt and shoes over there."

Lord Buckley laughed and started the motor. "Just put your feet up, mon. I'll get the beachboy to fetch them. From here on you're my guest."

After retrieving Orient's gear, he skillfully guided his craft through a maze of jetmobiles and yachts, around a man-made jetty, into open water. Orient found the motor's deep throb oddly reassuring as they continued east, hugging the lush coastline. His guide also seemed relaxed after his initial flurry of suspicion. Lord Buckley sat with one hand on the wheel and the other holding a hand-wrapped cigarette the size of a small cigar. He lit the cigarette with a vintage Zippo, inhaled deeply, and grinned at Orient.

"You like reggae?" Without waiting for an answer, he

switched on a cassette player and reggae music came chugging through twin speakers. The music blended with the engine's lazy purr as they cruised past an impressive complex of dwellings rising along rugged green cliffs that cupped a white horseshoe-shaped beach.

"That the Sans Souci, mon. Fanciest hotel 'round here."

It remotely resembled the Olympia, but, as Orient recalled, the DEA enclave was smaller and much more difficult to spot from the sea.

Although it was still early morning, the sun beat down through the tattered awning, heating the interior of the boat considerably. Orient moved away from the large engine and joined his guide at the wheel. The man glanced at Orient.

"So what you lookin' for really?"

Orient was prepared for the question. "Looking for a place to build a house."

"Why you not say so? Lord Buckley know all the pretty places 'long this coast."

"I'll know it when I see it," Orient told him. "I want a place over past Goldenhead."

The boatman pulled out the throttle a bit. "That's right where I'm going to take you."

In a short time he called Orient's attention to the jutting knuckle of land that marked Orocabessa. The steep hill seemed to fold in on itself, then curve around to a majestic point. Past Goldenhead the low cliffs extended as far as Orient could see. Judging from the stately villas crowning the rocky landscape, the area was well populated.

"That there's Goldeneye," the boatman announced. "Ian Fleming's old place. My buddy Ramsey still works up there."

At first all Orient could see was a verdant, private beach with a stone mosaic patio. There were stairs cut into the cliff leading up to a shaded flower garden. The arbor was graced by a pair of matching trees whose limbs formed a natural arch overlooking the sea. Then he glimpsed a low, comfortable house set back behind the garden.

However, as they continued past the area, Orient could tell from the sparse vegetation along the coast that the place he sought was elsewhere.

"Have any scuba gear I can use?" he asked, eyeing the calm, clear water.

The boatman grinned. "I got a boss place for divin', just up ahead some."

Five minutes later he cut the motor and steered the boat close to a small cove sheltered by an overhanging. A curtain of vines and flowers shaded the water. He hauled out masks and breathing apparatus for both of them and followed Orient over the side.

The water felt like cool silk as Orient adjusted his mask and ducked beneath the surface. Suddenly the world bloomed with the vivid patterns of undersea life. He saw Lord Buckley motioning and trailed after him to a wide cave that housed a dazzling array of fish of all colors, sizes, and peculiarities. A variety of coral also flourished at the back of the cave along with rainbow-tinted seashells, transparent crabs, and swarms of tiny luminescent creatures.

After lingering for about twenty minutes, Orient swam slowly back to the boat and pulled himself aboard. Lord Buckley followed and flopped down on a padded seat. For long moments neither of them spoke, listening to the sweet, lilting reggae coming from the speakers.

Curious, how the water seemed so clear and empty from the surface, Orient reflected. And how much life existed within the cramped boundaries of a single undersea cave. Imagine how much life must exist in the blazing vastness of the Milky Way.

"Lots of action down under," Lord Buckley droned. "Everybody busy. Eatin', lovin', gettin' born, dyin' . . .

wonder if fish cry too? I know they laugh. Ever see a shark smile?"

Orient laughed. "Matter of fact, I have. What say we haul anchor?"

The sea remained calm as they cruised eastward. But when they neared Galina Point, the wind swirled fitfully, stirring up the surf.

"Always blow up 'tween here and Port Maria," Lord Buckley explained, deftly guiding the pitching craft around the rocks. The wind whipped up a fine spray as it gusted across the water, casting a misty veil over the dense blue cliffs. The terrain had also shifted, becoming more rugged. It seemed oddly familiar despite the fact that it failed to reveal any recognizable features.

"This ain't no place to build a house, mon."

"Too windy?"

"Too much trouble. Government own this land."

Orient's interest perked up. "Oh? What's up there?"

"Nobody know really. Politics, mon."

As the boat rolled through the choppy water, Orient kept a close eye on the coastline. But the reflections from the glaring sun made it difficult for him to discern landmarks.

"Time for lunch, mon," Lord Buckley called, weaving closer to shore.

Orient didn't argue. It had been a long time since breakfast.

They pulled into one of the countless vine-sheltered coves that made Jamaica a pirate's paradise. Lord Buckley wasted no time setting up a small charcoal stove on the beach. Then he reached beneath the cockpit and came up with a large fish and two cold bottles of Red Stripe beer.

Orient started the fire as Lord Buckley scaled the fish and garnished it with oil, herbs, and garlic.

Afterward, halfway into his second Red Stripe, Orient considered a closer check on that government land.

"See anythin' you like yet?" Lord Buckley inquired.

"Not yet. Maybe farther up—"

"Shit!"

Surprised by his vehement reaction, Orient looked up and saw Lord Buckley in a half crouch, peering across the water.

"What is it?"

"Security boats," he muttered. "We're trespassin'. No big deal maybe," he added, looking at Orient intently. "All they do is take us back and check our papers."

Orient met his gaze. "That's no good for me. And I know it won't be good for you."

Lord Buckley hesitated, then turned to check the pair of approaching boats. They were still a few hundred yards away, but bearing down fast. Orient recognized the sleek black shapes immediately. They were the same security boats used by the Olympia Club.

"C'mon, then, mon!" Lord Buckley shouted, scrambling to his boat. "Leave the stuff!"

Chapter 23

ORIENT SPLASHED THROUGH THE SHALLOW WA-
ter, then swam the last few feet to the craft. As he hauled
himself onto the deck, Lord Buckley yanked up the crude
anchor and pulled a lever on the engine. Then he jumped
over to the cockpit and fired the ignition. The boat surged
forward as the motor came to life with a roar.

The twin pursuit boats were now close enough for Orient to see the pilots' faces. One of them was steadying a
pistol on his windshield. Lord Buckley's boat picked up
speed, its bottom slapping hard against the choppy water
as their pursuers split up. The man with the gun stayed on
their tail, while the other veered to one side, hoping to
squeeze them into the rocks.

Lord Buckley kept steering seaward, ignoring the pursuit
boat angling in on his prow. With a sudden charge of power
the vessel leaped forward, skimming the waves like a sailfish.
It landed with a smack and began cutting powerfully through
the surf, sending up a huge plume of water in its wake.

A bullet cracked past Orient's ear and punctured the
upholstered seat in front of him. He ducked down and
yelled for Lord Buckley to take cover.

Instead, the boatman flashed an exhilarated grin.

"Watch this, mon!" he yelled back.

Lord Buckley swung the boat to the right, narrowly missing a large rock. The pursuit boat stayed right behind him, the pilot aiming for another shot.

In one deft motion Lord Buckley swung right again to avoid a rock, then jerked back in time to squeeze past a jagged black reef on their left. The pursuit boat was following too close.

It slid around the first obstacle only to slam head-on into the second. The boat disintegrated in a great spray of black smoke and flying debris.

The pilot of the other pursuit boat gave up the chase and circled back to assist his comrade. Lord Buckley gunned the motor and the boat sped away, curving out to open sea.

After putting a safe distance between themselves and their pursuers, he glided expertly into a tree-shaded inlet and dropped anchor.

"Better sit here awhile," he said evenly. "Whirly-birds soon be comin'." He stretched out on the padded seat and began rolling a cigarette. "Too bad we out of beer."

"This boat of yours is very fast," Orient said appreciatively. "What sort of engine has she got?"

Lord Buckley beamed. Apparently Orient had touched on a point of pride. "Missy got the best motor 'round here. Fix it up myself, from an old airplane engine."

Then his smile hardened and he looked Orient over carefully.

"What you mean when you say it won't be good for me?"

Orient met his gaze. "Other people who tried to help me have wound up dead."

"You some kind of spy?"

"No. Why?"

"That's all they got at the Olympia Club. And you was lookin' for the Olympia, mon."

Orient nodded. "I'm looking for someone who works there."

They were interrupted by the ominous flapping of helicopters flying low over the water.

"Don't worry, mon. They soon get tired. Tell me 'bout this person works over the Olympia."

Orient weighed telling him. Perhaps he had already revealed too much. "Maybe you'll tell me something first."

"Like what?"

"Like what are these Obeah hexes doing all over your boat?" Orient pointed to the voodoo flags.

"Those ain't hexes, mon," Lord Buckley said indignantly. "They charms for protection. Against the evil eye."

His reaction seemed genuine enough to Orient. He decided to risk it. After all, the boatman had proved he could be trusted in a pinch. "I'm looking for a man called St. George. Lucien St. George."

The boatman tilted back his baseball cap and took a long drag on his cigarette. "Why you want him?"

"I heard he's an Obeah priest."

"So what, mon?"

"He's an evil priest."

Lord Buckley continued to study Orient. "You gonna stop him, then?"

"Maybe. But I need some information first."

"You need an army, mon. St. George put a bad hex on you sure."

"You know St. George, then?"

"Know about him. Seen him around sometime. Know plenty of his people."

"His people?"

"Yeah. His followers. They mostly from Ocho, Port Maria—all over Middlesex."

"Then he has lots of followers?"

"Lots, mon. Could start his own county. Some say he may do just that."

"What do you think?"

"I think I was wrong about the whirlies," the boatman groaned as the helicopters swooped past again. "Somebody must have tell them you were comin' to visit. Too much trouble over a fish fry."

"They lost a boat," Orient reminded him.

"Why they shoot at Missy anyway? Ain't no cause. And why these damn whirlybirds won't go home?"

Orient was beginning to understand. Westlake had decided to cover himself by throwing him to the wolves. No matter who survived, Westlake got his share of the meat.

"So what do I call you?" the boatman asked.

"Name's Owen Orient."

"And you're sure you're not a spy?"

"I'm . . . a doctor."

"So what you gonna do when St. George hexes you, doctor man?" Lord Buckley chuckled, relighting his cigarette.

"He already did."

The boatman's lighter paused in midair.

"And so what happened?"

"I'm still here."

Lord Buckley swung his feet to the deck. "Think maybe I take you to see somebody."

"Who?"

"A friend."

The answer chimed in Orient's brain and he smiled. "I'm ready anytime the helicopters are."

"Screw them whirlies." Lord Buckley stood up and went to work on the motor. "After I fix it so nobody can steal Missy, we walkin' out of this."

The boatman removed a small part from the oversized engine, rendering it inoperable. Then he reached down into the compartment below the cockpit and came up with a well-used machete. "Let's march, mon," he said, waving Orient out of the boat. "We got a ways to go."

With Lord Buckley hacking a path through the dense vegetation, they slowly made their way around the side of a steep hill until they reached a narrow trail.

"From here up it's a breeze," Lord Buckley said, pointing the machete toward the summit far above them.

The trail widened as they climbed higher, then cut into a crude dirt road at the crest. They trudged along the pitted road until they reached a paved stretch that wound along the base of a hill and eventually curved around a wind-stirred bay. Orient saw a few scattered houses and some cars in the distance. Within a half hour they were crawling through a traffic jam in front of Port Maria's outdoor market.

Orient followed Lord Buckley into the teeming market. His recent hike up the isolated trail had left him unprepared for civilization. Which in this case consisted of a large outdoor marketplace, a bank, a post office, a movie house devoted to Kung Fu operas, and some dingy bars. Lord Buckley headed directly for the closest bar and ordered two Red Stripes.

Sitting in the shade, sipping his beer, Orient felt a vague stiffness from the long trek over the hill.

"What else do you hear about St. George?" he ventured, after a few minutes of street-watching.

"Mainly that he run the kitchen at the Olympia. They say he gonna open up a fancy place over Ocho Rios way."

"How do you know so much about him?"

Lord Buckley took a swig of beer. "People here don't have much TV," he said mildly. "So we watch each other."

The sun was starting to drop as they left the bar and

walked along the narrow main street, dodging cars, bi-
cycles, and goats, as well as hordes of loiterers. Orient
was relieved to see Lord Buckley take a key from his shorts
and insert it into the door of a shiny black Ford 4X4.

"You down for some food?" the boatman asked as he
drove slowly out of town. "I got a good place up the
mountain."

"How far up?"

"Far enough to find a friend."

Orient stretched out and closed his eyes. "Lead on,
milord. I'll just take a catnap."

When he opened his eyes about five minutes later, they
were on a narrow, unpaved road that seemed to be winding through the jungle. Then the road turned steeply uphill
and the terrain became rockier. Orient also noticed that
the air had cooled as the sun went down and he wished he
had brought along a jacket.

"Here you need the four-wheel drive." The boatman
chuckled as the vehicle bucked and lurched uphill. Finally
the terrain leveled off and Orient glimpsed a sliver of blue
sea through the trees. Abruptly the vegetation cleared away
and Orient found himself staring at an epic panorama of
nature's raw beauty. On one side, far below, the darkening
sea fanned out to the edge of the red sky. On the other
side the leafy mists of a deep valley rolled like a smoky
carpet to the blue mountains beyond.

"My house is right over there," Lord Buckley said.

Orient turned and saw a lovely brown wood house with
a large bay window, set beneath a cluster of giant trees.
As they neared the house a pretty Jamaican girl of five or
six, wearing pink hair ribbons to match her dress, came
racing toward them.

"Daddy—Daddy!" she cried, charging straight at Lord
Buckley, who caught her in his arms and swept her high
in the air.

"And how's my Ginny-gin been, huh?" he said, laughing. He gave her a big kiss and set her down facing Orient.

"This here is my Ginny. Say hello to the doctor man, hon."

Ginny studied Orient with grave, unfrightened eyes.

"Hello, doctor man," she said, before retreating to the safety of her father's arms.

Lord Buckley carried Ginny back to the house and put her down on the front porch. "Go tell Mommy we got company," he whispered. She immediately scooted inside.

He turned to Orient. "You want a Red Stripe? Or rum?"

"Tea maybe. No more beer for a while."

"How come, mon—you feel sick?"

"I've got work to do. I need a clear head."

"Maybe you right, mon." Lord Buckley patted a barely discernible bulge above his belt line. "Wife say I drink too much beer. Belly say the same."

A tall Jamaican woman came out on the porch.

"How come you don't phone ahead if we have company?" she scolded, smiling at Orient. "My husband's got no consideration for the ladies of the house."

"Doctor, I'm proud to introduce my charmin' wife, Violet, who is the flower of my eye."

Orient extended his hand. "Pleased to meet you."

"How do you do," she said, looking for a moment like her daughter. She was a handsome woman with a frank gaze and an easy smile, and Orient liked her immediately. In fact, he was starting to feel quite comfortable with Lord Buckley and his family.

"Please sit down, Doctor," Violet said. "I'll bring some refreshments."

"Iced tea, please, woman," Lord Buckley suggested.

Violet gave Orient an approving wink. "At least you're a good influence on him."

"You like cigars?" Lord Buckley opened a box beside his chair.

When Orient passed, he took one for himself and cut off the tip with the fisherman's knife he carried. Then he carefully ignited the cigar.

"Quite a busy day," he commented between puffs.

Orient waved at little Ginny, who was peering around the door. "Yes. Lucky thing you came along this morning."

"Wasn't much luck, mon."

"Oh? How so?"

"Somebody pay me to check you out."

His quiet words boomed in Orient's skull.

"Who are you working for?"

The boatman grinned. He had taken off his baseball cap, letting his sun-tinted dreadlocks fall around his head. He studied Orient through a haze of cigar smoke.

"I'll tell you after you meet that friend of mine."

Orient's response was interrupted by Violet's emergence onto the porch with a pitcher of iced tea and glasses.

"Shall I set another place for dinner?" she asked Orient.

"Of course, lady," Lord Buckley chimed in. "After dinner we takin' a ride up to see the Kid."

Violet glanced at her husband but said nothing.

"So you were paid to check me out," Orient repeated when they were alone. "Then why am I here? In your home?"

Lord Buckley contemplated the tip of his cigar. "Let's say I'm a fine judge of character." He looked up at Orient. "But not the final judge."

After that, dinner was a bit strained for Orient, but he couldn't deny Violet's cooking.

Little Ginny continued to stare at him throughout dinner. Then, while he was having coffee, she broke her silence.

"I had a dream about you last night," she confided.

"Tell us your dream, honey?" Violet asked playfully.

Ginny shook her head and backed away from the table.

"It was a very bad dream."

Chapter 24

LATER, AS ORIENT WATCHED THE FORD'S headlights tunnel through the dense foliage on either side of the dirt trail, he recalled Sybelle's warning in New York.

"Could use five-wheel drive up here," Lord Buckley muttered.

Orient remained wrapped in his thoughts as the vehicle hobbled up the steep incline for a couple of miles, then turned into a level area and stopped.

"This is it," the boatman said, getting out of the big Ford. Orient followed, poised to run if necessary.

A cool wind blew across the densely overgrown plateau as they walked along a pebbled trail that cut through the vegetation. The crescent moon floating overhead afforded little light, but the pebbles were easy to follow. In a few minutes they crossed a crude wooden bridge about ten or fifteen feet above a narrow river. On the other side of the bridge was a small house that seemed completely dark.

Lord Buckley paused at the far side of the bridge and called out softly, "Two friends comin', Kid."

A melodic, singsong voice called back from the darkness, "Come ahead, Lord Buckley. Bring your guest so I can see."

Orient warily followed the boatman to the house. When they neared he saw the door was open. He let Lord Buckley precede him, shutting his eyes tightly for a moment so that they would be accustomed to the lack of light inside.

"Pardon me for not risin'," the melodic voice hailed him. "They call me Kid Kismet. We never met. But Lord Buckley think you need advisin'."

Orient turned toward the sound. "Hello. I'm Owen Orient."

"Please sit down," the voice continued. "We'll have refreshments when my lady comes 'round."

As Orient's vision adjusted, he peered through the gloom and saw a seated figure nearby. A few feet away was the outline of a couch. He moved over to it and sat down. Lord Buckley sat next to him.

"Doctor man say he been hexed by St. George and still livin'," the boatman said casually.

"What does the doctor man say now?" the voice responded. "Does he care to tell us how?"

"The hex made me very sick. I cured it my own way," Orient said guardedly.

"Okay, Miz Laurie, please come in. And see about these gentlemen," the voice called out.

"Good evenin'. I expect you could use a light," a feminine voice announced. Then she struck a match and lit a candle. As the faint candle flame flared higher, Orient saw that the figure seated nearby was actually a boy no older than sixteen.

The boy wore metallic glasses and sat very still on the old-fashioned, overstuffed chair. On the table beside him were a Walkman and a large stack of cassettes, as well as a portable CD player and a smaller stack of CD boxes. From all appearances, Kid Kismet was blind.

After lighting the candle, the girl left the room and returned with a tray. She was slightly older than the boy, perhaps eighteen, wearing a blue kerchief that accentuated her smooth, Egyptian-like features. Orient noted that she and the boy shared a definite resemblance. She poured an iced, milky white liquid from a pitcher and gave them each a glass.

"Thank you, you're very kind," Orient said.

"My sister is kind. And by now you know I'm blind," the boy said mockingly. "But are you sure I have what you're looking for?"

Orient glanced at Lord Buckley. "I'm not sure what I'm looking for, actually."

The boatman nodded gravely. "Give us the word, Kid."

The boy smiled. "Doctor man thinks he's a fool to look here for truth," he said in a chanting voice. "But his feet are walkin' the golden route. If he has the sight, he will meet the friend he seeks this very night."

Lord Buckley lifted his glass. "Congratulations, doctor man. The Kid gonna help you.'

"With all due respect," Orient said quietly, "just how does the Kid propose to do that?"

"Well, he already do that. 'Cause now I'm gonna tell who's payin' me to check you out. 'Cause Kid Kismet already check you out, understand?"

"Maybe."

The boatman grinned. "See, the Kid has a special gift. Like second sight. He know from a word who's bad, who's okay, and who's special. He say you're special, doctor man."

Orient sipped his drink. The milky liquid was cool and sweet. He smiled at Laurie, who had sat down next to her brother.

"The drink is very good."

"It's soursap," she said shyly.

"Good for the stomach," Lord Buckley added. "So

what you say? Will you let the Kid take you to meet our friend?''

"You haven't told me who's paying you," Orient reminded him.

"Oh, that. It's the Cubans. They seem to think you're in the CIA. Like Lucien St. George."

"The Cubans?" Orient repeated disbelievingly. "How could they know I'm here?"

"Somebody must of told them, mon."

The boatman's casual answer burned in Orient's brain.

"A liar lies like a baby cries," Kid Kismet intoned. "You dealt with the devil, now deal with the wise."

Orient had to admit he made a strange kind of sense. "Okay," he said with a sigh. "When do I meet this person?"

"Right now," Lord Buckley said cheerfully. "The Kid can guide you from here."

It was dark outside. The tangle of trees and vines curtained off the meager light offered by the moon, rendering Orient quite helpless on the unfamiliar terrain. He had to depend totally on the senses of the blind young poet just ahead of him.

Kid Kismet seemed completely at home, moving easily through the the thick vegetation without benefit of eyesight or footpath.

From what Orient could gather, the route they followed started behind the house and wound gradually uphill. He still didn't know the name of the person they were about to visit. But, like the Kid, he had learned to depend on certain instincts. And he had faith that he was about to find the friend Sybelle had seen in his cards.

Lord Buckley had explained that to ensure their spiritual leader's complete safety, only the Kid knew exactly how to find him. And only a few people knew how to find Kid Kismet.

"We're nearly there, so have no fear," the Kid said after about twenty minutes. "Just hold your breath and say a prayer."

Orient didn't quite know what to make of the suggestion until they reached a clearing. Just ahead was a wide chasm cut through the rock by the narrow waterfall pouring down from the mountain above. The only way across was a crude rope-and-plank bridge that had seen better days—a fact that Kid Kismet ignored when he walked to the edge of the chasm, grasped the rope handrail, and started across the rickety bridge.

Heeding the Kid's advice, Orient held his breath and followed him onto the unsteady structure. The falling water threw up a fine mist that left the wooden planks slick with moisture. He gripped the slippery rope tightly and tried not to look down past the swaying planks as he gingerly eased his way across the chasm.

The Kid waited impatiently on the other side.

"C'mon, doctor man, try to hurry," he exhorted. "Soon I got to watch TV."

Puzzled by the remark, but grateful to be on solid ground again, Orient quickened his pace to keep up with his blind guide. They moved into a grove of trees and up a steep incline. Abruptly the Kid stopped and held a finger to his lips.

A moment later the silence was broken by a deep, cultivated voice with a decided English drawl.

"Come ahead, come ahead. Why are you dawdling?"

The Kid laughed and hurried to meet his mentor.

As Orient watched them embrace, he tried to get a glimpse of the mysterious leader, but all he could make out was his white trousers and flowing blue shirt. Then the man disengaged himself and strode toward Orient.

His long, snow-white dreadlocks partially obscured his patrician features. His translucent albino skin was wrinkled, but his pink eyes blazed with vitality. He fixed Orient with a piercing stare that seemed to penetrate past skin, blood, and bone to the core of his being. Then his eyes flashed as if taking a picture of Orient's soul for future reference.

"Welcome," he said with a small smile. "You have journeyed long to reach us."

Orient's brain sprang to attention.

He had sensed he knew the albino from somewhere. Certainly he recognized the greeting. It was the traditional salutation between master and neophyte that he had learned in Tibet.

"The journey is like the flow of water," Orient said, adopting the formal reply.

The elderly albino clasped his hands and bowed. "And water finds the thirsty man."

Orient remained wary, still trying to comprehend. He waited for the questions that formed the next phase of the secret ceremony.

Doubt shadowed the old man's creased features. "Why have you come?"

Orient hesitated. That particular question was not part of the recognition ceremony.

"I was brought here to meet a friend."

The man nodded and took Orient's arm. "You are my most honored guest. Please come."

He escorted Orient to a beautifully crafted, carved wood staircase to a large veranda with a curved roof that resembled a tortoiseshell. Kid Kismet followed them up the stairs to the veranda, which was lit by antique brass kerosene lamps. There were plants everywhere: flowerpots lining the railings, tall leafy plants standing on the floor, blossoms and vines hanging from the ceiling, not to mention a large vase of golden roses on the table. There was also a pot of aromatic tea on the table, along with three cups.

Orient's eye was drawn to a silver cigarette box beside the pot. The mandala design etched on its face resembled the one on his own cigarette case. However, it was not the same.

Still wary, Orient eased down onto one of the large pillows strewn around the table. The white-skinned man sat beside him and began pouring tea.

"Kid Kismet and I are alike. We both dwell in darkness. I cannot bear the sun, so I sleep by day," he explained. "Welcome to my home. I am Rastadamus."

Orient nodded, but didn't answer, waiting for a further sign of recognition.

"You've come so far to lose your faith," the Kid intoned. "If somethin's on your mind, say it."

"Why did you bring me here?"

Orient's question drew a look of uncertainty from Rastadamus. "Perhaps I have been mistaken."

The response nudged Orient's memory.

"The journey is strewn with illusions."

Rastadamus opened the silver box and picked out a hand-wrapped cigarette. "Then the journey will take a long time to complete."

Anticipation rippled through Orient's thoughts after Rastadamus had again responded correctly. "The journey will complete itself in time," he said quietly.

The old man's piercing red eyes burned into Orient's face. "Can you recall the name of the card that brought you here?"

"The card called The Devil," Orient said softly.

"My dear Kid," Rastadamus said, "would you mind leaving us alone for a few moments?"

Without a word the blind youth stood up and disappeared into the house.

"The Kid has great potential," Rastadamus told Orient. "However, he knows nothing of the path—or of the Nine Unknown Men."

Orient tried to keep his reactions in check, but his brain

was churning. There remained only one more question to ask.

"And you know the Nine?"

"I know of Ku."

Orient felt the tension drain from his body. No one but a follower of the path could know the name of his instructor in—and initiator of—the Serene Knowledge. No one save a master.

"I am of the seventh level," Rastadamus explained. "The eldest of the Nine."

The last statement took Orient by surprise, since he seemed much younger than his mentor, Ku. "I'm Dr. Owen Orient," he said formally.

Rastadamus lit his hand-wrapped cigarette. "Your coming was foretold. We have been waiting for you for a number of weeks."

Orient smiled. "I didn't realize I was so sought after."

"You are more than sought after. You are desperately needed."

"You can depend on my help."

The master beamed at him. "There are fewer than a handful on this planet able to accomplish this task. I am too old, too well known, even in seclusion. Jamaica is a small island. But powerful." His expression clouded. "Many covet this power—the Americans, the Cubans, and certain internal elements including the drug lords. Now one of these has allied himself with the Americans. One who dares channel the deep forces of Obeah. One who would use these unholy powers to turn this island into another Haiti—enforcing his rule with voodoo terror squads like the Ton Ton Macoute. Soon Jamaica would become a hellish anarchy of vice and murder."

"I take it you're speaking of St. George."

"You've met him?"

"I've *seen* him," Orient said. "I've learned to be quite reluctant to meet him."

Rastadamus took a long drag on his cigarette, then stubbed it out. "Enough for now. I must see to the Kid. We're watching TV tonight."

"He mentioned it on the way. But I still don't get it."

Rastadamus nodded. "You will. Come, join us."

He ushered Orient into the house. Like Lord Buckley's home, the interior was simply furnished with comfortable carved wood furniture. However, like the veranda, it enjoyed an abundance of plant life.

"I have a great affinity for growing things," Rastadamus said, leading him to the large living area, where Kid Kismet awaited them. "All of the herbs used in my healing are grown here. We also maintain a vegetable farm nearby." He led them to a smaller, glass-enclosed room that afforded a clear view of the sky and the waterfall. A six-foot long fish tank stood on one side of the room, its muted light providing most of the illumination. Looking around at the floor pillows and the thick, Tibetan patterned rug, Orient knew immediately that this was the master's meditation room.

"Please make yourself comfortable," Rastadamus said, seating himself beside Kid Kismet.

"The Kid is a potential," he announced after Orient was seated. "He is my apprentice in the telepathic technique. Every night we work together, and I communicate visual images of the life around us. It is in this manner that he can actually see."

"I understand."

"Good. Then let us link minds, and view some home movies."

As Orient began his breathing pattern, he felt sharply chilled in the high mountain air. Although still clad in his beach clothes, he didn't want to interrupt the preparations, so he went into a form of Yoga breathing known formally as hyperpyrexia.

This breathing pattern enabled him to raise his body

temperature to a comfortable level. However, by the time he rejoined Rastadamus and the Kid, they had already linked minds.

Orient entered their orbit tentatively, uncertain of his balance. He eased carefully into the major sphere of influence, then tried to flow with the gravity generated by their union. Almost instantly his senses lit up like a multidimensional movie screen. He saw a misty rainbow spilling over the waterfall in the morning light. He touched and tasted exotic flowers and herbs. He stood in the silent gloom of a sunless jungle, watching a brilliantly colored bird build its nest. As the vivid spectrum of Rastadamus's images rolled across his mind, Orient felt his fears evaporate.

He lost track of time. When he emerged from the orbit he was profoundly refreshed, as if his soul had taken a healing bath.

The albino master's eyes fluttered open. "Your technique is quite fluid, Doctor. I see you've developed over the years. Please indulge me. Show me a bit of the control you've acquired."

Orient looked around and saw a book of matches on the table. Tuning his concentration, he felt for the matchbook's specific pulse of energy. When he found it he focused his senses and pushed.

The matchbook slid across the table and stopped in front of Rastadamus.

"If you will," Orient said evenly, "please take one out."

Rastadamus removed a match and held it up. "Like this?"

Again Orient merged his senses with the specific pulse of the match head, but this time he generated an excess of body heat. The match burst into flame.

"Hold it there, please," Orient murmured. He focused

on the flame's frenetic pulse and slowed it to a standstill. Abruptly, the match flame went out.

Rastadamus nodded his approval. "You are to be commended. Your master would be proud indeed to witness such prowess."

"Doctor man got the power," Kid Kismet interjected. "But now's the witchin' hour."

"Ah, yes. Quite right, Kid," Rastadamus said. "Would you excuse us for an hour or so?"

Kid Kismet got to his feet and moved to the door. "In an hour or so, I'll be tuned to the stereo. When you're ready, let me know."

Rastadamus clasped his hands. In the dim light emanating from the fish tank, his patrician features seemed carved from bleached white driftwood. His pale red eyes burned inside darkly shadowed sockets as he studied Orient.

"St. George courts money and power. This is where you will find him. This is where you must confront him. His arena."

He paused to make sure Orient understood. "After you leave here, go to the place of wealth. Act part of the illusion. Do you have money?"

When Orient nodded, he continued. "St. George is a proud man, easily challenged. Sooner or later he will confront you. It's his nature. However, he is far from a fool. You will need great discipline, and great courage. And you will need deep knowledge of the Obeah art."

"I've been researching a bit—" Orient stopped, realizing how foolish he must sound.

"Ah, yes, I'm sure. Both your strong aura and your facility with psychic techniques attest to your discipline. But as I said, we are speaking of the Obeah *art*. Not everyone who can generate the energy has this art. It is the real power of Obeah."

He gave Orient an apologetic shrug. "We should not

see each other again, unless absolutely vital. So I'll take this opportunity to impress the inner rhythms of Obeah.''

Orient went receptive, allowing the master to link minds and begin feeding raw information directly into his memory. But unlike computer feeding, this was *felt* information, meaning it could be true or false dependent on a hundred other variables.

The process of transferring information went smoothly enough, but afterward Rastadamus asked Orient to maintain his receptive state.

"Let me guide you to the crossroads," he said softly. "Where the past, future, and present all meet . . ."

Orient breathed deeply, allowing his awareness to bevel into the master's orbit of consciousness. Almost immediately his senses began to tingle and images formed in his brain . . .

A group of shadowy figures was coming up a hill, toward him. They carried something on their shoulders. As they came nearer, he recognized the gaunt features of Lucien St. George at the head of the group. A small, dwarflike figure walked beside him, moaning softly. As the group slowly advanced, he saw that they were carrying a casket.

Suddenly they stopped and silently lowered the casket to the ground. Then the tiny figure at St. George's side darted toward him, weeping hysterically. At the same time St. George began to laugh.

He bent to lift the coffin's lid and threw it open, his laughter rising like a cold wind that pushed Orient closer to the casket. As he stumbled forward, he could see the outline of a tall, slender man inside the coffin.

A raw gust of fear cut through his belly and he stopped. He tried to turn away, but an intense force drew him nearer to the man in the casket. St. George's laughter pealed louder, pulling his horrified gaze to the coffin . . .

Orient jerked out of orbit, shivering convulsively and

gasping for breath. Rastadamus immediately picked up an embroidered cloth covering a nearby table and threw it over Orient's shoulders.

"I'm sorry, my son. But better to grasp it now than too late."

"Grasp . . . what?"

"The man in the coffin."

Still shivering, Orient knew but tried not to hear, as sweat poured down his back and belly like ice water.

"The man in the coffin," Rastadamus repeated hoarsely, "is you."

Chapter 25

ORIENT WOKE UP LATE.

It was drizzling slightly, and the sea seemed gray and foreboding. Just like his future, Orient brooded, stalking around his hotel room. He went out onto the terrace and let the misty rain wash away the fears of the night before.

But even after an hour of stretching, breathing, and deep meditation, the residue of the previous night clung to his memory like a cold snake.

He took his time getting dressed, then wandered down for a late breakfast at the beachfront coffee shop. The fresh fruit, yogurt, and toast he ordered looked delicious, but he had no appetite. He could no longer ignore the psychic prognosis. He would very likely die on the island. Perhaps today, he added morbidly to himself.

It was still drizzling by the time he paid the check, so he decided to take a stroll through town. He had barely set foot in the parking lot when a familiar voice hailed him.

"Mornin', doctor man," Lord Buckley called. "Your car is waitin'."

He was standing beside a shiny black Jaguar, dressed in

a blue suit and yellow tie. His dreadlocks were covered by an oversized gray derby.

"I think you better give me some money, mon. And wait here in the car," he said quietly as Orient approached.

"How much?"

"Countin' the hundred you owe from yesterday, a week's rental on the car, and your extras—only a thousand."

Orient counted out the cash, then climbed into the car.

"Soon as I pay your hotel bill and have your things sent down, I'll be back." He squinted at Orient. "You okay, mon? I thot you be packed like we planned."

Orient shrugged. "Didn't think you'd be here so early."

Basically, the plan they'd formulated consisted of Orient making himself conspicuous as a big spender eager to invest in the area. Because Ocho Rios was a small community, eventually he'd be thrust near enough to St. George to make contact.

But as he watched Lord Buckley enter the lobby, he realized he really didn't want to go through with the plan he'd made with Rastadamus. He was on the verge of booking the next plane to New York. Every step he took in Jamaica was a step closer to his own death.

A woman's face appeared at the car window. "Mr. Orient, is everything all right?"

He recognized the hotel clerk and forced a smile.

"Everything is fine, thank you. I've enjoyed my stay. I've just decided to relocate to larger quarters."

"Well, we may not be as fancy as the Sans Souci," the woman said primly, "but we do our best to please."

Even in the rain the San Souci looked impressive.

"Here comes the easy part," Lord Buckley confided as the car rolled past the immaculate lawns to the entrance. "All you have to do is enjoy serious luxury for a bit."

It was ironic, Orient thought. For him, luxury was the most dangerous aspect. It tended to slow one's reflexes. Still, considering his bleak future, he had nothing to lose by indulging himself.

The lobby was spacious and richly decorated with polished marble floors, lush plants, eccentric furniture, and a talking parrot housed in an ornate cage.

Lord Buckley had done his work well. The desk clerk was expecting him and immediately dispatched a bellhop to take Orient's bag upstairs. He had been booked into a suite that ran close to five hundred dollars a night. However, that included a list of amenities from mineral baths to polo. His suite seemed extremely comfortable, if overdecorated, and featured a terrace with a sweeping sea view.

It stopped raining after lunch, and Orient spent the rest of the day lounging about the mineral pool. At about six he showered, changed into a newly acquired gray linen suit, and strolled to the bar. To get there he had to cross the gardens to a glass elevator that afforded scenic views of the plush surroundings.

The dining terrace outside the Balloon Bar smelled of fresh flowers and rain. Inside, the handsome horseshoe bar exuded the scent of expensive perfume and cigars.

He nursed a ginger beer and watched the parade of sleek women having cocktails with their slightly overfed men. As darkness settled, candles were lit outside, completing the illusion of an intimate oasis in the primitive wild. Like being on safari, Orient reflected. All the great white hunters hunkering down around the campfires to compare trophies.

Of course, the cuisine was far from primitive. He ordered a glass of white wine and scanned the menu while waiting for a table. His salad, grilled lobster, and curried rice were excellent, but halfway through the meal Orient's attention was drawn to a small group of diners being seated nearby.

Standing at the head of the table, dressed in a white suit, his eyes shaded behind mirrored sunglasses, was Lucien St. George.

The shock of seeing him so close smothered Orient's appetite. He picked up his glass, downed the rest of his white wine, and signaled for another. Fortunately, the waiter was busy, giving Orient time to collect himself. He went into a deep breathing pattern, and by the time the wine arrived he no longer needed it.

He ordered a bottle of mineral water and coffee, then resumed his surveillance of St. George's dinner companions. St. George's female companion sat with her back to Orient, but something about the way she laughed scratched at his memory.

Then she half turned and he knew.

The other people with St. George seemed to be having a good time. But then they were obviously used to it. The portly blond gentleman and the pretty Jamaican girl facing Orient, and the pudgy, red-faced man in the blue blazer seated across from St. George, all had the hand-groomed gloss of prize house pets.

The lady sitting with her back to him was a different breed. Her grave blue eyes and exquisite features suggested a regal innocence, but Orient recalled their first encounter at Jack Ruby's pub. Then she'd been sharing a laugh with a trio of hustlers. Tonight the players were different, but the game seemed the same.

St. George gave his guests his undivided attention, showering them with considerable charm. He had removed the mirrored glasses and his piercing gaze never wandered far from the blond man, on his right. Occasionally he'd address the pudgy man, who always appeared delighted at whatever was said. Actually, however, the pudgy man's real interest was focused on the lovely blue-eyed lady. To Orient's surprise, he found himself vaguely annoyed by the man's concern.

"Is something wrong with the wine, sir?"

Orient looked down and saw his untouched glass. Impulsively he decided to call attention to himself. "Yes. It's undrinkable," he said loudly. "Bring me a cognac and a fresh cigar."

"Compliments of the Sans Souci," the waiter said when he returned.

As Orient lingered over his cognac, he kept staring at the blue-eyed lady, much to the pudgy man's discomfort. Finally he said something to St. George, who turned in his direction. Orient calmly met St. George's steady gaze. After a moment he smiled and raised his cognac glass. His face impassive, St. George did the same. The blue-eyed lady had also turned and was looking at him with a curious expression. Abruptly she turned back to the pudgy man.

Orient decided to test the waters while St. George was at a disadvantage. Obviously he was trying to sell something to the blond man, so he'd be reluctant to make a scene.

Orient signaled the waiter. "Please send a bottle of Dom Perignon champagne to that table," he said evenly. "And convey my compliments to the lady with the lovely blue eyes."

The waiter glanced at St. George uncertainly, but the twenty Orient pressed into his hand erased all doubt.

Orient savored his cigar as he watched the waiters arrive at St. George's table with an ice bucket and a bottle. One of them said something, and everybody at the table turned to glare frostily at Orient. Everyone except the blue-eyed lady. She accepted the glass the waiter poured and lifted it in a brief toast before taking a sip.

Orient returned the toast. Then he stood and slowly walked out of the restaurant. He could feel their eyes on his back all the way to the garden.

The encounter left him strangely hyperactive.

Fueled, no doubt, by the cognac and coffee, he told himself. He breathed in the clear, rain-washed air as he strolled through the gardens. At least he had accomplished his primary objectives, Orient reflected. He had established himself as an intrusive boor and initiated a mild confrontation with his target, not to mention a mild flirtation with a most intriguing young lady.

He was still thinking about her as he walked toward the private beach nestled against the moon-tipped sea. Along the way he noticed a gazebo perched on a large boulder jutting out of the water, and wandered over for a look. The darkened gazebo seemed like an ideal spot to think things over. He stepped inside the shadowy structure and extracted a hand-wrapped cigarette from his silver case.

But when he struck a match he saw that he was not alone. An oddly familiar figure sat on the rail, back propped against a column. Her sea-blue eyes flared in the brief light.

"Are you always so arrogant?" she asked calmly.

"Sometimes I'm rude," he confided, letting the match go out. "Did your dinner party break up suddenly?"

"It was all your fault. After you left, my escort became quite annoyed with me for accepting gifts from a perfect stranger."

"No one's perfect. Anyway, we're really not strangers."

"I couldn't very well tell him that, could I? He doesn't approve of my being seen in certain places."

"He?"

She tossed her head back. "My lord and master."

"So you were banished from the royal table?"

"Nothing so blatant. He's discussing an important matter with that film producer from London. He simply dispatched me on an errand. So I decided to sit by the water." She turned to look at him. "Have we met before yesterday?"

"I believe I'd remember."

"Me too." She sighed, swinging her feet to the floor. "Well, time I rejoin polite society."

"Meet me for lunch tomorrow," Orient said impulsively.

"Why?"

The question hovered like a wind chime in the darkness.

"Because we both like to sit by the water."

She paused, lips pursed in a thoughtful smile. "My lord and master is a mean bastard. He might kill you. Four tomorrow afternoon. Same place."

Before Orient could answer, she was hurrying along the seawalk to the gardens.

The next day began as usual, but Orient knew it was different. During his meditation the image of her clear turquoise eyes kept emerging from the corners of his mind, teasing him with promises no lady could keep. He cut his routine short and decided to take a swim. As he walked to the private beach, he realized he didn't even know her name.

An attendant appeared as he walked past the pool. "Phone for Mr. Orient. Back at the bar, sir."

Orient walked quickly past a grotto that housed a giant tortoise, to a small outdoor bar at the end of the shaded walkway. The call was from Lord Buckley.

"Pick you up in an hour, Doc. We got to talk."

The line went dead. Orient wasn't overly concerned as he headed back to the beach. But he was curious. After a fifteen-minute swim in the choppy sea, he ordered breakfast on the way back, spent ten minutes in the sauna, and got to his suite just as his food arrived.

When Orient stepped out of the cool marble lobby into the glaring heat, he saw Lord Buckley waiting for him in the Jaguar.

"Air-conditioning," he said proudly as Orient stepped into the frigid interior.

"Good morning, your lordship. You have some news?"

"You sound pretty chipper for Johnny-on-the-spot."

"How do you mean?"

Lord Buckley put the car in gear and rolled out of the lot. "What the hell happened last night? St. George's people askin' about you all over the place this mornin'."

"He was having dinner with some guests at the hotel. One of them was a young lady. All I did was send her champagne."

"All?" The boatman snorted. "Around here Lucien St. George is like a Mafia godfather. Messin' with his woman like that could ruin your vacation."

"I'm meeting her this afternoon."

The car slowed. "Meeting who?"

"I don't know her name."

"About twenty, beautiful blue eyes, long red-streaked hair?"

"Sounds right."

He pulled over to the side of the road. "That would be Cool Blue."

"And she's St. George's lady?"

"Closer than that," Lord Buckley said quietly. "Cool Blue is his high priestess."

Chapter 26

LORD BUCKLEY'S NEWS SOBERED ORIENT CONSIDerably. They drove in silence for some time while he weighed the possibilities. He had set out to beard the lion in his den, Orient reasoned. Why not the lioness?

"Where are we going?" he asked finally, peering out at the vaguely familiar landscape.

"Past Orocabessa to Galina Point. I thought I'd show you the Olympia Club, then take you back to Ocho for a fancy lunch."

"I just had breakfast."

"Sure. Toast, juice, fruit, maybe yogurt. Right? That ain't but a snack. I'm talkin' real food. You're gonna need your strength, mon."

The drive was short and scenic. Goldenhead was only twenty minutes away, and Galina Point lay just beyond. Before they reached Galina Point, the boatman turned into a side road and suddenly Orient saw the signs marking it a restricted zone.

"The Olympia Club," Lord Buckley announced. He stopped, shifted into reverse, and turned back for the main road. "Now you know your way here. Just in case."

They continued on to Port Maria, stopped for a Red Stripe, then returned to Ocho Rios. Lord Buckley took his time, even insisting they stop to look at a roadside vendor's wood carvings. Orient admired the carver's skill but saw nothing unusual in the pieces, until Lord Buckley took him aside.

"We're bein' followed, mon. Ever since this mornin'."

"You sure?"

"That's why I stopped here. We lost 'em over by the Olympia, but they must have been waitin' for us to come back this way. Now they parked up the road."

Sure enough, when they pulled away a small black BMW eased out behind them. Lord Buckley maintained his leisurely pace, keeping tabs on the BMW in his mirror. Because of their slow speed, it was well past lunchtime when they reached Ocho Rios.

Actually, it worked out just as well, Orient noted. They had their choice of tables in the hilltop restaurant Lord Buckley recommended, enabling them to sit out on the terrace, overlooking the bay.

"The food is superior, mon," the boatman said proudly. "Nuccio knows how to burn."

After sampling Nuccio's penne and pollo al diavalo, Orient had to agree. Of course, the bill reflected the chef's genius with Italian food.

"Think we can lose our escort before my meeting?"

"I got it covered, mon. Listen up. The BMW probably pick us up at the base of the hill. Soon after there'll be a blind curve. That's where you jump out. I catch you later after I get rid of them." He leaned back and lit a cigar. "So relax, mon. They'll be sweatin' in their car while we're enjoyin' the view."

At twenty to four Lord Buckley started the car and began rolling down the steep hill. Sure enough, just as they reached the bottom, the BMW slipped behind them.

"Get ready." the boatman advised as they approached the curve. "Now!"

He braked hard, enabling Orient to step out, slam the door, and slip behind a tree moments before the BMW came squealing around the curve. Orient waited until the car was well out of sight, then moved off in search of a cab.

Cool Blue had picked her time well. There were only a few pedestrians on James Avenue when Orient walked down to Jack Ruby's bar. Inside, the sole occupants were the bartender and a couple huddled together at a corner table.

Orient sat at the bar and ordered a Red Stripe. He checked his watch and noted it was past four. It crossed his mind that she wouldn't show up. Then he glanced at the couple sitting in the corner and his thoughts stood still.

Cool Blue sat with her back to the bar, talking to a short, broad-shouldered Jamaican man who wore a gold cross in his ear. For a full two minutes Orient debated whether to go over or wait for an invitation. Finally he decided to say hello.

"Lovely day, isn't it?" he ventured, not certain about her companion.

She was wearing sunglasses and she kept them on as she studied him. When she spoke she was quiet, and terse. "This is my friend Eric. He's here so I can say we stopped to talk and you barged in. Now Eric is taking me to Jungle Hut. Follow us in ten minutes."

Orient moved back to his stool, mindful of the barman's disapproving scowl. However, he had been anticipating his appointment with Cool Blue since the morning, and the instructions she left were hazy. He waited out the required time, paid his tab, then walked leisurely outside and headed for the cabstand.

Before he got there, Lord Buckley stepped beside him.
"Your car is waitin', mon."

"She wants me to follow her."

"Yeah. I see her leave with one of her drummers."

"Drummers?"

"You know. In the ritual." He opened the door.
"Where we goin'?"

"Place called Jungle Hut."

Lord Buckley turned the car around and drove west
along a two-lane highway leading to Runaway Bay.

"Did you lose our friends?"

"Hope so, mon. Don't see anythin' back there."

About ten minutes outside Ocho Rios, he slowed the car
down.

"You'll be gettin' off soon now. I'll keep going 'case
there's a tail. Then I'll circle back."

He stopped the car at the side of the road. Orient stepped
out, somewhat bewildered by the fact that there was nothing in sight. Lord Buckley pointed to a crude dirt trail that
cut through the vegetation. "Down there, mon," he said
hoarsely. Then he pulled away.

The trail curved down to an open field. At the far edge
of the field, shaded by a giant tree, was a small wood
house. As Orient neared, he saw a man leaning on the
hood of a car that was parked behind the tree. It was Eric.

He nodded when he saw Orient and tilted his head toward the house. Orient walked to a small door in what
appeared to be the rear of the house. Inside was a large
flagstone kitchen and the scent of freshly brewed tea. As
he came around the serving counter, he saw her.

She sat on a long couch facing an open wall that looked
out on the sea, barely twenty-five feet away. On a low
glass table in front of her was a black teapot and matching
cups.

"Miss Cool Blue?"

She didn't look up. "The only people who call me that are outsiders."

"It's the only name I caught," he told her. "May I sit down?"

"Of course, Doctor."

While surprised, he offered no reaction. "You've done your homework."

She began pouring the tea. "Actually, it's Lucien doing all the research. You seem to fascinate him."

"How about you?"

As she turned, the afternoon sunlight streamed down her red-streaked hair, and a slow smile illuminated the mischievous glint in her clear blue eyes. For a fleeting moment she looked like a playful child, before the mask slipped over her finely etched features. "Obviously I'm here," she said softly.

"You still have the advantage."

She cocked her head, not understanding.

"Your name. Or am I an outsider?"

She searched his face. "You are an outsider. But I feel I know you." Then she looked away. "Tea, Doctor?"

"Thank you, Cool Blue."

His biting tone drew a response. "My name is Ezili," she said sharply.

"After the Loa goddess?"

A flicker of curiosity shaded her expression as she handed Orient his tea. "Then you know."

"That you're St. George's priestess. Yes."

She shook her head. "I'm afraid you're mistaken, Doctor. You see, I'm not his priestess—I'm his slave."

Orient stared at her, trying to separate truth from treachery. Still unsure of her motives, he put the teacup down without tasting its contents. "Look, I'm sorry. But I don't understand."

"Of course not—how could you?" she said gently. "In a way, it's simple. I have a natural ability in certain areas.

In order to force me to use this ability on his behalf, Lucien holds my mother hostage. Even if I could free her, there are things he could do . . . Maybe he'd decide to send out the black bird and she'd die.''

"The black bird?"

"Yes. Whenever he wishes to cast a hex, he attaches his curse to a black bird and frees it from its cage. When it returns, you know it's done its work."

As she spoke, Orient's mind went back to the three madly fluttering ravens in Shandy's crypt. Struggling to maintain his composure, he pushed the memory aside.

"Do the birds always come back?"

"Only once, very recently, a black bird failed to return. I took it as an omen."

"Of what?"

"That the power of the evil Houngan, Lucien St. George, has begun to erode."

Suddenly Orient believed her. He knew for certain that one of the birds had not returned. The one sent out in his name the night Shandy died.

"Why tell me this, Ezili?"

His question drifted in the long silence as she sipped her tea.

"Because," she said finally, "I know you understand. I knew when I saw you."

He wanted to believe her. Which worried him. He decided to try the tea. If it hadn't been poisoned, they could go on from there. After the first cautious swallow he found the brew delicious. "Very good. I don't believe I've tasted anything quite like it."

"It's my own blend," she said with a sly smile. "I put a love potion in it."

Orient hesitated, not certain she was joking. Then he decided it made no difference. "You seem very sure of me."

Her smile faded. "Yes. I've been hoping you'd come.

For a month now I felt . . . I also saw someone like you in my cards."

The memory of Sybelle's Tarot reading chilled his reaction. "How like me?"

Her grave blue eyes found his and held on. "Am I mistaken about you?"

"Just answer. How like me?"

"Someone who understands who I am. Someone who isn't afraid to defy Lucien, as you did last night. You did do it consciously, didn't you? You wanted to make him angry."

"Yes," he said softly.

"And you used me to do it."

"No. Not exactly. I did want to challenge him, but that's not why I'm here now. I'm attracted to you."

"Then you do understand me, Doctor. I hate Lucien St. George. And I'm strongly attracted to you."

"Then perhaps you'll call me Owen."

Her pale pink lips formed an apologetic pout. "With pleasure . . . Owen."

Slowly, as if by some prearranged sign, she leaned closer as he bent to kiss her. Her gentle touch rippled across his senses and he felt her tremble in his arms.

They both heard the sound at the same time.

Ezili reacted first. She sprang to her feet like a Siamese cat, looking around in panic. Then she saw it and shrank back against Orient.

A large black bird had found its way into the house. It was perched on a ceiling lamp, preening its wings.

"Oh, God, Owen. I'm afraid." She grabbed his wrist and pulled him through the open door.

"Calm down," Orient said hoarsely. "It's just a doctorbird."

But she wasn't listening. "I've got to get out of here. Where's Eric?" she said breathlessly, hurrying to find the car. As they rounded the corner, Orient saw Eric sitting behind the wheel. He moved closer and yanked open the door. It was then he saw the bloody hole punctuating Eric's wide-eyed stare like an exclamation point.

"Owen!"

As Orient turned, three things happened at once.

Something hard slammed into his temple. A dark shape roared out of the bushes like a charging beast. And Ezili's scream exploded inside his skull.

Chapter 27

ORIENT WAS JARRED CONSCIOUS WHEN HIS FACE smacked the cool, wet grass. Blindly clawing at screeching fragments of reality, he instinctively rolled away in time to avoid the full impact as the car shot forward. A squealing tire grazed his shoulder, roughly bumping him aside on its way into the swirling green mist.

Then suddenly it was quiet.

There was nothing except the painful throbbing inside his damaged brain. Sucking air through his nostrils and pumping it from his diaphragm, Orient managed to gather his balance. Vision reeling, he pushed himself up onto his knees. Dimly he made out the looming shape of a car.

As his eyes cleared, he saw it was Eric's Fiat. And Eric was still in it. He looked around for Ezili, but she was gone.

Half dazed, he grabbed the fender and pulled himself to his feet. Then he opened the door on the driver's side. Eric's body fell into his arms, and he staggered back under the weight. Lowering the body gently to the ground, he looked inside the car and saw the keys dangling from the ignition.

He squeezed awkwardly behind the wheel, started the motor, and sped off toward the dirt trail, rear end fishtailing on the grass.

When he hit the main road, he swerved to a stop and scanned the asphalt for tire marks. Then he saw Lord Buckley's Jaguar parked a short distance away.

He gunned the motor and skidded to a halt next to the Jaguar. Lord Buckley was behind the wheel, reading a magazine.

"Which way did the car go?" Orient yelled hoarsely.

Lord Buckley tossed the magazine aside. "Follow me!"

Tires screaming, the Jaguar zoomed away in the opposite direction. Ignoring oncoming traffic, Orient backed straight across both lanes, wrenched the wheel, and peeled out after the disappearing Jaguar.

Fortunately, Lord Buckley's car was built for speed. Cursing the Fiat's sluggish acceleration, Orient struggled to keep the Jaguar in sight. However, he was thankful that one of them had a chance to catch up to the fleeing car.

The road his attackers had taken led to Montego Bay and curved along the wind-flecked sea. The road widened into a long straightaway and Orient spotted a black car weaving in front of the Jaguar as if trying to shake it off. Then he saw the Jaguar surge forward and ram the black car's rear bumper. As Orient watched, Lord Buckley took advantage of the black car's momentary swerve to accelerate past the vehicle and throw the Jaguar into a controlled skid that blocked the two-lane blacktop. The black car slid into the Jaguar, bounced off, and headed directly for Orient's approaching car. His body jacknifed forward as he stomped on the brake and jerked the wheel to one side.

Orient braced himself, but the impact never came.

The black car stopped about two yards short, and a man popped out of the rear door brandishing an automatic pistol.

As Orient ducked he heard the sharp crack of gunfire, and someone yelled. When he peered over the steering wheel, he saw Lord Buckley leaning on the roof of the Jaguar, aiming a .45 at the black car. The automatic pistol was lying on the road, near a fresh puddle of blood. Suddenly both doors on the driver's side of the black car burst open. Two men, one clutching a bloody shoulder, sprinted wildly for the trees as Lord Buckley fired.

Fortunately, he missed, because a trio of tourist vans was approaching. Lord Buckley tossed his gun inside the Jaguar, then hurried to retrieve the dropped pistol before hopping into the black car and pulling it over to the side of the road. Traffic was stalled for a few moments while he returned to the Jaguar and eased it behind the black car. Meanwhile Orient also parked his vehicle off the road.

The tourist vans went on their way without ever realizing there'd been a shootout less than three minutes before they arrived. Orient moved swiftly to the black car and looked inside. Ezili was huddled in the back seat, her eyes wide with shock.

"Thank God it's you," she sobbed, falling into his arms. "They killed Eric."

"You're safe now," he whispered. "They're gone."

"She all right, mon?" Lord Buckley inquired, leaning inside the window.

Orient felt Ezili stiffen. Slowly she eased out of his embrace. "Who is he?"

"The person who just saved your life."

Orient's quiet response seemed to allay her fears. "Please forgive me. It's just that I saw you shooting . . ."

"Had to," the boatman said tersely.

Orient looked at him. "I didn't know you carry a gun."

Sensing his unspoken disapproval, Lord Buckley lifted his brows in regal indifference. "Hey, Doc, I ain't no holy mon. I'm a family mon. Anyway, I shoot over their heads mostly. Don't need no dead bodies on my hands,'' he added meaningfully.

Ezili glanced at Orient. ''I'd better drive Eric's car back. I'll be missed. And it will take a major explanation.''

''Just tell St. George it was the Cubans,'' Lord Buckley said dryly.

Her eyes narrowed, and she studied him with feline intensity. ''I'll do that. And thanks for your help.''

She paused to give Orient a polite kiss. ''I'll be in touch soon,'' she whispered.

As Orient watched her drive away, he was struck by her remarkable self-control.

''She recovered real quick,'' Lord Buckley mused, echoing Orient's thought. The boatman inspected the damage to the Jaguar, then wearily slid behind the wheel. ''We all need a rest,'' he muttered. ''I'll take you back to the hotel.''

''How can you be so sure they're Cubans?'' Orient asked as they drove back to Ocho Rios.

'' 'Cause one of them used to hire out my boat. The one I clipped. Good client too.'' He glared at Orient. ''Why? Think I lead them to Cool Blue?''

Orient smiled. ''I'm just trying to figure out why the Cubans are interested in her.''

''Maybe 'cause they know St. George's dealin' with the CIA. Anyway, one thing is damned sure. Now we got all three for enemies—St. George, the CIA, and the Cubans.''

A numbing depression oozed through Orient's limbs as his mind flashed back to Sybelle's Tarot reading. It was all as she had predicted, he reflected, staring at the sunglazed water.

He wondered how much time he had left before his death.

* * *

When Orient arrived at the Sans Souci, the desk clerk greeted him with startling news.

"Your wife took the key, sir. She's upstairs."

Orient kept his expression blank, but his brain whirred with possibilities as he went up to his room. If Ezili had sought sanctuary in his suite, St. George would find out within hours.

However, he didn't have to worry about Ezili. The first thing he saw when he entered was the halo of silver hair illuminating Tristan's face. She was curled up on the couch, fast asleep, her long hair framing her chiseled features. She looked very young, and very vulnerable.

He stood there for a moment, trying to regroup his thoughts. As he neared the couch he recalled their last night in New York. He touched her gently and her eyes fluttered open.

"Hello, my darling," she said, her voice husky with sleep. "I was just dreaming about you."

"A nightmare?"

"No, silly. It was a lovely dream. We were passionate castaways on an island paradise."

"Sounds like a movie."

Her arms snaked around his neck, drawing him closer.

"Kind of a blue movie," she whispered, kissing him.

"How did you . . . ?"

"Know you were here?" Tristan gave him a smug smile. "I saw you walking across the lobby this morning. I called but you didn't hear. So I thought I'd surprise you."

"What about the book project?"

"Sold. That's how I can afford this place. I came down for a week of pampering before I go into deep seclusion and write my screenplay."

She pushed herself up and regarded him gravely. "Maybe this wasn't such a bright idea after all. You probably had other plans."

"Not tonight. But I am surprised."

She nuzzled his neck. "Then you forgive me for barging in?"

"Only if you promise to be good from now on."

"Oh, I'll be good," she murmured, slipping her hand inside his shirt. "I'll be so good, my darling."

Her silken fingers set fire to his skin, searing away his resistance.

Later, as they lay side by side listening to the birds chatter in the lowering twilight, Orient's thoughts drifted back to the abduction attempt of only a few hours ago. It occurred to him that Tristan might be in danger as well. The Cubans might decide the widow of a CIA officer would make an ideal hostage.

It also crossed his mind that Tristan's lines to the Company might still be open. She had a knack of turning up at crucial times, Orient brooded. Like the night Duke had been murdered.

"What are you doing down here anyway?" she murmured sleepily. "Last time I looked, you were in New York."

"Came down for some real estate speculation. I've found some prime beach sites," he added, trying to sound enthusiastic.

Tristan wasn't convinced. "Funny, you never struck me as the real estate type."

"I've got a big meeting tomorrow," Orient said firmly.

She sighed, nestling closer. "Okay, I get the hint. But right now it's tonight."

It was as if the world had shut down for the evening.

They ordered room service and dined on the terrace by candlelight. Then they made love again.

Sometime about five a.m. Orient was awakened by the shrill call of a doctorbird on the terrace. He got up to shut the glass door, then returned to bed. Tristan was asleep, her long blond hair spread across the pillow like silvery feathers. Then a cold stab of memory punctured his well-being. An image of Tristan's dead husband crawling out of his crypt swept through his thoughts like an icy wind.

He slept fitfully for a few hours and when he awoke, Tristan was gone. He checked his watch and saw that it was barely eight. He also saw the note taped to the mirror when he went into the bathroom.

Darling,
  Don't want to intrude on your dealings—or feelings. I'm in Suite 14 whenever you need to see me.

Love,
T

Orient felt relieved. He couldn't be anchored by conflicting emotions while swimming in shark waters. He showered, dressed, then ordered breakfast and a newspaper.

One front-page item in the *Daily Gleaner* caught his attention. The Jamaican elections were only a month off. Orient wondered if St. George would figure in the race.

His speculations were interrupted by the phone. The desk clerk informed him that his car had arrived. Sensing something was wrong, Orient hurried downstairs.

When he reached the parking lot, he found Lord Buckley pacing nervously. His usual exuberance had been sapped by the same deep anxiety that drained the vitality from his eyes.

"Please, Doc, tell me somethin'. Just what kind of doctor are you?"

"What's wrong?"

"It's my Ginny. She got sick last night."

"How sick?"

"We can't wake her up. She's been asleep now over fifteen hours. I called Dr. Jameson, but he can't find nothin'. He wants to take Ginny to the hospital in Kingston. I sent word to Rastadamus, but he can't come down until after sunset."

"I don't have my medical instruments."

"Dr. Jameson say you can use his. I already asked."

"Of course I'll examine her. But I can't promise I'll do any better than Dr. Jameson."

Lord Buckley pushed him toward the car and opened the door. "Let's roll, doctor man. Everybody's waitin'."

Chapter 28

THE SCENIC DRIVE WAS CONDUCTED IN SILENCE, broken occasionally by Lord Buckley's swearing at various obstacles on the primitive mountain trail. As they neared the house, he turned to Orient.

"I haven't told Violet about St. George."

"I don't understand."

"It's possible Cool Blue hexed my baby."

"Why her?"

He glared at Orient. "She see me yesterday. She knows I know about her. She tell St. George and they put a hex on my little girl."

"Children get sick all the time," Orient reminded him. But he had to admit Lord Buckley's theory had a chilling logic.

Violet came out to greet them when they arrived at the house. In the space of twenty-four hours the tall, handsome woman had become haggard. Her cheeks were hollow and dark circles shadowed her pain-dulled eyes.

"She's still the same," she told her husband.

Lord Buckley stepped out of the car and put his arms around her. "It'll be all right now."

Orient tried to assume a positive bedside manner, but he hadn't practiced in almost ten years. However, a half hour later, after examining the child, he knew it made no difference. Whatever ailed Ginny wasn't a known disease. She required a full battery of hospital tests—or the services of an occult specialist. Fortunately, he could help with the latter.

The Jamaican physician looking over his shoulder was a rotund, white-haired gentleman with a benign smile. Dr. Jameson reminded Orient of the old-fashioned country doctor who gave dignity to the medical profession. And he, too, suspected that Ginny's malady had supernatural roots.

"I've heard of cases like this," he said hesitantly.

"I beg your pardon?"

Dr. Jameson adjusted his spectacles. "In these parts, many people are still quite superstitious. Sometimes they fall prey to their own beliefs."

"Hard to believe a child could practice self-hypnosis."

"Some of these superstitions include the use of little-known herbs, drugs, poisons—even secret curses."

"You mean like witch doctors."

"Yes. Except here they're known as Houngans, and their special herbs and potions are known as *macoots.*"

"You seem to have made a study of this."

"No more than the average Jamaican. Here the old ways are interwoven with the new."

"I understand, Doctor. And I appreciate what you are saying."

"I hope you can make Ginny's parents understand that the child needs to be taken to Kingston for tests." He shut his worn black bag and reached for his hat. "Their reliance on this Rasta man who's coming could prove fatal. Good day, Doctor. It's been a pleasure."

As he left, Orient turned back to Ginny. The little girl lay unmoving, her head propped up on the pillow. She looked thinner than the giggling child Lord Buckley had held in his arms two days before. And very frail. He vowed to do everything in his power to make Ginny well again. Even if it cost him his own life.

"Are you finished, Doctor?" Violet asked softly.

Orient gave her a reassuring smile. "I'll need just a few more minutes alone."

After she left the room, Orient sat in a half-lotus position on the floor beside the bed. He went into an exploratory breathing pattern and almost immediately he sensed the cloying evil winding around the child like a shroud. As he dowsed for the source, a frigid pang of fear pierced his awareness. Reflexively he pulled back as if stung by a jellyfish. He kept trying, but the dense, painfully noxious pocket of resistance drove him back over and over again. Finally he retreated into a deep meditative state designed to recharge his exhausted senses.

At least now he was absolutely certain Ginny didn't need medical tests, Orient noted grimly. He went out to the porch, where Lord Buckley and his wife were waiting.

"We need Rastadamus," he told them.

Violet began to weep softly. Lord Buckley put his arm around her and scowled at Orient. "I told you. That bitch . . ."

"Let's wait for Rastadamus before passing judgment," Orient said quietly.

Violet prepared lunch, but none of them was overly hungry.

At about three that afternoon Violet returned from Ginny's bedroom looking extremely distressed.

"She's running a fever, Doctor."

Orient knew what was happening. As the sun passed its zenith and began to wane, the occult virus feeding on Ginny's energy gained strength. It was time for him to erect a defense.

"Look, we don't want to alarm your wife," he explained, taking the boatman aside. "But I'll need six white candles, a cup of rice, an onion, a big water bowl, and a bag of salt."

"I'll have to go to the market," Lord Buckley said suspiciously. "Anythin' else you left out?"

Orient tapped his brow distractedly with a long finger. "Yes. Six saucers, a ball of twine, and a piece of white chalk."

"What do I tell the wife?"

"The truth. I'm trying to protect Ginny from whatever is attacking her. At least until Rastadamus can get here."

Grumbling a bit, Lord Buckley went inside to talk to Violet. Then he trudged out to his Ford and headed for the local market.

As Lord Buckley negotiated the torturous dirt road leading to the small outdoor market a few miles away near Browns Town, he had serious doubts about his Rastafarian faith. Particularly his faith in his spiritual leader. Rastadamus had served as priest, healer, counselor, and judge to his family for three generations. And the same could be said for his small community of followers. Indeed, not everyone who wished to join the healer's spiritual family was accepted. This created some resentment, but the master's reputation was beyond reproach. Rastadamus had always guided his flock to the ways of harmony and prosperity. But maybe this time the wise old man had made a big mistake, Lord Buckley brooded. Ever since Rastadamus had accepted this so-called Dr. Orient, things had started going bad.

For openers they had the CIA, the Cubans, and St. George on their case. And now his poor, innocent little girl.

The burly-chested boatman fought back the rush of emotion welling up at the thought of his little girl lying sick and alone. That doctor man damn well better know what he's about, Lord Buckley raged helplessly. Or he'd pay the price for allowing Cool Blue to endanger his family.

He arrived at the market a bit late. At least half the crude stalls had closed for the day. He knew most of the vendors and their customers by name, but today he had no time for small talk. He made his purchases quickly, but had some trouble locating the white chalk. As he walked across the market, he saw a familiar figure and stopped.

The long, red-streaked hair and crystal blue eyes could belong to only one female. Like it or not, Cool Blue seemed to be heading directly into his path.

Unwilling to make a show of avoiding her, Lord Buckley stood his ground, pretending to examine some mangoes. Cool Blue wandered slowly toward him, then paused to pick up a mango. As she brushed against him, Lord Buckley felt a tug at his pocket.

For a panicked instant he wished he had brought along the .45 holstered beneath his dashboard. He looked around for the usual bodyguards, but there was only one other woman walking with Cool Blue. Rather than call attention to the encounter, Lord Buckley continued his shopping. When he reached into his pocket to pay for the chalk, he found the note.

O   meet me at crossroad/midnight   E.

Lord Buckley debated whether or not to deliver the note, certain it was some sort of trap. He knew the crossroad could be a dangerous place at midnight. Crossroads were the gathering places of evil spirits, he noted grimly as he climbed into his vehicle. Before starting the motor, he made sure his weapon was still in place. During the drive back a combination of confusing emotions flooded his thoughts. The mounting frustration at his inability to help little Ginny churned into anger. Anger at Rastadamus for waiting so long to help his daughter. Anger at these so-called doctors who couldn't even cure a child's ailment. Anger at Cool Blue and St. George for inflicting their evil on his little girl. Anger at himself for not knowing what to do.

He decided to wait a while before giving the doctor man his note. Could be he was expecting a message.

The idea punctured his reverie like a dart. Also could be why the bastard sent me on a fool's errand, he fumed, one hand snaking under the dashboard. By the time he arrived home, he had calmed down. After all, Rastadamus had proved himself many times over. But as he carried the bags into the house, Lord Buckley resolved to hold the note back until the doctor man had proved himself.

Orient was waiting on the porch.

"Sun is almost down," he said, taking the bags. "Rastadamus should be here soon." Without any further conversation he took the packages to Ginny's room. Lord Buckley followed him, both curious and wary. Violet was sitting beside Ginny's frail, unconscious form, gently moistening the child's mouth with a wet handkerchief. When she looked up, he could see the suffering in his wife's face and his anger flared.

"Just why did you send me for that stuff?" he demanded.

Orient calmly handed him the glass bowl. "Fill this with water, please."

When the boatman returned, the doctor had removed his shoes and was measuring Ginny's bed with a length of twine. He stood and scanned the room before choosing a spot to place the twine. He gave Lord Buckley one end of the rope and pointed to the floor.

"Please hold this end right here."

Lord Buckley did as he was told. He held one end of

the twine firmly in place while Orient pulled it taut and traced a large circle with the chalk. Then Orient asked him to help carry the bed into the center of the circle.

When that had been done, the doctor placed the water bowl at the foot of Ginny's bed, just outside the circle. As Lord Buckley watched, his thoughts were buffeted by conflicting emotions. He had seen Rastadamus perform similar rites of purification, but tonight he felt neither reverence nor respect. There was only the bleak loss of faith—and the hopeless rage.

He watched in stony silence as Orient placed candles at the four points of the circle. At each point he set a burning candle on a saucer and intoned a muffled prayer. Then he did something Lord Buckley had never seen before. Using a kitchen knife, he sliced an onion into quarters. He carefully placed a quarter onion into each of the four corners of the room. Again he muttered some sort of prayer.

Having completed that phase, Orient took the bag of salt and sat cross-legged in front of the bowl at the foot of Ginny's bed. Holding a burning candle in his left hand, he poured salt into the water bowl with his right hand. This time the prayer was a bit more easily understood.

"I exorcise thee, creature of earth, by the Living God, by the Holy God, by the Omnipotent God, that thou mayest be purified of all evil influences in the name of Adonai, Lord of Angels and men . . ." Orient recited slowly, crossing the burning candle over the bowl.

"In the name which is above every other name, and in the power of the Father, the Son, and the Holy Ghost, I exorcise all seeds of evil, and all influences of evil. I lay upon them the spell of Adonai, that they be bound fast as with chains, and cast into outer darkness, that they trouble not the servants of God."

The boatman glanced at his daughter and sharply sucked in his breath. Ginny was beginning to stir.

Hope washed over his parched awareness as Orient left

the circle and placed a candle on either side of the door. The boatman watched with rising anticipation as the doctor took a handful of rice, then carefully placed four grains at each of the four points of the circle. Then he stood and mumbled a prayer over Ginny. To Lord Buckley's horror, Ginny stopped stirring and fell back into a deep sleep.

The boatman's huge fingers knotted into fists. "She was wakin'," he said indignantly. "Why you make her sleep?"

"I awakened an evil spirit—not Ginny," Orient told him. "Please stay calm."

"Bullshit. I see her wake up myself," Lord Buckley growled. Violet hurried to restrain him as he advanced on Orient, shaking his fist.

"There's evil in the air, and tempers flare," a familiar voice sang. "Have no fear, the Kid is here."

Lord Buckley whirled and saw the blind boy standing in the doorway. "Where's Rastadamus?" he snapped.

"I'm the master's guide. I stay at his side. I come to see everything's right. And I ain't bringin' him here to fight," Kid Kismet said emphatically. "Ain't no time for hate. We all need to keep the faith."

Lord Buckley's hands fell helplessly to his sides.

"Please . . . we need to see him."

"It's all right, my son, I'm here."

An odd note in the master's voice alerted the boatman that something was wrong. Then he saw.

Although Rastadamus was swaddled in a cotton sheet from head to foot, what could be seen of his albino skin was seared a bright pink by the late afternoon sun. Small blisters were also visible across his nose, lips, and hands. Suddenly Lord Buckley realized what a great sacrifice the master had made by traveling before nightfall. Even the rays of the setting sun had burned his ultrasensitive skin.

The boatman felt a deep pang of shame. "Master . . . you need help," he murmured.

"It's nothing," Rastadamus said, surveying the room.

"I see you've prepared for my arrival. How is the little one?"

"She started to come awake when the doctor was prayin'," Lord Buckley told him. "Then he stopped."

Rastadamus looked at Orient. "The exorcism?"

"Yes. It responded immediately."

The old man nodded and turned back to Lord Buckley. "You must have faith, my son. It was the evil duppez inside Ginny that came awake when the doctor tried to cast it out."

"I'll leave, Father."

"No. You are needed here," Rastadamus said gently. He sat down on the floor at the edge of the circle. Orient sat facing him, also at the circle's outer edge.

Lord Buckley hesitated. Rastadamus pointed to a spot a few feet behind him. "Sit there, my son. And bear witness."

The master turned to Orient. "After your visit I went into deep meditation. I felt the evil come over the little girl." He paused to remove the cotton sheet from around his shoulders. Underneath he wore a loose-fitting white shirt that covered him from neck to wrist, and white trousers. Still, every exposed area of his skin—face, throat, fingers, even ears—had suffered burns. The knowledge tempered Lord Buckley's reaction when he heard the master's next words.

"Who was the channel for this evil attack? It was you—the physician."

Orient's chiseled features seemed to waver in the candlelight. But his green eyes remained steady as Rastadamus went on.

"The animator of this evil force is a powerful rite which channels sexual energy."

A deep furrow creased Orient's brow, and he lowered his eyes. "So it's true. She came to betray me."

"To betray us," Rastadamus corrected him. "But this evil would have struck through any of a dozen others."

"Yet it struck through me."

"Now you know your true enemy."

Lord Buckley swallowed a surge of anger. His suspicions were well founded, he noted bitterly. Cool Blue had used the doctor to work her whorish voodoo. Heart pumping, he waited as the two men sat silently facing each other, their eyes closed. Lord Buckley couldn't be sure what they were doing, but he sensed a definite charge of energy pulsing between them.

Then a wave of static electricity prickled his scalp.

"Let us begin."

The master's words rippled through his mind as he watched Rastadamus enter the circle and make his way to Ginny's bedside.

After a few short minutes Lord Buckley realized that the master's warning had not been exaggerated. His self-control was being tested to the limit. To his mounting horror, he watched his little girl begin to writhe and growl like a cornered animal. He wanted to make them stop, but he knew she'd die without them.

Tears running down his cheeks, he clasped his hands in prayer as her shrieks battered at their chanting harmony.

"*Apage satanus . . .*"

"In the name of Adonai . . ."

"Creature of water . . . ," Rastadamus intoned, sprinkling water over Ginny.

Lord Buckley's heart froze as he saw a luminous froth bubbling from his daughter's lips. Immobile with terror, he stared at the gleaming bubbles as they drifted lazily toward the ceiling. Suddenly Ginny's body went rigid and she began to tremble convulsively.

Across the room a framed photograph of Ginny crashed to the floor.

Their droning voices rose to meet the squalling attack as they continued to sprinkle salt and water around the circle.

"By Gabriel . . ."

One of the bubbles floating overhead popped.

A lightning flick of energy lashed the air. The bed panel above Ginny's head cracked in half as if chopped by a giant ax.

Another bubble burst and Ginny shrieked in pain.

". . . I command you return now to whence you came—creature of abomination!"

A profound silence settled over the room. Sweating profusely, Lord Buckley gaped breathlessly as the glowing bubbles faded into the gloom, and Ginny fell back into blessed sleep.

The boatman's relief crumbled to disappointment when he realized that all they had achieved was a standoff. Whatever possessed Ginny's body was still there, feeding on her precious life.

Head bowed with exhaustion, Rastadamus stepped out of the circle. "All right, Kid," he said with a sigh.

Kid Kismet appeared at the door with a tray. Wordlessly he placed the tray on the floor, just beyond the threshold. On the tray was a pot of tea and three cups, as well as a jar of dark unguent for Rastadamus's raw skin.

"If only we had a point d'appui, something—anything—connected to the attacker," Orient ranted helplessly.

"We would have real leverage," Rastadamus agreed. He had begun to apply the unguent to his face, but paused when he noticed Lord Buckley staring at him.

"Did you say if you had something connected . . ." Lord Buckley glanced at Orient, then marched on. "Something connected with this woman could be a help against her?"

"That's true," Rastadamus said, studying him. "What do you have?"

The boatman reached into his shirt pocket for the note Cool Blue had given him. Rastadamus scanned the note, then handed it to Orient. The doctor looked up as if confused. "Where did you get this?"

"Cool Blue sneak it to me, over at the market," Lord Buckley said gravely. "Will it do?"

"Problem is—Cool Blue didn't hex Ginny."

The boatman stared at him, totally crestfallen. "But you and she . . . at Jungle Hut . . ."

"It was another woman," Orient said firmly. "She was at the hotel. After you left me yesterday."

Lord Buckley clapped his hands in frustration. "Damn! What about Ginny now?"

Orient looked at Rastadamus. The master nodded sadly.

"It's clear that even linking our powers against this force will not suffice. And yet, sometime ago, you managed to fight off St. George's hex all alone."

Orient shrugged. "Obviously he's forewarned. He's using a more potent rite."

"No. Every killing rite requires the full force of the Houngan's power. For should it somehow break down—the price for failure is the priest's own death."

"Then St. George should be long dead. Since I survived."

"Think, my son. Was there not another victim?"

Shandy's death-mottled face rising from his crypt danced across Orient's memory. "Yes," he said tonelessly. "The husband of the woman who betrayed me last night."

"Is there something else you want to tell me?"

The question hung in the flickering gloom.

"I saw him rise up and walk. Long after his death," Orient said finally.

"The husband?"

"St. George killed him—then brought him back to life."

"This Houngan St. George is a skilled controller of the living dead," Rastadamus said quietly. He cocked his head and squinted at Orient. "Are you afraid?"

A tight smile broke across Orient's candle-shadowed features. "Of course I'm afraid."

The master beamed and swept his hand toward the tray on the floor. "Please drink some tea while it is still fresh. We all need our strength tonight."

True enough, Lord Buckley felt refreshed after his first cup, but he remained anxious about Ginny's welfare.

"I believe the child will be safe until Saturday night," Rastadamus said as he applied the unguent to his blistered hands.

"What happens Saturday?" Orient asked.

"The voodoo rite," Lord Buckley blurted out. He glanced at Rastadamus. "Everybody hear about it around town."

The master furrowed his sun-reddened brow. "Yes. Saturday night is traditionally when Obeah ceremonies take place—and this Saturday is special."

Rastadamus put the unguent aside. "It's the feast of Baron Samedi, the Loa who rules over graveyards and burial places. Saturday the thirteenth also marks the new moon," he added, his face pensive. "But why does St. George want us to know this?"

As the question faded, he looked at Orient. "This woman who wishes to see you. The one who wrote the note. You must go to her."

"It could be a trap," Orient said evenly.

"You said yourself this woman did not betray you."

"Not yet."

Rastadamus weighed the doctor's grim logic. "We have no choice. We must find out how we can help the child. Strike a bargain, if need be."

Orient sipped his tea. "I'll try, Father."

Lord Buckley exhaled slowly, vastly relieved.

"There is one thing that has occurred to me," Rastadamus mused, refilling everyone's cup. "Did this other
woman take anything from you last night?"

"Perhaps. I didn't think to check."

"Something personal," the master persisted. "Anything that could be used as a point of contact, from priest
to you. It might explain St. George's sudden elevation of
power."

Orient's face clenched with anxiety. "There is something," he muttered, looking through his pockets. "No!
Here it is." His features relaxed into a small smile as he
handed Rastadamus a silver cigarette case.

"Fortunately, no one knows of the mandala," Rastadamus said, passing the case back. "Try to remember,"
he prompted gently. "Perhaps a gift or a token, from
someone dear?"

"Wait. There is something." Orient emptied all his
pockets, then rummaged through their contents piece by
piece. "Before I came here, my friend Sybelle gave me
an amulet. She claimed it was quite potent." He continued sifting through his things. "It's gone," he said finally.

"What form did it take?" the master inquired.

"A metal cross, made of coffin nails and human hair."

"Why was it not pinned inside your shirt?"

Orient looked away. "I was lax. I didn't think."

"Yes, you were lax," Rastadamus agreed. "Because
you lacked faith. You didn't believe this object could protect you."

"Perhaps you're right, Father."

"Remember it tonight—when you meet this woman at
the crossroads. Faith."

Orient struck a match to light his cigarette. In the flaring light his features seemed carved from smooth dark
stone. Except for a faint glimmer of uncertainty in his
green eyes.

"How will I know the crossroads?" he asked quietly.

"Don't worry, brother." Lord Buckley spoke up. "I'm goin' down the line with you." He clenched his fist in a gesture of support.

Orient gave him a lazy grin. "Hope you can handle zombis, brother."

A frigid pang of fear deflated the boatman's bravado. As he drew his hand back and crossed himself, he heard little Ginny moaning in her sleep.

Chapter 29

ORIENT WAS DEEPLY GRATEFUL FOR LORD BUCK-
ley's company as the Ford burrowed through the dense,
forbidding bush. The knowledge that St. George held a
weapon against him gave the trip a gallows twist, Orient
reflected morbidly. He hadn't been surprised to learn the
real reason behind Tristan's well-timed appearance. Just
depressed.

Lord Buckley squinted through the windshield. "We
soon arrive."

Orient checked his watch. "Eleven-forty. Better stop
here for a bit. No sense rushing in."

Lord Buckley rolled to a quiet stop and doused the
lights. Immediately the blackness closed in. When his eyes
adjusted to the dark, Orient saw they were parked on a
narrow trail that cut through the forest.

"Not much chance of company," Lord Buckley assured
him. "This ain't the main drag."

"How far to the crossroads?"

"Just up ahead maybe five hundred meters."

"Okay. Turn the car around, just in case. I'll go ahead
on foot. You follow in about three or four minutes."

As soon as Orient started out, he wished he had brought Lord Buckley to guide him. He heard the startled chatter of birds when the car motor started up behind him. In a minute or so the silence crept over the forest again. An overcast sky further limited Orient's visibility as he walked along the rutted trail. He tried to keep to the side, but the path had steep shoulders. As he plodded on, he slowly acquired his night vision and realized the trail was getting wider. About a hundred meters beyond the end of it stood a shadowy figure.

Carefully drawing closer, Orient made out the man's old-fashioned stovepipe hat and long coat. The man stood motionless in the center of a wide clearing, body slightly tilted as if he was peering through the darkness.

As Orient moved nearer to the clearing, the figure's head snapped back. Orient froze, certain the man had heard him. He slipped behind a tree and crouched down. Slowly the shadows seemed to recede and he could feel the movement of the jungle. The rustling breeze carried messages of a nearby presence. One much closer than the unmoving figure ahead.

Guided by his senses, Orient edged around the tree and took a few careful steps toward the presence. He paused when he saw the long-haired figure a few yards away, watching the clearing from a place of concealment. Moving very slowly, Orient crept closer, but he knew who it was long before she turned and he saw her blue eyes.

"Are you alone?" he whispered.

"Yes. Are you?"

"Yes," he lied, hoping Lord Buckley had the sense to stay back. "What about him?"

"Who?"

"The man watching the clearing."

She smiled. "That's no man. See for yourself. But bring this along." She took something from her pocket and gave it to him. "It's an offering," she explained softly.

Orient saw it was a piece of sugar cane. He walked slowly out to the figure and saw it was nothing more than a scarecrow, actually a voodoo totem set to guard the crossroads. But when he came closer, an apprehensive chill crawled across his belly.

The basic skeleton of the scarecrow figure was a crude wooden cross. A long black tailcoat with a rose silk lining was draped over the arms of the cross. Impaled at the apex of the cross was the bleached, hollow-eyed skull of some fang-toothed beast. The stovepipe hat perched on the savage skull added a darkly comic effect.

However, the humor was lost on Orient. He had approached the totem more in response to Ezili's challenge than because of his curiosity. It occurred to him that she might have sent him out into the exposed area to alert an accomplice.

He added the piece of sugar cane to the others like it that were spread about the base of the cross; then he moved back into the protective foliage.

"It's good you put the offering there to appease Kalfu," Ezili whispered. "He is the Loa of the carrefour, the crossroads. A very dangerous place. We need his protection tonight."

"Why?"

Her clear blue eyes narrowed as she considered the question.

"Because you lost your protection."

Orient stared at her. "What do you know about it?"

"Everything," she whispered, taking his hand. "Come."

He resisted gently. "Come where?"

Ezili's expression suggested he'd just confirmed her worst fears. "Don't you want to help the child?"

"How do you know about her?"

"Do you wish to help her?"

"Yes."

"Then trust me. Now come. We might be seen here."

Still uncertain, Orient allowed her to lead him through the dense underbrush to the base of a rocky hill. His main concern was that he had already lost contact with Lord Buckley.

Ezili led him up a rising path to a ledge about six feet above the forest floor. From there Orient had an excellent view of the surrounding area.

"This is a traditional place for lovers," she told him. "No one can sneak up unobserved."

"Unless they're already above us," he said.

"I don't mind checking. Do you?"

Orient extended his hand. "I'll go first."

He climbed to the next level above them and scoured the small cliff for any sign of recent occupation.

Ezili finally grew impatient. "Rather than waste time looking for evidence that I betrayed you, why not hear me out?"

"Why did you want to meet me tonight?"

She looked up at the sky in exasperation. "I know St. George cast a hex on the child. And I know how it was done," she said deliberately. "He sent the woman to use you."

"Did you help cast this hex?"

"I'm his mambo. A *Quatre Yeux*," she added proudly.

Orient knew the term referred to a master priestess with clairvoyant powers, but he remained unimpressed.

"Yet you use your rare gift to hex an innocent little girl."

Her eyes flashed angrily. "Remember, he holds my own innocent mother hostage. I do not have the CIA or the Cubans to act as my bodyguards. I am alone on this island." She took a deep breath. "Now I'm going to help you—because you are going to help me."

"Help you do what?"

"Free my mother."

Orient shook his head. "I can't."

"You, and your friends. The girl is your friend's child, is she not? The one who shot the Cuban. Surely he's willing to try in exchange for his daughter's life."

She lifted her hand to Orient's lips before he could speak. "St. George holds us all hostage. If we join forces, perhaps we will all be free one day."

Her feathery touch awakened a flurry of sensations. He smothered an urge to kiss her, trying to keep his mind clear. "You're absolutely certain you can cure the girl?"

"The girl—and you."

"What do you mean?"

"The first time you defeated St. George. That means your power is greater. But he found a weapon."

She held out a clenched fist, then slowly unfolded her fingers like flower petals. Nestled inside her palm was a crude metal cross. The amulet Sybelle had given him. And Tristan had stolen.

"How did you get it?"

"St. George had placed it on his Pe inside the Hounfor. I took it when I was alone. There are many things on the Pe. He won't miss it right away."

Orient understood she had taken it from the altar inside St. George's voodoo temple, or Hounfor.

"And you think now I can defeat him?"

"No. Your amulet still carries St. George's curse. As do you. Someday you may succumb."

"Trying to frighten me?"

A slow smile drifted across her face. "You know everything I say is true."

"Everything so far," he amended. "Not even *le Quatre Yeux*, the four-eyed priestess, always speaks the truth."

Her smile widened. "You are a most exasperating sort of man." She took his hand and led him down to the lower ledge, to the mouth of a small cave partially obscured by foliage.

Orient peered inside. "What's this?"

"The trysting place I told you about. It's quite private. We can even light a candle."

Actually, the lower level afforded more protection than the one above. It was also a superior vantage point. From there they had a clear view of the crossroads and the surrounding area. But without moonlight it was difficult to distinguish shape from shadow.

"Listen," Ezili whispered.

The monotonous trill of the doctorbirds mingled with the brisk chirping of crickets. Faintly in the background he could hear the wind rustling fitfully through the leaves. When Ezili spoke, her voice seemed to fade into the primal harmony.

"The woman Tristan—is St. George's mistress. She used your own sexual energy against you."

"I knew that before I came here."

"Did the old one tell you? The albino?"

"Who?"

"No matter. The only important thing is that I remove the curse. I can heal the child—and you. Right here and now."

"How so?"

"By performing the *Gros Bouzain,* a special technique designed to cleanse body and spirit."

Orient smiled. "Does that mean you intend to make love to me?"

Her expression wavered between amusement and admiration. "You know a great deal of our Obeah ways."

"I find them fascinating."

"And me?" She moved to the rear of the cave and took a red candle from the pocket of her long white dress. "Do you find me fascinating?" she prodded, striking a match.

The flaring light caught the fiery accents in her flowing hair and illuminated her pure-aquamarine eyes. She moved past him to make sure the entrance was curtained off by the foliage. In the process she brushed against him, igniting his senses.

"I'm still wondering about this deal you propose," he said, trying to stall.

"We don't have much time. And the child has no time at all," she reminded him. "My bargain is quite simple. I will cure the girl. When you're convinced she's well, I expect you to free my mother. Is that not fair?"

Orient could find little reason to disagree. Even if her offer contained some hidden clause, it made no difference at this juncture. In fact, the prospect of making love to Ezili was the sole bright spot in his doomed future.

"Yes. It's fair."

Before the words had left his mouth, she was leaning close to kiss him. Her soft, moist lips were like spring rain on winter earth. Her drew her closer and drank her in. Long minutes later she eased free and coaxed him down to the leaf-carpeted ground. "Lie back, my darling," she whispered. "I'll do it all for you."

As she spoke she reached behind her, and the long white dress fell away from her shoulders. In the dim, dancing light she seemed like a bronze Venus rising out of a gauzy white shell.

"*Woi*, Loa Guede . . ." she chanted softly. "Come to me, Guede."

Then she was tugging at his clothes. He tried to help but she gently pushed him back. The shock of her naked skin against his pulsed from the base of his spine to his brain. Suddenly the spring rain became a deluge, the candle flame a distant flicker of lightning, as her cool lips moved down his chest and slowly caressed his belly, sending electric ripples across his skin. The pleasure began to drum through his body as the breathless chant rose in the steaming quiet. "*Woi*, Gran Bois . . . *Woi*, Commere . . . hear my prayer . . ."

Then the words dissolved into a current of babbling

sound and overwhelming sensation that poured over his flesh like liquid satin. Waves of conflicting emotions flooded his awareness and disintegrated into a torrent of surreal images. He saw Ezili's face loom above him, her glistening, pink-nippled breasts swaying voluptuously. Hallucination and ecstasy bubbled up in a slow, moaning fusion that drained his body dry and left his naked skin drenched in sweat.

Suddenly the only sound in the small cave was the ragged heave of his own breathing. When he opened his eyes, it was totally dark.

"We needed the candle for the rite," she whispered. "But it's dangerous."

Orient sat up and felt for his clothes. "Will St. George come looking for you?"

"I'm supposed to be at the crossroads alone tonight. To perform a ceremony honoring Kalfu."

"Then why did you send me to Kalfu's totem, where I could be spotted?"

"So if we are seen together, I can say you were spying," she said calmly. "As I said, I'm alone on this island. You have resources. That's why we made a bargain."

"How do we find your mother?"

"I'm so pleased you finally asked. I've prepared a map with instructions." She pressed a folded paper into his hand. "Make sure you take everything before we leave."

Orient rummaged through his pockets and found his silver case as well as Sybelle's metal cross. He slipped the folded paper into the case and pinned the cross to the inside of his shirt. Ezili had put on her dress and paused at the entrance to reconnoiter the area.

By the time Orient was dressed, his vision had readjusted to the darkness. It seemed deserted outside the cave, but the overcast sky kept visibility minimal. There could have been a platoon lurking in the forest for all they knew.

"We shouldn't leave together," Ezili said softly.

Orient nodded. "You go first."

"Aren't you interested to know when we can meet again?"

"I gathered from this meeting you know how to get in touch."

"You gathered too much. My encounter with your friend was pure chance."

"What do you suggest?"

"Leave a message for me at Kalfu's totem, in the pocket of his coat. After dark tomorrow."

"Good."

She leaned back for a last, lingering kiss, her crystal blue eyes glowing. "Good night, my darling. Be safe." Then she slipped through the leafy curtain and faded into the shadows below.

Orient waited a few moments before he crawled out of the cave and made his way slowly down the hill, taking care not to dislodge any loose rocks. When he reached the shelter of the trees, he stopped to look around. He caught a glimpse of a hazy white figure moving through the darkness and began to follow.

He planned to trail Ezili at a distance until he located the crossroads, then get back to the car as quickly as possible. But after a few minutes the blurry white figure stopped and started to circle back.

The fine hairs on Orient's neck prickled and he ducked behind some bushes. As he watched the figure moving slowly in his direction, it became painfully clear it wasn't Ezili.

A huge man dressed in a tight-fitting white jumpsuit was edging through the forest as if searching for someone. Orient's blood began pumping faster as the man neared. He crouched low, trying to become part of the shadows. One of the man's trouser legs suddenly appeared through a gap in the foliage.

Orient remained where he was as the man continued to the base of the hill. When the man started to climb the hill, Orient emerged from his hiding place and moved swiftly in the opposite direction, keeping his body low.

Less than three minutes had passed before he heard a shouted curse behind him and knew he'd been spotted. Praying that his sense of direction wouldn't let him down, Orient broke into a run. Hobbled by the unfamiliar terrain and the lack of visibility, he soon slowed to a trot. The clatter of falling stones far behind him signaled the man's hasty descent from the ledge.

A shot cracked the darkness and Orient stumbled. Recovering his balance, he sprinted blindly through the undergrowth.

Breath heaving, he burst into the clearing and looked around wildly for the trail. He forced himself to calm down and remember the landmarks, especially the angle to the Obeah totem dominating the crossroads. Relief flooded his parched lungs when he loped around the edge of the clearing and saw the trail.

He also saw a flashlight beam sweep the far end of the deserted road. Without waiting to see more, he made a long dash for Lord Buckley's car, but he hadn't counted on his pursuer being mechanized. The rumble of a motorcycle shook the panting quiet.

He had almost reached the car when it suddenly started up and began rolling backward, skidding to a stop six inches from Orient. He scrambled inside, and before he could shut the door, the car lurched forward. Lord Buckley remained hunched over the wheel, peering through the darkness.

"What's up, mon? I heard a shot."

"Somebody's after us. He's on a motorcycle."

"Shit. Motorcycle can go where we can't."

Abruptly Lord Buckley braked to a stop, hopped out, and lifted up the rear seat, revealing a well-stocked tool chest. The boatman snatched up a length of rope and hurriedly looped one end around a tree. He strung the rope across the road, about waist-high, and secured it around another tree. Then he sprinted back, jumped behind the wheel, and gunned the motor. The vehicle lurched forward and began pounding along the crude, pitted trail.

"Just hope he follows 'long the road," Lord Buckley shouted. "If he takes the ridge, we soon be in trouble."

Fortunately for them, the motorcycle's headlights flooded the rearview mirror as it roared straight down the center of the trail.

Lord Buckley stomped on the accelerator, but the motorcycle swiftly devoured their lead until it reached the rope. Suddenly the light swept across the rearview mirror and vanished. Orient turned in time to see a riderless motorcycle wobbling up the ridge before tumbling back onto the trail.

"Guess we lose them," Lord Buckley muttered. "You hit?"

"I'm okay. You see anything?"

"After you go off with Cool Blue, I follow a bit. See nothin'. So I figure better stay by the car 'case there's trouble."

"Good thing. He was coming faster than I thought."

"What happen with Cool Blue?"

Orient weighed the question. "She performed a healing rite. She said it would cure Ginny."

"Think it's true?'

"I did until I ran into our friend back there. He definitely seemed to know I was coming."

"Like maybe she told him?"

Orient stared out at the rushing darkness. "We'll know soon enough, won't we?"

Lord Buckley used every shortcut he knew as the Ford shuddered and bounced along trails that were barely footpaths. By the time they arrived, Orient felt as if he'd been in a wrestling match. However, he also felt a sense of elation as they entered the house.

"Honey?"

As Lord Buckley's hesitant call echoed in the quiet, the place seemed curiously empty. The boatman hurried to the bedroom with Orient close behind.

"Oh, my God," he said breathlessly.

Orient whispered a prayer of thanks when he saw Ginny sitting up in bed, arms stretching out for her daddy. Then he realized something had changed. The candles were still burning, and all the artifacts of psychic protection were in place, but Rastadamus and the Kid were gone.

"They stayed here until Ginny woke up," Violet told them. "When they hear the car coming, they say we all better go. I decided we had to wait for you."

"I'm sure glad you did," Lord Buckley said, embracing her. "I needed to see both my girls are safe."

"Perhaps we'd best make plans to leave," Orient suggested "Rastadamus wouldn't have gone off unless it was important."

Lord Buckley sighed. "He's right, darlin'. Pack a bag for you and Ginny." He looked over at Orient, who was inspecting the onion quarters he'd placed in the corners of the bedroom. Picking Ginny up in his arms, he came over for a closer look. "What are those for anyway, Doc?"

"The quartered onion is there to absorb any strong evil force in the room," Orient explained. He held out his hand to the boatman. The freshly cut section of onion in his palm was gnarled and blackened. "As you can see, we needed it tonight."

"What about the rice?" Lord Buckley persisted.

"It's a slightly different form of protection," Orient told him, scanning the floor around the bed. "In order for a life-draining force to attack Ginny, it would have to consume each of the sixteen grains of rice I placed around the bed.''

''I don't see any.''

Orient pointed to the head of the bed. ''Over there.''

Holding Ginny tightly, Lord Buckley bent to examine the spot. Of the sixteen grains of rice, only three remained.

''I've got everything,'' Violet announced from the doorway.

After they had extinguished the candles, there was only one dim lamp in the hallway to guide them out. Violet led the way, while her husband followed with Ginny. Orient brought up the rear, alert for any sign of trouble. As Violet reached for the door, a sharp metallic click snapped through the quiet.

All four of them froze.

Orient and Lord Buckley exchanged glances, having recognized the sound of a weapon being cocked.

''Shit,'' the boatman hissed. ''Left my piece in the car.'' He passed Ginny to her mother. ''Go back to the bedroom.''

As she hurried inside and shut the door, Orient switched off the lamp. Standing there in the stifling darkness, he suddenly realized the night birds were still.

The area around the house was shrouded in expectant silence. Orient waited, his thoughts suspended between fear and frenzy. Then he heard the slow, muffled creak on the porch.

Chapter 30

ORIENT JABBED HIS FINGER TOWARD THE FRONT door and crouched down. Lord Buckley eased over to the other side of the doorway. Heart thumping, Orient cocked his fist and waited for someone to come through the door. A moment later a trio of flashlight beams pinned them where they stood.

"Freeze!" a voice barked. "Drop your weapons."

Both Orient and Lord Buckley extended their empty hands.

"Okay, turn around and assume the position."

Orient lifted his arms and turned.

"Hands against the wall, old sport. Feet spread apart. Don't tell me it's your first time."

Orient didn't answer. He waited until the body search was over, then turned around slowly. Lord Buckley stood with upraised arms, glaring at one of their captors. Something about both men's body language suggested they knew each other. And their knotted faces made their mutual dislike quite clear.

From where Orient stood, Lord Buckley's friend wasn't a likable man. He towered over the boatman by at least three inches, and his muscular body strained the seams of his soiled white jumpsuit. His shaven head sat on his beefy shoulders like a glass turret on a white tank.

A pair of mirrored, wraparound glasses obscured part of his face, but his brutish jawline had the contours of a bear trap. As he waved his pistol at Lord Buckley, his sneer revealed a row of sharp gold teeth.

"I owe you for two, my man."

"Get out of my house, Ramon."

Ramon's sneer widened. "First you shoot Cecil. Then you fuck up my motorcycle."

Without warning he smacked Lord Buckley's skull with the long barrel of his magnum. The boatman staggered and bounced off the wall. His raised fist stopped short at the sight of Ramon's magnum pointed at his eye. He slumped back against the wall, blood trickling down his cheek.

"Enough, Ramon!" a voice snapped.

The big man swiveled his head toward the flashlight beam.

"This is my business."

This time the voice was placating. "Later. We don't have much time. And we need them alive."

Orient squinted into the light. "What exactly do you want?"

"Information, Dr. Orient."

Orient was impressed by the accuracy of Cuban intelligence. He assumed they were the same people who had killed Eric and tried to kidnap Ezili. Obviously Ramon was the man in white who'd shot at him earlier at the crossroads and tried to follow on the motorcycle. What he couldn't figure out was how they had gotten to the house so quickly.

"Who is your control at the Olympia Club, Doctor?" the voice asked.

Orient briefly pondered the question. He felt no obligation to Westlake or the CIA. "I cut a deal with Commander Westlake on a specific job," Orient said carefully. "But I'm not an agent."

"Sure, he's a scumbag mercenary like this guy." Ramon pointed the magnum at Lord Buckley. "Work for everybody, don't you, scumbag?"

"This isn't about money," Orient corrected him. "St. George killed a friend of mine."

A barely perceptible hush told Orient his instincts were correct. The Cubans were trying to get at St. George. However, he was only half right.

"What about the drugs?" the voice demanded.

"I know nothing about any drugs," Orient said firmly.

The blow took him by surprise. Stunned, he dropped to one knee, his left ear ringing with pain.

"I told you, Ramon," the voice warned. "Now that's it. Get outside and secure the area."

As Orient got to his feet, the entire left side of his face felt hot and swollen. He gingerly touched his ear and was grateful to find it intact.

"Please accept my apology, Doctor," the voice soothed. "Ramon gets carried away. Now, you were saying?"

"I was saying I know nothing about drugs."

"Let's start over. You say you're on Westlake's payroll?"

"I accepted money from Westlake for a purpose."

"Which is?"

"I wanted him to think I needed the money."

There was a pause. "That's extremely unique." The voice chuckled. "I'm almost tempted to believe that one."

"Look, the point is, my deal with Westlake was to get a line on St. George."

"So?"

"Isn't he the man you really want?"

"What makes you think that?"

"You tried twice to get at his lady friend."

"Twice?"

"The day Cecil was shot, remember?"

"Oh, yes, Cecil. And when was the other time?"

"Tonight, of course."

"Of course."

"I can give you a way to get at St. George."

"Why are you being so generous, Doctor?"

"You have me at a disadvantage. I'm not used to dealing with a man I can't see."

"Or we're not dealing," the voice said. "You're talking."

"Then our discussion is at an end," Orient said calmly. "Better send for Ramon."

A tall, balding man wearing an olive-drab suit stepped into the light. "I'll listen to your deal, but I can't promise Ramon will like it."

Someone interrupted with a rapid flow of Spanish.

Orient looked over at Lord Buckley. "You all right?"

The boatman remained slumped against the wall. "Sure. Soon be dancin'."

"I'm told there are two females in the bedroom," the man in the olive suit announced.

Lord Buckley snapped to attention. "That'd be my wife and baby."

"I think Ramon may be interested in this."

Lord Buckley glanced at Orient.

"Don't do anything foolish," the man warned. "Innocent people could get hurt." Keeping his .45 trained on Lord Buckley, he opened the door and called Ramon inside.

"Better give me your weapon, old buddy," the man said.

Ramon glowered at him suspiciously. "My magnum? Why?"

"Because I said so."

There was no mistaking the edge behind the man's easy

drawl. Still glowering, Ramon handed his pistol to the man in the suit. During the exchange Orient had a moment to study him. Despite the two pistols he now held, he looked more like a Wall Street broker than a Cuban agent. His perfect American carried traces of a Texas drawl, and he carried himself with the assurance of a well-educated athlete. "You two come with us," he said quietly.

Something in his tone set off an alarm in Orient's brain. He braced himself against a turn for the worst. Flanked by Ramon and another, much smaller man holding an automatic rifle, Orient and Lord Buckley were ushered into the bedroom. As soon as they entered, Lord Buckley tried to go to Violet's side but was herded back by the rifle-toting Cuban.

"Tell me, Ramon." The man in the suit swept his hand around the room. "You ever see anything like this before?"

Ramon nodded. "Yes. It's voodoo." He turned to Lord Buckley. "I'm gonna kill you, voodoo man."

Orient stepped between them, arms upraised. "Wait a second. We can explai—"

Ramon didn't wait. Orient heard Ginny cry out, a moment after he was plucked from the floor. Then Ramon hurled him bodily against the wall and all he heard was a violent cacophony of sound.

There was a shrill shout, then a loud boom that echoed in the abrupt silence. Cautiously testing his bruised limbs, Orient tried to get up. "Hold it," he mumbled.

Someone helped him stand. It was the man in the olive suit.

"Sorry about Ramon," he said with a smirk, "but he has a real bug about voodoo. Seems someone put a spell on his son and he died."

Orient took a deep breath and looked around. Both Violet and Ginny were staring up at a large hole in the ceiling. The man in the suit was holding a still smoking magnum, but Ramon was no longer in the room. The other Cuban had his rifle leveled at Lord Buckley.

"Look," Orient said weakly. "St. George put a hex on the little girl. All of this was an attempt to cure her. We do not practice voodoo as you know it."

The man in the suit smiled. "Very good, Doctor. Very quick. No wonder Westlake has you on his payroll."

"Dammit, it's true!" Lord Buckley blurted out.

Orient remained calm. "Just check with Dr. Jameson. He treated Ginny before we figured out her real illness."

The man hesitated. Then he shrugged. "Does this Dr. Jameson have a telephone?"

Violet provided the number, and after a whispered conference the man with the rifle backed out of the room.

"You know, I still don't understand why your government is so intent on St. George," Orient said.

The man seemed confused. "My government?"

"I presume you're Cuban."

"Actually, I'm from Lubbock, Texas."

It was Orient's turn to look confused. A deep ache was creeping up his spine, and his brain throbbed like an outboard.

"So you're a mercenary?"

"I'm an American agent."

"I don't get it."

"I'm with the DEA—Drug Enforcement Agency."

"What about the Cubans?"

The man looked away. "At the moment, our interests coincide." His pained expression hardened when he looked at Orient. "I promise you, if this is some cute game, I'll feed you to Ramon."

"So far as I can see, we all have the same goal—St. George."

"Maybe."

"And I know we can help each other."

"We'll see."

"If he's an American agent, how come he's goin' against the CIA?" Lord Buckley demanded.

The man reached into his jacket and took out a laminated-photo ID which stated that one Frederick Groton Jr. was a special agent of the United States Drug Enforcement Agency. The man in the photo looked younger and his brown eyes hadn't yet developed their dark circles, but the receding hairline and stubborn jaw hadn't changed since the picture was taken.

Orient shrugged. "This still doesn't answer my friend's question."

Groton returned the card to his pocket. "Let's discuss it when Ramon gets back."

The agent did allow Lord Buckley to sit with Violet and Ginny while they waited, but the concession did little to ease Orient's concern. The fact that drugs were involved altered things drastically. More than likely Groton and the Cubans intended to hijack St. George's shipment. The question remained, to what end—personal profit or political gain? He found it difficult to believe Groton had an altruistic motive for terrorizing a mother and child.

Ramon's huge bulk filled the doorway. Groton went over for a conference, while the man with the rifle kept an eye on the prisoners. After a long discussion Groton rejoined Orient.

"It seems Ramon is inclined to believe you. This Dr. Jameson is well known in the community. He corroborates your contention that the girl was gravely ill. Which, I might add, doesn't prove a damn thing."

"You said we could discuss it when Ramon got back," Orient reminded him.

"You said you had a way to get at St. George."

"We haven't discussed terms yet."

"What do you want, Doctor?"

"First off, the immediate release of the woman and her child. They've been through enough. Second, you tell us why you're running this wildcat operation. That's all. If we can agree, I'll outline the entire plan."

Groton scratched his nose with the barrel of the magnum, then looked at Lord Buckley. "Is there another room?"

"There's my bedroom 'cross the hall."

"All right, then, Mrs. Buckley. Why don't you take your little girl in there?"

"I need to fix her somethin' to eat," Violet said, jaw trembling in defiance.

Groton sighed. "No problem. You can use the kitchen. But the little girl stays in the bedroom."

As Lord Buckley watched his family leave, he glanced at Orient and nodded his thanks. However, Orient knew their freedom was merely cosmetic. All they had gained was a little privacy, and basic comfort. If negotiations broke down, their position would be quite precarious.

"Tell me, Doctor, how come it's so important to you to know why we want to hit St. George?"

"Because I'm not a traitor. Or a drug dealer."

"I thought you said you know nothing about drugs."

"I got the idea from you, Mr. Groton. And if this is a hijack scheme, I want no part of it."

Groton studied Orient for a long moment. "Okay, here it is. We have reason to believe St. George is about to auction off a sizable amount of drugs. He's invited some sort of international cartel to his voodoo ceremony to consummate the deal. There's also an important local political candidate involved." He paused to light a cigarette. "Problem is, the CIA is protecting St. George. So anything I do through official channels winds up getting undone."

"You're saying Westlake has a piece of the drugs?"

"Not necessarily. But he's certainly willing to keep us from upsetting St. George's gravy train."

"So you threw in with the Cubans."

Groton gave him a sly smile. "They're the only ones on this island willing to take on St. George and his political cohorts. They see it as a blow against the CIA."

"What about the drugs?"

"They've already agreed to let us take the drugs as evidence."

"Suppose Ramon changes his mind?"

Groton chuckled. "It has occurred to me."

"So that's why you came here tonight. You thought we were part of the plan."

"Exactly. We figured you and Cool Blue were cutting a deal. It's still a possibility."

"Cool Blue helped us heal the little girl."

Groton looked surprised. "That's a switch. I thought she handles his hex work."

"Only under duress. St. George keeps her mother hostage."

"Where?"

"Will you help me do it?"

"Do what, Doctor?"

"Free Cool Blue's mother," Orient said carefully. "Without her, he can't keep his hold on the island."

Groton exhaled a contemplative cloud of smoke. "How do you know all this?"

"Cool Blue gave me an exact layout of the place where her mother is being held."

Groton took another puff. "You know this could very well be a trap?"

Orient smiled. "It has occurred to me."

"Okay, Doc." The agent sighed. "Let's hear your goddamned plan."

Chapter 31

ALTHOUGH TIRED AND HUNGRY, LORD BUCKLEY felt grateful for the way things had turned around. Ginny had been healed, and the Cubans transformed from enemies to allies. All due to the doctor man.

The man has got guts, Lord Buckley reflected as the car headed down to the sea. He wouldn't easily forget the way Orient had stepped between him and Ramon. The act saved him from being beaten in front of his family. Now he and Ramon were fellow soldiers on a mission.

Ramon's bulk seemed to spread all over the front seat, leaving little room for Orient. Lord Buckley sat in the back between Groton and the man with the rifle, whom they called Pago.

Of course, Lord Buckley had his doubts about the operation. He didn't trust the Cubans, and despite Cool Blue's help in curing his daughter, he had no use for anyone connected to Lucien St. George. He determined to keep a watchful eye on the doctor man.

Trying to be unobtrusive, Ramon drove slowly, taking an off road that led to a secluded section of beach west of Ocho Rios. The location was well known to Lord Buckley.

It was where he had concealed his powerboat. Now he would have to find another spot to hide Missy, Lord Buckley thought glumly. If he and the boat managed to survive the night.

When they reached their destination, Orient looked back at Groton. "Remember, we agreed. No shooting."

"Only in self-defense," the agent reminded him. "This is a high-risk, highly impulsive operation, Doc. And we still don't know exactly how we're going to pull it off."

Groton's words had an indisputable logic. "First we sweep the area," Orient ventured. "I trust you have walkie-talkies. Three of us check out the house while the other two wait in the boat."

"Which three?"

"You, me, and Lord Buckley."

"I thought so. Then what?"

"If everything appears as advertised, the same three move in, handcuff the guards, and liberate the woman. They won't be expecting anything like this."

"Okay, I'm convinced. Let's move out."

"What about the weapons?"

"I won't fire unless it's an emergency. But I don't go in without my weapon. Agreed?"

"All right."

Orient didn't look happy, but Lord Buckley felt a great sense of relief. He had left his own .45 back at the car. Still, for the next leg of their journey he'd be in charge as boat captain, which, under the circumstances, was a titular position. He enlisted Pago's help in pulling the tarp off the powerboat, then Ramon helped them push the vessel into the sea.

The man was strong, Lord Buckley noted as he guided the passenger-heavy craft through the shallow waters. Ramon had practically lifted the stern by himself. The boatman had never considered himself a lightweight, but he wondered if he could take the huge Cuban in hand-to-hand combat. No doubt the best way was to coldcock the bastard.

Out at sea, with a deck under his feet, Lord Buckley felt confident he could handle anything. As he steered the boat in a lazy course along the shoreline, he suddenly remembered the flare gun. It was clamped to the underside of the instrument board.

The sky was murky and the fine haze coming off the flat water obscured visibility, but Lord Buckley knew the waters well. Cool Blue's mother was being held hostage on the grounds of the Olympia Club.

They chugged slowly past the blazing crescent of hotels lighting the bay of Ocho Rios, then headed out into deeper water. Lord Buckley could see the bobbing lanterns of fishing boats strung along the horizon as they cruised toward Goldenhead.

As they neared their objective, a secluded cove between Galina Point and Port Maria, Lord Buckley slowed the boat and turned to Orient. "You know, this section be bugged with all kinds of alarms."

"We figured we might try going along the shoreline until we get to the house."

"Can't do it," the boatman said flatly. "Comin' up to the house is sheer cliff."

Groton pushed Orient aside. "You know the place?"

"I seen it once or twice from the water."

"What do you suggest?" Orient asked calmly.

The boatman took his time, just to irritate Groton. "The water's shallow 'round there. Maybe we can hide the boat nearby and walk to the place.'

Groton seemed incredulous. "Wade through this water?"

Lord Buckley throttled the engine down. "Don't worry, I show you the way."

He guided the boat close to shore and maneuvered it

beneath an overhanging tree that offered partial concealment.

Draping a long coil of rope over one shoulder, he threw
his leg over the rail. "All ashore who's goin' ashore."

As Lord Buckley swung himself over the side, he heard
Groton mutter some last-minute instructions in Spanish.
The waist-high water felt warm and oily on his legs. He
quietly edged his way along the rocky shoreline, followed
closely by Orient. Groton brought up the rear, holding his
walkie-talkie in one hand and his automatic in the other.

They continued to wade for about two hundred meters
until they reached a narrow gorge that slashed the sheer
cliff.

"What's this?" Groton hissed. "We can't climb . . ."

Lord Buckley hefted the coil of rope. "I'm climbin'—
you're waitin'." He wedged his bulky frame into the narrow crack in the rock face and started working his way
up. He made swift progress, pausing every so often at one
of the many alcoves along the way. When he reached the
summit of the low cliff, he carefully scanned the area.

Fortunately, there was a tree growing near the edge. He
secured one end of the rope around the trunk and dropped
the other end into the gorge. A moment later it tightened
and someone began climbing up.

Groton arrived first. He tapped Lord Buckley on the
shoulder and pointed toward the house. "Let's go."

The boatman glared at him. "I'll be waitin' for my
friend."

"Well, of course," Groton snorted, as if that was what
he'd meant.

Orient clambered onto the top of the cliff and looked at
them. "What's the matter?'

"Nothin'," Lord Buckley grunted. "Let's check the
equipment."

After a quick test of the two walkie-talkies, Lord Buckley led them to a small, isolated house a few hundred

meters away. The cliff afforded sparse cover, so Lord Buckley sent Orient first, then held Groton for a minute before letting him follow.

Situated on a rocky clearing overlooking the sea, the house was well protected against intruders. It could only be approached from a dirt road, unless one took the route up the gorge. The house's wooden shutters formed a cross when they were closed. Thin streaks of light filtered through the cracks, but the area was dead quiet.

Orient turned and motioned Lord Buckley to keep down. Then he crept along the side of the house and paused beneath the window. He remained there listening for a minute before moving back to rejoin the boatman.

"We've got to draw them out," he said tersely.

Lord Buckley shook his head. "No tellin' how many for sure. Or what they're holdin'."

In the dim light Orient's green eyes shone with intensity. The sharp angles of his face gave his expression the shadowy detachment of a stalking cat.

"Let's build a bonfire," he suggested. He began gathering dried twigs and leaves, scraps of paper, anything that would burn. Lord Buckley also went to work, and in a few minutes they had collected a sizable amount of debris, which they piled beneath the side window.

Orient got on the walkie-talkie and muttered some hasty instructions. When Groton was briefed, Lord Buckley crept to the corner of the house. He saw the flash of Orient's match and watched him move swiftly toward him in the mounting light of the flames. They stationed themselves on either side of the door and waited.

Someone shouted inside the house. Long moments later the door burst open. A man in khaki shorts carrying a bucket bolted onto the porch, straight into Lord Buckley's forearm. The short chop caught the man's throat, and he dropped in his tracks. Lord Buckley caught him before he hit the floor and lowered him quietly. For a few seconds it was silent. Then they heard a muffled sobbing inside the house.

Groton suddenly appeared from around the corner, brandishing his automatic. Orient held up a warning hand, but the agent brushed past him and stepped inside. Lord Buckley grabbed the water bucket and followed. Seated in the center of the room was an older woman with close-cropped gray hair and vibrant blue eyes. When Groton went inside, she held up her hands as if to ward off a blow. "No," she said weakly. "Stop!"

"Are you Ezili's mother?" Orient asked. The bonfire continued to smolder, so the boatman moved to the kitchen to refill the bucket. But as he turned on the faucet, a man appeared from behind the refrigerator. The noise of running water partially muffled the metallic snap as he cocked his Uzi. Neither Groton nor Orient saw him until it was too late.

Chapter 32

A STACCATO BURST OF GUNFIRE CUT ORIENT OFF in mid-sentence. He jerked his head back and saw a slender young man pointing an automatic weapon through the cloud of dust and shattered plaster still falling from the ceiling.

"Stand very still," the man warned. "I pop the first fool that moves. You—drop the gun."

Orient saw Groton tense, then relax, letting the .45 slip out of his hand. The man jabbed the Uzi at him. "Over with the others."

Orient realized that whatever had to be done should be done immediately, before the man on the porch came to. He glanced around the room and spotted a table lamp off to the side. He drew a long, slow line of air through his nostrils, inhaling deeply, then forced it out in a tightly controlled exhale. He took another breath and focused on the lamp, senses dowsing for its magnetic pulse. Slowly the lamp wobbled, tipped over, and toppled to the floor.

At the sound of the crash, the man swung his Uzi around and Orient leaped. He grabbed the man's arms and held on tight, wrestling him to the floor. Lord Buckley rushed in and wrenched the Uzi from the man's hand.

"Get the one outside," Orient yelled.

The man on the floor launched himself at Orient only to collide with Lord Buckley's knee. His head snapped back and his nose became a bright splotch of red.

"Check the rest of the place," Groton barked, dragging the other man inside.

"Are there any others?" Orient asked Ezili's mother, who had retreated to the far corner of the room.

She shook her head. "Who are you?"

"Friends of your daughter."

"We'd best move out," Groton muttered. "Those shots will draw heat."

Orient beckoned to the woman. "Come. You'll be safe with us."

She hesitated, then took his extended hand. Lord Buckley and Groton stayed behind long enough to bind and gag the guards, then caught up with them. The going went slowly with the woman, but their route was direct. Within minutes they were back at the cliff. Ezili's mother looked at Orient questioningly when she saw Lord Buckley testing the rope.

"Now, ma'am, you get on me piggyback and hold on tight, understand?" Lord Buckley instructed. "Don't you worry about anything else."

Although slightly overweight, Ezili's mother appeared to share her daughter's grace. She clambered up on Lord Buckley's broad back and wrapped her arms around his neck.

"Am I too heavy?" she asked timidly.

Lord Buckley grinned. "Light as a feather, ma'am."

Gingerly he lowered himself over the edge and made his way down to the shallow water far below. When the rope went slack, Orient started down, followed by Groton.

The quartet waded back to the boat, where Ramon and Pago stood waiting, their weapons poised.

"*Qué pasa?*" Pago asked hoarsely. "We heard shots."

"No problem," Lord Buckley grunted, lifting Ezili's mother into the boat. He went over to the cockpit and started the motor as Orient and Groton climbed aboard. Elizi's mother shrank back when she saw Ramon's menacing bulk looming over her.

"Now you tell us about St. George, eh?" the big man snarled, baring his gold fangs.

"Call him off, goddammit!" Orient yelled, glaring at Groton.

The agent seemed unconcerned. "Don't know if I can, old sport. We'll discuss it when we get back to your place."

Without warning Lord Buckley pivoted and whacked Ramon's shaven skull with the butt of a large handgun. The big man toppled like a felled tree. Pago started to swing his rifle, then realized the boatman's flare gun was pointed directly at his head.

"Kindly taken Groton's gun, Doc," Lord Buckley directed. "And you, throw the rifle in the *aqua*. Now!"

With an expression of profound regret Pago tossed the rifle over the side. Lord Buckley bent to retrieve Ramon's magnum, then gestured to Pago and Groton. "Get him off this boat."

The two men hauled Ramon's unwieldy bulk to the rail, then carefully rolled him over the side. He hit the water with a loud splash.

"Now you two better make sure he don't drown."

"You can't leave us here," Groton rasped.

"You be okay," Lord Buckley assured him. "Just keep swimmin' west. Better go now. I think your friend is drownin'."

Hurriedly Pago swung over the rail into the water.

Groton took his time, fixing Lord Buckley with an intim-
idating stare.

"I'm going to make it a point to look you up."

"You really want folks to know you been workin' with
the Cubans?" the boatman drawled, moving closer. "Now
take a swim and think it over."

Reluctantly Groton dropped into the water and began
helping Pago guide Ramon's staggering form to shore.
Lord Buckley moved back to the wheel and hit the throttle,
easing the vessel out to sea where he could open her up.

Ezili's mother was named Marie, and she and Violet
became friends immediately. However, Orient was still
deeply concerned for their safety. His fears were shared
by Lord Buckley, who announced his intention of taking
his family to a safe house.

"I got a sweet little place set up for emergencies. They
can live there a while till this mess blows over," he told
Orient. "You got any special plan?"

"I thought I'd wait here until Rastadamus shows up."

The boatman gave Orient a hard look. "Why you so
sure he's comin'?"

"I called him."

"How? The walkie-talkie?"

"Something like that." Orient decided to change the
subject. "Before you go anywhere, better check the car."

"My car, or theirs?"

"Yours. Groton and Ramon got here too quickly after
the crossroads. Chances are they planted a homing device
while you were following me."

"Damn. I think you got somethin' there, Doc. 'Scuse
me while I check."

He returned within ten minutes, holding a metal cube
the size of a matchbox. "It was under the boot," he said
indignantly. "Stuck it there with magnets."

Orient's reply was interrupted by the sound of a familiar voice.

"Right now things are clear as a bell. In a little while better run like hell." Kid Kismet strode into the house and sat down on a nearby couch. "I've been walkin' all night. Helpin' the master in this fight."

A few moments later Rastadamus came into the house.

"You've all done splendid work tonight," he said softly. "But you are still in grave danger here." His pale pink eyes fixed on Orient. "Where is the woman?"

"She's with Violet."

The old man nodded. "I wish to see her, please."

"Come with me, Father," Lord Buckley said.

Orient followed them to the kitchen and was mildly surprised to see the master embrace Ezili's mother.

"Dear, dear Marie," he murmured. "It's been so many years."

"Thank God," she said breathlessly. "I didn't dare believe I was truly safe until now."

"I'm going to take you away with me for a while. We'll find a way to get word to Ezili," he added, glancing at Orient. The old man smiled, radiating an almost tangible aura of strength. "You will be completely safe with us," he assured her. "However, we must leave this house immediately. I sense a storm brewing."

Lord Buckley looked at his wife. "You ready, hon?"

"Everything's packed," she said calmly. "I'll get Ginny."

As Lord Buckley went along to help, Rastadamus asked Ezili's mother, "Are you able to walk?"

"Why, yes, I'm fine. Why?"

"My apprentice, Kid Kismet, will guide you to my sanctuary. I'll follow presently. We need to discuss some matters in private."

Marie took Orient's hand. "I never had a chance to

thank you. You've done so much for me. And I don't even know your name."

"It's Owen. But I don't deserve all the thanks. Your daughter helped arrange this."

She looked at Rastadamus. "Will Ezili be waiting at your sanctuary?"

"I'm sorry. No."

A shadow fell across her face like a scythe.

"Then she's still with St. George."

"When she knows you're free, she'll make her break," Orient told her.

"Yes," Marie said, but she didn't sound convinced. She reached up and kissed him on the cheek. "Thanks for my life, Doctor."

"Go now," Rastadamus prodded gently.

Kid Kismet was waiting at the door to lead her to the master's mountain retreat. Lord Buckley came into the room carrying two large suitcases.

"You ready, Doc?"

Rastadamus shook his head. "The doctor is not going to your home tonight."

Both Orient and Lord Buckley looked at him in surprise.

"Can Violet drive your car?" he asked.

"Sure, why?"

"Please have her drive to your hideaway alone. You must accompany the doctor back to his hotel."

"Guess I could dump the car we borrowed from Groton back in Ocho Rios," Lord Buckley speculated. "But the doctor man's a sittin' duck back there at the hotel."

Although Orient said nothing, he definitely agreed with the boatman.

Rastadamus lifted his hand. "If you will, my son, please see to your family while we confer."

Orient regarded the snow-haired patriarch with a mixture of reluctance and curiosity. He had a feeling Rastadamus was about to ask him to risk his life—and he didn't feel lucky.

"Tonight you called me here," Rastadamus began. "And it was wise." He referred to the telepathic message Orient had sent. After dumping Groton and his cronies, Orient had decided he needed direction. He had no idea his direction led straight into the lion's mouth.

"You now have faith in our ability to sustain contact," Rastadamus went on. "So it is that you must muster all your faith—all the strength of your soul—for this test."

"Test?"

"In forty-eight hours, on the midnight of the new moon, St. George will perform his blood rite to Baron Samedi and his *Corps Cadavres*—the walking dead."

A cold snake of fear began winding around Orient's belly.

"St. George needs Ezili for this rite, and only you can stop him," Rastadamus was saying. "Now that you have freed Marie, St. George will come to you. Unless you meet him, your chance will have gone."

Rastadamus paused and smiled at Orient. "It's not only Ezili, or her mother. If St. George isn't stopped, none of us on this tiny island will be safe again. When the voodoo gods were unleashed on Haiti, there was no turning them back. So it will be here. We must fight, even if it means . . ."

His smile faded and he looked away, but the unspoken word rang in Orient's brain like a church bell. *Death*.

Lord Buckley kept to the back trails as much as possible, but he had to use the main road when they neared Ocho Rios. The night was waning and dawn tinted the edge of the sky. Orient suddenly realized he was exhausted. An endless parade of wounded thoughts marched through his brain, keeping ragged time to the throbbing ache in his bones.

Lord Buckley also seemed tired and drove in trancelike silence for most of the trek down from the mountains. When they neared the main road he became more alert, and Orient noticed him fingering the butt of a weapon stashed beneath the dashboard.

"Expecting trouble?" he asked casually.

"Never know. Remember, we drivin' a stolen car. Most likely belongs to Groton."

"You wouldn't shoot a policeman."

"Not worried about cops," Lord Buckley muttered. "Could be the Cubans put a bounty on this car. That puts twenty, thirty people on our case right away. I just want to ditch it and split."

"Where do you plan to drop it off?"

A quick grin flashed across the boatman's grim expression. "So happens I got an emergency vehicle parked over by Ocho Rios."

"You seem to have things stashed all over the island."

"Pays to be ready."

Lord Buckley turned into a deserted road leading to a secluded stretch of beach curtained off from view by a double row of trees. He parked the car and walked over to a large willow tree. In the half-light of the emerging dawn Orient saw the boatman reach inside a mass of vegetation growing beside the tree. As he watched, Lord Buckley removed a section of camouflage-patterned tarpaulin from the leafy mass. A moment later he made out the aerodynamic shape of a motorcycle being wheeled out of concealment.

Orient left the car and climbed aboard the motorcycle. For those precious fifteen or twenty minutes as they glided down the silent highway with the salt wind washing their weary faces, Orient felt more alive than he had in years. Even as each passing mile brought him closer to his promised death.

He half expected it to occur on their arrival at the Sans

Souci. But when they rolled into the parking lot, there were no assassins lying in wait.

"Anything you need later on?" Lord Buckley asked.

Orient shrugged. "Let's both take the day off."

"Fine with me. Let's hope our friends do the same. Take care, doctor man."

Orient was pleasantly surprised to find a clerk on duty at the front desk despite the early hour. The clerk gave him two phone messages along with his key. The names on the messages shattered his tired calm. One call had come from a Mr. Westlake. The other from a Mr. St. George.

His aching brain throbbed with possibilities as he avoided the scenic elevator and shuffled up the white stone stairway to his suite.

He unlocked the door carefully, making sure the room was empty before going inside. As an added precaution, he left the door open while he checked the other rooms. Finally he locked the door, wedged a chair under the knob, and went directly into the bedroom. He peeled off his clothes and was about to lower the blinds when he glimpsed a dark shape perched on a deck chair.

Staring at him through the glass with bright, angry eyes was a large black bird. The creature suddenly spread its wings and flew off, but as Orient eased his pain-stiffened body onto the bed, he knew his time was at hand.

Chapter 33

THE LATE MORNING SUN SPILLED THROUGH THE cracks in the blinds, washing away to cold dread of night. He had been dreaming, but couldn't recall the images. All that remained was a bitter taste in his brain.

Without pausing to brush his teeth, Orient put on his bathing trunks and headed directly for the beach. For the next half hour he swam in the clear, salt-scented water, feeling at one with the sea and sky. From there he went back to his room and ordered breakfast. It arrived shortly after he finished his shower. Not until he settled down on the terrace with a plate of buckwheat pancakes and a pot of Blue Mountain coffee did he begin to assess his position.

Even at best it was highly untenable. If St. George didn't get him, the Cubans would. Not to mention Westlake or old Groton. But, of course, Rastadamus had already informed him he would die, he reminded himself grimly. What difference who got the credit?

Feeling refreshed after his second coffee, Orient decided to take a stroll. But as soon as he stepped outside the lobby, he saw Lord Buckley leaning against a black Toyota, reading the *Daily Gleaner*.

"Says here somebody stole a U.S. Government vehicle," he announced as Orient approached.

"I didn't expect to see you today."

"Thought I'd make sure the Cubans didn't have you staked out."

Orient realized he'd have to try another tack. "Look, the whole point of my staying here is to let St. George contact me. If he smells a trap he might pass me by."

Lord Buckley squinted skyward. "St. George ain't afraid of no trap. Not 'round this county. It's you and me in the damn trap. Don't you worry, he soon come."

"There is a job that needs doing."

"Name it, then."

"Someone's got to leave a message for Ezili at the crossroads. She still doesn't know her mother is safe."

"I take care of it, if you do me a favor."

"Name it."

"Don't go walkin' around Ocho. Too many people after your ass."

A sense of solitude followed Orient through the afternoon. He treated himself to a leisurely lunch, then strolled about the hotel's spacious grounds. Among the more unusual amenities found at the Sans Souci were perfectly manicured croquet lawns and a grotto that housed a giant tortoise. There was also an oversized chessboard with huge pieces adjoining a thatched gazebo called the meditation hut.

Orient lingered in the meditation hut, smoking a hand-wrapped cigarette as he gazed at the flat green sea. He went into a slow breathing pattern designed to cleanse the mind of negative residue. But despite his efforts, an intuition of impending danger nagged at his awareness. Trying to shake it off, he decided to take a late swim.

The sea seemed colder than usual. The chill seeped into his marrow, and as he waded back to shore, a bank of clouds blocked the sun, deepening the cold. Shivering, he hurriedly put on his shirt and wrapped the towel around his neck, but the lingering chill stiffened his limbs. To warm them he broke into a trot, jogging slowly along the deserted beach.

As he neared the pool area, a small boy with a water pistol playfully squirted him. He waved and kept running. By the time he reached the stairs, the warmth was spreading through his bloodstream, and he headed for the outdoor bar.

One of the unique features of the hotel was the giant chessboard with human-sized pieces which dominated the area near the bar. As Orient passed, he noticed a game was in progress. He paused to examine the position.

From what he could determine, the white king was about to be checkmated by a combination of the black bishop and queen. But while contemplating the dilemma, he detected an escape hatch.

"Black bishop mates in three moves."

The resonant voice drew his attention. When Orient looked up, his blood turned to ice. Seated in the shade of a tree, his lean frame partially obscured by the black king, was Lucien St. George.

Orient tried to regain his composure. "There is an alternative," he noted calmly.

"Oh?"

"White knight takes black queen."

"You lose both the knight and the white queen."

"Yes. But the king is safe."

St. George regarded him with a pensive smiled. "Free perhaps, but far from safe."

Senses blaring like fire alarms, Orient glanced over his shoulder.

"Don't worry, Doctor, we're quite alone. The better to discuss our position."

"It is your game, after all."

A wry smile crossed St. George's impassive features. "You have one of my most valuable pieces."

"I'm afraid you'll have to move on without it."

"Then you're willing to sacrifice your queen?"

The question floated in the balmy quiet.

"Your blue queen," St. George prodded.

"I don't need the hint," Orient said evenly. "I understand why you're here."

"Actually, I've come to extend an invitation. To join us tomorrow night at our little ceremony."

"I'll consider it."

"I'm delighted. Well, then, shall we discuss Ezili?"

"What about her?"

St. George stood up slowly. He was taller than Orient by at least three inches, and his reedy frame and elongated features suggested an Egyptian carving.

"Ezili is the singer, I am the song." His bright black eyes fixed Orient with a cobralike stare. "Do you know anything of the *Corps Cadavres*—the living dead?"

"I've heard of zombis," Orient said softly. "I've even seen one."

St. George's mouth stretched into a mirthless laugh. "You are most refreshing, Doctor. But seriously, the most intriguing aspect of the so-called zombi is his—or her— infinite capacity for obedience to their master. In death the subject is stripped of personality—and when reborn, is imprinted with the will of the master."

"You, I take it, are the master."

"Yes, Dr. Orient. And I'll let you in on a little secret. In a short time you will be a zombi."

The faint strains of a reggae tune filtered through the sunset quiet as Orient struggled to comprehend. Then the cold certainty slammed his belly. "But how . . . ?"

"The little boy, Doctor. Who shot you with his water pistol. The toxin was actually absorbed through your skin. In less than an hour you will be clinically dead. But take heart, I do have an antidote."

Orient fought to maintain his calm. "What do you propose?"

"Propose?" Again St. George's features folded into an empty laugh. "Listen to me good, Doctor. In a short time you'll feel a numbness stealing up your legs. By the time it reaches your groin, you'll be eager to do anything I ask."

For a panicked instant Orient considered flight, then realized there was no place to run to. Or reason. This was exactly where he had to be. He gathered his resources and prayed for strength.

Suddenly he felt a tingling at the back of his knee, like an insect bite. But when he scratched he discovered there was no sensation. Both his knees were numb, and the tingling was creeping higher.

"Well, Doctor, I see it has commenced."

St. George's voice seemed to be coming from a room inside Orient's mind. "You have two choices." he was saying. "You can go with me now and learn my secrets— or you can stay here and die alone."

Orient felt perspiration sliding down his back. He blinked, trying to clear his blurred vision.

"Go where . . . ?"

St. George took his arm. "To your new home."

Even with St. George's help it took a long time to walk to the lobby. Orient became aware of another man when they went outside. The man half lifted him into the cool, dark interior of a car. Orient sank back against the leather cushions, heart thumping erratically. He was aware of the car moving, but with each passing second the darkness wrapped itself tighter around him. Soon the only part of him left open was the room that housed St. George's voice.

It came to him across a long corridor, hollow and compelling. Orient clung to the voice, knowing it was his sole link through the smothering darkness.

"Soon, Doctor," the voice promised. "Soon you'll be reunited with your love."

Chapter 34

THERE WERE LEVELS TO THE DARKNESS.

First was the fear. Foul and relentless. Swarming everywhere. Then the memory loss, which obliterated all time—or reason—and reduced him to nothing more than a rudderless wreck drifting on a vast, underground sea. And finally, the oozing slowness of thought.

The one clear note in the thick silence was St. George's voice.

"Don't despair, Doctor. I'm going to make you better in a little while."

Orient had the impression he was floating out of the darkness to a blazing red sky. By the time he realized he had been lifted out of the car, the darkness had closed over him again.

A sharp, pungent scent filled his brain like light, awakening dormant senses and forgotten thoughts. He blinked away the haze obscuring his vision. The scent stuffed his nostrils and he breathed deep, reveling in its strength.

"There now, Doctor. Isn't that better?"

St. George's voice loomed inside his skull. He blinked again and the gaunt features swam into focus.

"Please to see me again?"

It was a rhetorical question. Orient could not speak, nor could he move his limbs.

"Welcome to my temple," St. George continued. "This is my sanctum. And since you are a most learned scientist, I'm going to share a few professional secrets."

Orient's mind rolled over. Realizing this was probably his last opportunity to establish telepathic contact with Rastadamus, he attempted a breathing pattern.

"For centuries," St. George was saying, "the powers of the zombification toxin were limited to mere questions of life and death. Overlooked was the toxin's effect on the brain."

It was still difficult to breathe. Orient tried to relax and begin again.

"The toxin's main ingredient is the ovaries of the puffer fish. It's better known to Japanese gourmands as fugu. At least fifty of them a year fail to survive their expensive dinners. The puffer's ovaries are violently lethal."

Orient tried to focus, his breathing slow and shallow. Painfully his senses labored to pry open the psychic energy buried inside him.

"Other ingredients include the datura root, as well as its flowers. It's my contention that its hallucinogenic properties endow the toxin with its peculiar side effects." St. George peered at him. "Are you listening, Doctor?"

The mocking question triggered an idea. Obviously St. George enjoyed flaunting his advantage. Perhaps if he pretended to lose consciousness, Orient reasoned, the priest would offer another jolt of his special smelling salts. He closed his eyes.

It worked. St. George paused, and a few seconds later the pungent scent exploded in Orient's nostrils.

This time he was prepared. The moment the scent vitalized his sluggish functions, Orient went into an extended breathing pattern that pumped extra oxygen into his brain. For a precious instant his senses converged and broke free.

"Yes, breathe deep," St. George urged. "We are about to welcome some distinguished visitors. They've come especially to see you."

Orient's compressed awareness swung into orbit, reaching for a familiar gravity.

"Do you know anything about the science of aromatics, Doctor?" St. George passed a tiny blue bottle in front of Orient's face. "The ancient Egyptians actually refined aromatics to a high science. They could influence everything from sex to sickness by using special scents. Anytime I wish to call you back from the dead, all I need do is pass this bottle under your nose."

As St. George illustrated his point, the scent wafted through Orient's skull.

Orient flexed his will and suddenly connected. He felt a powerful rush of sublime energy pour into his parched cells when his mind merged with Rastadamus.

"Now that your mind is clear, Doctor, I'd like you to lift your head."

Despite his strong desire to defy St. George, and despite the renewed strength supplied by his link to the master, Orient found himself compelled to obey.

Numbly, his body responded to the command. Without any sense of effort—or control—his head lifted up, as if severed from his body.

"There's someone who wants to see you," St. George murmured, his gaunt features tight with anticipation.

Orient clung to his precarious link with Rastadamus, like some dazed rock climber dangling over the abyss. At the same time the strings of his consciousness were being manipulated by St. George.

"Ready, my dear?"

St. George had moved just outside of Orient's vision. When he returned into view, he had a companion. In his numbed state it took Orient a few moments to recognize the female standing just behind the priest. The silver-blond hair registered before his damaged memory could identify her face. It was Tristan, staring at him with a mixture of fascination and apprehension.

"Don't be afraid, he's quite harmless," St. George said.

"Is he . . . ?"

"Dead? Not quite. However, by the time my guests examine him, he will be clinically deceased—a living corpse."

Tristan gave a small shudder. "How long will he stay . . . that way?"

"Until he is no longer useful. Because of Orient, I was forced to dispose of your husband after the incident at the cemetery. I spent a great deal of time programming Shandy to be the perfect assassin. Now Orient will take his place. Fitting, don't you think?"

St. George bent closer. "You see, Doctor, we are about to embark on a global crusade. Tonight I will market one of the most lethal—and expensive—weapons on earth. A poison that does much more than merely kill. A drug that will completely enslave the strongest of men.

"Since the dawn of time the real war has been for control of men's minds. The Nazis, the Soviets, the Chinese, the CIA—all conducted extensive experimentation in mind control. And all still share an intense interest in the subject. With my zombification toxin, and the help of a few powerful political allies, I'll soon dominate the Caribbean." He put an arm around Tristan. "And your true love will be my queen. She is the one who helped me focus my powers, dear Doctor. She encouraged me to look beyond this tiny island. After all, the Obeah gods are equally at home in Rio, or Paris, or even Washington.

"In a short while envoys from seven major governments will arrive to examine your body. After they are convinced

you are dead, they will observe as you are taken outside—
and buried.''

The words crashed through Orient's awareness like
blocks of ice.

''The final proof will come when you are resurrected.
In twenty-four hours, at the apex of my ritual to honor
Baron Samedi—your casket will be dug up and you will
walk. On my command you will pick up a sword and
perform a sacrifice to Baka, Loa of hell.''

At first Orient's frozen thoughts failed to comprehend.

Then St. George made it horribly clear.

''Turn your head left, Doctor.''

Without hesitation, Orient's head swiveled, as if it were
an extension of St. George's will.

There was someone stretched out on a nearby table. A
woman with red-streaked hair lay as still as death.

''Tomorrow night,'' St. George promised, ''you will
behead my fallen priestess, Ezili.''

The darkness was squeezing in again. And the fear.

Orient could feel his link to Rastadamus dissolving like
cotton candy. The one thing that remained strong and clear
was St. George's voice inside his skull.

Orient's sluggish brain could respond only to primitive
reflex, while brute terror continued to pound at his awareness. With each passing second the darkness became heav-
ier, settling over him like concrete. Then time stopped.

''Are they ready?''

Vaguely Orient sensed he was floating. Like a dirigible
that had slipped its moorings, his body seemed to be
lifting. It moved very slowly at first, then gradually accelerated as if sailing on a wind current.

His consciousness spiraled upward toward a tiny glimmer of light. As he neared the glimmer, it became a
window. He drifted through without effort into a swirling
sea of color. Bit by bit, the pattern emerged, until he

realized he was hovering high above a large white room, looking down at his own body.

An ornate altar, decorated with red flowers, dominated one corner of the room. In the other corner was an open casket.

There were people in the room as well. He recognized St. George's skeletal figure, but the rest were unfamiliar. However, they appeared to be fascinated with his body, which lay on a long white table. He was naked except for a sheet over his hips, and from every appearance, quite dead.

An Asiatic gentleman in a black suit was puncturing his skin with a long gold needle while a bearded man listened for his heartbeat through a stethoscope. St. George stood back from the table, his gaunt features beaming approval, as if he were presiding over a diplomatic tea.

As Orient's consciousness cleared, he realized he was no longer afraid. The fear had been displaced by anticipation. He was eager to begin his journey to the next plane of existence.

Then slowly, as he watched them continue to probe and jab at his inert body, a profound sadness settled over him. He would never begin his journey. He was trapped between death and rebirth by St. George's demonic will. And he was powerless to resist. Every attempt he made to break through the bubble of consciousness floating above the room, to somehow contact Rastadamus, fell far short. All he could do was watch strange men haggle over his remains.

"I trust you are all satisfied his vital signs are extinct." St. George's voice shattered the silence, drumming tiny nails of fear into his brain.

"Then if some of you will assist with the preparations—to assure yourselves there is no fraud."

Despair shrouded his senses as he watched the men slide his body off the table and place it in the casket. Before the cover was put over him, St. George carefully painted the sign of Guede on his forehead, chest, and abdomen.

"Now he's ready," the priest murmured, screwing the cover shut.

As if still connected to his body by an invisible rope, Orient found himself following the coffin as they carried it outside. It was then he saw that St. George's altar room was actually located in an abandoned church. Just behind the church was a cemetery with a scattering of tombstones and one open grave.

The despair wound tighter as Orient watched the men lower his coffin into the moist earth. His fragile link to Rastadamus had been severed. He was powerless to prevent St. George from forcing him to kill Ezili.

Then he saw someone step forward, pick up a handful of dirt, and throw it on the coffin.

Although the man was dressed in a nondescript suit and hat and wore dark glasses, something about him seemed familiar. By focusing his awareness, Orient found he could come closer to the man, who was now walking away.

Then memory and recognition collided and he plummeted into a vortex of abject defeat. The man leaving the gravesite was Commander Glen Westlake.

The agent's masked expression and hurried stride were the last fragmented images Orient saw before he tumbled slowly into his grave and was swallowed up whole by the suffocating darkness.

Chapter 35

LORD BUCKLEY DIDN'T LIKE WAITING.

Too many things could go wrong. The sentry could stumble over one of the men staked around the perimeter of the churchyard. Or the dogs might hear something. The longer they remained, the greater their chances of being discovered. And of being slaughtered.

He had no illusions as to what might happen if they were captured by St. George's boys. He once had the misfortune of viewing a ravaged human carcass found at the site of their inhuman rituals.

He gripped his .45 tighter, but the weapon afforded meager comfort. There were only four of them, including Kid Kismet and Rastadamus. And he was the only one armed.

Armed with a real weapon, Lord Buckley amended. The Kid had a blowpipe, but darts wouldn't stop a pussycat, much less the pit bulls trotting at the sentry's heels.

Rastadamus had positioned Tosh, the fourth man in their party, too near the sentry. One of the damn pit bulls could pick up his scent. Fortunately, the sentry wasn't walking around much. The boatman wondered how Rastadamus intended to deal with the dogs. One guard could be taken out easily, provided he didn't have a buddy somewhere, or a special alarm system. But the dogs could do serious damage, Lord Buckley speculated unhappily. Especially since Rastadamus wouldn't allow them to be harmed in any way. However, despite his reservations, he did trust Rastadamus to run the operation safely. Wishing he could light a cigarette, he settled back on his perch in the crook of a tree and waited.

Suddenly his confidence in the master's tactical skills evaporated. Stunned, he watched Tosh rise up and creep closer to the sentry. His heart began to race when he saw the guard cock his head as if listening. He slipped the safety on his .45 and kept the guard in his sights.

The dogs had also been alerted. They paced nervously, sniffing the night air. Lord Buckley saw something else that caused his finger to tighten around the trigger. The sentry had donned a set of goggles, probably night-vision lenses.

At that moment the scene took on a surreal, nightmarish cast. The guard's space goggles and black jumpsuit formed a ghostly counterpoint to the crooked tombstones scattered about the deserted churchyard. The ominous tableau was amplified by the glowering pit bulls, straining at their leashes.

In absurd contrast was Tosh's feeble attempt to storm the gates. The dogs saw him before the guard did, and began snarling. Tosh stopped and raised his hands. The guard turned, his Uzi trained directly at him. Without warning the guard stiffened, one hand pawing at his neck. He dropped the Uzi and slowly sank to the ground.

Unfortunately for Tosh, the sentry also lost his grip on the leashes. Instantly the pit bulls sprang forward, powerful legs catapulting them toward the intruder with savage speed, their jaws yawning hungrily.

Just before the frenzied beasts reached Tosh's retreating

figure, Rastadamus emerged from the shadows, arms
raised like some bloodless apparition.

The frail, white-haired master stepped directly in front
of the charging dogs. Abruptly they drew up short and
began circling each other in confusion. Rastadamus remained completely calm, answering their whines with a
low, soothing murmur. Soon they stopped pacing and
curled up at the master's feet, watching him expectantly.

Rastadamus turned and beckoned.

Still somewhat unnerved, Lord Buckley dropped from
his perch and advanced toward the dogs, his .45 at half-
mast. Tosh gave him a toothless grin. "They gentle now,
mon."

Rastadamus put a finger to his lips, then motioned for
them to follow. The dogs padded behind him as he strode
into the churchyard.

From the corner of his eye the boatman saw a familiar
figure step out from behind a tree. Kid Kismet brandished
his blowpipe. "The master mixed the sleeper—my dart
put down the keeper," he whispered proudly.

Rastadamus moved purposefully among the gravestones
and half-buried sepulchers, looking for something. He
paused at what appeared to be a freshly covered grave.

"Here," he rasped. "Here is where we dig."

Tosh produced a small military spade, generally used
for digging foxholes, and began removing the loose top-
soil. Lord Buckley scoured the area and found a discarded
shovel. Working together, they soon uncovered a black
wood coffin at the bottom of the shallow grave.

"Open it quickly," Rastadamus ordered.

Tosh used his spade to pry the top off. But Lord Buckley
was not prepared for what he saw when they pulled off the
cover.

The doctor man lay inside, his skin parched and yellowed like old newspaper. Orient's aristocratic features
sagged, as if they had deflated without the luminous in-

tensity of his will. Lacking the fire of his personality, the flesh that remained was nothing more than a hollow construction of sticks and strings. Seeing him there, shriveled and still, the boatman felt his eyes flood with tears.

"Move aside," Rastadamus muttered, clambering into the grave. "Get up top and keep watch."

Lord Buckley crouched at the graveside, while Tosh and the Kid took up positions near the gate.

The master had his *macoot* bag open beside him. Lord Buckley knew the traditional shoulder pouch of herbs and roots was an essential weapon in the occult war against St. George. As he watched, Rastadamus bent over Orient's corpse, passing a small blue bottle under his nose.

Lord Buckley saw him pour liquid into Orient's mouth. Then the boatman heard a low, chanting sound. The chanting went on as he restlessly paced the edge of the grave. Oddly, the dogs lay quietly nearby, peering down at the white-haired master.

When Rastadamus stopped chanting, he touched the side of Orient's neck. Then he passed the blue bottle under his nose again. The master continued to work over Orient's corpse for long minutes. Finally he beckoned Lord Buckley to join him.

"We're too late. Neither my herbs nor my prayers can bring a soul back from the dead," Rastadamus said, his voice thick with fatigue. "But at least we can make sure St. George will not use this corpse for his zombi slave."

"How, Father?"

Rastadamus stared at him, his pale pink eyes dull with loss. "We must burn the doctor man's body, and return the ashes to the sea."

Suddenly the pit bulls appeared over the lip of the grave, baring their sharp teeth and growling threateningly. At the same time Lord Buckley heard something that turned his blood to water.

Chapter 36

A LOW MOAN SNAKED ACROSS THE STILLNESS.

It grew louder, squeezing his awareness with unholy intensity until abruptly it burst, shooting up into the darkness like some noxious geyser from hell, catapulting him into the sudden glare.

He woke up screaming.

As his blurred vision slowly focused, he saw the rabid dogs glaring down at him.

"It's all right."

The melodic voice cooled his boiling terror and he closed his eyes. When he opened them again, the beasts were gone.

"Can you hear me?"

He turned his head and saw a wizened, pink-eyed albino at his side. A slow smile eased the old man's knotted expression. "Try to speak, my son."

He tried to shake some words loose from the sticky quagmire of the memory. His lips struggled to form sounds, but all that came forth was a dry, broken croak.

A pungent scent slashes his awareness, loosening fragments of thought. Then suddenly Orient remembered.

307

"Ras . . . tadamus . . ."

"Sit up," the old man said gently, wiping Orient's face with a scented cloth.

The sweet perfume seemed to disperse the flaring terror, and he took a deep breath. As his brain cleared, he became aware of the others. He recognized Lord Buckley and the Kid, but the stranger caused the fear to bubble up again.

"It's all right," Rastadamus whispered. "Tosh is our friend. He helped us find you."

Lord Buckley bent closer and helped Orient into a sitting position. His limbs were still too numb to support him, but the damp night air revived his senses.

"Thanks . . ."

"Easy now, doctor man. Soon gonna get you outta here."

"I must speak to Dr. Orient alone. Now."

The master's urgent tone penetrated even Orient's dulled perception. Curiosity tugged at his thoughts as he watched Lord Buckley, Tosh, and Kid Kismet move away from the grave. Seconds later the dogs were back, peering down at them.

"Now, then, can you remember your primary breathing pattern?" the old man asked softly.

Orient nodded.

"Then let us begin."

Patiently, the master guided him through the basic breathing technique. While it was difficult at the outset, the compressed flow of oxygen to his brain and bloodstream dissolved the paralysis clogging his muscles. He was able to move freely and felt the strength ebbing back into his limbs.

Rastadamus then moved him into the advanced patterns which concentrated the oxygen in specific sections of his brain, stimulating certain synaptic connections. From there a subtle shift of rhythm and intensity would charge the telepathic sensors.

The master stayed with him at every stage, his pale pink eyes flaming with energy. At one point he passed a small bottle under Orient's nose, and the familiar scent rushed through his being like a cleansing rainstorm, washing away the foul dregs of death.

Although still weak, Orient tried to stand.

"Not yet," Rastadamus said gently. "I have something to teach you."

"Here?"

The master smiled. "You are ready. I am ready. Let's go back to the Om pattern. Seventh degree."

Primed by their earlier exercises, Orient moved easily into the advanced telepathic pattern. Within moments his awareness lit up like a radar map. It was then that he sensed the master's great inner turmoil.

A heartbeat later, all that was overshadowed by the awesome recognition of a new level of existence. As the experience dawned across his consciousness, he glimpsed fragments: a white spider spinning a webbed cathedral; a lizard's lazy tongue snatching a crimson dragonfly; dolphins mating beneath the sea; the eye of a blackbird staring at a snowy mountain . . . Suddenly he understood more than he had ever dreamed possible to comprehend.

And it all flowed through Rastadamus.

The wizened master had become a conduit between source and shadow, music and harmonic, death and rebirth. All the master's knowledge was becoming part of him. But with the revelation came responsibility—and the price was much more than he could bear.

"No!" he said sharply. "I can't."

Rastadamus didn't answer, but his link to Orient remained unbroken. The silence widened.

"I can't do it," Orient repeated.

As he spoke, all the reasons why he would gusted over

his awareness like snow. And it made him afraid. But even when he tried to disconnect his telepathic link to Rastadamus, the truth remained frozen in his thoughts.

"Not now. Not right away."

"It must be now," Rastadamus said gently. "While body and will still hear death's quiet."

Knowing it was true, Orient dreaded what had to be done.

"I will put you in a deep sleep. When the hour comes, I will wake you. Until then I will remain with you, inside with you." He leaned closer to Orient. "This I promise."

What if you should die? Orient thought.

Rastadamus smiled. "If I should fail to wake you, St. George most certainly will."

Orient wasn't amused, but he couldn't deny the master's logic.

"All right," he rasped, heart booming in his throat. "Let's do it." He lay back, took a long breath, and prepared to be buried alive.

Lord Buckley almost quit.

He had seen the doctor man sit up and talk. Beyond any doubt, Orient had recovered. So to find him unconscious again, and to be told to reseal his casket for burial, were horrifying. Were it anyone else but Rastadamus, he definitely would not have gone through with it. As he helped Tosh screw down the cover, he kept looking at Rastadamus to make sure there was no mistake.

The master surveyed their work with serene approval.

When Lord Buckley reluctantly tossed the first shovelful of dirt into the grave, he glanced at Rastadamus. The only response he received was the hollow thump of earth striking the casket.

Chapter 37

It had been all night and all day.

Lord Buckley felt completely wrung out and hung up to dry. By noon he thought he was about to drop.

The whole endeavor was taking on the absurd aspect of a drunken civilian challenging a platoon of troopers. Counting Tosh and the Kid, they had six men. Quen and Harry had joined them sometime during the morning. But even Quen's formidable size and Harry's experience as a professional boxer were a poor match against armed guards. To be sure, some of them were packing guns, despite Rastadamus's admonition against violence. Lord Buckley still had his trusty .45 and he knew that Quen and Harry each carried a pistol. However, there were now four guards posted around the deserted churchyard, and very soon the site would be teeming with St. George's followers.

The sole saving grace was their new relationship with the pit bulls. Rastadamus made sure they all got friendly with the fierce beasts after they finished covering Orient's grave.

Fortunately, the guard Kid Kismet took out with his dart

never did realize what had happened. From his hiding place Lord Buckley saw the guard come to, yawn, look around for his weapon, and go about his business as if awakening from a catnap.

Shortly after dawn the guard had been relieved by two men in khaki uniforms carrying holstered side arms. The first guard put the dogs inside the church that now served as St. George's Hounfor. Then he drove off on a motorcycle.

About ten hours later the guard returned in a jeep driven by a man wearing a black jumpsuit. He too carried an Uzi. From the distinction in weapon and uniform, Lord Buckley could only assume this guard belonged to an elite squad within St. George's organization. Something like Hitler's SS, he noted grimly.

The four guards remained at their posts through the afternoon. Toward sunset, others began to filter into the area.

Lord Buckley burrowed deeper into his hiding place—a leafy trident of tree limbs about twenty feet above the ground—and tried to sleep. It didn't work. Despite his being awake for over thirty-six hours, the tension had him in a state of total alert. He was even automatically keeping a head count of everyone at the site. Twenty-six so far.

Apparently Quen, Harry, and the others were well concealed. He hadn't seen any of them for hours.

He took a sip of fruit juice from his canteen and munched on a slice of the carrot cake Violet had packed in his survival bag. He also carried water, binoculars, morphine, bandages, a compass, and a combat knife, as well as extra clips of ammo. Added to his gear were the night-vision goggles he'd nicked from the sleeping guard.

But as long velvety shadows curtained the crimson sky, Lord Buckley realized he wouldn't need goggles. Torches were being fired all around the churchyard. In the flickering glare he could clearly make out the faces of St. George's congregation as they entered the gates.

He recognized a number of Jamaica's elite among the growing crowd. Many prominent lawyers and politicians, a few entertainers, two or three doctors, even a minister, were among the arrivals.

An air of expectancy hovered over the gathering.

As the time neared for the ceremony to begin, he could feel the excitement mounting. The drummers had set up and began a slow, loping beat. A black goat was led inside the gates and tethered to a pulley device in front of the Hounfor.

People were still arriving for the ceremony, including a man he recognized as Westlake, the American CIA director at the Olympia Club. With Westlake were several foreign agents, as well as representatives from China, Iran, and Syria.

It occurred to Lord Buckley that the odds were heavily stacked in St. George's favor. Especially in light of the fact that Rastadamus had given them no definite plan of action. His only order had been to remain hidden until he came forth to make his challenge. As plans went, this one left much to be desired. Were it not for his deep, abiding faith in the albino healer, he would have been long gone.

The drumbeat shifted, becoming deeper and slower as a file of turbaned women entered the church that served as their temple. When they came out of the Hounfor, they were accompanied by their priest.

St. George wore a flowing scarlet shirt over tight black trousers, and a long strand of rosary beads around his neck. The large black crucifix that dangled from the beads hung upside down. In his left hand he carried a machete.

He walked slowly to the tethered goat and stood before it. Pressing the machete against his forehead, he intoned a prayer. Two of the priest's followers grasped the goat's horns. With a slow, almost languid motion, St. George lifted the machete and brought it down across the beast's neck.

As the severed head rolled at their feet, the men hoisted the goat into the air, using the pulley. One placed a large bucket under the carcass to catch the blood spewing from its raw, gaping neck.

Through it all the drums continued their loping beat, and as the goat was lifted, St. George rocked back and forth. His little dance was imitated by some others who gathered around the twitching carcass. One of the women lifted the gore-matted head and carried it over to the gate. Laughing, she impaled the goat's head on a sharp iron post at the entrance. Body swaying, she moved back to rejoin the others.

Lord Buckley heard the drumbeat quicken as the crowd parted. Another woman came forward holding a silver cup, which she gave to St. George.

The gaunt priest went down on one knee and dipped the cup into the blood-filled bucket. As the boatman watched, St. George brought the glistening red cup to his lips and drank. Then he dipped his finger in the blood and drew a cross on his forehead.

His worshippers began to dance in earnest, moving around the headless carcass in a slow, weaving circle. One by one, they drank from the bloodied cup. St. George drew away from the circle and walked back to the Hounfor. When he emerged a few minutes later, he had Cool Blue with him. She trailed behind the priest woodenly, as if drawn by an invisible chain.

Night had fallen, and as Lord Buckley peered through the dense shadows surrounding the churchyard, he hoped he'd be able to spot Rastadamus and the others when the time came.

If it ever came, the boatman amended, watching St. George lead Cool Blue to the headless carcass. The priest dipped the cup into the bucket and handed it to her. Hesitantly, she took the blood-oiled cup and drank.

The acolytes cheered when she sipped the blood, as if

the rite had reached some turning point. The women hurried to set up a long table at one end of the churchyard. They filed into the Hounfor and came out bearing trays of food, rum bottles, cakes, flower bouquets, boxes of cigars, plates, glasses, and everything else needed for a proper feast.

After the table had been prepared, two men stepped out of the temple carrying a large black cross which bore a garish effigy of Christ, crucified head down. They carefully placed the cross at the head of the table.

Abruptly the drums stopped. At the same time St. George's voice rose through the deep hush. Lord Buckley couldn't hear the words, but there was no mistaking the priest's harsh, guttural tone. St. George was calling the forces of evil to dinner.

The civilian observers, which included most of the politicians and other assorted Jamaican gentry, as well as Westlake's group, had separated from the worshippers. They stood huddled near the church, as if wary of the ritual's side effects.

St. George's guttural chanting was cut off, and he strode back to the Hounfor, every step punctuated by the thick silence. Then he disappeared inside the small church. For a few moments the entire gathering held its breath.

The priest emerged carrying something against his chest. Lord Buckley strained to see what it was, before an icy finger tapped his heart.

Cradled in St. George's arms were the yellowed, parched remains of some long-dead corpse. The mummified figure was dressed in an old-fashioned swallow-tailed coat and tattered striped trousers. A battered stovepipe hat topped its grinning skull.

Carefully St. George propped the skeletal figure at the head of the table, facing the inverted cross. Then he sat beside it and poured out two glasses of rum. One he placed before the ragged corpse, the other he drank. After draining the glass, he refilled it and lifted it high. The drums began again, rolling into an ominously infectious rhythm that drew the worshippers closer to the table. The priest ignored them and offered the glass to Cool Blue.

Head bowed, she came forward and accepted the glass. She drained its contents in one swallow, then stepped back. She lifted her head as if slowly awakening and walked toward the drummers, her hips swaying to their rhythms. As she neared them, her body seemed to absorb the intricate percussion and she began to dance.

Her back was turned to everyone except the three drummers, and from his lofty perch Lord Buckley watched the priestess remove her white turban and shake loose her long, fire-tinted hair. The drums grew bolder as her dancing intensified, her arms and body tracing sensual patterns on the galloping beat. Then she turned.

Lord Buckley's thoughts froze when he saw her face.

In the space of minutes Cool Blue had been transformed into another person. Her once fine features had thickened into a coarse mask, and a dull glaze deadened her blue eyes. Her hair hung in limp, sweat-greased strands as she stalked to the table and greedily swallowed another glass of rum. Skin glistening with perspiration, she snatched up a cigar, bit off the tip, and spat it out. After lighting the cigar with a candle, she stepped back between the graves and continued to dance, her movements crudely suggestive.

She moved back to the table, plucked the high hat from the corpse's skull, and put it on her head at an absurd angle. St. George leaned back and laughed as the priestess went into a swaggering parody of dance while puffing on her cigar.

Lord Buckley understood that Cool Blue had been "mounted," or possessed, by one of the gods in the Obeah hierarchy. Exactly which one he couldn't really know. But from her rough manner and crude gestures, the Loa who possessed her was obviously male.

The other worshippers were also imbibing the rum and foodstuffs spread out on the festive table. The entire ceremony in the torchlit churchyard had taken on a carnival atmosphere with much raucous laughter and spirited dancing between the graves.

Lord Buckley put on the night goggles and peered into the shadows away from the churchyard, hoping to spot Rastadamus or one of the others, but they were still well concealed. His legs were getting stiff and he wondered if they'd hold up in a fight. Or in flight, he mused, watching the revelers build up to a fever pitch.

The power generated by the drums was undeniable. The energy steamed off the dancers like heat waves. Completely possessed by the god, Cool Blue reeled drunkenly, her hair disheveled and her face contorted in a bestial grimace, while St. George sat at the big table beside the grotesque mummy.

Abruptly the priest stood up and walked slowly to the burial ground. At the same time the drums cut their tempo, shifting into a martial dirge. But before he reached the graves, Cool Blue blocked his path.

She stood swaying defiantly, hands on her hips and cigar clenched in her teeth. Impatiently, the priest gestured to one of the men standing nearby.

The man took Cool Blue's arm and gently nudged her aside. With a stunning burst of strength she wrenched her arm free and drove her elbow into his belly. As the man dropped, two others moved in to restrain her.

The first collided head-on with her wild swing, cracking his nose. The second managed to grab her from behind, but only for a moment. The slender priestess suddenly twisted away and clawed at her would-be captor until he fell back, arms protecting his blood-streaked face.

Seeing the commotion, a guard hurried over with the

two pit bulls. He stopped short when he saw St. George's upraised arm. The priest turned and waved the others away from Cool Blue. Then he began to chant in a deep, soothing tone. Lord Buckley understood nothing of the words but he could sense the hypnotic effect of the priest's voice. Almost immediately Cool Blue appeared to calm down.

St. George approached her slowly, his droning chant cutting through the hush. Cool Blue's arms fell to her sides. As her eyes closed, the bestial snarl twisting her features dissolved. And when she reopened them, she again seemed young and fragile.

And very frightened, Lord Buckley noted. Anxiously, he looked around for Rastadamus. Then he saw someone emerging from the church.

A beautiful woman wearing a black silk gown and red sash strode into view. Her long silver-blond hair shimmered in the torchlight as she walked past the gaping congregation to St. George's side. The priest's hollow smile echoed the skeletal grimace of his table guest when he took the woman's hand.

Cool Blue stood passively, head bent in submission.

St. George led the blond woman to the gore-soaked bucket beneath the headless carcass. He dipped his finger and traced a bloody cross on her forehead. Then he offered her the cup.

She drank greedily, oily red trickles staining the corners of her mouth. The drums began a quick, insistent beat that pushed the dancers back into motion. All except Cool Blue, who remained where she stood, head bowed.

The priest waited until the drumbeat neared a frenzied pitch before finally moving toward the burial ground.

He paused at one of the tombstones and pretended to read the inscription. Then he started to dance around the grave, fingering the rosary beads dangling from his neck. He chanted something unintelligible and threw a handful of red powder over the grave.

As if on signal, three men carrying shovels came forward and began to dig.

When they brought up the casket, Lord Buckley rummaged through his survival bag for his field glasses. The compact Nikons were more properly opera glasses but served him well at short distances. He could clearly see the men unscrewing the casket's lid.

He could also see the blue vial in St. George's hand as the priest reached into the open coffin. Seconds later he saw something he did not wish to see.

The death-mottled face of a male corpse lifted into view.

The grisly figure sat up and struggled painfully to its feet. The moldered condition of its skin and clothing suggested the corpse had been buried for a long time.

"Baka!" the priest cried out, as if greeting an old friend.

St. George's face was no less grotesque than that of the corpse, Lord Buckley decided, zooming in close on the priest's taut features. Despite heat and exertion, St. George's skin was bone-dry. However, his eyes shone wetly deep inside their hollow sockets. It was his fixed grin that set off alarms in the boatman's brain.

Thick white flecks of foam dotted the corners of his rigid smile. It suddenly occurred to Lord Buckley that the priest was possessed. No doubt he'd been mounted by Baka himself.

"Baka!" St. George repeated, leading the shuffling corpse to the festive table. The worshippers parted to let them pass, hushed by a mixture of fear and fascination as the decay-pocked zombi shambled after St. George.

The priest guided the creature to a chair beside the mummified guest of honor. When the zombi was seated, the blond female came forward and knelt in mock reverence.

St. George laughed and called out to the drummers. Lord Buckley recognized their insistent tempo from the previous grave-opening ceremony. Sure enough, the priest stalked to the burial area and began dancing around another tombstone.

Lord Buckley heard his voice rise and watched him mark the site with red powder. Just as the three men began to open the grave, he turned in time to glimpse Rastadamus weaving through the dark forest.

From his vantage point he could also make out a large, shadowy shape trailing the white-haired master. Lord Buckley hastily put on the night goggles and probed the darkness away from the torchlight.

He spotted Rastadamus first. The shape was about fifteen or twenty yards behind him. But even at that distance there was no mistaking the hulking girth and gun-turret head.

Ramon was stalking the master, a 9 mm pistol clutched in his huge fist.

Chapter 38

THE ROLLING THUNDER AWAKENED HIM FROM A deep dream.

The booming continued to vibrate around him and he dimly realized it was the pounding of drums.

Then he remembered, and the fear crushed his awareness. He fought to push through the terror but its massive weight pressed down, filling the smothering confines of his tomb. As he struggled for breath, a rotting stench filled his nostrils.

Suddenly a familiar chord radiated through his being, melting away the fear. His mind unwrapped like a winter flower. He knew why he was there and what he must do.

He shut his eyes against the oppressive blackness and began a shallow breathing pattern. In time it came easier. As his mind cleared, he could sense the supportive presence of Rastadamus.

His breathing merged with the drums and he heard the sound of metal chopping the earth above him. Soon, very soon, he'd be face-to-face with St. George. He had to prepare himself.

Orient charged his senses, opening his mind to Rastadamus. He let the master's power pour into his parched consciousness, and felt his strength swelling until he believed he could burst through the wood, rock, and dirt entombing him. Then he heard St. George's voice cutting through the drums. The words were a babble against the galloping drumbeat, but Orient understood.

"I'm coming to free you, Doctor. To free you. But you will owe me a service. You must obey the god Baka, ruler of the *Corps Cadavres* . . . ruler of hell itself . . . You will be his *servitor* . . ."

To Orient's horror, the voice seemed to envelop his consciousness, strangling his contact with Rastadamus. He squeezed his concentration and fought the seductive drone, but he was tired. He wanted so much to sleep . . .

The section of his mind that remained lucid struggled helplessly against the looming void. He ransacked his brain for something, anything, that would help him keep fighting. In an effort to remain alert, he flexed his fingers and tried to move his arms. His hand brushed a sharp metal object and it pierced his skin.

The pain shot through his awareness like an electric shock, dimming St. George's voice. In that instant he realized he had touched the metal cross Sybelle had given him.

The sharp chopping noises drew closer and he breathed deep as a mist of new air filtered into the casket. Focusing his being on the channel of pure energy generated by Rastadamus, he expanded his awareness.

When the metal tool scraped the lid of his coffin, Orient felt totally alert. An image of the scene above formed in his mind. He saw St. George dancing at the edge of his newly opened grave. The gaunt priest appeared changed somehow. Orient understood St. George had been possessed. The crackling yellow aura around him signaled extreme danger.

The telepathic flow of information expired the moment

the coffin lid was pried open. For an instant Orient felt weightless, as air and light flooded through the crack. A dazzling rush of sensation burst onto his senses when the lid was lifted. Fire and movement, battering drums, faces contorted by bestial lusts . . . poured over him like lava from an erupting volcano.

The priest's voice sliced through the chaos.

"Come," he chanted hoarsely. "Come to Baka now!"

Stiffly, Orient raised his head into the blinding glare.

"Come to Baka," St. George repeated.

Orient awkwardly pushed himself erect. He blinked, trying to clear his vision. A mass of people crowded around his casket, gaping at him. Orient shut his eyes. In that fraction of a second he felt Rastadamus reconnect, and when his eyes reopened, they saw everything with vivid clarity.

St. George stood a few feet away, his face glazed with triumph. A yard behind him hovered six or seven armed bodyguards, including one holding a pair of pit bulls. All of them, especially the dogs, appeared quite crazed by the bloody ritual. They stared at Orient in slack-jawed terror.

Beyond them stood two parallel lines of worshippers, men on one side, women on the other. Most held torches aloft, forming a blazing archway. At the end of the human corridor was a flower-laden table with three guests: a mummified skeleton in a frock coat; a moldering, undead corpse; and Tristan.

Her long silver hair framed a dark red cross on her forehead, and an air of bemused expectancy.

"Come to Baka," St. George whispered, his hoarse voice cutting through the drums.

Orient intended to play dead until he found an opportunity to disrupt the ritual. It proved to be a wise choice. When he struggled to his feet, he found his limbs were stiff and his balance very uncertain. As he followed St. George he tried to locate Ezili, but she was nowhere in sight. Slowly he shuffled after the priest, holding tight to his link to Rastadamus. With each step his mental faculties grew more acute.

Orient was walking with more confidence by the time he reached the festive table. He noticed a knot of people standing in the shadow of the church. A few seemed familiar, but he recognized one scowling face in particular. As usual, Commander Westlake was observing from a safe distance.

Tristan's sculpted features remained impassive as he neared. Only the skeletal figure in the frock coat was smiling. And, of course, St. George.

His rigid grin widened as he turned to issue an order.

"Bring the priestess."

A few moments later two figures appeared in Orient's peripheral vision. One of the black-uniformed guards was leading a disheveled female with blood-smeared lips. When they reached the table, the guard withdrew. The woman stood there, swaying slightly, arms limp at her sides. Her face had a numbed, battered quality, as if bruised on the inside. It took Orient some time before he was certain she was Ezili. Only the copper-streaked hair was the same. Something foul and obscene had devoured her pure spirit, leaving only a flaccid shell.

Orient breathed deep, feeling the circulation return to his cramped limbs.

St. George barked a command and someone brought him a machete, its thick, curved blade gleaming in the torchlight.

The priest turned to Ezili, chanting softly in a singsong voice. Extending the sharp tip of the machete, he slit her gown from neck to waist. Ezili stood passively as the gown fell to her ankles, exposing her smooth, naked body. St. George muttered something and she stepped forward. At his command she knelt before the undead corpse and kissed its crusted groin.

Orient smothered his emotion, channeling all of his energy into finding some way to abort the ritual, and to survive. Someone brought St. George a bloody cup. The priest dipped his finger into the cup and drew a bright red talisman on Ezili's back. He dipped his finger again and traced an oily line along her neck. Then he picked up the machete and held it out to Orient.

"With this sacrifice may my power multiply," St. George droned, his voice rising with the booming drums. He gestured toward a large bamboo chest on the ground. "May my curses fly and my enemies die. Come, Baka!" The priest placed the machete in Orient's hand and stepped back. "Now execute her in the glorious name of Baka."

Orient could hear his heartbeat above the drums as he lifted the machete. He hesitated, hoping for some sign from Rastadamus, but none arrived.

"Strike!" St. George rasped. "Bring it down on her neck."

As the priest reached for the machete, Orient wrenched it away.

"No!"

The one word stilled the drums and brought the frenzied ceremony to an abrupt halt. Suddenly everyone in the churchyard stood motionless, staring at Orient in awed silence.

"Come, Baka," St. George hissed, pointing at the undead corpse. "Come kill your enemy."

In that instant Orient knew what had to be done. Focusing his combined powers, he exerted his will on the mottled zombi slowly lifting from its chair.

"No," he said sharply. "Stay."

Orient felt the raw hatred seething from St. George's inflamed will as the priest brought his power to bear. The corpse hovered inches off the chair as the two men stared at each other, wills locked. As Orient's concentration teetered, a surge of pure energy restored his balance. And he saw the corpse fall back into its chair.

Orient's vision fragmented. He caught a quick glimpse of Tristan getting up from the table. Then a flicker of movement on his right drew his attention. He turned and saw a gang of worshippers advancing toward him, brandishing torches.

Without hesitation he lifted his arm and pointed. His amplified senses responded instantly. Using his core-squeezed focus as leverage, he swung the full weight of the master's power toward the flames.

First he snuffed the lead torch. Then, one by one, he put out the others.

As if on signal, the entire congregation silently retreated, faces sagging with panic. Tristan, too, was backing away. Only St. George remained where he was. The gaunt priest grinned at Orient triumphantly, but his gaze was fixed on a point beyond him.

Orient heard a rapid scratching sound and jerked his head back.

The pit bulls were charging directly at him, fangs bared in frenzied anticipation, their rabid attack fueled by the scent of fresh blood.

At the same time, someone began shooting.

Chapter 39

THE NIGHT GOGGLES WERE A REAL ADVANTAGE.

One he sorely needed, Lord Buckley noted, circling Ramon's position. The big Cuban had stopped about seven yards behind Rastadamus, who was crouched near the gate.

Although Lord Buckley was aware of a disturbance inside the churchyard, the master's safety was his prime concern. He stepped behind Ramon and pressed the .45 against his neck.

"Drop the piece. Now."

He retrieved the fallen automatic and checked the safety. It was still on. He prodded Ramon's bulk against a tree and gave him a quick frisk that turned up two extra clips and a switchblade.

"What you want here?" Lord Buckley hissed.

Ramon shrugged.

"Why are you followin' him?"

The huge Cuban's scowl was both menacing and confused.

"Voodoo bastard—who is he?"

"You ass. He's no voodoo—he's with us. Groton here too?"

The Cuban nodded.

"What's up?"

"Groton got a tip there's drugs in the church."

"You havin' a goddamn raid?"

"Maybe."

Lord Buckley pulled the hammer on his .45. "Don't fool with me, Ramon."

"I ain't foolin'," the Cuban whined. "We came up here with a squad of local police. Then the police see all the big honchos." He jerked his head toward the group standing near the church. "All of a sudden they take off."

"How many you got left?"

"Me, Groton, and Luis. Listen, who's this albino anyway?"

The boatman automatically glanced back at Rastadamus, but he had disappeared into the shadows.

"*Madre . . .*"

Ramon's disbelieving gasp drew Lord Buckley's attention to the churchyard. He saw the naked woman kneeling in the torchlight. He saw Orient take the machete from St. George. Moments later he saw something incredible.

As the boatman watched in openmouthed wonder, Orient seemed to challenge St. George. Then he pointed at the torches circling closer and snuffed them out. One by one. Like blowing out candles.

Lord Buckley shouted a warning when he saw the guard unleash the pit bulls, but it was lost in the eruption of noise and confusion. Gunfire exploded a few yards away and suddenly Groton burst out from the shadows at a dead run, followed by a short man armed with an automatic shotgun.

"Give me my piece," Ramon demanded. "They need backup."

Lord Buckley made an impulsive decision. He handed Ramon his 9 mm, then followed the huge Cuban as he plowed toward the gate, hoping Quen and Harry would join the charge.

Having Groton and the Cubans certainly improved the odds, Lord Buckley calculated as they approached the churchyard. Most of the worshippers and guests were scattering for cover, leaving the battleground to St. George's bodyguards. He counted at least ten, perhaps as many as fifteen, armed men. And maybe two or three feisty worshippers. Six men might be just enough to pull it off, the boatman decided. Counting Orient, there were seven of them.

Lord Buckley hit the gate firing, and dove behind a tree. Ramon managed to find a friendly tombstone, but Groton and the short man were cut off from cover by three bodyguards who pinned them down between the church and the graveyard.

At the same time, he saw Orient grappling with St. George while the pit bulls nervously darted back and forth, crazed with excitement. Abruptly one of the bodyguards stepped into view, to get a clear shot at Groton, whose gun had jammed.

Lord Buckley reflexively aimed and fired, clipping the guard, who went down clutching his leg. A moment later another of the guards ran to within a few feet of Groton and fired. Somehow he missed. Before he could try again, Luis blew his arm off with two quick blasts from the shotgun. Thinking Luis would have to reload, the third man popped out from behind a tombstone, machine gun extended. Fortunately, he popped back in time to survive Luis's three-shot barrage. As it was, the tombstone disintegrated. The man barely escaped by rolling into an open grave. Suddenly a group of men located behind the church started shooting.

Both Groton and Luis ducked for cover and returned their fire, but it was soon clear that these boys had major weapons, including a machine gun that sprayed chunks of concrete, turf, and wood inches away from Lord Buckley. Then he spotted St. George sprinting madly through the tombstones, his entire body drenched in blood. Right behind him, thick necks straining in hot pursuit, were the pit bulls. A guard jumped out from behind a tree and opened fire on the dogs.

Lord Buckley turned and saw Orient leaning against the festive table, head bent as if sharing a secret with the zombi seated there. Orient pushed himself erect and ran after St. George, exposing himself to gunfire from two directions. One of which was coming at point-blank range.

The doctor man didn't have a chance.

Lord Buckley jerked his weapon toward the man shooting at the dogs. But it was too late.

Chapter 40

WHEN THE FIRST SHOTS RANG OUT, ORIENT WAS TOO busy trying to ward off the attacking pit bulls to comprehend.

Still connected to the master's power, he calmly met their snarling charge and exerted his will. The beasts came to an abrupt stop, whining frantically. He looked up and saw St. George edging around the table, taking the same escape route Tristan had used. Instinctively he scrambled after the priest and brought him down with a hard tackle.

St. George bounced up kicking, clawing, and punching. The lanky priest was all knees and elbows, limbs pumping like metal pistons until he wrenched free. Orient started to rise, but St. George lashed out with his foot, catching him in the belly. As Orient fell back he glimpsed the growling dogs at the edge of his vision.

An instant later St. George loomed up before him, grinning wildly, the machete clutched in both hands. Instinctively Orient rolled away and struggled to his feet. Machete held high, St. George advanced, his eyes burning with hatred. Frantically looking around for a weapon, Orient

331

seized a nearby bucket and flung it full in the priest's face, spilling its contents over his entire body.

Dazed by the blow, St. George staggered back, drenched with blood from neck to knee. He saw Orient slump over the table, near exhaustion, and lifted his machete. They both saw the dogs at the same time.

St. George stiffened, aware that something was wrong.

Snarling ominously, their powerful jaws salivating at the musky scent of fresh blood, the pit bulls eyed the priest as they pawed the dirt, torn between their training and raw instinct. St. George took a step back as the sullen beasts worked up the momentum to attack. He took another step backward and stumbled over the large bamboo chest. He managed to recover his balance but the chest overturned, suddenly releasing a cloud of wildly fluttering birds. Momentarily panicked, the dogs jumped away.

But in that broken instant, amidst the chaos of screams, shooting, and frightened birds wheeling crazily in the torchlight, Orient met St. George's eyes.

They were cold sober. His ecstatic grin sagged under the weight of a horrifying truth.

Like physics, the law of occult ritual decrees that every action has an opposite and equal reaction. Having released the birds bearing his death hex without properly consummating the ritual sacrifice, St. George himself would have to suffer the curse.

Pawing nervously, the dogs circled the priest, their muscular shoulders gathering to spring. Before they could leap, St. George suddenly bolted, scrambling madly for the safety of the Hounfor. The dogs bounded after him and were swiftly cutting down his lead when one of the guards stepped into view and opened fire.

He wounded the lead animal but failed to stop it. The charging pit bull veered and leaped at the guard, bowling him over. The guard screeched as the beast's crushing jaws clamped his shoulder, sending up a spray of blood from a severed artery. Orient was stumbling after St. George when the second pit bull sprang.

The dog's teeth ripped into the priest's calf, tumbling them both into an open grave. Orient started to follow, then skidded to a halt when he saw the short man pointing a shotgun in his direction. The man fired.

The blast caught the pit bull gnawing at the fallen guard. The beast jumped convulsively as its rib cage shattered.

Orient started after St. George, then saw the blood spurting from the guard's partially severed shoulder. He stopped to treat the man's wounds as best he could, applying a crude tourniquet and bandages made from torn clothing. Suddenly a familiar figure sprinted toward him, pistol extended. He dimly recognized Groton as the DEA agent ran past him and began firing into the open grave.

By the time Orient reached Groton's side, it was too late.

Even in its death throes the pit bull maintained its pitiless grip on St. George's throat. Part of the priest's abdomen had been slashed open like a paper bag, spilling its contents. There was little doubt St. George was dead.

Groton looked as if he was about to throw up.

Orient whirled and ran back to Ezili. She was still kneeling on the ground, head pressed against the earth, as if praying.

He found the remnants of her gown and threw it over her shoulders. He tried to pull her up but she seemed drugged. Finally he dragged her to her feet and looked around for Groton.

The agent was crouched beside the grave. Orient couldn't tell if he was sick or returning fire. He saw the short man race to Groton's side and pull him behind a tombstone just as a hail of bullets tore up the earth around them. Then he spotted Lord Buckley galloping directly toward him, waving frantically.

"Take cover, mon!" the boatman shouted. "They comin' . . ."

Orient swept Ezili up in his arms and scrambled behind

the large table. When Lord Buckley arrived, they both heaved the table over, spilling food everywhere and throwing both corpse and skeleton to the ground. The skeleton shattered, its skull rolling into the path of a huge, sweating figure lumbering toward the table. Ramon's foot landed directly on the skull, crushing it before it brought him down. He sprawled on his belly a split second before a spray of bullets tore into a nearby tree. The giant Cuban crawled the rest of the way to the improvised barricade.

"Bastards make counterattack," he wheezed.

Lord Buckley snapped a fresh clip into his automatic.

"Here they are now."

There were five of them, three on one side, two on the other. They all had Uzis and kept firing alternating bursts as they advanced. The boom of the shotgun on Groton's side of the churchyard only drove the attackers closer to their own flimsy barricade. Their bullets began chopping at the table.

"Make every shot count," Lord Buckley warned as they neared. Suddenly the distant sound of gunshots froze the attackers. The shooting grew louder and Orient could see three men closing in on the attack force.

"Goddamn, it's them—Tosh, Quen, and Harry," Lord Buckley muttered. As the attackers scattered, two shotgun blasts dropped one guard and drove another behind a tombstone. Ramon and Lord Buckley began shooting in earnest, and another attacker fell. Caught in a vicious crossfire, the remaining three threw down their guns and raised their arms. Groton and Lord Buckley came out to collect their weapons, closely followed by Ramon. Orient cautiously brought up the rear, sensing danger. As they neared, one of the guards reached behind him.

"Don't move!" Lord Buckley shouted.

"Wait."

The familiar voice turned Orient's head. He saw Ezili staggering toward him, arms extended.

"Don't move!" Lord Buckley repeated.

Orient whirled in time to see the guard produce a grenade and grab the pin. Before he could pull it, Ramon reached out and smothered his hands with one huge fist. With the other he hooked the guard's belt and swung him overhead like a sack of coffee. But as Ramon tossed him aside, the grenade exploded, dismembering the guard and sending shards of hot metal everywhere. Ramon toppled like a felled tree, blood streaming down his face.

Groton ran to his side, then, satisfied he'd survive, herded the remaining prisoners together.

"Who are these people?" Groton yelled, waving his weapon at Lord Buckley's companions.

"They're ours," Orient assured him firmly.

"Cover the prisoners," Groton told Lord Buckley. "I'll locate the dope."

On instinct, Orient followed the drug agent as he ran to the chapel.

The worshippers had long since fled, leaving the churchyard deserted. As Orient sprinted after Groton, he wondered why Ezili had called to him. But it was too late to turn back. When he reached the chapel he came to a stop and peered around the entrance. Groton was already inside, rummaging through the plaster saints, flower vases, fruit baskets, and rum bottles decorating the altar.

Groton smashed the saints during the course of his frantic search for drugs. Orient already knew there were no drugs.

"What St. George was dealing is as lethal as nerve gas," Orient told the agent. "But it's not illegal."

"That is not what my informants tell me," Groton said through clenched teeth. "There were people here to make a big buy."

"Yes. But not to buy street drugs."

Groton gave him an exasperated stare. "Then what kind of drug, Einstein?"

"A zombification drug," Orient said evenly. "As in the living dead."

Groton dismissed the information with a wave of his gun.

"Where the hell is Luis?" he snapped. "We have to take this place apart."

As he turned he saw Ezili in the doorway and reflexively lifted his weapon.

"Hold fire, damn you!" Orient yelled.

"She's St. George's woman."

"He was about to kill her. Or didn't you notice?"

Ignoring their heated exchange, Ezili lurched to Orient's side. Somehow she managed to secure the torn gown around most of her body, and her eyes had cleared. "Darling . . . I was so afraid . . ."

"Tell us where St. George stashed the drugs," Groton cut in impatiently.

"Drugs? There's nothing here." She looked at Orient. "But there is a secret room behind the Pe, where he keeps the toxin."

"Dammit, what toxin?" Groton moaned.

Orient smiled. "I already explained . . ."

"Sure, sure, zombi toxin, right? C'mon, lady, let's go. This is serious. Where's this Pe?"

Ezili hesitated as if steeling herself, then went to a large wood panel behind the altar table. She tugged at a cornice and the panel slid back. Groton entered first, followed by Orient and Ezili.

Inside was a short stone stairway leading to a small, round room. When Orient entered he understood Ezili's reluctance. He recognized the room as the one where he had been laid out for inspection, prior to his burial. Except now the table was decorated with a tall white cross and black candles. The tiny dancing flames provided the only light in the room. Like the Pe upstairs, this altar was also strewn with offerings from egg baskets to rum bottles.

Orient pointed to a narrow door across the room.

"Where does that lead?"

"Outside," Ezili said softly. "It—"

"C'mon, let's see where he stashed this damned toxin," Groton rasped impatiently.

As Ezili moved past the narrow door on her way to the altar, Orient shouted a warning.

It was too late. Westlake stepped out, wrapped one arm around Ezili's neck, and pressed a gun against her head.

"Drop it, Groton," he said sharply.

"Why should I? She's my prisoner."

Westlake gave him a tight smile. "Boy, you don't know dick from Dick Tracy. This is a Company operation all the way. You have zero jurisdiction. We know all about your little Cuban deal, so back off—before you get blown away."

To Orient's dismay, Groton lowered his gun. "Look, the Agency knows all about your drugs," he countered weakly.

"Wake up, kid. There's no drugs here. Just a pair of traitors. Now put away the weapon. We have work to do."

"Don't," Orient said quietly. "He'll kill us for sure. He can't afford any witnesses on this."

"I don't have to kill you, Doctor," Westlake scoffed. "When I'm finished feeding your file to the computer banks, you'll be a landslide for public enemy number one."

"So you did murder Duke."

"St. George terminated the man."

"With some help from Tristan."

A woman's voice suddenly chimed into the conversation. "Never talk about a lady behind her back, darling," Tristan chided, easing behind Westlake. "It isn't gallant."

"Put the weapon away, Groton," Westlake repeated. "We've got to locate that toxin. Our country needs it."

Groton nodded, and started to reholster his weapon.

"Thank you," Westlake said.

The gunshot sounded curiously flat in the small room. Groton hit the wall and slid to the floor, leaving a shiny trail of blood.

As Westlake turned the gun on Orient, Ezili twisted free

and stumbled between them. "Wait! Don't shoot. I'll give you the toxin."

Westlake smiled. "Very well. I can wait."

"Really quite touching," Tristan purred acidly as Ezili hurried to the altar.

Ezili pressed the top of a wall panel behind the altar and it slid open, exposing a space the size of a small safe.

She started to reach inside but Westlake stopped her.

"Step away, right now," he barked. "Tristan, check it out."

Tristan moved over to the panel and removed a thickly wrapped package that resembled a cigar box.

Westlake waved his pistol at Ezili. "Is that it?"

She shrugged, sea-blue eyes intent on Orient. They both seemed to share the same thought.

Orient had already prepared himself. With an abrupt surge of will, he toppled one of the rum bottles on the altar. As it fell over, it struck a burning candle, igniting the high-octane alcohol spreading across the white linen altar cloth. In the sudden flare Orient saw Ezili shove Tristan into Westlake. At the same time he glimpsed Groton aiming his weapon from a sitting position.

Tristan was stumbling against Westlake, the package clutched in her outstretched hands, when Groton fired.

His bullet missed both of them but went squarely through the package. A cloud of yellow dust erupted, spilling over Tristan's black dress.

"No!" she screamed in horrified disbelief. "Get it off! Please get it off me! Please . . ."

Frantically she tore at her dress, trying to remove it, but it was no use. Her arms, hands, and ankles were streaked with the yellow powder. Within seconds her efforts became weaker. She turned to Westlake. "Glen . . . help me, for God's sake . . ."

"No! Get away!" he shouted, scrambling back through the door in panic as Tristan reached out to him. She tried to follow, then slowly sagged to the floor.

Orient started toward her.

"Wait!" Ezili cried. "If that powder touches you any-where—you die!"

Orient paused, knowing it was true. The smoke from the burning altar began to fill the small room. He saw Groton trying to crawl to the door and hurried to help him. With Ezili's help he dragged the wounded agent up the stone stairs to the chapel. Lord Buckley and Luis were waiting for them.

"What about the drugs?" the small man demanded.

"Ask your boss. Where's your car? He needs a doctor fast."

Westlake's bullet had passed cleanly through Groton's side, missing the vital organs. Still, the agent had lost plenty of blood and could easily go into shock. Orient did what he could to stem the bleeding, then helped get him into Luis's Land Rover. Ramon's face was a raw mess, but he managed to make it aboard under his own power. As they sped away, Orient surveyed the carnage in the churchyard.

"We better get some doctors over here," he muttered wearily.

Lord Buckley grinned. "They already on the way. I sent Quen and Harry after them."

"Oh, my God, look," Ezili whispered.

Orient turned and saw the bright orange flames oozing from the chapel window.

"Time we split, mon," Lord Buckley said firmly. "Po-lice, firemen—everybody soon come."

The flames shot higher as they climbed into the vehicle, casting gold-and-silver tints across the white tombstones. For some reason, as the car roared off into the shadows, Orient was reminded of Tristan's moonlit hair.

Chapter 41

IT WAS NOT EASY GETTING OFF THE ISLAND.

After hiding out with Lord Buckley in the mountains for a few days, Orient finally managed to contact Groton and cut a deal. In exchange for a private flight to New York for him and Ezili, he agreed to tell Groton what he knew about Westlake and St. George. However, he carefully avoided mentioning Rastadamus, or the scope of his own work.

He received one message from the master while at Lord Buckley's mountain retreat, reassuring them that he was safe. But his prolonged exposure during the stakeout raised the possibility that he might be recognized by St. George's people. He had definitely been spotted by Ramon, which seriously frayed his mantle of anonymity. In time he would resume his work among his devoted followers. Should the need arise, he could always contact Orient telepathically.

Orient also made certain Groton gave Senator Jacobs a full, notarized statement concerning the events in Jamaica, in case of reprisals by Westlake.

"He is partial to hit men," Orient observed. "And Fred here can attest to his moral character."

"The lying bastard shot me in cold blood. After pulling rank on me, no less," Groton said vehemently. "I don't care if I lose my job on this. I'm going after him with everything I've got. He should be put away."

"Chances are he won't be," Andy Jacobs rumbled. "But I'll make damned sure he backs off while you state your case."

Orient stared down at the Hudson River through the senator's bay window. "There's still the disk they stole from Duke. Once Westlake runs my file through the computer banks, I'll be public enemy one through ten."

"We'll cross that bridge," Andy assured him. "But right now you deserve to get on with your life. And so does that lovely lady of yours."

He was, of course, absolutely right.

Orient couldn't remember being happier than during those first few weeks with Ezili in New York. They explored odd corners of the city from Chinatown to the Cloisters. They went jogging in the park and made a serious effort to find the best Italian restaurant in town. Sometimes Orient and Ezili wandered over to a tiny playground tucked away in Cherokee Square, near the river, and spent the twilight hours sitting on the swings and talking.

Ezili encouraged Orient to resume his telepathic research, despite the specter of Agency intrusion.

"If people like Westlake drive you, and your work, into hiding, they win the war for the human spirit," she reminded him while rubbing his back. Somewhere during the excitement he'd pulled a muscle, and it still bothered him.

"A little to the right."

She paused. "Are you listening?"

"I said maybe you're right," Orient amended hastily. "Please don't stop."

"Sybelle told me you set up a lab when you first moved in. Down in the garage."

"It's still there. But we might need the space."

"Space for what?"

"Your mother. Senator Jacobs arranged for her to fly in tomorrow with a bodyguard. In case St. George's enforcers are out for revenge."

"I have a feeling you took care of that." She leaned closer and kissed his neck. "Thanks for my mom. But maybe she'd be happier with her sister in New Jersey. You know what I mean."

"Actually, I don't know what you mean."

Her hand slipped under the sheet and caressed his thigh. "What I mean, Mr. Sensitive, is I love my mom but I want you all to myself."

On Saturday they drove out to Kennedy Airport to meet the plane. Ezili's mother seemed much younger, and stronger, than the last time Orient had seen her. Her graceful carriage and vibrant blue eyes suggested that she and Ezili were sisters. After embracing her daughter, she gave Orient a heartfelt hug.

"I'll never be able to thank you," she whispered.

"There's no need, Mrs. Buchanan."

"Please call me Marie."

"Now I know she likes you," Ezili teased. "Even my father called her Mrs. Buchanan."

"Child, you know that's not so," Marie scolded. "Don't you pay her any mind, Owen."

In fact, he wasn't. His attention was drawn by a tall man with long dreadlocks and a huge grin, who was approaching them.

Lord Buckley hurried over and grasped Orient's hand. "Real good to see you, mon. We miss you back home."

"So you're the bodyguard Andy mentioned."

"Figured I'd come in for the reunion. Business been

slow ever since the operation got shut down. Anyway, we never got time to talk that talk.''

"If we keep talking we're going to spoil Sybelle's dinner,'' Ezili said. "You two can start bragging when we get there.''

As promised, Sybelle was waiting with a sumptuous repast. She opened a bottle of champagne on their arrival, and kept the wine flowing through the evening.

"You know, dear, Ezili shows great ability as a psychic consultant,'' Sybelle confided to Orient during dinner. "I'm thinking of retaining her as my associate. I have far too many clients and she's just perfect, don't you agree?''

Orient didn't, but decided now was no time to discuss it. However, Sybelle had other ideas.

"Come now, darling, don't look so glum. After all, if it wasn't for me, you'd never have met her at all. Incidentally, that reminds me. There's something I still don't understand. Why did St. George sabotage Craig's submarine?''

"From what I gathered from the DEA man, Groton, a cousin of St. George's on the sub was selling secret information to certain Cuban agents.''

"That would be Harold Patterson,'' Lord Buckley said. "He was known to be dealin' with the Cubans.''

Orient nodded. "The Cubans told Groton that St. George double-crossed them. Commander Westlake of the CIA told me he had men aboard that sub. My guess is Westlake sent them to persuade Patterson to reveal his source. Which was most likely St. George. Except St. George had already set a human time bomb. He managed to remove cousin Harold and Westlake's boys at the same time.''

"If Craig hadn't been aboard, he would have succeeded,'' Sybelle mused.

"So then St. George got tight with Westlake at the

Olympia Club and double-crossed the Cubans,'' Lord Buckley added.

Ezili shuddered. ''It didn't take him long to attract people to our ceremonies. They were so eager for evil. At first I thought I could make it different. But when I tried, St. George took my mother hostage.''

Sybelle lifted her glass. ''Thank God we're all here to tell about it.''

Ezili's mother touched her glass to Sybelle's. ''Here's to the men who were so brave.''

Lord Buckley and Orient looked at each other and laughed. ''I think, ma'am, that the doctor man and me were runnin' scared most of the time,'' Lord Buckley admitted cheerfully. Then his mood turned solemn and he raised his glass. ''But I never could have braved the things this fella did.''

Orient felt his ears redden with embarrassment. ''Uh . . . I'd better call Andy Jacobs. He's due back from Washington.''

''Make sure you invite him over,'' Sybelle called after him. ''There's plenty of food and wine.''

Senator Jacobs declined the invitation. Instead he asked Orient to join him for breakfast.

''I have good news, I have bad news,'' was all Andy would say on the phone.

The next morning Orient went to the West Side expecting the worst. Andy Jacobs was waiting in his study.

''Well, let's get goin', Owen,'' he droned, ushering Orient to a sideboard laden with fresh juices, bagels, smoked salmon, scrambled eggs, cream cheese, and fragrant Blue Mountain coffee.

''So what's the problem?'' Orient inquired.

''First the good news, there's more of it,'' Andy said, heaping salmon onto his plate. ''It seems, through efficacious management, the residue of your estate is worth over three hundred thousand. Quite a nice nest egg for a young couple starting out."

Orient spread cream cheese on a slice bagel. "Thanks, Andy. I know how well you've taken care—"

"Forget the bullshit, boy, and listen. Or perhaps you're no longer interested in Commander Glen Westlake."

Orient looked up. "What about him?"

Andy gave him a devilish grin. "You remember the computer disk he stole? The one with your file? Well, you were absolutely dead right. Westlake plugged the disk into every computer bank from the FBI to Interpol."

"Is that supposed to be good news?"

"Hear me out. You see, it seems the disk had what they call a virus. Sort of a self-destruct program. So when Westlake entered your file, this little virus erased all information concerning you from every computer in the damned system."

"Duke," Orient muttered. "So that's what he meant. He said he made sure the disk couldn't be used against me."

"Well, he did a hell of a good job. Not even the Pope's record is as clean as yours is now. Which reminds me. I had some discreet conversations with some friends on the Hill. Seems Fred Groton is making some pretty big waves up there. All under the table so far, but some important people are scared it may surface and spill over on them. As a result, Westlake is about to be transferred and retired. In that order. Some of Groton's allegations will be entered in his record, to cover the big boys."

The ex-senator reached for a cigar. "There's even an outside chance Groton can make the shooting charge stick. At any rate, Commander Westlake's career is on permanent hold. He'll never get near a Cabinet post, thank God."

Orient looked out the bay window, thinking about Duke. "What about the bad news?"

"Seems old Westlake isn't completely finished. He does have the support of certain factions within the CIA. And from what I gather, he wants you bad."

"Ezili told me something," Orient said, sipping his juice. "If I let Westlake drive me underground again, he wins."

"She's damned right too," Andy declared. "Westlake's barely hanging on by his fingernails after this fiasco. Groton has the DEA and a few congressmen hot on his ass. Whatever he throws at you will be unofficial."

"Like his voodoo assassins?"

Andy sighed and lit his cigar. "Whatever happens, you'll always have my support. But for Ezili's sake, be careful. Those bastards get real nasty when they lose."

Orient didn't answer. He was still thinking about Duke.

During the weeks that passed after Ezili's mother settled down in Short Hills, Orient took to his research with renewed enthusiasm. He furnished the garage laboratory with a maze of equipment, including a computer.

Sybelle finally convinced him to begin working with Ezili on developing her psychic potential, and she proved correct. Not only did Ezili make remarkable progress in a short time, but her talent brought his research to a new level.

The only aspect of this new stage that concerned Orient was Ezili's involvement with the occult.

However, it was a very small ripple in a vast river, Orient reflected while meditating one morning. And the river was moving out to sea.